A SCANDALOUS KIND OF DUKE

MIA VINCY

Inner Ballad Press

E-book ISBN: 978-1-925882-06-3

Print ISBN: 978-1-925882-07-0

CONTENT NOTES: *Parental abandonment of a child (in the past); divorce due to adultery (in the past)*

Cover: Studio Bukovero

Development editing: May Peterson, Melinda Utendorf

Proofreading: Deb and Debbie of DP Plus

This book was written on the lands of the Dja Dja Wurrung people, and I acknowledge them as Traditional Owners. I pay my respects to their Elders, past and present, and the Aboriginal Elders of other communities.

A SCANDALOUS KIND OF DUKE

Never seek to tell thy love
Love that never told can be
For the gentle wind does move
Silently invisibly.

— WILLIAM BLAKE

PROLOGUE

I t was a chance encounter, as all their daily meetings were, the pair of them somehow treading the same woodland paths in the first hours of daylight, while Juno's family slept. Early morning was the best time of day, they agreed, when the air was crisp and unsullied and full of hope.

The meetings were not secret, but neither ever spoke of them. It was simpler that way. Leo was a guest, visiting at seventeen, eighteen, now nineteen; Juno was two years younger. Erroneous assumptions would be made, accusations hurled, punches thrown. Even Juno's family would not understand the innocent fervor of their friendship: their wide-ranging conversations, their free laughter, their sense of belonging found nowhere else. And honor demanded Leo never take it beyond friendship, not when he was heir to a duke and Juno his friend's low-born cousin. Quite the little joke Fate had played, putting Juno Bell in his path, close enough to touch, yet forever out of reach.

That morning, their rambles ended in a meadow, chaperoned by an ancient oak and excitable birds. They were arguing, playfully, about whether the delicate pink wildflowers were called "cuckoo flowers" or "lady's smock." They were everywhere, amid splashes of blue and yellow, red and white, the masses of English wildflowers carpeting the fields and just now opening to greet the sun.

"Cuckoo flowers," Juno said, holding one aloft, its four pale petals quivering. "Because they bloom when the first cuckoo arrives."

"Lady's smock," Leo insisted, though he didn't care about the name. He cared about the laughter dancing in her eyes, bluer than the morning sky behind her. He cared about her air of a pagan goddess, with wildflowers woven through her fair, unbound curls.

He cared about the way he felt when he was with her: free, alive, whole.

Dancing backward, she brandished her flower at him like a sword. He plucked one of his own to accept the challenge and, laughing, they dueled with the flowers. Until she broke through his guard and brushed the petals over his cheek. Their eyes met. Their smiles faded. His breath stopped. His heart thumped.

Then she stretched up and leaned in and pressed her soft lips to his. Sensations cascaded through him, warm and hopeful, magical, sensual, as nothing he had ever known before. How he welcomed her kiss, wanted it, *needed* it, closing his eyes, moving his lips against hers, burying his hands in her hair. He hadn't a clue what he was doing, but she had already taught him there were times to stop thinking, to surrender to one's senses and simply respond as felt right.

When they parted, they were breathless, sharing shy, astonished, delighted smiles. Reborn into a world forever changed.

It was his first-ever kiss, and the sweetest moment of his life.

Then Juno said, "I love you."

And Leo said—nothing.

His throat froze. His mouth opened, shut, opened, shut, his

words held prisoner by the war raging inside him. He had duties and obligations: *This must stop now*. He had her kiss lingering on his lips: *This must never stop*.

His torn silence dragged on until it filled the meadow.

Juno's expression dimmed. Her shoulders slumped. And now she was backing away from him, her lips twisted, perhaps in a bitter smile, perhaps in a fight against tears. All the while, she was nodding sadly, as if to say, *What else did I expect? Of course*.

He reached for her hand, savored a desperate, desolate brush of skin before she pulled away.

"We cannot be together in any way," he finally croaked, his throat tight, icy, aching. "I must consider my duty to my family when I choose a wife. You are my friend's kin and Sir Gordon's niece, so honor demands that I never touch— Even a kiss is not —" He tried again. "The future—"

"Oh, enough with the future, duty, honor, family," she snapped. "Why must you carry them all with you? Why can we not be two people alone in a meadow, without you bringing everyone else along too? Do you think me so simple? I *know* we can never be together."

Then she laughed, softly, bitterly, even as she blinked away tears. "How stifling and miserable your life is, that you may not even kiss a girl in a meadow. I—" She paused to consult the old oak tree, before facing him defiantly. "I shall be an artist, and no one's wife or mistress. I only wanted to kiss you and tell you that I love you, because I'm alive and you're alive, and we're young and beautiful and here. I know better than anybody that nothing lasts forever. Nothing ever stays. Not even this."

She flung her crumpled flower at him and whirled away, her dew-soaked skirts clinging to her legs as she carved a path through the grass.

Leo wanted to surge after her and cry that of course he had to bring it all with him. His ancient family, his name, his duty, his honor—they were as much a part of him as his own skin and bones. He had to choose them, didn't she see? He had to put his duty first.

He might never make her understand, but perhaps he would have tried, had she looked back.

She didn't look back.

CHAPTER 1

Ten years later

Leopold Halton, the Duke of Dammerton, was a man of many pleasures.

He took pleasure in caressing the smooth, graceful curves of exquisitely shaped porcelain. He took pleasure in stroking the silken threads of the embroidery on his clothes.

And on this day, he took great pleasure in stripping off his coat and seducing secrets from a wooden crate with a hard, iron bar.

Very gently, mind. Its contents might be fragile.

"Don't you have people to do that for you?" Hadrian asked, pausing his prowling just long enough to watch Leo pry a plank off the crate and toss it aside. "You have staff in there—" He waved at the doorway to the main office of the Dammerton Foundation, where the director and two clerks were pretending to ignore their employer rampaging through the box room with a crowbar and no coat. "Shouldn't they be in here working up a sweat instead of you?"

"I never work up a sweat," Leo said absently. "Sweating is for horses and gamblers, and I am neither. Besides…" He spun the crowbar in his hand. "Nothing like tearing open crates full of decorative objects to work off a mood."

"Most men work off a mood by boxing. Only you would choose *un*boxing. What's with the mood?"

"Odd day, I suppose."

He levered up the second plank. With his bare hand, he ripped it off and dropped it onto the floor beside its friend. The crowbar soon clattered down beside them.

"And I have people to do things I don't enjoy doing myself," he added. "Opening boxes is something I enjoy very much."

Packing straw frothed up out of the newly opened crate, just begging him to plunge in his hands and uncover the treasure within. Leo rolled up his sleeves, slowly, *slowly*—anticipation was to be savored like an aged scotch—then in he dived, fingers venturing through the prickly straw to identify the prize: intricately carved wood. He eased the item out and raised it, reverently, hopefully. It was a bookend, beautifully weighted, scrolls and curlicues carved from gleaming walnut.

"Pretty," Hadrian said, obviously humoring him.

Leo deflated with a sigh. "It's skillfully carved, but the design is ordinary. Uninspired. Unremarkable."

Remarkable—that was what he craved. A decorative object that made his breath hitch and his eyes linger, that made his insides ripple with excitement and his imagination spark to life.

Such finds seemed to be rare these days, though he supposed they had always been few and far between. He used to hunt down the treasures himself, inspecting goods at markets and fairs across Britain, talking to locals, following clues—to a hut where a former soldier carved whimsical figurines, to a cottage where a widow embroidered birds that seemed to fly off the cushions, to the backroom of a print shop where the blind son of a bookseller tinkered with ornate clocks.

Now the treasures came to him. Word had spread of the Dammerton Foundation and, uninvited, artisans had taken to sending samples in the hope of securing a grant. Leo admired their initiative, but it wasn't the same.

He nestled the bookend back in the straw with a pang of regret. Its maker had packed their hopes in there too. A grant from the Dammerton Foundation could make all the difference to a workshop. If only he could do more.

Once more his limbs tensed with the restlessness, the agitation, the *something* that had plagued him ever since that morning's meeting about his finances.

Ever since his decision.

Leo straightened and waved the crowbar at the remaining crates. They seemed to perk up at his attention, like ladies at an assembly with a shortage of men.

"There should be an inventory on the table," he said to Hadrian, who was peering out the window.

"Hmm?"

Turning, Hadrian scrubbed a hand over his closely cropped hair. Daylight stumbled over the scar twisting his lower lip, which Leo still wasn't used to. It was good to have his friend back in London after nearly a decade at the embassy in Vienna, but time had changed him. Once earnest and studious, Hadrian Bell had acquired a cynical, watchful air.

Well, time did tend to change a person. Leo was certainly no longer the same as when he last saw his friend.

"Inventory," Leo repeated, gesturing at the papers on the table. "Should say where these crates came from."

Hadrian shuffled through the pages. "What does the inventory look like?"

"It's a list. It'll look as dull and vexing as every other infernal list."

"There are four lists here."

"Of course there are," Leo muttered. "The bloody things pop up like mushrooms."

Leo hired people to organize his life, and they punished him for it with countless lists. Countless to him, anyway. His clerks probably counted them eagerly, giggling while they dreamed up more of the wretched things.

Hadrian scanned a page. "This list is not an inventory, but an accounting of the costs of expanding the Dammerton Foundation and whether you can afford it." He looked up. "Apparently, you cannot afford it. You're not broke, are you?"

Leo levered the crowbar under the top of another crate. Nails tore through wood with a satisfying crunch. "No. But I need a large lump sum to expand the Foundation, and they tell me I have a big hole where the money should be."

"Too many pretty waistcoats?"

"Too many divorces. I gave Erika back her dowry. It was a very substantial sum, as my man of affairs reminded me with a tear in his eye."

No law had required him to give Erika anything; learned men had forcefully advised against it. But it saved Erika from returning to the family she had married him to escape, and that eased the guilt, at least.

"And how does a duke go about raising a large lump sum?" Hadrian asked.

"There is only one way, my friend. The time-honored, traditional, tried-and-true way."

"Ah. Marriage."

"Yes. Marriage."

Hadrian gave a low whistle. "Brave of you, to dive once more into those shark-infested waters."

"I want to get married again." Leo ripped off the plank and tossed it aside. "I have to get married again. The entire point of the divorce was so I could get married again."

Yet here he was, still no closer to being wed than when Parliament passed the Act finalizing his divorce two years earlier. Surely finding another bride ought not to have been so difficult? He was a *duke*, for pity's sake, not yet thirty, with London's finest collection of decorative objects, the world's prettiest waistcoats, and hair that fell so effortlessly into the coveted Windswept style that it evoked sighs of envy from gentlemen across the land.

He could not even blame his unwed state on the scandal of his first marriage and subsequent divorce. England, after widespread debate across coffee houses and taverns, parks and assembly rooms, had magnanimously chosen to forgive him for his youthful mistake. Besides, he had been in Vienna when he married so impulsively, and all young men made bad decisions when abroad, the nation had agreed. Of course, most tourists brought home tawdry paintings as a souvenir, not a hedonistic Hungarian princess.

Nor was it for lack of suitable ladies. Leo had waltzed and strolled and dined with any number of eligible women: diamonds and originals, wallflowers and bluestockings, widows and companions. Any number of times he had nodded at a lady and told himself, *Yes, she will do nicely*. Only to somehow neglect to ever speak to her again.

Such behavior bordered on *dishonorable*, came the outraged whispers of those whose greatest pleasure was finding something to be outraged about. When a duke showed an interest in a lady, only to abandon her, everyone wondered what was wrong with her.

When it happened enough times, with enough ladies, everyone wondered what was wrong with him.

Leo tore another plank off the crate with more vigor than was required.

Nothing was wrong with him. He had simply been waiting for the right moment, the right lady, the right motivation. A little push, that was all he'd needed, and that little push had come today when his man of affairs bombarded him with numbers, such as the number of pounds, shillings, and pence he needed to obtain in order to expand his Foundation, and the number of ladies he needed to marry in order to obtain that sum. Thousands of pounds. One lady.

"I was curious why you hadn't remarried," Hadrian mused. "It's unlike you to delay once you decide something. I'd wondered if the divorce caused you pain."

"All the divorce caused me was great expense and even greater embarrassment."

Chuckling, Hadrian flipped to the next page. "Ah, this is interesting. Criteria for your bride, it seems: 'Twenty thousand pounds. Of child-bearing age. Suitable to be a duchess. Likes decorative arts?' That last one has a question mark."

"My secretary included it as a nice-to-have, but not necessary."

Hadrian blinked at him. "Your *secretary* dictated these criteria? You open your own boxes but let your staff advise on marital affairs as well as financial ones?"

"My dear chap, marital affairs *are* financial affairs," Leo drawled in affected ducal tones. "And yes, as we already established, I hire people to do things I don't enjoy, and that includes making lists and doing sums."

"And choosing brides?"

Leo ignored him.

"What about…" Hadrian flung aside the pages and roamed again, scraping his fingers over his scalp. "I don't know… Passion?"

Leo snorted derisively. He had yielded to passion once, and it had chewed him up and spat him out. He was still tidying up the mess.

"I made mistakes," he said. "Marrying properly is the final step in fixing those mistakes."

"But if you marry wrongly again…"

"It'll be different this time."

"How so?"

"This time when I choose my wife, I'll actually be sober."

No more delay. He would begin his courtship at tonight's ball. He'd be engaged within a month, married within three. There was one lady in London who met all four of those criteria. Her name was Susannah Macey, and she would make him a good wife.

And Leo would try, very hard, to make her a good husband. He would do whatever necessary to ensure his marriage worked this time.

"I like her," he said quietly, as he reached into the straw.

"Who?"

"The lady who meets those criteria."

Yes, he liked Susannah Macey. She didn't fire up his imagination or any of those other traits he sought in decorative objects, but she wasn't a decorative object, so that was all right.

"Does she like you?" Hadrian asked.

"She doesn't run at the sight of me, which is always an encouraging sign."

Searching in the crate, his fingers touched cool porcelain. He gently extricated a vase. Excitement poked up its head like a curious kitten, then sank back down with a sigh. Not quite, he thought, as he inspected the brushwork through his quizzing glass. It was technically good, but it lacked that spark, that heart, that *something* that stirred him up inside. He imagined Juno's merry laughter if he told her that. "It's called 'emotion,' Leo," she would tease him. "It's emotion that makes art, not technique."

Hadrian wandered to his side and tapped the vase. It rang hollowly. "I don't understand, Dammerton," he said. "This seems so superficial. That's very pretty, I'm sure, but it's a *vase*. Today's newspaper is dissecting your last speech on voting reform, yet here you are, surrounded by…" He waved an arm at the waiting crates.

"Frivolous fribbles and fripperies?" Leo suggested dryly. "To quote my critics."

"You established an embroidery workshop. What sort of duke establishes an embroidery workshop?"

"The sort of duke who seeks to safeguard those with the skills to create beautiful things." He glanced down at his waistcoat, made by a talented embroideress at that workshop, and brushed off a piece of impudent straw clinging to the bright riot of flowers adorning the silk. No surprise the decorative arts seemed superficial to Hadrian, who was up to his ears in secret affairs of state.

"The objects in our lives aren't mere things. They connect us to each other." Leo raised the vase to the light. "Someone shaped and painted this vase with their own hands. Someone fired the kiln, using wood someone else cut, carted by a horse someone else fed, with corn harvested by someone else." He waved his free hand at the mess around him. "Someone sawed the planks to make the crates, someone sailed them down the canals, someone baked the bread to feed the men who built those canals. Countless steps, involving countless people, each with their hopes and fears, losses and loves. One simple object, a thousand complex lives. There is nothing superficial about that." He returned the vase to its bed of straw. "How often do you look at everyday objects and think about all the people involved in making and moving them?"

Hadrian shrugged. "Approximately never."

"Try it some time."

"Then I'll become as mad as you are."

"Nonsense. Dukes are far too rich and important to be mad." Leo grinned. "I am merely eccentric."

WHEN LEO and Hadrian emerged onto the street, they were greeted by the sight of a jaunty peddler's cart. Propped up against the cart was Woodruff himself, packing tobacco into a crusty pipe. At Leo's approach, the peddler grinned, causing his long, luxurious beard to quiver. Woodruff oiled his whiskers as devotedly as he adorned his cart with ribbons and bells. Leo lived in hope that the peddler would similarly adorn his beard with ribbons and bells, but, alas, was disappointed again.

"Well, if it isn't my favorite duke!" Grinning, Woodruff twirled his pipe. "Fancy meeting your lordship here."

"Fancy," Leo agreed dryly. "Haven't seen you for a couple of weeks at least."

"I've been traveling the world. I've been hunting down such marvels as to bring a tear to a fine man's eye."

"The whole world? In a fortnight? I'm impressed."

His feet carried him toward the cart with its dizzying display of goods.

"You're not buying something from him," Hadrian said.

"You never know. He might actually have a treasure here."

"Oh, I do," Woodruff offered. "Such treasures that are sure to steal your breath."

"Not to mention your purse," Hadrian muttered. "I'll leave you to it. See you at dinner. And good luck with the courtship!"

With a wave, he jogged across the street and leaped into a hackney cab.

Woodruff's eyes gleamed, as the pipe disappeared into the depths of his greatcoat. "Courting, is it, Your Grace? You'll find a special gift for the lucky lady here. Consider these handkerchiefs, the silk so soft you'd think it were spun from the locks of angels. Or these combs…"

Leo let the familiar patter wash over him, as he poked through wooden toys and copper pans and a tangle of shiny satin ribbons. And then he saw—

"I'll take that," he said.

It was a conch shell: huge, polished, flawless. Entirely useless, of course, but entirely right.

With a sorrowful shake of his beard, Woodruff reached for the shell. "'Tis the end of days, verily the end of days, when a duke eschews diamonds and silk to give such a thing to the lady he's courting."

Leo fished some coins from his pocket. "Calm yourself, good fellow," he said. "This is not for the lady I mean to court. This is a gift for a friend."

CHAPTER 2

The drawing felt almost alive under Juno's fingers. Stormy waters crashed around a mermaid's fishtail as she laid claim to a muscular sailor, who had not only been shipwrecked, poor fellow, but had somehow managed to lose all his clothes in the process.

"That's the least of your worries, though, my friend," Juno cheerfully informed her sailor, "since that beautiful mermaid is about to drag you to your doom."

The sailor remained stoically silent, but a feline burr came from the red-cushioned window seat, where the cats were curled up together in a puddle of late-afternoon sun. Artemisia was ignoring her, striped paws crossed over her eyes, but Angelica blinked sleepily, and yawned when Juno scratched her soft gray ears.

The drawing was good, she marveled, with the faint surprise she still felt after completing a pleasing piece of work. Somehow, she had done this: captured the turmoil of the churning waves, the tautness of the sailor's muscles as he battled nature, the sleek ribs and waist of the mermaid as she reached for him.

And yet. Her eye turned critical. The sailor's unclothed figure was satisfactory, but his face required further changes, to disguise the model's identity.

Humming a sea shanty, Juno went back to work, gradually becoming aware of someone watching from the studio door.

Mr. St. Blaise, presumably. Bother. She had hoped her model had left.

"You had better have your clothes on this time," she said sternly, without looking up from the easel.

"I am happy to report that I have committed all my sins today in a state of full dress."

The familiar drawl, dryly amused, sent warm pleasure bubbling up through her.

"Leo!" She turned with a smile. "Forgive me. I thought you were someone else."

"Someone more naked, I presume? I am sorry to disappoint."

"Oh, you could never disappoint, not while you blind me with your ducal splendor."

He had arranged himself like a painting: his slender figure lazily propped up against the doorjamb, booted legs crossed at the ankles, posed just so with the light teasing his burnt-umber hair and gliding over the long angles of his face.

She let herself take him in: his artfully tousled hair and deceptively sleepy eyes, the jeweled pin glinting in his flawless cravat, the ornate embroidery on his waistcoat, the doeskin hugging his thighs. His form-fitting coat fairly smirked at her shapeless smock, and the gleam on his boots made her scuffed wooden floorboards blush with shame.

Leopold Halton, the Duke of Dammerton, looked as out of place in Juno's humble, chaotic studio as some glittering creature from fairyland, yet his presence always felt right. Even after four years, she never tired of his unannounced visits, just as she never tired of looking at him. And why should she? Any artist would appreciate the elegance of his form, the grace of his movements, the wizardry of his tailoring.

To say nothing of the gifts he brought her. He held one up now, a lump covered by a linen handkerchief.

"My offering to the Muse," he said.

"Very well. You may enter."

She wiped her grubby hands and threw the cloth over the sketch to conceal it, while Leo navigated through her forest of easels to present his gift. It was his own handkerchief draped over it, and a hint of lemon verbena teased her nostrils as he folded back the linen to reveal, of all things, a conch shell.

"Oh, but this is unbelievable!" she laughed, reaching for it eagerly.

Her fingers brushed his warm palm; a pleasant tingling ensued. She carefully focused instead on the shell: the rough bumps of its spire, the smooth coolness of its inner lips.

"You find the conch shell amusing?" he asked, watching her thumb slide over the shell's glossy pink lip.

Her grip tightened. "I find it wonderful you knew I wanted one."

"I knew nothing. I was passing a peddler's cart and it caught my eye."

"And still you refuse to believe in magic. Here, look at this."

She whipped the cloth back off the drawing and directed his attention to where a second mermaid bobbed in the waves, holding an indistinct shape to her mouth.

Juno tapped the shape. "This poor darling is meant to be blowing into a conch shell, but I realized I'd only the vaguest idea what one looks like. And right while I was wondering how to get one as a prop, you were buying this from a peddler."

"Coincidence."

"Magic."

He did not insist. He was frowning at the drawing, suddenly, palpably taut. Surely the near nakedness of the figures would not bother him? What was he— Oh. *Oh.*

With fresh eyes, Juno saw what she had not seen earlier, what had sailed from her imagination to the page without passing through her conscious mind: the sailor's raw yearning as he gazed at the mermaid, and— Good heavens, the mermaid! Her expression was fierce with possessive hunger, as she laid desperate claim to a prize she could only destroy.

Even Juno felt a little unsettled by the Muse's mischief. All that passion! No wonder Leo looked disturbed.

She whirled away and carried the conch shell to her crowded prop cabinet, negotiated a space for it between the porcelain doll and the brass sextant, also gifts from Leo over the years. It seemed to amuse him to present her with whimsical items. Some were fine pieces—the Chinese lacquer box, the Persian chess set, the Genoese globe—but most he picked up from fairs and peddlers and the curiosity shops he poked about in. They cost him mere pennies and were more valuable to her than all the jewels in the realm.

"This drawing is magnificent," he murmured. "But it's different." He jerked his chin at another easel, holding a partly painted portrait of a banker's wife dandling an infant on her knee. "To your commissioned work, I mean."

His gaze flicked back and forth between Juno and the sketch, Juno, the sketch, as if trying to find the connection, as if she had pulled some trick and he wished to see how it was done.

An unfamiliar shyness washed over her. How silly. Shyness was for other people, and there was no reason to feel exposed. She certainly wasn't ashamed of such drawings, any more than she was ashamed of the shadowy corners of her mind from whence they came. Everyone had such corners, even those who insisted they didn't, and finding the courage to plunder such places was essential for creating art. Of course, one must be careful, especially as a woman. This mermaid drawing was destined for her secret collection, artwork she created only because such images gathered in her mind like storm clouds, until she had to release them or go mad.

But she should never have shown it to him, not to Leo.

Not when the drawing revealed something intimate about her, and he took such care never to reveal anything about himself.

She waved the cloth, as if waving away her discomfort. "There is something you should know about my model for the sailor," she said brightly.

"I already know he is a very muscular fellow." Leo's tone also became jauntier. "Can you guess how I know this?"

"Because you are very observant and pay meticulous attention to detail?"

"Yes. And because he is notably devoid of clothing." He slid her a sideways look. "Am I to believe you drew such accurate and detailed musculature from your imagination?"

She matched his look coolly. "I have a very vivid imagination."

He laughed then, and she did too, and their unease vanished from the room like smoke through an open window.

"Drawing nudes again, really." He tutted at her with mock solemnity. "A grave risk, Juno. Your feeble female brain will explode and they'll cart you off to Bedlam. 'Tis what happens to women when faced with a nude, you know. Scientific fact."

"And yet my brain has not exploded. Perhaps I am particularly robust."

"I fear not. You already exhibit the adverse side effects of drawing nudes: You are not married, you are not tidy, and you talk to your cats." He nodded at the drawing, more serious now. "Not to mention the risk to your reputation. Your clients will abandon you and Mrs. Prescott will withdraw her patronage. You'll never be able to show or sell the final work."

"But I am able to paint it," she said defiantly, "and that is the point."

Though it was a shame she could never exhibit such excellent work under her own name, while men displayed similar works with pride. But society had strict notions about what subjects were appropriate for the so-called gentler sex. One could not have London's art world collapsing in a collective faint at the discovery that a woman actually knew what went on under a person's clothes.

Moving away from him, Juno untied the scarf protecting her hair. Her curls made a break for freedom; she corralled the mass into a coil and stabbed it with a pair of mismatched combs. The heavy smock soon joined the scarf on their hook. She stretched her arms over her head and breathed deeply. Oh, but that felt good after hours of stillness.

Twisting her spine with a groan of pleasure, she caught Leo watching her. With a curt shake of his head, he looked away and took to leafing through her sketches, all studies for the final drawing. Poor Leo, how he suffered at the sight of her work dresses. The gowns were loose-fitting for ease of movement, in a dark print to hide stains, and made of sturdy cotton to endure for years. They were practical, comfortable, and unavoidably dowdy, an affront to poor Leo's sensitive eyes.

"Meanwhile," she said, "I really must warn you about my new model."

"Who, I gather, is still wandering around your house without his clothes on."

"He enjoys that far too much. I had to send him to get dressed several times. I've not seen him for a while, so he must have left. But he— Ah."

There was no need to continue, because Leo had uncovered the one sketch that revealed her model's identity.

"Please say it isn't so." His expression was an amusing mix of vexation and disbelief. "*St. Blaise?*"

"He's actually very good. Stands perfectly still and never complains. I should have started hiring soldiers years ago."

"Clearly your mind is already addled, if you hired my scoundrel of a half-brother as your new model."

"What a beastly thing to say of me, Polly," came the voice of that half-brother from the studio door.

Juno turned with a sigh, as Mr. St. Blaise came swaggering into her studio like he was leaving a brothel at dawn. His dark hair was rumpled, and he had still not managed to get dressed. Although, to give him credit, his breeches and boots were on, and his other clothes trailed from one hand, so he had made some progress since the last time she sent him away.

Perhaps hiring St. Blaise was a mistake. The former cavalry officer was, after all, a notorious rake, and the eldest son of Leo's late father by his long-time French mistress, the famously beautiful Marguerite St. Blaise. But when she met him in a salon a few nights previously, he had just looked … right.

It was not Juno's habit, normally, to engage in the careful weighing of decisions. Things felt right or not, after which there was just a lot of making up reasons to justify doing what one already wished to do. Her family, that horde of clever darlings, worshipped at the shrine of something called "rational thinking," but it struck Juno as a tremendous waste of energy to debate something that was already settled in one's heart.

Of course, sometimes her intuition did make spectacularly unwise decisions. But as far as she could tell, others' endless cogitations did not deliver notably superior results.

"And of course Miss Bell hired me, for she is a woman of taste," St. Blaise was saying to Leo. "Come, Polly, even you must admit I have a magnificent physique and my face is uncommonly beautiful."

Leo flicked him a glance. "Your face is also uncommonly punchable," he said mildly.

St. Blaise grinned and collapsed onto the daybed like a lover in a folk song.

"I have had the most fabulous nap. Modeling is exhausting," he said, with a dramatic yawn and stretch of those bare arms and chest. "Miss Bell, I have dreamed up a wonderful idea: I shall live in your studio and become your kept man. I shall bring you tea and cake, charm your guests, and pose whenever you please." He winked. "I am very talented at taking off my clothes."

"But rather less talented at putting them back on again," Juno said pointedly.

"Your wish is my command."

In a flurry of energy, he pulled on his shirt and waistcoat, then hurled himself back onto the daybed, limbs flung out, eyes soulful, lips curved into the smile that lifted a thousand petticoats.

It was an impressive display. But alas, Juno was no longer easily impressed. St. Blaise's body would only ever be a prop to her now. She glanced at Leo: He didn't mind, really, did he?

To her delight, a tiny smile teased Leo's lips, and delicious devilry danced in his eyes.

"What a fabulous opportunity for you, Juno," he drawled. "Haven't you always wanted a kept man?"

"I'm afraid I haven't the cabinet space in which to keep one."

"You could roll him up and store him under the bed."

"Or in a cage in the window like a songbird."

"And in all fairness," Leo added, "you'll find him more useful than, say, a pet monkey."

"Here's an idea." Her eyes widened. "I could dress him in a pet monkey outfit, with a little hat and an adorable jacket."

"Hmm, pet monkeys don't wear trousers, though."

"A kept man shouldn't wear trousers either, or what's the point in keeping him?"

He smiled at that, and they took a moment to enjoy their shared nonsense, until St. Blaise interrupted.

"I say, Miss Bell," he broke in. "Polly isn't your kept man, is he?"

"Leo?" Juno burst into astonished laughter. "Heavens, no. I could never afford him. A single waistcoat would beggar me."

"Then why is he here?"

"I do not wish to upset you, but I must inform you that a man can call on a woman without intending to bed her," she said.

"Can he?" St. Blaise sounded genuinely curious. "Can he, really?"

"He came to give me a gift."

"Actually," Leo corrected lazily. "I came to fetch you."

"Fetch me where?"

He raised one eyebrow and said nothing. He raised the other eyebrow and still said nothing.

"Oh, good heavens—Hadrian's dinner!" she remembered, slapping her cheek. "I completely lost track of time." She glared at the window with its deceptive daylight: The days were so long this time of year. "Thank you. I should hate to be late."

"Dinner?" St. Blaise said. "Who's going to dinner?"

"It's a family dinner, to celebrate my cousin Hadrian's return to England," Juno explained, as she gathered up the finished mermaid drawing and her other sketches. She locked them in the heavy armoire, where she hid most of her secret things. "It will be the first time we are all in the same room in years."

And how she was looking forward to it, all of them together: her aunt Hester and uncle Gordon; her cousins Phoebe and Livia, one married and living apart from her husband, the other resolutely unmarried and living at home; young Daniel, now studying at Oxford; and Hadrian, finally come home from Vienna.

"If it's a family dinner, why is Polly invited?"

"Because he is Hadrian's oldest friend." She grabbed St. Blaise's coat and snapped it at him like a toreador at a bull. "I must dress for dinner, and you must leave."

"I could help you dress."

"You will help by leaving," she insisted firmly. "Out. Now."

"I suppose you've not seen Hadrian since we were all in Vienna," Juno said to Leo, once she had shooed St. Blaise out the door and was washing her hands with lavender-scented soap. "That must be… How many years ago now?"

"Eight," Leo said shortly.

"I'll always remember Vienna with such fondness. I had such a wonderful time there. Do you remember—"

"I prefer not to remember Vienna," he said with startling chilliness.

Without looking at her, he dropped onto the window seat beside the cats. Artemisia stoutly ignored him, but Angelica, the darling little flirt, launched herself at his ribs. There followed some negotiations between duke and cat, as Leo explained that his outfit was already perfect and would not be improved by cat hair. "My valet will skin you and turn you into a hat," he warned, so Angelica flopped against his thigh and grinned at him upside down. Her efforts were rewarded when Leo's slender fingers raked through the gray fluff on her belly.

Juno tore her gaze off his hand and turned back to the wash-basin to attack her grubby fingernails with a boar-bristle brush. How careless she was. Of course Leo did not wish to speak of Vienna, for it was in Vienna that he had met his former wife, the youngest daughter of a minor Hungarian prince, whom he had married after a whirlwind romance.

When Hadrian told Juno that Leo was coming to Vienna, she had been eager to see him again. By that time, she had been studying in Vienna for two years, while devouring the manifold delights of that city's bohemian world. It would be her first meeting with Leo after that embarrassing display in the meadow, and she had hoped to repair their friendship, which she had surely ruined with that foolish kiss.

They had walked together in the gardens, where Vienna's autumn foliage had dazzled with its display of orange, ochre, and red. Even after more than two years apart, chatting with Leo had felt so *right*. Juno happily kicked up the leaves and listened to Leo's news, and when Hadrian left them alone to greet a colleague, she seized the opportunity to apologize for her behavior in the meadow. He need not fear any more unwanted declarations of love or kisses, she had assured him, for she thought of him now as only a friend!

Alas for her: Leo had shown no further interest in her company. Instead, he ran wild with his German cousins, their reckless behavior shocking even Viennese society. Juno traveled south to Florence soon afterward, seeking a new tutor and a milder winter. She did not learn of Leo's sudden marriage until some months after it was done. The news had surprised her; she could only assume he had been very much in love.

With a sigh, she dried her hands on a clean linen, her eyes wandering back to him.

Once more, he had managed to arrange himself like a painting, his head framed by the window, with the sunlight gilding his eyelashes and caressing his smooth-shaven cheek. The light shimmered over the vibrant flowers embroidered on his waistcoat. *Unknown Gentleman with Cat*, Juno would title it.

He was so carefully curated, so artfully presented, as if to ensure that if he was subject to the world's stares, it would be on his own terms. He had turned himself into a piece of art, and nothing touched art.

It vexed her sometimes, the way he used his manner and dress to hold the world at a distance. Or perhaps she was merely piqued he held her at a distance too.

The invisible lines between them had been drawn during Leo's first visit, just over four years ago, barely days after Juno moved into this house. She had been turning in circles in her empty studio, deciding what to put where, and between one turn and the next, Leo had appeared, glossy and untouchable: older, still married, so newly a duke he still wore a black armband for his late father. Hadrian had sent him to check on her, he had explained, and Juno hadn't minded, for she'd never expected to see much of Leo again at all.

How easily the conversation had flowed, and yet how carefully. At that time, London was abuzz about his wife's scandalous behavior, so Juno had tactfully waited for him to mention her first. Four years and a divorce later, she was still waiting.

Indeed, one might think the scandal had concerned a different man entirely. Even during the circus surrounding the trial of his wife's lover and the ensuing divorce, even as the published trial transcripts sold in the tens of thousands, as increasingly bawdy cartoons lined every shop window, as he became a comic character in puppet shows and the subject of songs sold on street corners— Leo had strolled through his days as if none of it had anything to do with him.

In many ways, Juno knew Leo. She knew he took his tea with lemon, and he liked a nice pork pie, and he preferred the sort of theater that made one laugh. He delighted in embroidery and artisans and arguments for reform. He despised lists, numbers, and small-mindedness. He admired his mother, adored his siblings, both respected and resented his late father.

But she did not know if he still loved his former wife, or how their lack of children made him feel. She did not know what future he dreamed of, or if he took lovers, or if he would ever love again.

She knew what people said about Leo, because people were *always* talking about him. "Such *sprezzatura*," some cried, citing that Italian virtue of effortless skill and style, while others insisted the duke was cold and aloof.

Aloof? Cold? *Leo*? No: With her, Leo was playful and fun. Eyes that shade of blue could seem cold, perhaps, but Juno only saw their sparkle when he was enjoying a joke. His quietness could be mistaken for aloofness, but in fact he was shy; despite his high status and the constant glare of attention upon him, he preferred to observe than be at the center of a group. With his friends, however, he was amiable and relaxed.

Yet she couldn't help but sense that he carefully kept a wall between them.

And why wouldn't he? He was a splendid duke, and she was a shabby artist, and they lived in different worlds, and she must not let herself forget that, because no one else ever would.

He glanced up, caught her studying him. She unfurled the cloth from her fists.

"Thank you for ensuring I'm not late, but you need not have come yourself," she said, a little stiffly. "I'm sure a duke has more important missions than to remind an artist of her appointments."

"My motives are entirely selfish," he drawled. "I must ensure you are there on time so I have someone to rescue me if Livia and Phoebe talk at me in Latin."

"Not talking at people in Latin has always been one of my more appealing traits. As patience is yours!" she added. "I'll dress quickly, if you don't mind entertaining yourself—" She stopped short, taking in his boots and doeskins. "Oh, you're not dressed for dinner either."

He tipped Angelica off his thigh, stood, and brushed down his coat. "I'll make my own way there. A carriage awaits you outside."

She forced a smile. "Of course."

Of course a duke could not be seen traveling across London alone in a carriage with an artist. Not when the duke was divorced and seeking a wife. Not when the artist was an unmarried woman. Gossip would not affect him, of course; a duke would be forgiven all manner of things. But even though artists and other bohemians were not held to the same rules of behavior as the *ton*, Juno was an unmarried woman who had excellent connections but earned her own living, and no one knew quite what to make of someone like her.

"That is very thoughtful," she added. "Thank you."

"My pleasure."

Juno watched him go, a secret treat she liked to give herself, her breath hitching at the graceful taper of his shoulders, back, thighs, the almost feline energy of his movements. Her fingers twitched. He could be captured only with sweeping, fluid lines.

In the doorway, he twisted unexpectedly; she straightened guiltily. He whisked a searching glance over her, as if to catch her transforming behind his back. It was new, his faintly troubled expression when he regarded her. The drawing of the mermaid had unsettled him.

Satisfaction bloomed in her chest as his footsteps crossed her parlor and faded down the stairs.

Serve you right if my art affected you, Leopold Halton, she thought. *Serve you jolly well right.*

CHAPTER 3

"Ten pounds says we'll not even finish our port before my father starts nagging me to get married," Hadrian had grumbled to Leo when inviting him to fill the eighth seat at the Bell family dinner.

As it happened, the tricky topic of marriage did not arise until after the gentlemen had finished their post-dinner port and joined the ladies in the drawing room. And it was not Sir Gordon who started it, but Juno, when she innocently asked her cousin, "What are your plans now you are back in England, Hadrian? Do you mean to stay this time?"

She was seated on a settee across from Leo, beside her cousin Phoebe, or rather, Mrs. Grayshott as she was now, who, at five-and-twenty, had acquired an air of sophistication along with a failed marriage. Juno sat with one foot tucked up under her. When the gentlemen arrived, Lady Bell had automatically admonished her to sit properly, and Juno had automatically obeyed. But here she was again, that foot tucked up, heedless of her exposed calf and abandoned slipper. If Lady Bell had noticed, she was saving her breath, for everyone knew Juno always went her own way in the end.

In all other respects, she appeared every inch the genteel lady her aunt had raised her to be, in a pretty pale-blue gown trimmed with shiny darker-blue ribbons. Even her hair was tamely piled on her head, save for a few renegade spirals that fluttered about her neck.

The change from her dowdy work dresses was startling. Leo was not used to seeing the rounded lines of her bare arms, golden in the candlelight, or the expanse of skin above the generous swell of her bodice. Although, to be fair, while those hideous day dresses had long sleeves and high necklines, their loose-fitting folds tended to offer tantalizing hints of Juno's curves when she stretched in her luxuriant way.

Yet neither version of Juno—neither artist nor lady—looked capable of the furious passions swirling within her drawing of the mermaid with the sailor.

That drawing. That bloody drawing.

His mind kept coming back to it throughout dinner, while Phoebe and Livia debated Greek translations over the pea soup, while Sir Gordon and young Daniel dissected law over the lamb cutlets, while Hadrian and Lady Bell discussed economics over the duck ragout, while Juno regaled them with gossip from the art world over the gooseberry tart. Conversation flowed energetically, but no one mentioned Hadrian's mysterious scar, or Phoebe's estrangement from her husband, or Livia's increasing withdrawal from society, or—mercifully—Leo's failure to contribute much to the conversation at all.

The drawing was not lewd, and even her terrible choice of male model could be forgiven, as she'd changed the features so much. But their expressions! The mermaid's fierce, hungry possessiveness, the sailor's confused longing, knowing the siren would drag him to his death, but wanting her anyway.

It was only a drawing, he told himself. Just charcoal lines on paper. Yet those feelings had coiled off the paper and nestled under his solar plexus, turning it peculiarly cavernous and achy. *Sehnsucht*, as they said in German, that intense yearning for he knew not what.

And there was Juno, the mastermind of this sensation, blithely nibbling on a chocolate truffle, pausing to savor the taste, to meet his eyes, smile wickedly, and pop the remaining morsel into her mouth.

"Or will you be looking for another position abroad?" This time, the question for Hadrian came from Livia, bright-eyed, coltish, and looking much younger than her twenty-three years.

"He'll be looking for a wife," Sir Gordon inserted sternly.

Stunned silence clattered through the drawing room, chased away by bright laughter.

"Oh ho," Phoebe laughed. "You're in for it now, Hadrian!"

"This is hardly the time to discuss this," Hadrian protested. "Mother, please ask——"

Lady Bell raised her palms in surrender. "Do not appeal to me, my boy. I wash my hands of the lot of you," she cried, laughing too. "If I have failed in my duty as a mother, then so be it! To have raised five children to adulthood, and only Phoebe married."

"And Phoebe does not even speak to her husband," Hadrian pointed out.

Phoebe widened her eyes. "Oh, are we meant to keep talking to them after we wed?" She aimed a walnut at her elder brother. "And do not use me to deflect attention from yourself, you beast," she said, and let the walnut fly.

Hadrian caught it with lightning-fast reflexes. "Then I shall use Juno as a distraction," he said unrepentantly. "Come, Father, why not nag Juno to get married instead of me, as she is next in age? Haven't you heard? She is nearly twenty-*eight*."

Sir Gordon eyed his eldest son over the top of his glasses. "Because you are my heir, and while I am happy to hand down the law firm to Daniel—"

"And I am happy to take it," said Daniel.

"—you will inherit the baronetcy. Besides, Juno has made her own choices and followed through on them with admirable resolve."

"I have made my choices too." Hadrian turned serious. "My current position does not allow for married life."

"Then find a new position."

Father and son locked eyes in a silent battle. Tension sliced the room, softened only by confusion. None of Hadrian's siblings knew what his work for the government entailed, but Leo and Sir Gordon knew, and there was very little paperwork involved.

From the corner of his eye, Leo caught Juno giving him a curious, thoughtful look. He knew she had questions about his marriage; he sensed them at times, teasing the edges of their conversations like a breeze teasing the ribbons on a bonnet. He also had questions, but he dared not ask. If he asked Juno why she had not married anyone, she might ask him why he had married Erika. Leo would rather be boiled in oil than discuss Erika with Juno, so he would have to hurl himself out the window to avoid answering and it would all get rather awkward after that.

It was Livia who broke the tension, saying, "I do want to know about Juno, though. You never give a satisfactory reply."

Juno froze like a thief, hand poised to steal another truffle from the red Venetian glass bowl. "Reply to what?"

"Why you are not yet married," Livia said. "I'm sure there are many men who want to marry you."

Juno's lips quirked. "And I'm sure men want to marry me for the same reason they want to dance with me: for a chance to bump up against my glorious bosom."

This scandalous sentence was greeted with shrieks of

delighted laughter. Even Lady Bell fought a laugh as she said, "Juno Bell, behave! One does not speak of such things in polite society. Whatever will Dammerton think?"

She flashed him her crooked smile. "If Leo were to be shocked by anything I say, that day has long since passed."

Leo raised his glass in a mock salute. "I confess I near fainted the first time I heard her speak that way, but I am now made of sterner stuff."

Such was the effect of her years among the bohemians of Europe: a lack of restraint in word and gesture, bawdy humor, and her matter-of-fact attitude toward bodies, nudity, and other topics that proper English ladies avoided like a groping drunkard at a ball.

Juno selected a truffle and leaned back, seated properly now. "Besides, marriage requires a great effort. My art and ambition consume all my time."

"But what about when you have achieved your ambitions and can rest on your laurels?" Livia persisted.

"By then I shall be so old my bosom will be resting on my laurels too, and what man will fancy me then?"

"Certainly no respectable man," Hester sighed through the laughter.

Juno grinned at her impishly. "Just as well I do not aspire to respectability."

Hadrian set his glass down with a thump. "I don't believe it," he said. "I recall when your art overflowed with romance. What have you become, sweet cousin—a jaded cynic, or a hopeless romantic who is difficult to please?"

"What I am is my own mistress," Juno said defiantly, waving her truffle about as she spoke. "When I want quiet, I have it. When I want company, I have it. I can work all day without inter-ruption, or sleep all day without judgment. I earn my own way, do as I please, and am beholden to no one. Where would a husband fit into that life? He will demand attention and pester me about his boots or his dinner, then take my money and disrupt my schedule and steal my time."

She nibbled the edge off her chocolate truffle and swung one foot back and forth. Her scuffed slipper dangled from her toes, and her hem slipped back to reveal the flower motifs embroidered over the ankles of her darned stockings.

Daniel snorted. "We men are not so rotten. You haven't a shred of evidence for these claims."

"Oh, the young lawyer demands evidence, does he?" Juno said. "Very well: Consider the case of Elisabeth Vigée LeBrun. She painted portraits for Marie Antoinette and all of Versailles until... Well."

"Well, indeed." Hadrian chuckled darkly. "Beheadings must really put a damper on the portrait-painting business."

This earned a round of groans and another walnut flung at his head, after which mayhem Juno continued.

"After fleeing Paris, Madame LeBrun moved around Europe, painting royals. She even had a studio here in London for three years, painted the Prince of Wales, as he then was. She earned a fortune from her paintings—and her husband gambled it all away. I earn considerably less than a fortune, so why should I give it all to some man?"

"But maybe she was in love," Phoebe argued. "You used to proclaim the superiority of emotion and sensation over what you call our 'thinking.' Surely you've not changed so much. Do you never fall in love?"

For the length of a heartbeat, Juno's foot stilled, as did Leo's breath. But then she continued, her eyes elsewhere, her tone light.

"On the contrary. I make it a practice to fall in love at least three times every day. One must take love lightly and drift down into it, as a feather onto a cloud. Land too heavily in love and one will get stuck there, like a carriage in a bog."

She swung her foot so hard her slipper flew right off, executed a somersault, and landed with a slap by Leo's shoe. He herded the slipper back across the floor to her. She hooked it with her toes, shot him a bright smile, and went right back to swinging her leg, completely at peace with her free-spirited ways, her rakish views on love.

Her cousins were wrong: Juno's carefree philosophies were not new at all. Leo had learned how she truly viewed love eight years earlier, when they walked together in the gardens in Vienna that crisp autumn day.

It had been the first time Leo saw her since that fiasco in the meadow. The moment was painted in his memory: the blue sky, the orange leaves, the way his chest had swelled at the sight of her after so long apart. He had endured two long years since their first kiss and her promising words of love, two painful years of waiting for the chance to fix his mistake and put matters right.

But she had spoken first, there among the bright colors of the dying leaves. How earnest her smile had been, as she squeezed Leo's arm and assured him her youthful nonsense had passed. "I promise to never again importune you with kisses or protestations of love," she had laughed, adding, "I was so young! I suppose every girl of seventeen must have a silly infatuation and you were mine. How awkward it must have been for you!"

A silly infatuation. Youthful nonsense. That was all their first sweet kiss had meant to her, while for him it had meant the world. Thus were Juno's words of love: easily spoken, soon forgotten.

And that same night, in that red salon, with that older man, the Czech violinist...

The long-buried memory from Vienna suddenly shone in his mind like a freshly polished silver plate: the red brocade walls, the overwrought chandelier, the scented air, and in a corner, half obscured by velvet draperies, Juno and the violinist, sharing an intimate look.

Juno tilting her chin.

The violinist bending his head.

The violinist kissing Juno.

Juno kissing him back.

Leo shook his head and shoved the memories back down into the dank cellar of his mind where they belonged. Where everything from Vienna belonged.

Back in the present, Hadrian was cheering Juno's sentiments, with a rowdy "Hear, hear!"

"May we all avoid getting stuck in the bog of love," he said, raising his glass. "A toast to our parents for demonstrating the perfect marriage, so that none of us dare try it for ourselves."

"Be brave, my son," Sir Gordon said dryly. "You may know love yet."

Hadrian laughed. "If I am to marry, Father, then I shall borrow Dammerton's list of criteria for his next wife: well bred, well behaved, and well dowered. That sum it up, Dammerton?"

"Pretty much."

Sipping his port, Leo risked a glance at Juno, but her attention was on the chocolate truffles, and her choice of which to eat next.

THE PARTY SOON BROKE UP, as the Bell family scattered to prepare for a ball. Leo waited for them in the drawing room, with Juno for company. She would not attend the ball, for hers was the world of risqué salons and soirees instead.

She paused to study a painting; he joined her at the wall. It was her own work, from her youth, depicting a young Phoebe and Livia clad in togas and lecturing in a Greek agora, while renowned philosophers listened at their feet.

She tilted her head to look at him. "You've been quiet this evening. What are you thinking about?"

Leo shrugged.

"More of your secrets," she said softly, and turned back to the painting.

It felt oddly unsettling, like she was slipping away.

"How old were you when you painted that?" he asked.

She pursed her lips, considering. "About sixteen, I think. They must have been about fourteen and twelve."

"Your affection for them shines through."

"They were already so learned, even back then. I never could keep up with their clever arguments."

"Not one of them can do what you do and they know it."

She traced a corner of the frame. "It's peculiar, isn't it? I do not lack confidence, yet a small part of myself is still ashamed and frightened like that grubby ten-year-old who showed up on their doorstep, not knowing which fork to use and hardly able to read, while my bluestocking cousins were already studying Greek. Sometimes, that little child tells me I'm not good enough."

"Showed up," Leo thought. The family always phrased it thus, as if little Juno had arrived at the Bell's country home in Longhope Abbey of her own volition, like a stray cat, rather than being left there by her artist parents, who had decided that a child no longer fit into their plans.

On one of their morning walks, Leo had said, *You never mention your parents,* to which she replied, *I never think of them. They had no time for me, so I have no time for them.* Her jaw had turned uncharacteristically hard, her shoulders stiff, her eyes flinty, so he'd known not to mention it again.

In many ways, Leo knew Juno. He knew she craved experience and chased sensation, and avoided the written word whenever she could. She enjoyed long walks in nature, but hated the way exertion turned her cheeks pink. She believed in superstitions, but worked hard and left nothing to luck. She followed rules only when they suited her, and never tried to hold anything that did not want to stay.

But he did not know what future she dreamed of, or if she still took lovers, or what she thought of in the night, when she woke up alone.

Her merry laugh bubbled between them. "Listen to me, getting so pensive! 'Tis the effect of this reunion, I suppose, stirring up that old feeling that I didn't belong, though they welcomed me from the start. Do we ever outgrow our younger selves, I wonder, or do they remain within us like ghosts, misbehaving at the slightest provocation?" She studied his profile. "Then when I met you…" Her hesitation pulsed between them. "Well, I suppose that's why I felt comfortable with you, the first time I encountered a truly like-minded soul."

"Until you went to Vienna," he reminded her. "Which abounded in like-minded souls."

"Yes. Of course."

"You were thriving in Vienna. Among your own people, immersed in art. I had never seen you so radiant."

Her brow creased with confusion. Warmth crept over his neck. He ought not to have said anything.

But that was part of his tangled memory of Juno in Vienna: how he had admired her, been happy for her, even as her blithe words tore his heart to shreds.

Light glinted off her silver earrings as she swung back to the painting. "I was so very proud of this, but now I cringe at my poor technique. I've changed much since then."

"Your choice of subject matter has certainly changed," he said pointedly.

Again she laughed. "Oh dear, I really should not have let you see that drawing today. I never show ones like that."

"Then you have others like it."

Foolish to insist. Wiser by far to keep distance between them. And yet... That drawing had left him ravenous.

"Is it so important to keep such artworks secret?" he asked.

"All secrets are important. One's secrets reveal what one values, or what one fears." She faced him again, chin raised in challenge. "I'll show you mine if you show me yours. Why do you never tell me your secrets, Leo?"

Her eyes pierced him, but he could never confess. Waste of breath, confessions.

Instead, he offered a lazy smile. "Because I have no secrets. Everyone in Britain knows everything about me already. In fact, people have to invent new secrets for me. I pick up the papers each morning astonished to learn what mischief I have been up to."

She was not fooled. "Then we are both keeping our secrets tonight," she said softly.

Sorrow shadowed her features, as if she grieved for something lost. For an unwanted moment, that loss echoed through him too.

Yes, something had been lost, many years ago. And some things that were lost could never be regained.

Their pensive mood was shattered by the amiable bickering and footsteps of her cousins returning. Juno wandered across the room, saying brightly, "'Tis ages since I attended a grand ball. Are you very thrilled to go?"

Another secret: his list of criteria, his need for money for his Foundation, the lady he meant to approach this very night, at the ball.

He spread his hands. "Ribbons, reels, ratafia, perhaps a scintillating scandal over supper? How could one not be thrilled to bits?"

CHAPTER 4

"Thrilled to bits," Leo murmured, as he entered the ballroom, with its heated, eddying swirl of frothy gowns and feathered heads. Orchestral music floated over the tinkles of glass and gossip, while flower arrangements burst from uninspiring vases and leafy palms stood guard in woefully bland pots.

And there was his target: Miss Susannah Macey. She caught his eye over her fan, smiled demurely, and turned away. He headed for her, yet was almost immediately accosted by—oh, so help him, it was her brother Thomas, who had apparently elected to liven up his evening by insulting Leo's clothes.

"What was that you said, Macey?" Leo asked amiably. "Something about my waistcoat, I believe?"

Tonight's waistcoat was indeed worthy of comment. The base was peach-colored silk, upon which was embroidered a cluster of primroses, whose upper edges transformed into a cloud of colorful butterflies bursting up over his chest.

But young Thomas Macey was not looking at the exquisite art that Leo wore. His attention darted to his trio of friends, who were watching their exchange with the eagerness of boys at their first peep show.

Ah, yes, Leo knew that set: They had been discussing him at their club that morning, speculating on ways to stir him out of his habitual unruffled calm. He had been seated within earshot, but they apparently believed that if they did not look at him while discussing him, he would not be able to overhear.

Unfortunately for everyone, sound did not work that way, so he had been forced to overhear, as they dared each other to provoke him into losing his temper in public, with a pot of cash for whoever succeeded in baiting him.

Duke-baiting. Really.

No reasonable person would expect a duke to tolerate such insolence. No reasonable person would object if Leo were to squish Thomas Macey like the annoying gnat he was. Leo was not, however, in the business of ruining young men simply for being immature numbskulls.

But Thomas Macey did not need to know that.

"I said, Your Grace," Macey explained smugly, flicking another glance at his friends, "I learned at a lecture that the purpose of a peacock's plumage is to attract a mate. It put me in mind of your fondness for ornate embroidery, yet two years divorced and you've not yet attracted another wife. Methinks your strategy does not work. For whom do you make yourself so beautiful?"

Leo raised his quizzing glass and examined Macey from brown top to black toe. When he lowered the glass, it was with a disappointed sigh.

"And for whom do you make yourself so … drab?" he countered. "Tell me, does *your* strategy work? Is your lady even now sighing, 'Oh, Mr. Macey, he's so delightfully dowdy. Dear Mr. Macey, he's so deliciously bland.'"

The younger man smirked. Leo could not abide a smirker. They were almost as bad as the color beige.

"I don't require bright colors to be noticed," Macey said. "I have my wit."

"Wit? Hmm. Perhaps if you dressed your wit in bright colors, I might have noticed it."

Leo tucked his quizzing glass into the pocket of his waistcoat, took the time to arrange the chain just so, then presented his most ducal stare until Macey looked away. He stepped closer and brushed a speck off his shoulder.

"My dear boy, you'll have to do better than that if you wish to rile me up enough to win your group's little game," he said softly. "And you do need to win, don't you? A few hundred pounds would help nicely with supporting that secret wife of yours. Daughter of a warehouse clerk, I believe? What will your father say when he learns about her?"

This speech had the interesting effect of turning Thomas Macey into a hooked fish: bulging eyes, gaping mouth, pale clammy skin. "How… How do you know about her?"

"Oh, my dear boy, I know everything." Leo smoothed down the lad's lapels, then stepped back, his fingers recoiling from the inferior fabric. Grandson to an earl and the boy could not choose a decent superfine. "Enough of this impertinence. Run along now, and tell your friends not to bother me again."

"You won't tell anyone…" Macey gulped. "Your Grace, I beg you, forgive me."

"Run along, I said."

Macey ran along.

Leo shook his head and sighed. Not yet thirty and already addressing younger men as "my dear boy."

It occurred to him, as he eased through the crowd, that if Miss Macey accepted his suit, he would assume some responsibility for her fool of a brother. Or not: The lad was twenty-one, which was old enough to tidy up his own mess.

Leo knew a lot about tidying up one's mess.

The old feeling bit him: that sense of failure where Erika was concerned. Their marriage had been foolish, impulsive, reckless, but he had been well beyond caring at the time. At first, he and Erika shared similar tastes: They had both enjoyed getting drunk and indulging in raucous diversions. But by the time they returned to England, Leo was bored with endless entertainment, while Erika was bored by everything that wasn't endless enter-tainment.

You misled me, she had said. *About the sort of man you are.*

His second marriage would succeed, he vowed. Not just for the Foundation, but for his title, his family, his future heirs. For his wife, for himself.

If he was fortunate enough to win Miss Macey's hand, he would make their marriage work, whatever it took.

SUSANNAH MACEY, who knew balls as a bird knew trees, had come armed with a beautiful fan, which she spread wide as they spoke. It was hand-painted with yellow daffodils and green swishes, the perfect complement to the yellow flowers and vines embroidered over the bodice of her white gown, and the braided green-and-gold headdress tucked into her pile of sable-brown hair.

The fan served three purposes, as far as Leo could tell: to fashion a cooling breeze, to demonstrate her taste and wealth, and to inspire conversation. *His* conversation in particular, he suspected. Conceited of him, perhaps, but in his defense, he was a duke, and while his title was of no interest to, say, an artist, it would be very interesting indeed to the nineteen-year-old grand-daughter of an earl.

"That fan is exquisite," he said dutifully.

Though it, too, failed to spark his ardor. Perhaps it was simply his mood these days, and he could not blame a fan for that.

Besides, it *was* lovely. Miss Macey had excellent taste. That was, her taste mostly aligned with his, and everyone knew the best taste was that which aligned with one's own.

She turned the fan this way and that, twirling its emerald-green tassel between the gloved fingers of her other hand.

"I thought you might like it," she said. "It is hand-painted by a very talented woman in Spitalfields. I had wondered..." She hissed in a little breath, then added in a rush, "If she mightn't be a candidate for a grant from the Dammerton Foundation."

He smiled. "Certainly worth considering."

The fan snapped shut. "Last time we spoke, you mentioned plans to expand the Foundation's work. More education, appren-ticeships, and markets, I believe?"

"If possible, though it will require a very large sum."

He looked at her. She looked at him.

Susannah Macey would bring to her marriage twenty-five thousand pounds. Leo knew she had twenty-five thousand, and she knew he knew, because not all gossip was useless.

"A gentleman as resourceful as yourself will no doubt find a way to secure that sum," she said. "The Dammerton Foundation does such admirable work, I'm sure you'll not have to look far to find someone willing to be part of it."

She held his gaze for a stitch longer than was proper.

Well. That sounded remarkably like an invitation to make a marriage proposal. Worded very subtly, and as a business transac-tion, but Susannah Macey was surprising that way.

"Indeed," she went on, more confidently now, "I have been thinking of other skilled craftsmen and women who might benefit. Forgive me for being forward, but I was so inspired as to make a list of criteria."

"How fortuitous," he said. "I too have a list of criteria."

Her face lit up. "I do adore a good list. There's nothing quite so satisfying as imposing order on the world, don't you find?"

"Order," he repeated. "That is it *precisely*."

Since his birth, his life had been unfailingly orderly—until those heart-stopping minutes in a meadow a decade earlier, when Juno Bell's kiss sent him into a downward spiral of chaos: his fights with his parents, his behavior in Vienna, his mess of a marriage, the greater mess of the divorce.

But now he was tidying up the last of his mess and restoring order in his life, thanks to Susannah Macey.

She adored lists. He abhorred them. She loved to impose order. He tended to make a mess. They complemented each other. She was precisely what he needed.

Unfortunately, he rarely managed to speak to her for more than five minutes before someone in her family whisked her away.

And right on cue, here came Lady Renshaw now, bursting out of the throng, wearing a yellow turban that did no favors to her gray hair or anxious expression. The countess gripped her granddaughter's elbow like it was the last bolt of silk on sale.

"Susannah, dear, there you are," Lady Renshaw said. "Do come show your new fan to the other ladies. If His Grace would be so kind as to release you." She offered Leo a tight smile. "Good evening, Your Grace."

"Lady Renshaw."

Miss Macey did not move. "Grandmother, we were discussing the duke's Foundation and the grants he provides to craftsmen."

"How very interesting." Lady Renshaw's brow darkened. "Tell me, Your Grace, do you also provide grants to artists? I understand you enjoy passing time in artists' studios."

Her tone was mild, but her look was as sharp as a grumpy tailor's needle. As the English made a sport of not saying what they meant, Leo had to guess her meaning; he guessed they were discussing his visits to the studio of one particular artist, namely, of course, Juno Bell.

Ah, bless the gossips. They were as hardworking as smugglers, tirelessly moving their goods around in the dark.

"I enjoy many things," Leo said. "Yet when gossip favors excitement over truth, it reports things that do not exist."

Lady Renshaw offered another insincere smile. "Attention is unavoidable for people in our position, yet we do try to avoid it where possible, especially the sort of gossip that is likely to cause my granddaughter embarrassment. I'm sure you understand, Your Grace."

Miss Macey was passing this conversation in close examination of her fan. The fan's construction must be fascinating, the way she studied it so intently.

"Indeed, my lady, I understand you perfectly."

Nevertheless, Lady Renshaw added, "We leave in a fortnight for Lord Normanby's estate, and we must speak to his mother, who is so very fond of Susannah." She nudged her granddaughter's shoulder. "Do go ahead, dear. I should like a word with His Grace."

Miss Macey opened her mouth as if to protest, but closed it again, for well-behaved young ladies did not quarrel. Instead, she obeyed with an apologetic smile and small curtsy, leaving Leo alone with one very disgruntled countess and feeling rather disgruntled himself.

"I was about to ask your granddaughter to dance," he said impatiently. "And invite her on a drive in the park, and then perhaps to share my box at the theater. Need I make my intentions more clear?"

Lady Renshaw maneuvered him into a triangle of privacy with a potted palm and fixed him with a sharp glare.

"The attentions of a duke are very flattering for a young lady, but when those attentions are accompanied by ceaseless gossip and potential humiliation, they lose their shine. Your visits to *that artist*—"

"Completely innocent," he said. "That is the truth."

She shook her head. "We both know the truth matters little if there is delectable gossip to be had. Your calls on *that artist* may pass with little notice now, but they are sure to excite great interest once you become engaged. Everyone remembers how your father chose to live with his French mistress, thus leaving your poor mother abandoned and alone."

Leo nodded solemnly, trying not to smile at the image of his robust mother as poor, abandoned, or alone, given the way she filled her house in Lincolnshire with European musicians and was right now having a wonderful time in Berlin.

"Should you keep seeing *that artist*, the world will wonder if you mean to emulate your father by favoring a long-term mistress over your wife, and I'll not have Susannah mocked as your mother was." She sniffed. "Susannah's other prospects may appear less grand than a duke, but will lead to a more contented future. The Earl of Normanby, for example, is very satisfactory. If you wish to court my granddaughter, you must reform your behavior first."

Leo raised a very ducal eyebrow, which served to chasten her a little.

"Forgive me, Your Grace, I mean no insult. But your connection with *that artist* does give one pause, and makes one wonder, well, what else might he do? Good evening, Your Grace."

And with that, she hurried off to take Miss Macey by the elbow and lead her safely away.

Leo scrubbed a hand over his face, suddenly weary of this

ball and its cloying air. Susannah Macey was his nearly-ideal bride. If she chose someone else, he would have to start all over again.

He did not have the energy to start all over again.

It was downright absurd that he, a duke, was being forced to choose between his friendship with Juno and his marriage to Miss Macey. All for the sake of some narrow-minded nonsense.

Yet, narrow-minded nonsense or not, Lady Renshaw made a valid point. Leo's engagement *would* spark more gossip, and his activities *would* attract more attention, and that gossip *would* embarrass his betrothed, and quite possibly Juno too.

So perhaps it would be wise to, say, call on Juno a little less frequently. And the gossip would affect her, so it would only be right to warn her it was coming.

He considered leaving, but spied Livia Bell, alone and awkward against a wall, and went to ask her to dance.

CHAPTER 5

Bounding up the stairs to Juno's parlor, Leo heard cheers and whoops, and he cursed under his breath to learn she was not alone.

The cheers, he discovered, came from a half-dozen guests, poets and the like. They were lined up against the wall with the furniture, and they were cheering because Juno was fencing, of all things, with Tristan St. Blaise.

Perhaps not fencing exactly, but they both brandished foils, fine Italian pieces with long, flexible blades. Juno wielded hers like a cross between a paintbrush and a poker, now sketching motifs, now jabbing at air, while she skipped back and forth along the worn blue rug as freely as her skirts would allow.

Those skirts belonged to one of her hideous work dresses—today's was a dull brown with a black-leaf print—yet even so, she made a beguiling picture, there under the windows, where the sunlight bathed her in its honeyed glow and made a halo of her flyaway curls.

Unnoticed, Leo leaned in the doorway, scheming ways to get her alone like some debauchery-minded rake. Chance would be a fine thing: Juno's studio saw more traffic than a coaching inn. Those sitting for portraits brought their friends; artists, poets, and musicians visited to avoid doing their own work; and studio tours were popular among people of all classes. Like many artists, Juno hung a dozen or so paintings for such tourists, including a still life of vibrant flowers, a portrait of Arabella, Marchioness of Hardbury, and her newest painting, of the mythological Pandora.

Leo would not see the next painting she added. He would not return to relax into her voluptuous settee, or share nonsense jokes, or sit in the window seat and watch her work.

Well. No need to be dramatic about it. No one was dying or getting exiled to the other side of the world. He'd return one day, when talk had settled down and interest had moved on. When he was wed.

In the middle of the room, St. Blaise was spinning around and flipping his foil, earning oohs and aahs from their poetic audience, who were too easily impressed by a pretty man doing showy tricks.

What the devil was his half-brother doing here again anyway?

"Such admirable style you possess, Miss Bell!" St. Blaise said. "I am amazed by the strength and steadiness of your arm."

"Such hyperbolic style *you* possess, sir," Juno returned. "My arm must be strong and steady, to draw and paint for hours. Or had you not realized that is what an artist does?"

"No! Is it? I thought artists did nothing but get drunk, moan about the Muse, and complain that it's always the least talented people who have the most success."

Mischief lit her expression. "You're confusing us with the poets."

The watching poets yelled their protests. Juno spun toward them, giggling cheekily, lips parted to riposte, when she spied Leo. She lowered her foil, and her smile softened to one of welcome. He straightened under her warmth.

"Behold! My fair brother Polly!" At St. Blaise's cry, every head turned. "Let the Duke of Dammerton serve as your tutor now."

Without warning, St. Blaise sent his foil spinning through the air toward Leo. The blade stayed upright, quivering like a ballerina as it rode its arc across the room. The guests pressed into the wall, even as they awkwardly tried to bow to Leo, murmurs of "Your Grace" warring with yelps of self-protection.

In a single movement, Leo stepped toward the flying sword and caught its grip. The momentum propelled him onto the rug, where he demonstrated that he, too, could swish a blade like a preening cavalier, as he presented himself to Juno with a bow.

Her crooked smile kicked up. The exertions of swordplay had pinked her cheeks, and several curls tumbled free of her lopsided pile of hair.

"We must not impose upon His Grace, with his hair so superb and his waistcoat so splendid," she said, offering him an exit, even as her eyes sparkled with challenge. "He might want to let another man have a turn."

"My hair always looks superb and this is only my fifth-favorite waistcoat," Leo said lazily. "I think I can bear to duel with you."

He handed his foil to a grinning St. Blaise and turned away to tug off his coat and hang it over a writing desk.

What *was* his half-brother up to? Nothing good, surely. Sowing mischief was one of St. Blaise's greatest skills, up there with fencing, riding, shooting, boxing, and damn near every other athletic pursuit. He was Leo's superior in all of them, always had been. Back when they were boys, Papa Duke spent his quarterly visits to Leo gushing about his beloved Tristan's accomplishments, like a boy boasting about his new puppy.

And then Tristan showed up here, with his famous beauty and superior fencing skills, eyeing Juno with undisguised admiration. The fool. She would never be interested in the likes of him.

Would she?

Not Leo's concern.

Did she still take lovers?

Also not his concern.

He reclaimed the foil and faced Juno. "*En garde*, Miss Bell!"

Gazes holding, they put up their swords. The blades crossed, slid down each other's length with a shriek of metal on metal.

"Why the interest in swordplay?" Leo asked, cross-stepping around the small space. She mirrored his movements. "Are you turning pirate? Or have you a score to settle tomorrow at dawn?"

"I'm inspired to paint a scene with a sword fight." She danced backward and swept her blade through the air, the spectators leaning away like a row of trees in a gale. "My tutor in Florence insisted that an artist should adopt the pose of the subject, to portray them from the inside out." She came to a pause before Leo. "So St. Blaise sent for blades and offered his tutelage, and here we are. He says I have a natural talent for it."

He lowered his foil, resting its tip on the rug. "You have many natural talents, but you seem to have confused fencing with dancing."

"Surely the whole point of fencing is to give men an excuse to dance with each other."

"It's more about men trying to stab each other."

"Then I shall just have to stab you," she said, and extended the foil straight at him.

Chuckling, Leo spread his arms wide in invitation, ready to flick the blade out of her hand. "Try it. I'll easily disarm you first."

"Leo, you disarmed me years ago."

The words startled him into stillness. Memory of another duel flashed, a decade ago, flowers and a kiss and—

Juno lunged. The blunt tip of her blade stopped a hair's breadth from the gleaming green birds embroidered on his waistcoat. Then, with that strong and steady arm, she closed the gap, pressed the tip against his sternum as gently as a finger's touch. The foil's blade arched up between them like a rainbow.

Their eyes met. Her triumphant smile faltered, then reasserted itself rebelliously.

"I win!" she cried. "The duke is slain!"

THE BLADES WERE SOON PACKED AWAY and the furniture restored to its usual position. Juno trotted down the stairs with St. Blaise and her other callers, then returned to the parlor where Leo lingered.

He was still in his shirtsleeves, hands clasped behind his back as he studied her painting of Pandora.

She tangled her fingers together to keep from grabbing his elbow and yanking him away. He could not possibly know of the secret compartment in that frame, nor could he ever guess the nature of the papers hidden in that compartment. But she greatly misliked his attention on it all the same.

Although, if she were to grab his elbow, well, she'd get a fine handful of linen and … arm. It was her first-ever sighting of Leo without his coat. What a revelation, to at last see clearly the shape of his shoulders, the tapering of his ribs and waist, the leanness of his hips. And what a revelation to watch him wield the foil with such effortless grace and strength.

How she had longed to touch him, to experience the sensation of his warm skin and firm muscle under linen and silk. Perhaps that was why she had stabbed him with the foil, as a proxy for touch.

Be careful, she warned herself. It was unwise to get ideas about touching Leo, because if she were to act on such ideas, he would be appalled and then she'd never see him again.

"It's lovely to see you again so soon," she said.

"And yet you ruthlessly stabbed my waistcoat."

"Oh, hush. 'Tis only your fifth-favorite waistcoat. Had it been your favorite, or even your second favorite, I might be moved to remorse." She laughed, suddenly delighted. "Don't feel too badly about it. I was training with that foil for a whole fifteen minutes. 'Tis no wonder I gained such mastery."

"I shall take comfort in that as I lie in my grave."

His gaze flickered away from her, then back again. Silence fell. It felt strange and new, this silence, as though barbed with unspoken words. He looked at her differently now, she thought, his expression searching yet wary. All during dinner the night before, she had noticed him stealing covert glances at her, and she was just vain enough to suspect he had been admiring her in her evening gown.

It was that mermaid drawing, she thought. Something had changed since he saw it yesterday. Perhaps the artwork's passion made him see her anew.

"There is a matter I wish to discuss with you," he said.

"Will you finally tell me your secrets?" she teased. "I do hope so. A man of your caliber must have the most opulent secrets."

His chin jerked up. Oh dear, had that sounded like flirting? He began to speak, then he stopped and muttered a curse.

Juno heard it too: footsteps, whistling, and the rattle of china. Then St. Blaise was sauntering in, carrying a tea tray; he must have gone into the kitchen to charm Mrs. Kegworth, rather than gone out the front door as she'd hoped. He dumped the tray on the table and sprawled in a chair. Bother and blast, Juno thought. As entertaining as St. Blaise was, she desperately wanted to hear what Leo wished to say.

But the moment had passed.

Without looking at her, Leo crossed the room and sank down

onto the settee. Impulse had her leaning over behind him to place her lips close to his ear.

"I shall winkle your secrets out of you," she whispered.

He turned; she froze. Their faces were suddenly very close. Close enough for her to see the fine hairs of his brows, the dark-blue rim around his irises, the smoothness of his cheek and jaw. Close enough to catch a faint scent like wood shavings and citrus groves.

Close enough that she could press her lips to that cheek and run her fingers through his hair.

Her breath snagged in her chest, where it fluttered helplessly. Then the fluttering spread down, down through her body, to where it fluttered persistently, right where a fluttering ought not to flutter.

At least, not when she was serving tea.

She stumbled away and busied herself with setting out the tea things, fumbling the cups with unusually clumsy hands.

"I thought you'd gone, St. Blaise," Leo said pointedly. "Please don't feel constrained to stay on my account."

St. Blaise nestled back in his chair. "But I am parched after my exertions. You would not send me away without some nice restorative tea."

The rising steam from the tea danced before Juno's eyes. Her mind raced. Leo had called twice in two days. He wished to be alone with her, to discuss something privately. He had been stealing glances at her last night. He disliked his brother flirting with her.

And now everything she said felt like flirting too.

She glanced up to catch St. Blaise's gaze volleying back and forth between them.

Attraction was a curious beast. St. Blaise was, objectively, the more handsome of the two. Not that Leo was plain by any stan-dard, but St. Blaise was one of the most beautiful men she had ever seen, all chiseled cheekbones and sultry pout. And she had seen all of him while he was modeling, save what the loincloth covered. Yet it was Leo in shirtsleeves who made her insides flutter. Possibly because that glimpse was the most she had ever seen of him, the most she could ever hope to see.

"How was the ball last night?" she asked brightly, as she handed Leo his tea, taking great care not to let their fingers touch. "Livia sent me a note this morning, saying you were the only person whose conversation did not make her want to drown herself in the ratafia, so I must thank you for saving her life."

"Happy to serve. Death by ratafia sounds gruesome indeed."

"And did you have any delightful conversations, Polly?" St. Blaise asked, as Juno handed him a cup. "A sweet tête-à-tête on the balcony, perhaps? A heart-stopping waltz? Lingering looks over supper?"

Again Leo's gaze briefly met hers before sliding away. "Only some idiots seeking to provoke me to anger as part of a stupid game." He snorted softly. "They are not very good at it."

"Of course not," Juno said, pouring her tea. "You are always so in control."

"The tedious part is that they haven't the mettle to risk actually offending me. So instead I get mealy-mouthed insults and smug inquiries into why I dress so prettily."

"We all know why you dress so prettily: because you can."

"Yes. And because I am exceedingly good at it." A self-mocking smile drifted over his face. "But I concede they have a certain evil genius. As dearly as I would love to knock their heads together, doing so would win their game for them and make them rich."

"Rich?" St. Blaise perked up. "For making you angry? I might excel at this game."

"Fifty pounds if I yell, two hundred for violence, five hundred if I challenge someone to a duel."

"Five hundred pounds," Juno repeated wistfully. "You could challenge me to a duel."

"I could, but then I'd have to shoot you, which would ruin your dress, and you know how I feel about crimes against fabric." Then he scowled at her gown: long sleeves, high neckline, loose fit, dull print. "What am I saying? That dress *is* a crime against fabric."

Delighted, she laughed. "Then my dress could win the bet, if you call it out for offending your eyes. Although if you do mean to shoot my gown, please be so kind as to warn me first, so I can take it off."

St. Blaise made a strangled sound in the back of his throat. Leo's gaze raked down her length, then he hastily looked away.

Oh no, that definitely sounded like flirting! Cursing her wayward tongue, Juno grabbed her tea and retreated to another chair.

St. Blaise hardly mattered; he would flirt with the furniture, and she could not take him seriously. But Leo? In four years, he had not betrayed the slightest hint he was even aware of her body. But now…

She exhaled. Her tea rippled.

Leo had been provoked by the image of her taking off her gown.

Was that why he had called today? Was that what had changed?

The idea tingled through her.

Might he? Want to? With her?

Surely not.

But if he did? Would she? With Leo?

Oh my.

No. They were friends. Friends must not.

But if he did want to… Would she…?

What an experience that would be! And one must seize opportunities when they came, for they might never come again.

She would never dare proposition him, though. The wound of his first rejection was ten years old, but the scar remained tender and tight. She could not bear it if he were to reject her advance.

But if he were to suggest it first?

It was a terrible idea, and, like most terrible ideas, it was terribly tempting.

The embarrassed silence persisted. Juno sipped her tea and scrounged for a safe topic of conversation. Yet she did not trust herself to speak, not when everything she said today made her sound like a flirt.

Her gaze strayed back to Leo, who was tracing the rim of his teacup with his thumb.

He glanced up suddenly. "Your tea service is looking tired. Shall I send over a replacement?"

"How very charitable of you."

"Not at all. My housekeeper informs me I have forty-two tea services. She demands I stop acquiring them as she cannot fit more in the house."

"Simple solution to that," said St. Blaise.

"Yes. Buy another house."

"Tut tut, Polly. You don't need a house to solve your problem with the excess porcelain. What you need is a wife."

Juno looked back down at her teacup.

"How romantic you are," Leo drawled. "Do you advise I mention that in the proposal? 'Marry me and sort out the china cupboard, would you?'"

St. Blaise spread his hands. "Merely seeking to help my beloved brother. I do so worry about you, all alone in that big house."

"Or you worry you'll lose your wager on the date I get

engaged. I am aware the betting books are full of speculation."

"You wound me, Polly." St. Blaise's hurt expression was very convincing until he added, "Although if you *were* to announce your engagement in the next fortnight, I would be much obliged. It'll win me two hundred pounds."

"It is not my concern if you choose to make senseless wagers," Leo said.

"Ah, but it wasn't senseless. You see, most of the fellows bet you'd propose to someone early in the Season. 'Man of action, the Duke of Dammerton,' they said. 'He makes a decision, he goes after it, wastes no time.' But I knew better," St. Blaise added smugly. "'Oh no,' said I, 'in the case of his second marriage, my dear brother Polly will not seize the moment. In the case of his second marriage, my dear brother Polly will hesitate and vacillate and ruminate and mastur—'"

"When I marry again," Leo cut in smoothly, "it will be on my own schedule, not yours."

"But why not now? Come, use your famed eloquence to answer me that."

Leo used his famed eloquence to say, "Sod off."

Juno listened with half an ear, unbothered by their crude language; she had experience enough of men and the manner in which they expressed their feelings.

But how interesting to glimpse this other side of Leo, and how fascinating to consider his life as a duke, the male aspect of it, wagers and so forth, and how very intriguing to return to the question of why he was here, and what his stolen glances meant, and if he too felt a certain fluttering, and whether they might—

He shot her a look, but before she could decipher its meaning, her hand was moving and her teacup clattered into its saucer.

"Oh, how silly not to see it before," she said. "That's what you wished to discuss, isn't it? You're engaged."

CHAPTER 6

Giddy laughter rippled through her. Juno pressed a hand to her mouth to keep it in. She shoved her cup and saucer onto the table, where they rocked unsteadily.

Her intuition led her astray sometimes, but this took the prize! To think she'd fancied Leo intended to seduce her, when his only intention was to wed.

Her head swam. Her mouth felt dry and her knees shaky, as if she'd narrowly avoided being hit by a speeding carriage. How mortifying if she had expressed her lascivious thoughts. Thank the heavens she'd not said a word.

"Tristan," Leo said, sliding his cup onto the table with an enviably steady hand. "I'll give you five pounds if you leave us now."

"You wish to be alone with Miss Bell? Hmm, not a good idea. I should stay to chaperone."

"Ten pounds."

"Twenty."

"Done."

St. Blaise bounded to his feet, winked at Juno, and strolled from the room. She followed him to the doorway and watched him hurtle down the stairs.

When she turned back, Leo was standing, imprisoning her with an inscrutable stare.

She forgot, sometimes, how compelling his eyes were, that promising blue of the morning sky in summer, the forget-me-nots in spring, the distant Alps in winter, and all those other sights that made her soul expand.

Suddenly, every inch of him seemed sharply defined, as if outlined by every fragment of the room's light.

Just as suddenly, she became aware of a fizzing in her muscles, as though she had run down a hill and the wind itself was swirling through her limbs.

What an odd reaction. She could not account for herself at all. It was hardly a surprise for Leo to be engaged. No sooner had he divorced his first wife than everyone was speculating about the identity of his second.

But two years had passed since the divorce, and the knowledge that he would remarry had faded into the walls like a dull painting one hardly noticed anymore. Suddenly that painting was very interesting indeed: the portrait of the lady he meant to marry. The future Duchess of Dammerton.

She freed herself from his gaze to focus on the debris of their unfinished tea. Leo was right: Her tea service was looking tired. And what of it? All her furnishings were shabby and mismatched. *She* didn't care.

"He fancies you," Leo said. "St. Blaise. Is he bothering you?"

"Will you protect me? My own knight in shining armor!"

That sounded like flirting too, albeit with an edge. She must not flirt with him, or he would run away and hide. She must not flirt with him, when he was soon to be wed.

"I don't know why he called today," she said. "To me, he is no more than a prop. I know you don't like him much, but I didn't think you'd care."

"I don't care."

"Besides, he doesn't meet my criteria."

"Your criteria? For…" He frowned. "Liaisons?"

Juno shifted uncomfortably. She had truly lost control of her tongue today, alluding to her affairs. But what of it? She didn't have to explain herself to anyone, and certainly not to Leopold Halton.

"Have I shocked you?" she said.

"It's not my concern."

He picked up his coat and shrugged into it, once more hiding those intriguing shoulders and arms. How like Leo, to give her a glimpse of himself and then take it away.

A surge of energy pushed her aimlessly around the room. "Then last night's ball was more interesting than you let on, if you are betrothed," she babbled. "Congratulations. Or is it felici-tations? My aunt did try to teach me the right phrases, but they never stuck."

"I am not engaged. Not yet."

"But you mean to become engaged soon," she guessed. "You have chosen the lady and believe she will accept your offer."

"Yes."

She bumbled to a stop, nearer to him than she intended.

"That cannot be a surprise," he said.

"Not at all. Everyone talks about it."

He began to speak, stopped, raked a hand through his hair. He seemed to be at war with himself, wanting to say something, not wanting to say it. How unlike his usual unflappable self. She'd never seen him perturbed before. Except— Yes, once. In the meadow ten years earlier, when her declaration of love made him stammer awkwardly, not wanting to hurt her, she supposed, but wanting to be very clear he had no place for her in his life.

A single gray cat hair clung to his lapel, unnoticed. Juno felt a wicked stab of glee at this tiny flaw, a fierce urge to grab those otherwise flawless lapels and just *shake* him, a savage longing to tear those fancy clothes right off him.

Figuratively speaking, of course. Not literally.

Well. Maybe a *bit* literally. But *mostly* figuratively.

He wore his clothes and attitude like armor. If only she could tear it away, his armor of silk and words and other slippery things better at hiding truths than revealing them. Nature, the senses, the body—*they* were real. If Juno could get to Leo's senses, get to his body, then maybe, just maybe, she could get to *him*.

Figuratively speaking, of course.

Pointless thoughts, figurative or literal. Leo was a duke, soon to be married to a lady who was surely as well bred, well behaved, and well dowered as a duke's wife ought to be.

Besides, he had made it plain ten years ago that Juno was not good enough for him.

"Why so mysterious, Leo?" she teased, somehow achieving a light tone. "You are a duke, and it is your duty to remarry and produce baby dukes. What else is there to say? I cannot fathom why you needed to tell me yourself. I could have read the announcement in a newspaper along with everyone else."

"You don't read newspapers."

"True, but other people read them, and someone would have told me, sooner or later."

Once more he raked his tousled, untouchable hair. Once more he stopped himself from speaking. When he did speak, it was to curse, with a vehemence that startled her, until she heard the sounds from below: the front door closing, voices greeting Mrs. Kegworth.

Juno cursed too. Usually, she loved that people came and went from her house all day, unless she asked Mrs. Kegworth to bar the doors. But not now, as Leo turned inscrutable and unflappable again.

Footsteps came skipping up the stairs and then, in a flurry of yellow skirts and swaying ringlets, Juno's patroness Beatrice Prescott was bursting into the room.

"Juno, darling, I have the most exciting news!" Beatrice cried, taking both of Juno's hands in hers. "I have brought along—" She stopped short as she caught sight of Leo. Moving very carefully, she released Juno and sank into a curtsy.

"Good day, Your Grace," she said.

As she rose, she shot an awed look at Juno. "It's the Duke of Dammerton," she whispered.

"Yes," Juno said. "I know."

A moment later, in marched Mr. Prescott, London's foremost art critic. Mr. Prescott's compact form was clad in black, his reserved manner a stark contrast to his young wife's colorful exuberance. He too stopped short at the sight of Leo.

"Dammerton," said Prescott.

"Prescott," said Dammerton.

Having thus reminded each other of their names, they fell into the silence of two men who disagreed on nearly every topic and chose to say nothing rather than risk a quarrel. Then, with a curt nod, Mr. Prescott peeled away to subject the wall of paintings to his fearsome scrutiny, with Juno left to introduce Beatrice to the duke.

"Mr. Prescott has come to examine Miss Bell's new painting of Pandora," Beatrice said to Leo, her eyes shining. "I have told him of its excellence, and if he agrees with my assessment, he might even find a buyer."

Excitement and trepidation waltzed along Juno's spine. Mr. Prescott's expression remained impassive as he brandished his quizzing glass at her work. Every artist in London clamored for

Prescott's attention, every buyer sought his advice. He tended to ignore London's small circle of women artists, but Juno had secured the patronage of his wife, a coup that was working in her favor today.

Leo, naturally, remained unimpressed. "The great critic himself," he murmured.

"Behave!" Juno mouthed at him, and a conspiratorial smile curled the edges of his lips.

Oh, she did enjoy Leo's smiles, the way his eyes took on that playful glint, the way he spoke without saying a word. What about his future bride, she wondered: Did that lady enjoy his secret smiles, his subtle looks? Did she know how to kindle that light in his eyes?

What a foolish thought. All his acquaintances would know; Juno was no one special.

"Bringing Miss Bell's work to the attention of London is an important part of my role as her patroness," Beatrice was telling Leo. "She has completed the most marvelous portrait of me. Marvelous thanks to her skill, that is. I'm sure I make a very poor subject!"

Beatrice Prescott, with her eye-catching prettiness, could never make a poor subject; Leo gallantly murmured something to that effect.

Perhaps encouraged by his compliment, Beatrice continued. "Indeed, I am unveiling the portrait two days from now, during a garden party held especially to introduce Miss Bell to the finest art lovers in society. Only a modest garden party, but everyone who enjoys art is welcome. Perhaps, Your Grace, if you have no other claims on your time…"

Her eyes were wide and expectant, the invitation plain in her voice. Prescott shot his wife a quelling look at her impertinence, but Leo's expression didn't change.

"What an excellent endeavor," he said, politely sidestepping her invitation. "I wish you every success." He inclined his head. "Mrs. Prescott. Prescott. Miss Bell."

Having once again reminded everyone of their names, Leo strolled out of Juno's parlor without a backward glance.

～

No sooner had Leo disappeared than Beatrice, beaming, clapped like a child.

"How exciting! I wondered if I might ever encounter him here, and there he was! A duke! Oh, how impertinent he must think me. But wouldn't it be wonderful if he did come to our garden party?"

Prescott fired an irritated look at his wife, who grinned at Juno.

"Prescott's wearing his grumpy face. Let us leave him in peace, while you show me what wonders you're working on now."

Poor Beatrice. How she longed for attention from the peerage. She was determined to establish herself as a grand patroness of the arts, but despite winning over art-loving ladies in the gentry, peeresses continued to ignore her. From the day she and Juno became friendly, Beatrice had been dropping hints: Would her friend the Marchioness of Hardbury be around? Might her acquaintance the Duke of Dammerton call? Unfortunately for Beatrice, Juno had no sway over the comings and goings of her friends. Besides, while she knew her connections were part of what attracted Beatrice, she refused to use her friends that way.

In the studio, Beatrice lowered her voice. "I caught a glimpse of Dammerton at a ball last night. Can you guess which lady he was flirting with? None other than Miss Susannah Macey. Do you know her, Juno?"

"No," said Juno.

"Well. Her father is heir to the Earl of Renshaw, and she has twenty-five thousand pounds. They say the duke is courting her, but then he is always courting someone. It's a wonder anyone can keep up. Has he spoken of it, Juno? Will he marry Miss Macey?"

"I couldn't say," she said. "We don't speak of such matters."

"No, of course. He would reserve such matters for his intimates."

Miss Susannah Macey. Now Juno had a name. And no doubt the unknown Miss Macey was perfectly lovely. Perhaps Juno would meet her one day. Perhaps Leo would bring his new duchess here and he would say, "This is Miss Bell, whom I first met years ago when we——"

Silly Juno. He would never introduce her to his wife. He would never bring his wife here. In a flash, she understood his odd manner: He had called today to tell her he would never call on her again.

Sadness washed over her. She impatiently shook it off. She was no naive fool. She knew how the world worked.

There would be gossip following his betrothal, because there was always gossip about Leo, which meant there would be gossip about her, and Juno did not need gossip of that kind. He was an honorable man, and honor meant guarding his future wife's reputation. Honor meant putting his wife above her.

Well, never mind. She hadn't moped when he broke her heart ten years ago, and she most certainly would not mope now.

"Miss Bell."

Mr. Prescott's summons cut through her thoughts. The critic had reached his verdict.

Heart pounding, Juno went back to the parlor and clasped her hands nervously. At her side, Beatrice fairly bounced with excitement.

Mr. Prescott's expression was impassive. "*Pandora Trapping*

Hope," he said, repeating the artwork's title like a butler announcing guests at a ball.

At the center of the painting was Pandora, illuminated by the light radiating from a glass jar. Open at her feet was an empty wooden chest, and surrounding her were spring blossoms, holding back the leering, shadowy crowd of miseries and demons released from that infamous box.

"An unusual interpretation of the myth," Prescott went on. "Most artists choose to depict Pandora giving in to temptation and releasing the evils from the box. Yet you chose to show her after the evils are released, when she manages to hold on to Hope."

Most artists chose to vilify Pandora; as far as Juno could tell, the gods had set the poor girl up to fail. "That was the part of the myth that most strongly resonated with me," she said.

He nodded, uninterested. "As usual, my wife's judgment is sound. This is a superb depiction, as fine as anything in London. You continue to improve," he added, with a dismissive glance at her earlier works. "I should be happy to suggest this piece to a buyer, and expect it to fetch a fine price."

Juno tried to stop the smile from conquering her face. "Thank you, sir. You are too kind."

Her mind raced with arithmetic. What with the sale of this painting, and the fee owing for her full-length portrait of Beatrice, as well as whatever else Beatrice sent her way, why, Juno would be *rolling* in gold this quarter. Well, maybe not *rolling*, given she was already rolling in bills for her latest deliveries of colors, canvases, and brushes, and Mrs. Kegworth had been waving about a sheaf of household bills. Not to mention the amount owing to the frame maker.

Speaking of which…

She caressed the ornate giltwood frame holding Pandora. "It must not be sold with this frame, however."

Prescott barely glanced at it. "Seems fine."

"This one is old. It has … sentimental value." By which she meant: *It has a secret compartment in which are hidden private drawings I do not wish anyone to see.* "I've ordered a new frame, but it won't be ready for another week."

"No matter. You're unlikely to find a buyer so soon anyway," Prescott said impatiently, already heading for the door.

ALONE AGAIN, Juno tumbled onto the settee with a sigh. Angelica came bounding in and landed on her lap, and together they studied the abandoned teacups.

She reclaimed her cup and lay back to sip at it, staring up at the painting of her darkly beautiful Pandora, illuminated by the glow of Hope.

"Well, my lovely girl," she said, absently keeping her tepid tea away from Angelica's nose, "you have done me proud. I have done me proud."

Her focus shifted past the canvas, to the frame that held it, huge and ornate as was the fashion these days. She thought guiltily of the drawings hidden within.

"The fact that I draw him now and then means nothing," she told Angelica, who purred loudly in agreement. "And the fact that I keep them means only that…"

What? Nothing. It meant nothing at all.

And as for the mystery of why Leo kept her at a distance? There was no mystery. He must dread her falling in love with him again. How awkward it must be for great men such as himself, having low-born women throwing themselves at his head. He had made it plain ten years ago she was not good enough for him. Good enough for secret walks in the woods. Good enough for a kiss. Not good enough to make her part of his life.

Yet he liked her, she thought defiantly, and he enjoyed visiting her studio. Whatever else, she would never believe they were not friends.

But she would only ever get crumbs from him, and it was a waste of precious time to wish for more. She had always known she could never hold on to Leo, but only enjoy him, the way one enjoyed a sunbeam on a winter's day, or a cool swim in summer, or a nightingale's song in the dark.

Let her continue to satisfy herself with the occasional indulgent thought, and the occasional indulgent drawing, after which she would tuck the thoughts back into the shadowy part of her heart, and slide the drawings into the secret compartment in the frame, and carry on.

After all, she was perfectly content with her life.

Artemisia, in one of her rare affectionate moods, bounded up too, and the two cats vied for her cuddles, which she was more than happy to give.

Look at her: She had the endorsement of London's leading art critic and the patronage of his wife. She had clients lining up to commission portraits, and a studio in which to receive them. She lived in a pleasant house in the vibrant city of London, with a cloak of respectability thanks to her lodgers Mr. and Mrs. Kegworth, who claimed to be her mother's kin in exchange for room and board. She had a supportive family and dozens of friends and "yes," she added out loud, "I have two wonderful cats, though I have so spoiled you, you spend more time sleeping in my studio than mousing in the kitchen."

She had everything she needed, and she certainly did not need a duke.

If Leo's impending marriage meant she never saw him again, there was no reason for that to bother her at all.

CHAPTER 7

W hy so mysterious, Leo? It's your duty to remarry, Leo. Everyone is talking about it, Leo.

That evening, Leo wandered restlessly through his house, scowling at the decorative objects as he passed. He was irritated with himself. More than irritated: disgusted.

Why the devil had he not spoken?

The opportunity had been there, when they were alone, to say his piece. But did he speak? No. He had stared at her like a bull staring at passersby.

He paused before the marble bust of some dead duke, and said, "I expect news of my engagement to intensify attention on my activities and connections, at least temporarily, so for that temporary period, it would be better for all concerned…"

The marble bust cringed. Leo sighed.

He'd have sounded like a pompous prat saying it, but at least it would have been said.

Life was full of difficult conversations, but one did what had to be done, one said what had to be said, and one never cowered from uncomfortable moments or shirked one's duty.

Except, in his case, where Juno was concerned.

She alone inspired his silence, his wretched hesitation. In the meadow ten years ago. In Vienna eight years ago. In London, six bloody hours ago.

Order, he thought, resuming his rambles. Everything in his life had a place. Then Juno, with a single smile or word, threw the lot into upheaval. She waved a foil and he threw away decorum to fence with her, a poor decision that could make its way back to Lady Renshaw's ears. She quipped about taking off her dress and he immediately imagined her taking off her dress. She whispered in his ear and stood so close until all he wanted was—

His Foundation, he reminded himself firmly. His heirs. Peaceful domesticity. What he wanted was to share his oversized houses with actual human beings, rather than wandering through them alone.

And Juno? Free-spirited, misbehaving Juno, she who took love lightly, selected lovers like chocolate truffles, shunned marriage, drew nudes, lived for art, craved experiences, chased sensations. She had no place in his life. She ought never to have been part of it.

But one morning, many years ago, while staying at Hadrian's house, Leo went out for an early morning walk and found his friend's cousin traipsing through the woods like a pagan goddess of spring, singing softly and smiling at him as if he were the brightest part of her day. She had been so at ease, so eager to share the myriad pleasures around them, that he had relaxed into her presence and, for the first time ever, felt fully himself.

Countless morning walks later, she was kissing him and saying she loved him.

For Leo, that morning had changed his life.

For Juno, it had been just another day.

The old bitterness twisted through him. No, not fair.

Resenting Juno for not loving him forever was like resenting the blossoms for falling from the trees or resenting the sun for setting. It was simply her nature.

Perhaps it had been a mistake to call on her when she moved back to London. But when Hadrian had written, obliviously asking Leo to "keep an eye on her for me, would you?", curiosity had won. To his relief, he'd felt completely at ease in her company, with none of the old feelings at all. Again and again, he had gone back, until her studio had become a regular haunt.

His ramblings took him to the dining room, with its enormous table and sideboard carved with wild beasts. The housekeeper, in a display of either humor or pique, had laid out all the tea services in a colorful city of fragile towers.

Point made. Forty-two was a bit excessive.

Had he really purchased this much? Surely not. Perhaps it got frisky in the china cabinet and started breeding.

Lucky porcelain.

A wife would bring more than money. She'd bring the sweet intimacy of another body, the sanctuary of domestic companionship, the delight of discovering his own children.

Leo ran his hands over a chair's carved crest, polished like everything else in this room. Yet for all the gloss and gleam, it felt barren and dusty.

No matter: This feeling would pass once he married. Courting Susannah Macey was the most sensible course of action. Leo liked taking action and he was, in the end, a sensible man.

The leaning towers of china eyed him skeptically.

"Oh, sod off. Nobody asked you," he said to them, and pivoted to continue his perambulations elsewhere, away from judgmental porcelain.

And almost collided with St. Blaise in the doorway.

"Twice in one day," Leo sighed. "What did I do to deserve this?"

"I need somewhere to stay."

"I thought some woman gave you a bed."

"She has since kicked me out of said bed. Lucky for me, my little brother is a duke and has more rooms than he knows what to do with." St. Blaise peered past him. "Egad. I see what you mean about the china. How much could I get for all of this?"

"Nothing. Because you're not selling it."

Leo brushed past him and wandered on.

"This space is wasted on you," St. Blaise said, trailing after him. "Do you know what this house needs?"

"You gone from it?"

"About a dozen courtesans. You are terrible at being a duke," he added. "Your life could be one endless, divine debauchery, drinking all day and bedding a different woman every night."

"I've never seen the appeal of sleeping with strangers."

"The fact they're strangers *is* the appeal."

Leo glanced over his shoulder. "Wouldn't you rather sleep with a woman who knows you well?"

"Any woman who knows me well wouldn't want to sleep with me."

"Fair point."

Three steps later, St. Blaise gripped his shoulder. "Polly, wait. What? Do you mean to say... Your wife... You've lain with only one woman? No! Can it be?"

Leo didn't bother answering. St. Blaise was rendered momentarily speechless.

Only momentarily, alas.

"But don't you want more experience? Didn't you get bored in bed, doing the same thing over and over?"

"Who says we did the same thing over and over?" Leo tugged himself free. "Sounds like you need more experience, if you know only one thing to do with a lover. One can achieve more variety with a single partner and a bit of imagination."

In the study, Leo set about lighting candles and briefly indulged in a fantasy of turning his half-brother out onto the streets. But among their father's last words to Leo was a plea to "Look after Tristan for me. He's a good boy, really."

It was not Tristan's fault he had been their father's favorite. Nor was it Tristan's fault their father had chosen to live as he had: in a cozy cottage with his mistress and their children, and paying quarterly visits to his duchess and their children.

It *was* Tristan's fault that he was so bloody annoying.

The "good boy" was now prowling around the study, opening cabinet doors and poking in drawers.

"What are you looking for?" Leo asked.

"Anything I can steal and pawn. Don't sack the servants if the silver spoons go missing. It will likely just be me."

"I hear your gambling debts have become bad."

"No! What? They're not bad. They're in excellent health, plump and merry and stomping all over me." At Leo's look, he shrugged. "What can I say? I was bored."

"That's what you get for selling your commission. Find an occupation."

"I have an occupation. I rack up debts, and then I develop ingenious schemes for paying them off."

"Such as betting on the date of my engagement?" Leo said. "Two hundred pounds of winnings won't cover your debts."

St. Blaise kept rummaging through drawers. "I'll win double if you get engaged to the lady I've nominated. I think you should marry Miss Susannah Macey. Rumor has it she likes decorative arts too, so if all else fails, you could spend the rest of your days discussing teapots, and really, what else does marriage need?"

Leo found himself in front of the drinks, studying crystal

decanters that glinted in the light. "Thank you for that enlightening perspective," he said.

"I can't be far wrong: You do seem to have singled her out for attention. Though you've been singling ladies out for years." St. Blaise's voice became muffled as he stuck his head in a cabinet. "Everyone is talking about your serial courtships. It's bordering on a scandal."

Leo had to laugh. "Hardly. I've not debauched a single one of them."

"I can help with that, if you like." St. Blaise slipped a small crystal fox into his pocket and continued to the next cabinet. "Speaking of debauchery," he went on, "have you never been tempted by the luscious Miss Bell?"

"No." Leo poured a brandy and downed it in a gulp.

St. Blaise picked up a snuffbox and turned it dreamily in his hands. "I couldn't stop thinking about it, while she was drawing me yesterday. There I was, in nothing but a loincloth, and she saw me only as an object. 'Naught but lines and shadows,' she said. I cannot decide if it was utterly debasing or utterly thrilling." He sighed. "I do believe I'm in love."

Leo snorted and poured another drink. "Only a fool would fall in love with Juno Bell. She has so much appetite for life that she cannot stay long in one place or devote herself to one person. It is part of her charm, the way she immerses herself in something, then dances away like a will-o'-the-wisp. She would tell you she loves you, and at the time she would mean it, but then she'd find something else, and in the end, you'd be nothing more to her than a passing fancy."

And the fool who believed her words and decided he loved her in turn? Leo knew that fool, knew him too well.

That was the fool who'd been a lustful virgin and confused his pleasure in her company with the frantic desires of his changing body. The fool who had decided this desire must be love.

That was the fool who had lurked in the cold, dark streets of Vienna, staring at silhouettes in windows, ready to sell his soul for a mere glimpse of her. Hiding in the shadowy corners of glittering salons, wishing hell upon the Czech violinist who won her kisses, then doing sums so he would not weep. Making friends with the bottle and a fast crowd of hedonists, his evenings a disjointed kaleidoscope of nightmarish grotesqueries, until mercifully there was nothing. Until he awoke again, putrid and empty and sick.

He laughed ruefully at the memory. How earnest he had been. How self-righteously he had bided his time, and never once considered that Juno might not feel the same as he did.

"If I did attempt to seduce Miss Bell, would you mind?" St. Blaise said. "Would you, Polly?"

Leo relaxed his fingers on the glass. "Juno makes her own choices and treads her own path. Always has, always will. Don't be fooled by her warm smile and amiable manner."

"And that goddess's body. Glorious!" Then he added, in glum tones, "Thwarted lust. Messes with a man's mind. It's like being very hungry or very tired, making easy actions difficult and turning simple matters confusing."

Leo wheeled away from the drinks, toward the desk. He had no wish to discuss Juno's body.

"A man should have more control," he said.

"Of course he should," St. Blaise agreed. "I'm talking about how his thoughts get confused, like shipwrecked sailors who are so thirsty they drink seawater though they know it'll make everything worse. When one gets too lustful, one cannot think straight for all the delusions and fancies."

St. Blaise might, for once, have made a useful point.

"And Miss Bell is surely no maiden," he added, and Leo went right back to wanting to punch him.

Yet Juno *was* very sensual, and she would surely be bold and playful in bed. She would enjoy exploring her lover's body, and having her own explored, and she would—

Don't think about it, he told himself.

His mind immediately began thinking about it.

Desperately, Leo seized a list of numbers: the Dammerton Foundation's account. Leaning on his knuckles, head bent like a Catholic penitent, Leo mumbled the numbers out loud until they iced his imagination like a midwinter swim.

LEO HAD ALMOST FORGOTTEN his half-brother was there, until a soft sound of interest caused him to look up.

St. Blaise was examining a ring box, whose dainty panels were adorned in colorful Viennese enamels.

Or, as Leo liked to call the ring box, "The Coffin."

The first pretty little thing he had ever bought.

The second if one included the ring inside it. Leo did not.

"Not your usual thing," St. Blaise mused. "It looks cheap."

"Don't open that."

St. Blaise opened it. "A bit tawdry."

In three strides, Leo crossed the room and grabbed the box from his brother's hand. He caught his first glimpse of the ring in eight years, those simple knots of silver, before he closed the box, dumped it in the drawer, and slammed the bloody drawer shut.

He had forgotten about the ring. He'd meant to get rid of it. That was why he had bought the ring box and dubbed it "The Coffin." He had intended to bury it in a graveyard in Vienna, in a ritual symbolizing the death and burial of his loving heart.

How very dramatic of him. In his defense, he had been only twenty-one at the time.

The only saving grace was that Juno never knew Leo's true reason for traveling to Vienna eight years ago, setting off as soon as he turned twenty-one and could legally make decisions for himself. She never knew of his aching regret for rejecting her after she kissed him in the meadow, or his arguments with his father and mother, or the letters he wrote and never sent because he did not have her address.

She never knew about the ring burning in his pocket, or the question burning in his throat.

The question that was never spoken, the words that had turned to ice when she stood in the park in Vienna and laughed about youthful nonsense and silly infatuations, and before he could even think about changing her mind, she was kissing some bloody violinist from Prague.

"I say, Polly, were you in love?"

Leo said nothing.

"That ring is too simple for Erika's taste though," St. Blaise mused, because he was not quite the pretty idiot he pretended to be. "And it looks cheap, so you must have bought it before we lost Papa Duke."

"It was just some girl I knew. Before I met Erika."

"The girl didn't like the ring?"

"I misjudged her feelings."

"And let me guess—Erika found out and that's why she strayed?"

"No. Erika knew about her before we married."

St. Blaise hooted with delight. "No wonder you have trouble with women, if you are actually honest with them."

Erika, taking his hand one night in Vienna, wherever it was that Leo and his German cousins had washed up in a drunken haze.

Erika, with flashing dark eyes and a gown the color of apricot schnapps.

Erika saying: "Why so sad, English lord? If you wanted to be sad, you could have stayed in England. Did some silly English girl break your heart?"

Erika laughing.

Erika saying: "I shall make you forget this girl. What an excellent game that will be! Come with me, sad English lord, and I will make you laugh."

And she had.

"Are you still in love with her, this girl?"

"No."

"And you're not still pining after Erika?"

"Never did."

Leo returned to the lists of numbers, to his plans for the Dammerton Foundation.

It was that ring box that had sparked his passion for decorative arts.

In the little workshop, in an alley deep in Vienna, Leo had found himself moved by the delicate hand-painted scenes, charmed by the notion that one person could create an object that would become woven into the fabric of another person's life. Best of all, whole minutes passed when he forgot his heartache over Juno. He went back to buy a snuffbox, and then a music box; each item soothed him for a few days. But it was never enough; he kept seeking more. Then, back in London, he helped a talented seamstress set up an embroidery workshop, and he hunted treasures across the country, and he established his Foundation, and he hired staff, and yet—

Yet somehow, it still wasn't quite enough.

I shall winkle your secret out of you, Juno had said.

His secret was not an exciting one. No murder or treason, no blackmail or secret heirs. It was simply that he had loved a woman who had stopped loving him, then married another woman whom he would never love.

Our secrets reveal what we value, she had said. *And what we fear.*

What he valued was his sanity. His pride. What he valued was his Foundation and his family, both the family he already had and one he would make with his next wife.

What he feared was feeling as wretched and wrecked as he had in those weeks in Vienna after Juno broke his heart.

He glanced up just as his half-brother slipped a silver cigar case into a pocket.

"Sainted stitches. If you're that desperate, get some money from my secretary," Leo said.

"I don't want your charity." St. Blaise picked up a jeweled music box, with a mechanical bird perched on top. He found the key to wind it up. "Besides, I like finding diverting ways to make a living. Finding a woman to keep me, stealing from you."

"You'd rather be a whore or thief than a beggar?"

"Why not? I became a murderer for money. Why not a whore and thief too?"

He released the key and the little bird began to turn on its perch. Tinny music jangled through the room.

"Tristan," Leo said softly. "You were a soldier, a cavalry officer. It isn't murder if you're a soldier."

"If you say so." The jaunty tune wound down. The bird bobbed one last bow. "Can I have this?"

"No."

"Fine." St. Blaise tossed the music box back on the shelf. "Just do me a kindness and get engaged to Susannah Macey."

Suddenly, Leo was grateful to St. Blaise for digging up that silly little ring. That ring box was a timely reminder of what mattered.

This went beyond Lady Renshaw's condition to reduce gossip before courting Miss Macey. This was about leaving the past behind and embracing his future with his whole heart.

This was about cleaning up his youthful mess.

And Juno Bell—sensuous, vibrant, warm, welcoming, passionate, fickle Juno—was at the heart of that mess.

Whatever it takes, he thought. This time, his marriage would succeed.

He must sever his connection with Juno entirely. No more calls. No more gifts.

A pang stabbed him like a dagger. He did not want to end their friendship, but neither could he bear to continue in this limbo.

But simply ceasing to see her did not sit right with him. He would see her one more time, he decided, just to say goodbye.

And this time, he would not hesitate to speak.

CHAPTER 8

I t turned out that Beatrice Prescott's notion of a "modest garden party" differed considerably from Juno's own.

"Granted, it is a *party*," Juno whispered to her aunt Hester.

"And it is taking place in a *garden*," her aunt replied, her eyes sparkling behind her spectacles.

But modest? Words were not Juno's forte, but she was fairly sure the word "modest" did not apply to a string quartet serenading the forty-odd guests from their spot under a white marquee. Nor did "modest" describe the dozen Roman-style pedestals arranged across the lawn, each covered in a colorful assortment of sugar flowers, marzipan fairies, and leaning towers of macaroons.

And "modest" most definitely did not explain the leafy bower in which five actors, in elaborate costumes, were arranged in a tableau from Shakespeare's *A Midsummer Night's Dream*: a noble fairy king Oberon, a mischievous Puck, an unknown Bottom—no doubt sweating in his donkey's head, poor man—and a starry-eyed couple suffering from love. Notably absent was the fairy queen Titania, for she appeared in the full-length portrait Juno had painted of Beatrice.

The portrait claimed pride of place at the top of the steps, where it presided over the lush lawn and the milling guests. It was, for now, concealed by a curtain the color of emeralds, and flanked by Mr. and Mrs. Prescott. On Beatrice's far side stood Juno, grateful for her aunt's presence and more than a little bemused by the spectacle before her.

What would Leo think of this? she wondered. He might well appreciate Beatrice's creativity, but he had a fine sense of the absurd. Of course, other society events likely eclipsed this in grandeur. "By some standards, this *is* modest," he might say, and, with that devilry dancing in his eyes, regale her with descriptions of—

Memory shadowed the thought like a cloud blocking out the sun. She might never speak to Leo again, let alone share amused, conspiratorial looks and encourage him to poke fun at the *ton*. Perhaps they might exchange polite greetings at an exhibition, or discuss the weather, should her aunt invite him to a family dinner.

With his wife, naturally.

Juno understood. He had to put his future wife first, certainly above a shabby artist he only saw once or twice a week.

But never mind, she didn't need him. She had her dear cousins Phoebe and Livia down on the lawn, engaged in a heated debate. She also had the cheeky sun, playing peekaboo with the clouds. She had the cool breeze, the tinkle of the fountain, the scent of the jasmine, the call of the birds. She had these pretty people, in pretty clothes, come to admire her work. Heavens, she even had a string quartet! Who needed a duke when one had a string quartet? And her aunt. She tucked her arm through Hester's, whose thin face lit up with a warm smile.

Everyone was in high spirits when Mr. Prescott silenced the

musicians and called the guests to attention. Beatrice launched into a speech, praising Art, Nature, and Juno, while a breeze teased the edges of the curtain, offering a tantalizing glimpse of the frame. The guests stood poised, quizzing glasses at the ready.

Beatrice's enthusiasm even infected her husband, who adopted a theatrical air as he tugged on the tasseled cords to open the curtain and reveal the portrait. Even Juno craned her neck to look at it, until she remembered herself and turned to watch the guests. They exploded into gasps of admiration and a smattering of applause, and Juno schooled her face to modesty, though she secretly told herself it was her best portrait yet.

It was outrageous, the entire party, but she reveled in her triumph anyway. None of it would last long, because nothing ever did, so she must wring out every drop of enjoyment while she could.

She elbowed her aunt, who elbowed her right back.

"We are so proud of you," Hester said quietly. "To think, our little Juno, feted by society."

"I would never have come this far without you," Juno said.

After all, it was Hester who had hired drawing masters for her, as attentively as she hired Latin and Greek tutors for her cousins, Hester who took seriously Juno's petition to study in Europe. But what battles they had fought at first! Juno had been accustomed to her parents' laxness and neglect, while Hester imposed routines and rules. Worst of all, Hester insisted Juno finish every drawing, with no fresh paper until she did, and no amount of temper tantrums or broken pencils would sway her.

But thanks to that discipline, Juno had learned to finish what she started, to be patient enough to improve, to be present for her own work.

"We knew you were talented the moment you put pencil to paper," Hester said. "I simply had to convince you of the benefits of learning to read first."

"I believe you also had to convince me of the benefits of using a comb and wearing shoes."

"Then I congratulate myself on a job well done, for you clean up very nicely indeed."

Before Juno could reply, a hush drifted over the crowd. The guests' attention was no longer on the portrait; it was directed at something or someone on the other side.

Juno stepped forward to the edge of the steps to peer around the painting, just as someone murmured "Dammerton" on a note of wonder.

The whispered title rippled through the group like the wind in the trees. Quizzing glasses fell from fingers to swing on their ribbons, as ladies sank into curtsies and gentlemen folded into bows.

Warmth infused her, as if the sun had sent down a special ray of sunshine just for her.

Leo was here.

Just when she was thinking she might never speak to him again, Leo had come.

Even in this refined crowd he stood out, as though he were the art on display. As always, the sunlight favored him: It burnished the reddish highlights in his tousled brown hair, traced the shape of his lips and jaw, and caressed the sheen of his waistcoat, the palest pink silk embroidered with twisting vines and tiny blue birds.

His sleepy gaze swept over the awestruck guests and garden, taking in every detail, pausing for none. His eyes skated over Juno too. Her buoyancy deflated. Perhaps he did not recognize her, in this stylish gown the color of the summer sea, with her hair in a compliant honey-colored pile.

This man was that cool, aloof duke she had heard about—grand, elevated, supercilious, one of society's arbiters of taste. She saw it in his air of command, in the demeanor of the guests, who all looked ready to roll over and show him their bellies.

It was hard to believe this was the same man who sat in her window seat and bickered with her cats.

Mr. Prescott was hovering at his side, looking faintly vexed by the arrival of this august guest. By comparison to the duke, the critic's stark outfit rendered him as prosaic as one of his own essays.

Meanwhile, Beatrice had sunk into a deep curtsy. The duke inclined his shoulders ever so slightly, like a sapling bending in the wind.

"Mrs. Prescott, a pleasure," he murmured to the pink flowers adorning the top of her head.

Beatrice rose, lips parted, blinking rapidly. "Your Grace, I am so honored that you chose to grace... That is, I mean, to take part in our humble gathering."

He nodded graciously. No one dared speak, nor even so much as breathe, as they awaited the duke's next move.

Leo looked at Juno's portrait of Beatrice Prescott, and then at the actual Beatrice Prescott, dwarfed and outshone by her own image. In the portrait, as Queen Titania, she floated through an English woodland in a long white gown, radiating blissful content. In reality, she was flushed and excited. She almost trembled with it, like a puppy trying not to wag its tail.

He raised his quizzing glass to examine the portrait, though he had already seen it in Juno's studio. He ignored everyone as he examined it: up close, from afar, from top to bottom and lingering on a few details in between.

He would make a good lover, Juno thought, with that attention to detail, the way he took his time. And then there was that surprisingly thrilling air of command under his polished indolence, as if a wave of his hand would send everyone rushing to do his bidding.

Good heavens, there she went again, indulging this foolish fancy of Leo as her lover. Best not forget he meant to marry soon and had no interest in her that way at all.

His inspection complete, he replaced his quizzing glass in his waistcoat and carefully arranged the silver chain.

"Mrs. Prescott, this is all quite splendid," he said. "You are to be complimented on your exquisite taste."

A gust of wind rippled through the leaves, as if the guests had let out a collective sigh. The Duke of Dammerton had complimented Mrs. Prescott! By extension, he had complimented every single person who had demonstrated the good taste to attend today.

Then he turned away from the crowd and directed a comment to his host, signaling that he was done with them, and they could return to their mundane affairs.

CHAPTER 9

At an insistent wave from Beatrice, the musicians shoved aside their sweating glasses of lemonade and resumed their playing. The guests, energized—they had a duke in their midst!—were invited to partake of tea.

As Juno wandered down onto the lawn, guests clamored to greet her, praise her, share their thoughts on art. She chatted with them amiably, feeling special and alive.

They melted away when Beatrice came trotting toward her, radiating pleasure. Her peony-pink skirts billowed around her like she was a flower fairy herself.

"Oh, Juno, I cannot believe it!" Beatrice gushed, catching both her hands. "A duke at my garden party! Did you see? Of course you saw. Everyone saw. He's right there; one can't help but see. And how they'll talk! 'The Duke of Dammerton praised Mrs. Prescott's exquisite taste,' they'll say. And there I was, all in a dither! Did I look very foolish?"

"Not at all."

"And he just shows up without so much as a by-your-leave! What a naughty fellow he is. I shall have to give him quite the scolding. Oh, to think I have a duke at my garden party!" She released Juno, opened the fan hanging on her wrist, and took a deep, calming breath. "I must compose myself. Mr. Prescott will not be pleased by my gauche excitement." She fanned herself, the picture of serenity restored, then shot Juno a gleeful look. "I am excited, though. I declare this afternoon a success. Am I not the best patroness you could dream of? Today, the Duke of Dammerton. Tomorrow, everyone else. Just you wait and see. This party will pay off, with a dozen commissions for you. *Proper* commissions."

"I had not realized my other commissions were *im*proper," Juno said dryly.

"Oh, portraits of bankers' wives and the like." Beatrice waved dismissively. "With your talent and connections, and my patronage, you can do much better than that."

For the most part, Juno liked Beatrice Prescott. She enjoyed her enthusiasm, admired her knowledge, and sympathized with her ambitions in a society that was notoriously judgmental and unyielding. But Beatrice, like so many set on improving their position in society, suffered from a distasteful snobbery.

Those "bankers' wives and the like" had kept the roof over Juno's head these years, and she had enjoyed painting each and every one.

"The middle classes deserve nice things too," she said.

"Oh darling, of course, of *course*. But they don't have the same eye for art that we do. The same—what shall we call it?—sensibility. As for the lower orders, they have no sense of form or color at all. But Juno, you are one of us! Why, your uncle is a baronet and your other connections—" Here she glanced at Leo and her aunt Hester, Lady Bell. "You should claim your rightful place as an artist in higher society."

Juno bit her tongue. An artist's life was always precarious, especially for an unmarried woman. Beatrice's patronage mattered, she reminded herself, so she had best refrain from pointing out that most artisans came from the lower classes, that not one gown or teacup here had been made by an aristocrat.

Indeed, Juno had not been made by an aristocrat either. True, her paternal grandfather had been a baronet, which was as high in the gentry as one could get, but her other grandfather had been a shipwright, and both her parents had been cut off from their respective families in disgrace. If not for the welcome of her uncle, Sir Gordon Bell, and his family, this genteel world would never have invited her in.

"I am so proud of you, Juno," Beatrice continued. "All your work comes to fruition today at my little party."

Juno smiled. "And is it quite the party!"

"Well, it certainly required considerable expense and..." Beatrice took to fanning herself energetically, her gaze bouncing around the garden. "I fear Mr. Prescott grew a *little* stern when he saw the bills and insisted I economize. But given the success of this party, you'll surely agree it was an *inspired* idea to use your fee for the portrait to cover the bills."

"I..." Juno blinked at the string quartet, the actors in their leafy bower, the leaning towers of macaroons, the elegant ladies whispering about Leo. Juno willed him to look her way. He hadn't so much as glanced at her since he arrived. "I beg your pardon?"

A faint flush stained Beatrice's cheeks. "But you must see this is a good use for your money. These art lovers are influential, and now they've seen your work, they'll tell their friends."

Still Beatrice's fan fluttered. Each stick of the fan was intricately carved. That fan had not been cheap.

"The portrait, there were costs involved," Juno ventured. "The paints, the canvas..." At least the frame maker's bill had gone straight to Mr. Prescott, but her time!

Silence simmered between them, then Beatrice surrendered,

crestfallen and crushed. "Oh, it's awful, I know. I am a terrible patroness. I ran miles over my budget and Mr. Prescott made me divert your fee to pay the bills. I'll make it up to you, I promise." Her face brightened. "I shall nag him *relentlessly* to sell your painting of Pandora, and I'll donate my pin money to buy you new paints. Then you'll pass summer painting up a storm, and in the autumn, I shall exhibit your work in a room that is completely bare. It will cost me only a pound and everyone will be amazed." She bounced under another wave of excitement. "Do you think the duke will attend that too? And oh! Imagine if he and Miss Macey are married by autumn. What a coup if the new Duchess of Dammerton comes to our exhibition!"

Juno's gaze crept back to Leo, who was chatting with her cousins and aunt. Briefly, their eyes met. An odd expression crossed his face, as if she pleased and vexed him all at once, and then his gaze skated on.

Beatrice was looking at her expectantly, so Juno forced a smile. But her joy had deflated, leaving nothing but a wrinkled, withered feeling. She tried to identify the cause, but her mind writhed around it unhelpfully, touching on the lost fee, her fickle patroness, Leo's impending marriage, his presence here.

"There's something about the duke, though, isn't there?" Beatrice was eyeing him coquettishly. "He draws the gaze so effortlessly. A certain … magnetism. One longs for his attention; one yearns to know his secrets. Very handsome, don't you think?"

Juno made a noncommittal sound.

"His sleepy look doesn't fool me! The lions in the Tower have that look, and they might tear us to shreds. Leo, like a lion! Rawr!" Beatrice's eyes widened at her own daring in speaking a duke's given name. "His mother named him well."

Juno was suddenly irritable. "His mother is Prussian and Leopold is a German name, not Latin."

"So?"

"So his name has nothing to do with lions."

"Well, look who knows so much!" Beatrice laughed, not unkindly. "You may claim some acquaintance, but the duke doesn't belong to you, you know."

"I know."

Beatrice snapped her fan shut. "Never mind my teasing. I am so very nervous. A duke is my guest and I must go converse. Juno, darling, you will stay by my side, and kick my ankle if I say anything too gauche."

ANOTHER GUEST CLAIMED Beatrice's attention, so Juno was alone when she reached Leo's side, just as Aunt Hester and Phoebe excused themselves to greet someone else, and Livia bounded off to badger the poor actors.

Once more, Juno glimpsed that expression fleeing from Leo's face, as if she pleased him and grieved him in equal measure.

The scraps of their odd, unfinished conversation the other day fluttered across her memory. She waved them away like a pesky fly.

"I am equal parts amazed and delighted to see you here," she said. "You had not mentioned any intention to come."

"I like to be unpredictable, keep the gossips on their toes."

She shook her head. Standing closer in no way dispelled the sensation that he was both familiar and new: that cool, aloof duke laid over her playful friend.

"You look like your own identical twin brother, as if in some Gothic novel," she said. "Leo and the duke. The only question is which one of you is evil."

"The duke, obviously."

"Evil or not, you are still my favorite duke."

She would swear he winced, as if her words had bitten him.

But when he responded, his tone was light. "Your favorite? Do you rank your dukes like I rank my waistcoats?"

"It would not matter if I did, for you would have the top twenty spots."

"And where do I rank today?"

"Just for being here? Definitely in the top five. Beatrice is delighted by your presence, but upset you didn't warn her. She threatened to give you quite the scolding."

Leo turned an amused look on their hostess. Poor Beatrice was trapped in a conversation and fairly straining to escape. "It's astonishing the number of ladies who chastise me for some terrible naughtiness I was not aware I had committed."

"They're flirting with you! How exciting!"

"If they must flirt, could they not simply compliment my superb hair or shapely calves or something, rather than telling me how naughty I am?"

"Perhaps some women harbor a fancy for scolding powerful men." She eyed the crowd suspiciously. "Who knows what secret proclivities these people might conceal beneath genteel manners and fine clothes?"

Leo chuckled. "Juno Bell," he said, in thrillingly stern ducal tones, "you are not fit to be taken anywhere. Keep such bawdy comments for your bohemian circles. One does not speak of secret proclivities at this sort of party."

"I should be permitted to speak of whatever I please at this party, considering I helped pay for it."

At his questioning look, she explained how Mr. and Mrs. Prescott had directed part of her painting fee toward paying for this celebration.

"The scoundrels." Leo glared at Mr. Prescott's straight, black-clad back. "I'll have a word with him."

"No!" she said hastily.

"Or scowl at him menacingly?"

"As dearly as I would like to see that, it would only make matters worse. They would turn it against me and paint me as some greedy conniving diva."

"We could leave in a huff," he suggested. "That's always fun."

"We could, but I must debase myself, for I am promised a look at Mr. Prescott's newly acquired Botticelli, and my desire to see that painting quite obliterates my pride."

"And perhaps Mrs. Prescott is not wrong." He jerked his chin at the clump of gentlemen studying the portrait. "This party might lead to some lucrative commissions, given the wealthy gentlemen here known for their interest in art."

"Art?" she scoffed. "Chances are they only attended in the hope of seeing pictures of naked women."

"We-ell, to be honest, that's all I'm here for." He lifted his quizzing glass, peered around. "They promised paintings, yet nary a naked nymph to be seen. It's terribly disappointing. Is it even an art exhibition if there are no breasts or buttocks on display?"

Juno laughed. "Thank you," she said.

"For?"

"For coming today. For cheering me up. For being a friend."

His gaze grew thoughtful. A chill shivered through her.

Then his aloof mask fell into place again, as Beatrice arrived, gazing at Leo with awe.

"Your Grace," she said. "Might I say again how honored I am that you chose to attend?"

He eyed her coolly. "How fortunate you are, to possess something so *valuable* as a portrait by Juno Bell, which is worth its weight in *gold*."

"She is a wonder, isn't she?" Oblivious, Beatrice squeezed Juno's arm. "And how proud I am to have discovered her. The other ladies will be so envious!"

"Careful, or they'll all be wanting one," Leo said. "A woman artist will become the latest fashion accessory among the ladies of London."

Beatrice giggled. "Oh, Your Grace, you are too droll!"

She was still giggling when Mr. Prescott joined them and curled a hand around his wife's elbow.

Leo acknowledged him with a nod. "We were just discussing the portrait of your wife, and what a talented, *valuable* artist Miss Bell is."

"We are very pleased with the portrait," Prescott said blandly. "It is my opinion that England has not seen so fine a woman artist since Angelica Kauffman."

Angelica Kauffman, one of the two female founding members of the Royal Academy. In the half-century since, the Academy had not seen fit to admit another woman, although some, such as Mrs. Green, Mrs. Carpenter, and Juno, had paintings accepted for exhibition.

"I do not wish to detract from Miss Bell's accomplishments, but there are many talented artists among England's women," Leo said. "Miss Linwood's embroideries are admired as far as Russia. On a more modest scale, consider the artistry of my own waistcoats."

"Such women's skills are useful," Prescott opined. "But it is laughable to imagine one would ever find a true artist among uneducated, low-born women who can hardly spell their own names."

Their corner of the garden suddenly became very chilly, as Leo studied their host.

"What a fascinating perspective," he finally said. "I do hope you'll publish one of your essays on the topic, for all of society to pretend to read."

Mr. Prescott's face tightened. Juno hid her gloating smile.

"Will you hold any further art exhibitions?" Leo went on easily, as though he had not just insulted their host. "Your personal collection is much famed, but it's a tragedy you do not show it. I understand you recently acquired a Botticelli, which I am eager to view."

Prescott's chin lifted. "I regret that will not be possible. It is not here."

Beatrice frowned at her husband. "But Prescott, darling, I promised—"

"I regret it is not possible." He bowed slightly. "If you will excuse us, Your Grace, Miss Bell, I have come to collect my wife on a matter that requires our attention."

Leo released them with a nod. Beatrice mouthed "I'm so sorry!" to Juno, bobbed a curtsy, and then they were gone.

Juno sighed at their retreating backs. No Botticelli, no fee. She felt childishly disappointed, as if a promised treat had been withheld.

"Well. Mrs. Prescott *discovered* you," Leo said. "What does she mean to do now she has discovered you? Patent you?"

Juno had to smile, his nonsense melting her hurt. "Present her findings to the Royal Society, perhaps."

"Just as well she didn't discover you in a foreign country," he added. "She might have put you in a museum and charged everyone a shilling to gawk at you."

"Just as well I'm not a foreign country. She might have stuck a flag in me and populated me with criminals." But her humor didn't last. She sighed and shook her head. "And insult to injury, no Botticelli either. I was so looking forward to seeing it."

"I remain unconvinced this Botticelli exists," Leo said. "Prescott has been boasting about it for weeks, yet no one has seen it."

"I believe it exists."

"Yes, but you believe fairies exist."

"And you'll never prove they don't." She wrinkled her nose at his teasing. "I also believe he told you a bald-faced lie and it is sitting in this house now."

A rueful expression crossed his face. "My fault, I suppose, for insulting him like that. Still, does anyone actually read his essays?"

"He wields considerable influence. With a single letter to *The Times*, he can endow half of London with firm opinions on a matter that, until then, they had not given a moment's thought." She made a sound of irritated frustration. "Now I long to see it even more."

"Your longing is childish and irrational."

"Exactly. A sensible longing is easily put aside, but an irrational one is not. I fear there is nothing to be done but to indulge the desire or to sulk."

"I cannot bear to see you sulk, so let us indulge it."

She laughed. "And what do you propose, Your Grace? He'll have it locked away. Will you break down his study door? Or scowl at it menacingly?"

He considered. "I have an idea. Go powder your nose, and then meet me outside Prescott's study."

CHAPTER 10

Leo lounged by the door to Prescott's study, at one end of the drawing room. The door at the far end opened and Juno slipped through. Smiling, she crossed the long room toward him.

He could not take his eyes off her.

He wondered if she realized how the other ladies had looked at her in the garden, their fascinated, admiring, slightly nervous looks. The way their necks arched a little when she was near, as if they knew they became more interesting merely by being in her presence. She managed to be just the right amount of disreputable: daring enough to give ladies a thrill, but not so much they were forced to shun her.

Where they had delicate flowers in their hair, she had three lapis lazuli hairpins, which, of course, did not match, in an apparently haphazard arrangement, which, of course, pleased the eye. Then there was that cerulean-blue gown, its capped sleeves and bodice trimmed with white ribbons and embroidery that shimmered in the sunlight. A proper lady walked with careful inhibition, but Juno moved freely, as her body wished, the fluent sway of her hips sending the blue fabric swirling around her calves.

Suddenly, the sway of those hips was full of promise, the crooked smile full of allure, the white embroidery on her bodice full of invitation. And she—

No. Stop. Enough. How vexing his mind was: In the wake of his decision to stop seeing Juno, it demanded to see her even more.

All of her.

When she reached him, she glanced over her shoulder, to check for witnesses to their crime. When she spoke, it was in a whisper.

"He's sure to keep it locked."

"You do not think I am to be thwarted by a lock?" Leo said. "This door will not hold me, for I have a special tool."

Her jaw dropped. "No! How on earth would you know how to... You have a *picklock?*"

"I have a key." He waggled it. "Courtesy of an entrepreneurial footman. A duke always retains the dignity of a duke, even when he is committing a crime. Come on, then. Let's see if this painting exists."

The key worked and Leo stepped back to let her pass. As he relocked the door and pocketed the key, he heard Juno sigh. The sigh was so fervent it was almost a groan, rich with relief, pleasure, delight, pain.

It was the most sexual noise he had heard in years.

The Botticelli did, indeed, exist.

She was leaning hungrily toward the painting, like a lover hoping to steal a kiss, her body tense like a prowling cat.

And her expression! It was as complex and layered as the artwork itself: desire, greed, adoration, possessiveness. Like the expression of her own mermaid, yearning to consume the sailor.

"You like it, then," he murmured.

"It's exquisite, masterful. I ache with it, right here." She pressed her knuckles to her chest, the embroidered motifs shifting over her breasts. "I want to breathe it in."

She did breathe in, breathed out, and he would swear there was something sexual about her breathlessness, something that skipped right past his brain to his loins. Perhaps that was why she took lovers, because art filled her with so much feeling she needed release. Then she abandoned the men, because they were never the point.

What a tableau they formed: Juno staring at the painting, Leo staring at Juno. There were two objects of desire in this room, and he was not one of them.

"Prescott is a monster," Juno said suddenly, her eyes still on the painting. "He hoards dozens of marvelous paintings such as this and never lets the world see. It's shameful, for a critic to chatter incessantly about art yet never show his own."

Leo had dozens of opinions about Prescott, but now was not the time. Now was the time to tell her why he had come today.

But barely had he said "Juno—", barely had she turned with a questioning glance, than they both froze, heads cocked, alert.

Someone had entered the next room. Voices. Men. Two voices, muffled. Growing louder. Nearing the door.

He cursed under his breath—would he never get her alone? —then, with an exchange of panicked looks, he and Juno scrambled for a place to hide.

LEO'S HAND closed around hers and tugged. The firm warmth surprised her, but then she saw his intent: a space between a large cabinet and the window, occupied only by velvet curtains. They slid silently into the space. His back was wedged against the wooden cabinet; her front was pressed against him.

They had only sounds to inform them. A key slipping into the lock. Jiggling. "A bloody nuisance." That was Mr. Prescott's voice. A click as the lock gave. A moment's pause. Their own breathing, suddenly too loud.

Juno squeezed further into the space, checked her feet, her skirt, hidden by the curtain. Leo still held her hand, and as they jostled for position, each helping the other hide, their fingers briefly tangled as they might while making love. His hand was warm, and reassuring, and then gone.

THE DOOR OPENED. Prescott again, saying, "Lord Renshaw has mistaken the date. I would not have made an appointment at the same time as my wife's party." The other man, his secretary perhaps, saying, "I'll check the schedule." Scrape of a chair, rustle of paper, Prescott's voice: "Don't bother. I cannot send away an earl. Just find the paperwork." A drawer opening. "We don't have much time."

TIME STOPPED. Leo's world narrowed to this tight space, with the oak of the cabinet hard against his skull and Juno's softness warming his arm and hip and thigh. Her hand rested on his sternum, under his racing pulse. Lowering his eyes, he saw— Oh, so help him, her breasts truly were glorious. Her whole body was. Her skin looked almost golden, as a strip of sunlight bathed the side of her face. Her lips were parted; she moistened them briefly. Then she glanced up with a jaunty lift of one brow, merriment dancing in her eyes. Leo had to breathe, so he breathed her in, capturing her warmth along with the reassuring hint of linseed oil under her floral scent.

"Here's the provenance sent from Milan," came the secretary's voice, then Prescott: "Have you the original bill of sale? Damn, I wanted time for this later." "You've made a note of the price here," said the secretary. "Show me? Ah yes. But Renshaw will pay more than that. He doesn't know any better."

If she didn't know any better, Juno would swear her skin was vibrating like a leaf in the wind, fancied something similar emanated from him. Never had they stood this close. She basked in the pleasure of sharing air with him, of sharing this adventure. How wicked she was, to keep her palm pressed to his chest. She was taking advantage of the situation like a rake with a debutante, but she was not sorry, because his closeness was just that delicious and she was just that wanton. He smelled so good, his scent and heat sliding right through her skin and into her blood. Poor Leo was probably mortified. But this was a once-in-a-lifetime experience and, besides, he would never know of her wicked thoughts.

"What was the price on the one we sold to Renshaw's crony?" More paper shuffling, an exasperated huff, fingers drumming on wood, and "damned nuisance, though I suppose my wife will be pleased."

LEO COULD NOT STOP his wicked thoughts. But sensation was in charge now and— Sod it, it was delicious, this desire, and, oh so help him, all the places where he could plant a kiss: her earlobe, her neck, her collarbone, the swell of her breasts. *There,* he thought, *I would touch her there and there and there.* He gripped the wooden carvings behind him. If he were to touch her, would she welcome him? What would she enjoy? She would be a selfish lover, he thought happily, and he would give her everything she asked.

"WE CAN'T EXPECT him to pay us what we ask, so nudge it up," Prescott was saying, "then he'll feel good when he bargains me down." The scratching of a quill, a pause, then, "Yes. Right. I'll fetch his letters from upstairs. Can't keep him waiting much longer."

JUNO MIGHT NOT SURVIVE MUCH LONGER, but it was almost over. Her body was awash in sensation and desire. Later, tonight, when she was alone, she would think about how much her body wanted to be with Leo and what she might do about it. Nothing, of course: He did not want her that way, and he meant to marry soon, and besides, he was a *duke.*

PAPER SHUFFLING, wood knocking wood, the door opening, closing, the bite of the key in the lock. Silence.

Leo's brain was in a fugue. His body was in a state. Juno was no innocent; if she looked down…

She didn't. She glanced up, with her tempting smile, her laughing eyes.

"I think we're alone now," she whispered, and peered around the edge of the cabinet. He dragged his eyes off the smooth skin of her neck to somewhere safer: her hairpins. But then he could see how her hairstyle was constructed, and how he might bring her wayward curls tumbling down.

Yes, they were alone. Alone in a locked room. No one to see if he touched her, kissed her, hiked up her skirts.

Her palm was still flat against his ribs, pressing harder as she used him for balance, casually, heedlessly, as if their closeness did not sear her from the inside out, as if the air in her lungs was not sultry like a hot summer's night, as if he was someone easy to her, someone comfortable.

A piece of the bloody furniture.

Then she looked back at her hand, and then up at his face. For three wild thuds of his heart, the air seemed to buzz like the hours before a summer storm and the space closed around them like a feather quilt, and Leo thought he could do it, she would welcome him, they could enjoy each other right here. The thought stunned him with its vulgarity and urgency and rightness and wrongness because this was Juno and they didn't, he mustn't, it wouldn't—

"What an unexpected adventure that was," she said brightly. She tilted her head and studied his chest. "Standing this close, I see you're broader than I realized. Did that happen when you became a duke? Do you dukes receive special feed supplements, like prize stallions?"

With an impish grin, she slipped away, around the cabinet and out of his sight.

Leo let his head thump back against the big, solid cabinet. A hard lump of oak dug into his skull. Perhaps it would knock some sense into him. He breathed, once, twice, three times, studying the fall of the curtains, the play of shadow and light.

Here he was, stewing in a fugue of desire, ready to tup her senseless, and she— She was making jokes.

Thank heavens he had not acted on that desire. Better he escape her presence, and soon; the fugue still hazed his brain.

And yet still he had not spoken. He had yet to explain Lady Renshaw's ultimatum and that he must sever their connection in order to marry his nearly-ideal bride.

Perhaps she would make jokes about that too.

Ah, sod it. London would be abuzz with the news once his engagement was announced. She'd put the pieces together, if he never called on her again. She needed nothing more from him.

"Leo? Are you coming out? Or did you so enjoy our hiding spot you're nesting there permanently?"

Huffing and grimacing, he extracted the key from a pocket. He walked straight past her and unlocked the door.

"You go first," he said. "I'll follow."

He watched her cross the long drawing room, with that unrestrained sway of her hips, watching her all the way until she reached the next door and, without a backward look, she was gone.

CHAPTER 11

L eo's pace faltered as he returned to the garden. The party continued, but everything seemed at a remove, as if viewed through a glass.

Desire, he thought, dulling his brain like opium smoke. St. Blaise was right: Thwarted lust did mess with a man's mind.

Mercifully, she was nowhere to be seen. He cast around the garden for something—anything—to distract him. Salvation took the form of an elderly gentleman, who was sitting alone at a wrought iron table, fidgeting with a teacup.

Lord Renshaw. Here for a mistaken appointment with Prescott. Miss Susannah Macey's grandfather, and her guardian while her father was abroad.

There was Leo's solution.

The haze faded. Clarity sparkled in his brain. He headed for Renshaw with a purposeful stride.

As he walked, he renewed his vow: He would not jeopardize his future. He would secure his marriage and his Foundation and his heirs. He would do things right this time. He would not let himself be distracted by Juno Bell's smile or body or verve.

Whatever it took, he reminded himself. Whatever it took.

THE EARL OF RENSHAW had been a so-called macaroni in his youth, devoted to the flamboyant wigs, cosmetics, and fashions of the time. Despite the new plainness of men's fashion, Renshaw still delighted in lavish lace at his cuffs, and frequently touched his bald pate with regret.

He was patting his head now and jiggling one knee as he sipped his tea. His harried expression cleared as Leo approached.

"You're here too, Dammerton. Jolly good. Yes. Bit of a surprise." Renshaw's perplexed gaze lingered on the living Shakespearean tableau. "Bit of a surprise," he repeated. "Yes."

"Ladies always try to outdo themselves at such events," Leo said. "Not your usual thing, I suppose."

"Not… No. I didn't know." He shook his head. "Came to see Prescott about some Roman painting he's acquiring, didn't know there was a thing. Said I got the dates muddled. Or the time. My diary…" He patted one coat pocket, sighed. "Maybe Prescott forgot."

The old man's confusion made Leo uneasy, as did the thought of Prescott whisking him away. Not to mention the risk of encountering Juno again.

"Fancy a turn around the garden?" he asked Renshaw, who agreed happily enough, and they strolled down a shady path covered with wisteria vines, whose plump purple blooms hung about them like grapes.

"Here is the matter," Leo said. "I would like your permission to court your granddaughter."

"Well." Renshaw stopped walking and turned to face Leo. He steepled his fingers. "Well."

Leo clasped his hands behind his back. "I believe Miss Macey would welcome my suit, but Lady Renshaw has made it plain she does not approve. Let us discuss your objections."

"First, there is your own … indecision." Renshaw, too, seemed to have relaxed, having lost that confused look. "In the years since your divorce, you have demonstrated a tendency to show an interest in a lady, only to abandon her. It does not look good, Dammerton. We do not want Susannah's name added to a list of ladies who weren't good enough for the duke." Renshaw pursed his lips, and then added, "It also raises questions of how you might treat a lady after marriage. If you might … abandon her then too."

Leo nodded. "Let us be clear that, in my previous marriage, my wife was the only one of us seeking entertainment outside the marriage bed."

Renshaw looked mildly taken aback by the confession. "One does wonder," he murmured. "Your late father. My friend, of course, and a great man in many ways and yet…"

And yet, a man with two families. Was that one of the ways in which the previous Duke of Dammerton had been "great"? Did taking a Prussian noble as a wife, and keeping a French woman as a mistress, with some eight children between them, add to or subtract from a man's claim to greatness? It was the mistress he had loved, with whom he was living before he even sent away to Prussia for a bride. *Why did you not simply marry Mme. St. Blaise, given your affection for her?* Leo had wanted to know. His father had seemed astounded by the question. *An English duke could never marry a French Catholic, my boy*, Papa Duke had said. *It simply isn't done.*

Leo said nothing. He would not apologize for his father.

Renshaw continued. "I suppose your father's more immoral tendencies display themselves in your half-brother. One often hears implications about Mr. St. Blaise."

Leo sighed. "There is always some implication about St. Blaise. The fellow was born with an implication."

"I wonder you acknowledge him at all. There are only rumors of what he does, for he is remarkably tight-lipped, but rumors do not come from nowhere. I should not like Susannah to be exposed to the likes of him." Shaking his head, Renshaw walked on. "And one does wonder why your mother took your younger sister to the Prussian court for her debut, instead of presenting her at court here as befits the daughter of an English duke. Rumor suggests that one or other of them has something to hide."

Leo refused to be baited. "You have thus far complained about my father, my half-brother, my mother, my sister, and my former wife. Restrict yourself to comments about my own behavior."

The main objection remained. Sure enough, Renshaw raised it next.

"My lady wife already discussed it with you. What is your relationship with this artist, this Juno Bell? I am informed you made two visits to that woman's studio just this week."

"Many people visit artists' studios."

Once more, Renshaw came to a stop. "Do not play the innocent. It beggars belief that you are merely looking at her *paintings*."

"If you wish to consult with my secretary, he can tell you everyone else I visited this past week too. Do you imagine I am swiving them all?"

"There is no need for such vulgarity."

"Why single out Miss Bell?"

Renshaw's lips tightened. "I do not wish to speak ill of Sir Gordon Bell's niece, but, well, a professional artist." He shook his head. "No respectable woman would put herself on display like that. A woman, making a living as an artist, and not married? It is an aberration, Dammerton."

"I'll thank you not to refer to any person as an *aberration*," Leo said coldly. "Miss Bell is respectable and hard-working, without a hint of immorality staining her name," he added. "I trust you do not intend to ruin a woman's livelihood out of sheer idleness and spite? I thought you a better man than that."

Renshaw looked momentarily chastened, before rallying. "As my wife said, it would be humiliating for my granddaughter to be engaged to a man who is involved in a liaison with another woman, especially given your father's choices and your previous marriage. Being a duchess will be no consolation for that."

Leo's impulse was to defend Juno again, but this was precisely why he was here. And precisely why he had to deflect attention to protect both Juno and Miss Macey from the gossips.

He had made his choice. He had chosen marriage to Miss Macey and his Foundation over his friendship with Juno and their tangled history. He had chosen to return his life to order. Now he had to make that choice stick.

He had to betray his friendship with Juno, right here, in the dappled sunlight under the wisteria vines.

"I haven't the slightest interest in a liaison with Miss Bell." He spoke clearly, deliberately. "I call on her merely out of duty to my friend Hadrian Bell, who requested I stand in his stead as her brother figure for the duration of his posting abroad. Now Hadrian is back in England, the visits will cease. I assure you, my acquaintance with Miss Bell is of no consequence whatsoever."

He felt strangely better for having uttered the lies. More in control of his feelings, less threatened by that desire, less haunted by the past.

"Well." Renshaw nodded. "The truth is, Susannah is amenable to your attentions. She sees herself as a great patroness of the decorative arts. You'll find her expensive," he added with a chuckle. "Call upon her at your leisure. But one word of misconduct on your part, Dammerton——"

Leo inclined his head. "I will treat her with respect."

"See you do. Yes. Well." Renshaw looked up and down the wisteria bower. Confusion wrinkled his brow. "This garden looks all the same," he said with a nervous laugh.

"You are here to acquire a painting from Prescott, I understand," Leo reminded him gently.

The other man's expression cleared. "Ah yes, Prescott." He nodded. "Yes. Got an appointment with him about a painting. I wonder if Mrs. Prescott might get me a cup of tea while I wait."

"No doubt she will," Leo said, choosing not to mention the tea Renshaw had already received. With a friendly hand on the older man's shoulder, he turned him in the right direction, then added a nudge. "Head back to ask her, or perhaps Prescott is ready for you now. I shall enjoy this garden a while longer."

Leo watched Renshaw toddle back along the bower, his coat coming and going in the dappled light. Then he pivoted and continued his walk in the other direction.

It was a pleasant garden, especially on an early summer's day, with the occasional cry of birds and the buzzing of bees. Music and voices floated through the air, distant like a dream, and he relaxed into the feeling of being apart.

So, he desired Juno: no matter. Desire burned hot and urgent, but it always passed. Desire alone did not mean he was doomed to fall in love with her again, and have his heart smashed to smithereens again, and find himself moping and pining and lurking on the street outside her window again.

This lust for Juno—surely it was no more than a hangover from the past. He was no longer a callow boy in the first throes of affection for a charming, pretty girl. No longer the foolish virgin who had exploded his life by spinning a web of fantasies from one brief adolescent kiss.

What was it Juno had said, about whether one's younger selves still lurked within? That was all this was, his younger self, that naive, broken-hearted fool, wailing in his mind like a ghost on the castle walls.

Indeed, Leo was feeling almost content as he strolled into a small garden, fragrant with the jasmine growing exuberantly over the walls.

Until Juno herself stepped through the shrubbery and planted herself on the grass before him.

Her complexion was both pale and pink. Her eyes were wide. Her mouth trembled.

"Leo," she said, her voice tremulous with accusation and hurt.

His first thought was to pull her into his arms and demand who had hurt her, that he might mete out punishment.

In the silence came the sound of violins and voices riding on the breeze.

Which led to his second thought: She had overheard his conversation, and this time the person who had hurt her was Leo himself.

"Is that true, what I heard you say to the earl?" Juno demanded. "That our friendship means nothing?"

Leo could not tell the truth. He was not ready to lie. Shame at his own behavior transformed into annoyance at her ambush.

He inspected his cuffs coolly. "You know what they say about eavesdroppers."

"Yes, eavesdroppers hear their friends deny their friendships. I was looking for Livia, who has disappeared, and I was thinking how happy I was that you are here today, and I was thinking—" She bit her lip. "But you do not care what I was thinking, do you? Not if we are not friends."

Her distress tugged at his heart. He could heal this rift. He could find a way to explain so they might part as friends.

It was so tempting.

And if he was tempted now, he would be tempted again. Some day he would be tired, restless, bored, and he would seek her out, as he always did. And she would welcome him, as she always did.

And he would jeopardize the new, orderly life he was trying to build.

He wished to safeguard her happiness; he wished to safeguard his future marriage. He could not do both. He had made his choice. Now he must enforce it.

The only safe measure was to burn the bridge of what lay between them and ensure he could never go back.

Whatever it takes.

He fingered the hard stone of the ruby pin nestled in the folds of his cravat. "You forget, perhaps, that I am a duke and not at your beck and call," he said coldly. "I have more pressing concerns than your passing sentiments."

She looked baffled. "What nonsense is that? Not half an hour ago we were laughing together, and now you are spouting this rubbish."

Leo said nothing.

"Why are you putting this distance between us?" she went on, seeing too clearly, too deeply, yet not clearly or deeply enough. "It is as though in the past half hour something has caused you to despise me, and I cannot fathom what I have done."

He was hurting her; he hated hurting her. Yet her bewilderment needled him, as if she could not fathom that he too could be hurt. How careless she was, bandying around words like friendship and love, as if she were the only one who ever felt them.

None of it would matter in the end. Juno may weep now, but she would forget him. She embraced all of life's delights and sorrows, and never dwelled in the shadow of the past or the glare of the future. Such was her nature. It would never change.

In that moment, he did despise her. It erupted from nowhere, the searing, raw bitterness and hurt that had consumed him in Vienna. He found that years-old thread of hurt and longing, and he spun it out and wove it into a broader tapestry of resentment. He wrapped himself in it like a blanket.

"It can be no surprise that I wish my second marriage to succeed," he said. "Maintaining a connection with a woman such as yourself would be disrespectful to the lady I make my wife."

"A woman such as myself." Her tone was flat.

"Do you require me to elaborate?"

"Oh, I think I comprehend your meaning. They'll assume I am your mistress, if they don't already. Because, after all, what use has a gentleman for a *woman such as myself*, except in his bed? Yet we are not lovers, and never have been, and never will be, except in their puerile, prejudiced minds. What a fine jest, when naught lies between us but a single kiss ten years ago that meant nothing at all, and was gone and forgotten before the summer was out."

Startling, really, that such an old wound might still prove tender. That somewhere inside him, that sensitive youth had just cried out in pain.

"I find myself grateful for your eavesdropping, madam," he made himself say. "As you save me the trouble of seeing you again to explain the situation. In the circumstances, I shall not be at liberty to call at your studio again."

In that moment, Juno detested him.

The playful friend who lit up her studio was in hiding. The

earnest boy she had once loved to distraction had grown into this glib, remote creature spun out of silk and lies.

So aloof, so ornate, and about as warm as a marble statue on a winter's day.

And if she painted him now? There, with the sun favoring him, framed against the wall of jasmine trembling in the breeze. *Beautiful Liar*, she might title it.

She never had painted him. She would need burnt sienna and burnt umber, a touch of Prussian blue for his eyes, and—Oh, what did it matter what colors she would choose? She would never paint him. Already she had wasted too much time and paper, drawing Leopold Halton's face.

Ten years ago he had rejected her, making it clear she was not valuable enough to keep in his life, and here he was, doing it again. He had tossed aside their friendship, crushed it under the heel of his impeccably crafted boot.

She hated those boots. Hated his waistcoat and his coat and his cravat, his eyes and his hair and his face.

He looked away, as if this interview had become vexing and tedious, as if called by some terribly important ducal matter. He had discharged an unpleasant task, but one did what one had to do. Honor and duty and such, don't you know?

Then he met her eyes and bowed, a deeper bow than a duke ought to give to a woman such as herself. Such excessive courtesy. Such wondrous condescension.

Such an insufferable beast.

Juno refused to curtsy, but he did not wait for it. He turned on his heel, and she said, "You do not even see it, do you?"

He paused, head cocked as if he had heard a distant voice in the wind.

"You have betrayed our friendship, yet again."

He turned back. "Again?" he repeated, sounding genuinely baffled. Sounding human and like himself again. There: a small tear in his facade. She would rip it open, as ruthlessly as he had torn her.

"I understand you must marry," she said. "I understand you must sever our connection out of respect for your future bride. I do not like it, it grieves me terribly, and I hate that our society is made thus, but I understand it. I understand we cannot be friends in the future, but I do not understand why you must deny our friendship of the past." She extended one hand in supplication. He glanced at it, looked away. She let her hand drop. "These words of yours, I don't only lose you now, I lose every moment we ever shared in the past. I do not understand why you must do that."

"And I do not understand why you persist. Madam."

"You lied to Lord Renshaw," she said, desperately needing it to be true. "And if you did not, then look me in the eye and tell me now our friendship meant nothing to you. I thought—" She laughed, but it was not a merry sound. "I deluded myself that I provided for you a haven, where you could relax and be yourself. And I fancied I could be at ease with you, and not hide— I never knew you were judging me for my choices."

She stopped short. Some things were better not spoken out loud—the fact she took lovers, she painted nudes, she made bawdy jokes, she did not *behave*. Yet not once had he made her feel unworthy of his respect.

Until now.

"All this time, you have been scorning me, and—" She shook her head. "No. I cannot believe it. You were happy in my studio. You—"

Tears pricked her eyes. She would not weep. She must return to Beatrice's party and act the grateful protégée of her treacherous patroness. But after that, she would be safe at home, and there, alone with her cats, she would release his image onto the page.

Then she would burn every drawing she had of Leo and dance on the ashes.

Something surged inside her, something savage and fierce. It surged through her chest and her limbs, so powerful and violent it propelled her toward him. She grabbed his coat lapels, hauled herself closer. Words failed her. She could express herself only with her body.

With a fierce, angry kiss.

Her mouth landed on his and— Oh! The blessed sweet warmth of his lips under hers! In that warmth, those very human lips, she found the man—not the duke, not the carefully curated work of art. Just the man. She savored his taste and inhaled his scent, before lowering down and stepping away. Their matching ragged breaths unfurled around them.

"Leo," she whispered.

He said nothing. His coat was askew. His posture was rigid.

His face was like granite.

"Oh no."

She pressed a hand to her careless, greedy mouth. Chills spiraled through her, icing her blood with horror at her own wantonness, at the unprecedented, unacceptable act.

"Forgive me," she stammered. "I ought never have— That was— Oh, please forgive me."

She whirled around to flee, every inch of her now burning with hot shame.

Then a hand closed around her wrist. Pulled her back, firm and gentle.

She turned, time slowing, the air moving about them like molten honey, as his body stepped into hers. His hand caught her face. His gaze seared her. Yes! There he was! His eyes were hot and hard and fierce; *that* was what she craved, that glimpse of his dark, passionate corners, his own wildness and mess. She felt a thrill of triumph, a bolt of desire, a gust of affection, all in those desperate, dazzling heartbeats until his lips claimed hers.

His kiss was savage and raw, and as angry as her own. He was offering a piece of himself; she would seize every bit she could. To taste the man behind those glib words, to feel the man under those pretty clothes. Such delicious sensations, and they ought not to be so delicious, because this was Leo. Oh, what madness, she was kissing Leo!

And an army of angels would not make her stop.

She curled a hand around his neck, hauled him closer, her breasts crushed against his chest, their thighs meeting, their tongues dueling. If this was the only taste of him she'd ever have, then she would take it all and give herself, all her anger and loss and longing for—something, something could not name.

Somehow, the fury passed. They stopped, entwined like a statue, if a statue could be made of savage lava. Her hand cupped the strong column of his neck; his fingers pressed into her waist. Eyes closed, she rested her forehead on his jaw. Ragged breaths passed between them. Two lava beings holding each other up as the world shook and shuddered around them.

Then she moved, or he did. Her hands slid down his chest; his palm caressed her cheek. Their eyes dared not meet, but their mouths raced toward each other again.

If the first kiss had been a blizzard of hail and fire, this kiss was the shelter from the storm. This kiss was a warm room, and two naked bodies on a soft rug before the hearth.

Its tender truth seared her, soothed her. His mouth gently explored hers, while his fingers sketched languorous circles on her waist. She pressed deeper into him, and his arm swept around her, his hand curving around her buttocks to hold her tighter, as if he needed to consume all of her at once.

Then he left her, in a series of small losses, first his mouth, then his arm, then his body. When she opened her eyes, he was facing away, head bent, one hand planted on the wall, crushing the delicate jasmine blooms and sending their perfume into the air.

Juno trembled with bittersweet yearning, longing coursing through her body with every wild thump of her heart.

Was that desire? She had no other word, but it was more powerful than any desire she had known before. This sensation was to desire what an oil painting was to a cartoon.

Slowly, it subsided, as everything did. Leo was still melded to the wall, hiding his face.

Who are you? she wanted to ask.

Then: *Who am I?*

And then: *If that was a kiss, I have never been kissed before.*

Finally, he pushed himself off the wall. Straightened. Performed a series of movements, stiff as an automaton, arranging his coat, smoothing his cravat, raking his hair. When he faced her, he was once more impeccably put together.

While she felt all in pieces like a mosaic.

He looked untouchable. *But I touched him,* she thought fiercely. *Not just his body or his senses. That kiss… I touched* him.

She felt almost drunk with it. A tipsy-sounding giggle escaped her throat.

Oh, how silly they were. This was Leo! They were friends! They could laugh about this, then dash off to some secret place to explore what came next. Tumble into bed together, enjoy a few days before they parted.

If they were friends.

"Friends do not kiss like that," she said.

Leo said nothing.

Anger lashed her again. "But we have established we are not friends. Tell me, Your Grace, you who knows so much, what are we?"

Leo said nothing.

"Nothing," she said, translating his silence to answer the question for them both. "Ten years, yet nothing remains."

She whirled around and stumbled away.

As she headed for the shrubbery, she focused hard on the leaves, on tracing their shapes with her mind's eye. Anything to keep from weeping. Anything to keep from indulging her cartwheeling feelings.

Anything to keep from looking back.

CHAPTER 12

Beatrice insisted on taking Juno home after the garden party, which meant she had to endure for what felt like years, pasting on a smile, making trite conversation with guests, waving away concerned inquiries from her cousins and aunt ("I'm merely tired," Juno assured them. "It has been quite a day!").

And, of course, suffering through Beatrice's oblivious enthusiasm.

"I have the most exciting news for you, Juno darling!" Beatrice said. "I shall tell you when we reach your house. You are in for the most marvelous surprise!"

Juno wasn't sure she could tolerate any more surprises today.

But at her house, she was too drained to resist when a beaming Beatrice dragged her into her parlor and pointed at the wall.

At an empty spot, right where Juno's painting of Pandora had hung.

Her stomach plummeted through the floor. She stared at the space in horror. "Beatrice, what have you done?"

"Prescott has sold your Pandora painting! And for a lovely price too." She caught Juno's shoulders in a brief hug. "I insisted he act with speed for I am so ashamed of how we treated you over your fee, and there was Lord Renshaw, happy to take any piece of art that Prescott recommended."

"Lord Renshaw."

Juno smothered her laugh. If she started laughing now, she might never stop. The man who had insulted her today now owned her painting and its frame.

Which meant he also owned her secret cache of drawings of Leo.

Oh, dear heaven, she was going to be sick.

"Lord Renshaw would never buy art by me."

"But of *course* he did. Prescott recommended it, and everyone listens to Prescott when it comes to art. We sent over his secretary with a note for Mrs. Kegworth to collect it. Renshaw is happy to acquire a new painting, you are happy to get a fine price from an earl, no less, and I am happy that you will forgive me. Isn't this marvelous? Look at you, you are quite speechless."

Juno forced her brain to work. "It was the wrong frame. We must get that frame back." She gripped Beatrice's shoulders urgently. "Tell Lord Renshaw there has been a mistake, take back the painting, and next week when the new frame is ready——"

"Whatever are you suggesting?" Beatrice yanked herself free, her expression appalled. "That I embarrass myself in front of an *earl*?"

"He'll have secretaries or butlers to manage such matters. If you or Mr. Prescott simply explain——"

"I expected you to be grateful, Juno. Prescott supported you. Prescott! Every artist in London clamors for his attention, and he staked his reputation on you! And you want us to tell an *earl* there has been a *mistake*? I would sooner *die*."

Juno scrambled for an excuse. "That frame is old. The new frame I ordered is much better suited to that painting, and since Renshaw has paid for the frame too, he deserves—"

"Prescott approved that frame. Perhaps the one you ordered is better, but you need not be perfect every time." Beatrice's expression softened. "Do calm yourself. You know these men. They like the idea of art more than the art itself. They show off a painting to their dinner guests once and then forget all about it."

"I—"

"Not another word. Let's speak again tomorrow when you are calmer, and you'll see you've made a big to-do about nothing."

Wearied, Juno gave up. Arguing was only making it worse, and besides, she'd had enough of Beatrice for one day.

Alone again, she paced, shooting glances at the wall as if the painting might miraculously reappear.

Even now, someone in Renshaw's household might be inspecting the frame. If she was very lucky, they would notice only that it was not new and ask Prescott to change it for another. If she was very unlucky, they would notice the cunningly concealed mechanism by which the frame split open to reveal papers inside. And if she was very, very unlucky, those papers would become known.

Papers covered with drawings of the Duke of Dammerton, each signed with her name. Humiliation would follow, possibly ruin. Leo would learn of it, of course, and he would think—

He would think she was in love with him.

Ha! Chances were the vain, arrogant duke already believed she was in love with him. That would explain his unkindness earlier, freezing her out as if he feared she might become emotional and—oh, the horror!—make matters *awkward*.

Well, she had become emotional and made matters awkward, and serve him right.

With a sniff, she wandered into the studio. "Liar," she muttered at the prop cabinet, crammed with gifts from Leo, then threw herself discontentedly onto the window seat. A simple gift, an hour or two a week: What did such things mean to a wealthy, busy duke? How she had cherished his visits—while he only ever gave her crumbs.

She hauled the curtains shut, kicked off her slippers, pulled up her feet, and hugged her knees.

Was he thinking of her now? Was he reliving their kiss, craving more, lost in a turmoil of emotions? Or had he shrugged off the whole episode? Perhaps he had gone home to place an order of flowers for Miss Macey. Perhaps he was calling on his future wife even now.

Closing her eyes, she relived the kiss. Relived those moments when he released some deep, wild part of himself that soared into the deep, wild parts of her.

Now she burned with wanting more. Her breasts were tender. Her belly was tight. Longing pulsed between her thighs. She rubbed her feet together, a futile attempt to relieve the pressure in her quim.

This is Leo, she scolded herself, trying to be sensible. Or rather, the Duke of Dammerton, who had insulted her, denied their friendship, disdained her. Yet he had also kissed her, with searing passion and tenderness, and how easy to imagine his hand around her breast, his mouth closing over her yearning nipples.

His eyes meeting hers as he honored her, pleasured her, and never rejected her again.

It was his slender, deft hand sliding up her leg, not her own. His fingers tracing designs on the soft skin of her inner thigh, while his eyes trapped hers, those blue eyes as full of promise as the morning, as his fingers feathered over—

Bang! A door slammed below. Juno's eyes flew open. She

froze, listening: voices, laughter, footsteps stampeding up the stairs.

With a yelp, she tumbled off the window seat, scrambled to her feet, shook out her skirts, and dashed into her parlor, just as a pack of her artist friends hurtled into it from the other door.

They were brandishing cheap brandy and bad jokes and promises of an entertaining night. "A new literary salon!" cried one. "Dancing!" cried another. "All of them!" cried Juno, almost in tears in frustration and relief and desperation to be rescued from her own confused thoughts.

JUNO'S WEIGHT pressed down onto him, her naked body heating him down to his eager bones. Her soft, plump breasts, her round, lush buttocks, and her mouth on his, her hand gripping his cock, her eyes, laughing, blue like a forget-me-not, a butterfly, a Wedgwood vase. Yes, yes! Her mouth so hot, her hand so frantic, her hair tickling him, smothering him, choking him—

Leo's eyes flew open. He sat up, gasping, spitting out the sheets that covered his mouth, sucking in air and painful reality. No naked Juno lying atop him, no mouths or breasts or buttocks, and the only hand on his tortured cock was his own.

Like a wounded wolf, Leo yowled into his dark, lonely bedroom. Squeezing his face with his spare hand, as if to crush his own bones, he finished himself off in a rage of despair.

Then he collapsed back onto the pillows, stewing in his own sweat and seed.

Hell.

One kiss at a garden party, and he was as delirious as a man with a fever, guiltily groping himself under the covers as he had when he was nineteen.

But that kiss…

He knew why she had kissed him: She had been angry and hurt, and one might do anything in such a state, especially someone as physically expressive as Juno.

What was his excuse? One touch of her lips, and he forgot everything but the flames of desire roaring into life like a furnace under the bellows. He could have taken her up against that jasmine-covered wall, where the scent of the flowers mingled with the scent of their bodies. He could have buried his face in her neck and nipped her skin and tugged down her bodice. He could have fallen to his knees and shoved up her skirts and tasted her and teased her until she—

Aargh! He hurled a pillow across the room.

Thwarted lust, messing with his mind.

Again.

No. Desire would *not* disrupt his life again.

He bounded out of bed and poured the entire pitcher of cold water over his head. Once dressed, he rode down to the river to row for an hour, then broke his fast at his club, taking refuge in the company of other men.

Hadrian was at breakfast, in deep conversation with a colleague. They exchanged greetings: Hadrian was leaving London that day, he said, to "look into something" along the coast, and Leo felt a guilty relief, given Hadrian saw Juno like a sister.

But all in all, it was a most satisfactory program, he decided, as he began his walk home. With enough cold water, vigorous exercise, and robust conversation, the vexing matter of Juno Bell would soon be exorcised from his mind and his courtship could begin.

His contentment did not last long, however, for as he strolled through St. James, someone called, "Your Grace! If you please!"

and then trotting by his side was Thomas Macey, the numbskull whose greatest—and only—contribution to the world was that game aimed at making Leo lose his temper.

"Are you heading home, sir?" Macey asked boldly. "Might I walk with you?"

"Been thinking up new ways to irritate me, have you, Macey?" Leo said. "Let's hope you've something more diverting than your stupid game of duke-baiting."

"Please accept my apologies for that—that horrendous impertinence." Macey was walking sideways, hands clasped in apparent repentance.

"And what about the impertinence of ruining my pleasant walk?" Leo said.

"I mean no impertinence, Your Grace. I wish only to beg your help. You are the only one who knows of my—" He lowered his voice. "My difficult situation."

Well. That was one way for a gentleman to refer to his secret wife.

"My father is returning to England." Macey swiped at the sweat beading on his upper lip. "My grandfather, Lord Renshaw, he is... He sometimes becomes confused and his memory is not what it was."

"I've noticed."

"My father has been recalled from Constantinople to take over my grandfather's duties as earl and he—" He gulped audibly. "Do you know my father?"

"By reputation. As I recall, his favorite pastime was finding new reasons to have poor people hanged or flogged."

Macey nodded so vigorously his hat tumbled off and he had to chase it several steps down the street.

"I worry what he will say. Will do. To her." He spun the hat over in his hands with dizzying speed. "He'll ruin her. Please,

Dammerton, what shall I do? You're a duke. My grandmother says you wish to wed my sister, which means you'll be my brother by marriage. Perhaps you could…"

"Could what?"

"Protect us somehow? My wife and me."

"How?"

"I don't know. You're a *duke*," he repeated in a wail.

Leo stopped and spun his walking stick in his hand. Macey's mouth quivered, as he continued to punish his undeserving hat.

"You're twenty-one, are you not, Macey?"

"Just, sir."

"Then you are no longer a boy. As adults, we can do as we please, but we must face the consequences of doing as we please. When our mistakes result in a mess, we clean up that mess. If you are old enough to marry against your father's wishes, then you are old enough to stand up to your father."

"Yes, but——"

"Good day, Mr. Macey."

Yet barely four strides later, the youth was once more trotting at his side. Again Leo stopped, rested both hands on his walking stick, and sighed.

Macey released a nervous laugh. "Honestly, Your Grace, I was walking home too, and our paths are the same…"

Leo said nothing.

"But I'll just, er, pause here a moment, shall I? And maybe, uh, choose a different route?"

"Good lad."

Leo kept walking, mercifully free of hangers-on. Unfair to judge the boy so harshly, given his own mistakes at that age. He still carried those mistakes with him. Hence his embarrassing overreaction with Juno the day before.

He had been unkind to her, unnecessarily so, driven by his

panicky, youthful fear that desiring her would mean losing his head over her again. An apology was in order. Surely it would do no harm. A five-minute call to apologize and then—

Oh, how right she had felt in his arms, how perfect her mouth had tasted under his and the warmth of her skin under his hand—

He smacked a gatepost with his walking stick, as if bludgeoning the memory. This was precisely the kind of temptation he had sought to avoid by insulting her and turning her against him.

Calling on her would be a mistake, he reminded himself, as his legs carried him onto the square where his house lay, and he would make no more mistakes because he would never see Juno again.

Only to see her coming down the stairs from Lord Renshaw's front door.

Leo stopped short.

Not possible.

There was no way the female figure in the plum-colored pelisse and straw bonnet could be Juno. It must be some other woman, who just happened to have a similar figure, and similar hand gestures, and a similar way of moving. And a companion who was very similar to Juno's lodger, housekeeper, and sometime chaperone, Mrs. Kegworth.

Sainted stitches. First the dream, then this. Juno could have no earthly reason to set foot in this part of town, let alone visit Lord Renshaw, of all people.

Until the woman turned his way. She, too, stopped short. Shock rippled through him, galvanized by wonder, panic, rage, delight.

"Juno," he breathed. She would smile at him, warm and welcoming, and he would toss her over his shoulder and haul her up to his bedchamber, and there they would laugh and chat and make love until the rest of the world disappeared.

He wanted her. He wanted Juno Bell as he wanted nothing else, and a thousand cold baths and hard exercise and dull breakfasts would never make that wanting stop.

CHAPTER 13

Juno had arrived at Lord Renshaw's house with renewed optimism.

Sometime during the previous night's diversions, between playing parlor games and dancing a reel, a simple plan had formed: She would seek permission to assess whether her Pandora painting was ready for varnishing, and hope to deal with a bored housemaid who neither knew nor cared that the painting would not need varnishing for months.

With good cheer, she had gathered up Mrs. Kegworth and climbed into a hackney cab for the journey across London, fortunate to get a driver who knew on which grand, elegant square Lord Renshaw lived.

Only for her plan to fall apart with a single poke from the earl's secretary.

"If someone were here to vouch for you, Miss Bell, it might be a different matter," Renshaw's man repeated, not unkindly. "But I cannot allow a pair of strange women to enter his lordship's house to inspect a valuable piece of art without proof that you are, indeed, who you say you are. If Mr. or Mrs.

Prescott had accompanied you, or even Sir Gordon or Lady Bell…"

Bother and blast. The man was being courteous, and not at all unreasonable. Reluctantly, Juno admitted defeat. She was just taking her leave when an elderly man entered and said, in affable tones, "There you are, Eccles. Who's our guest?"

Juno's stomach sank. It was the earl himself.

"This woman says you bought her painting from Mr. Prescott yesterday," said the man called Eccles.

"Ah, yes. *Pandora Trapping Hope.*" Lord Renshaw smiled pleasantly at Juno. "An excellent piece, excellent. Recommended by Prescott himself, you know. *And* by an English artist. Do you know the artist, young lady?"

"I am the artist, my lord."

Mr. Eccles said, "This is Miss Juno Bell. She is niece to Sir Gordon Bell."

The earl studied her blankly, and then he repeated, "Miss Juno Bell?" and his affability vanished as quickly as her optimism. "So Dammerton was lying. I knew it."

"This matter does not concern His Grace," Juno said hastily. "You bought one of my paintings—"

"What rot." Renshaw made a derisive sound. "The idea that I might purchase something by Dammerton's doxy!"

"I beg your pardon, my lord," Juno said, very sharply.

"Taking a tone, are you? Let me guess: Dammerton ended his liaison with you, as I requested, and instead of graciously accepting his decision and parting gifts, you came here to make trouble for my Susannah."

Juno stood as straight and tall as she could. "My lord, I have no interest in your family. I am a respectable artist, and I shall not—"

"Respectable! If you were respectable, you'd have a husband here to vouch for you."

"What a shame I forgot to get married before calling."

Mr. Eccles cleared his throat. "My lord, this lady's uncle is Sir Gordon Bell, so perhaps we—"

"Perhaps he should be ashamed to acknowledge her." He shook a finger at her, lace cuffs quivering. "I'll have a word with Dammerton about this."

"Please," Juno said. "This has nothing to do with him. I do not want any trouble, I—"

"Trouble's exactly what you want. I know all about women like you. In my day… Oh-ho, oh yes indeed."

"My lord, you know nothing about me."

"Enough. Eccles, shut the door."

Mr. Eccles shot her a rueful look and did as he was told.

For five stunned seconds, Juno stared at the painted wood and the brass ring, before turning to traipse unevenly down the steps to the street.

Mrs. Kegworth was looking worried. "Not went as you hoped, then?"

A broken laugh escaped Juno's throat. "I could not have achieved a worse outcome if I had delegated the planning of this to my cats."

Now Leo would hear of this—the Earl of Renshaw's version, that was. In one move, she had jeopardized both her own reputation and his courtship.

One option remained: to seek her aunt's help, and beg her to ask no questions about why, exactly, she had a score of drawings of Leo hidden in a painting frame.

"We must call on my aunt next," she told Mrs. Kegworth, and looked left and right to orient herself.

Only to be immediately disoriented when her gaze fell on Leo himself, standing like a statue, walking stick clutched in one hand.

Oh, dear heaven, could this day get any worse?

She briefly entertained mad visions of dashing to the garden in the middle of the square and hiding in the bushes until he went away. But her feet were like stone, and Mrs. Kegworth said brightly, "Why, it's His Grace," and then Leo was striding toward her, freezing her in place like a rabbit before a lion.

Warmth burst over her, which was immensely annoying, because she was neither shrinking violet nor blushing virgin, and he was nothing but an insufferable, vain, arrogant beast who had denied their friendship and treated her as a blight upon his day.

And kissed her so thoroughly she still felt him sizzling through her veins.

He stopped abruptly. His coattails flapped from the momentum. He remained at a courteous distance, but there was nothing courteous in his heated gaze as it roamed over her face and scorched her dry lips, or in his harsh tone as he said, "What the devil are you doing on this street?"

"For crying out loud," Juno muttered.

She spun around and hurried away, away from Renshaw and Dammerton and every other pestilent peer that infested this place.

Leo easily kept pace with her, though poor Mrs. Kegworth was soon left behind.

"Juno? Explain yourself."

"It is no concern of yours." She fixed her gaze on the street in front of her. "I had business with Lord Renshaw."

"What possible business could you have with Renshaw? If this is connected to what you overheard yesterday—" He stopped short. "Bloody hell, you did not come to see Miss Macey?"

Juno threw up her hands and whirled to face him. "I am sick of the lot of you. As if anything less than an emergency would induce me to set foot in this dreadful part of town."

Eyebrows raised, he let his gaze roam pointedly over the grand, polished houses that lined the square, with their judgmental doors and self-righteous windows and condescending flower boxes.

"Dreadful?" he repeated dryly.

"Dreadful," Juno confirmed with a haughty sniff. "I might catch a nasty case of arrogant presumptuousness. There seems to be a lot of it around here."

Oh, but his cool composure was irritating. How she wanted him discomposed!

There were a million other things she wanted too: to explore the contours of his body, to tear open his heart and discover what made him tremble and what made him howl, to solve the riddle of why he treated her as he did.

She whirled about and marched on.

"Where are you going?" he asked, once more at her side.

"As far from here as possible." She twisted to check on Mrs. Kegworth, who trailed behind them, gawking up at the houses. "For your own good. You do not want Renshaw to catch you talking to your *doxy*, as he calls me."

"He insulted you thus?"

His sharp tone made her snort. "What will you do? Call him out? Lords like you don't fight duels over women like me."

"That's not fair. I don't fight duels over anyone."

He caught her forearm. Fireworks crackled off the pressure of his touch. Time stopped as they both stared at the point of contact. Slowly, carefully, he removed his bare hand and curved his fingers over the head of his walking stick. One slender finger traced the intricate rosettes carved over the stick's head, just as his fingers had traced shapes on her body the day before.

She looked away from his hand, only to meet his eyes, and that was even worse.

"Careful, Leo. You wouldn't want to harm your courtship. Miss Macey is welcome to you."

"No one in Renshaw's household can see us now. Explain

why you're here."

She tossed her head. "You explain why *you're* here. Courting Miss Macey, I presume? I do hope you have not neglected to bring flowers. Or have you a sweet sonnet tucked in your pocket?"

"I was walking home," he said mildly. "My house is…" He twisted, pointed at the stately building that dominated the other side of the square. "Right there."

"Oh." With a groan, Juno covered her face with one hand. "I shall stop talking now before I embarrass myself further."

"Or start talking before either of us jumps to more conclusions."

He slipped his fingers around her hand as gently as if it were a newborn kitten and lowered it from her face. A heartbeat too long he held it, then once more let her go. "Why did you call on Lord Renshaw?"

She nursed her hand against her stomach and vowed to display calm and poise.

"If you must know," she said, in a most dignified tone, "Lord Renshaw has come into possession of certain papers of mine that would embarrass me if they were to become public. I sought to retrieve them."

A frown slowly formed and deepened on his face. "Am I to believe the Earl of Renshaw is *blackmailing* you?"

Her dignified facade crumbled. "*Blackmail?* Why on earth would you think—? Oh, yes, it does sound like that, doesn't it? In his defense, he does not know he has these papers."

"He's not the one you need to defend right now. Forgive my *arrogant presumptuousness*, but you have no connection to him, except a very tenuous one through me. I'd know of any connection, as we know so much about each other."

"We don't, though, do we?" she said quietly. "Until two minutes ago, I did not even know where you live."

Suddenly, it hurt to look at him. She didn't belong here, in this stately square. "Niece to Sir Gordon Bell," they described her, in that excruciatingly polite way, defining her by what they chose not to say.

Once more, Leo was an untouchable work of art—*Arrogant Stranger*, she would title it—whereas her cheeks felt flushed, and her best walking dress felt too tight, and she kept saying too much and speaking too freely. Mostly, she did not mind her own flaws: Life held too many delights to bother with such things. But now her flaws made her feel clumsy and plain. It was Leo's doing. He had the power to make her feel happy and at peace; he equally had the power to make her feel like dirt under his boot.

"It is not your concern, Your Grace," she said coldly. "We established that yesterday. I bid you good day."

Then she marched on. This time, he did not come to her side.

Just keep walking, she said to herself. *One step, then another, then—*

"Juno, wait."

She spun around. "Yes?"

He was tossing the walking stick from one hand to the other. The sunlight glinted on his ducal signet ring like a lighthouse warning.

"You are clearly in some distress. Perhaps I can offer assistance with your situation." A tiny smile tugged at his lips. "I am a duke, remember. We are not entirely useless. At the very least, I could offer you and Mrs. Kegworth a cup of tea and a carriage home."

Tears threatened. She chased them away with an unconvincing huff of laughter. "You are the last person whose help I'd seek with this."

He stiffened. The tiny smile vanished. "I see."

"I mean… That is not what I mean."

A cup of tea. In his house. Explaining her problem—an

edited version, of course. Receiving his help.

As if they were friends.

Yet their friendship had unraveled like a moth-eaten tapestry, until it was barely a heap of frayed threads, and she still did not understand how it had fallen apart so fast.

It was so tempting to stay near him a while longer. He was like a bowl of chocolate truffles, when she would say, "I'll have just one more, and *then* I'll stop. Just one more."

"You must apologize," she said, to her own surprise. "For how you spoke to me yesterday."

"I see." His gaze briefly dipped to her lips. "Anything else from yesterday I need apologize for?"

"No," she squeaked. She swallowed and added, "Everything else was perfectly … tolerable."

"Tolerable?" A rakish glint lit his eyes, as if she had issued a challenge. "So gratifying, to know it was *tolerable*."

He stepped closer. Her breath stopped. His gaze dipped to her mouth. Her lips parted.

Then the moment passed. He huffed out air and straightened.

"I apologize for the way I spoke to you yesterday," he said. "It was unkind and unnecessary, and I greatly regret my mistreatment of you."

"Why did you do it?" she whispered.

"I panicked."

"*You* panicked? I saw your brother throw a sword at you and you didn't panic."

"Swords are easy. One simply avoids the pointy bits. In conversations, the pointy bits are not always clear."

His sincerity had slipped back into glibness. She was losing him again.

"I still don't understand what is happening," she said.

He said nothing. Yes: She had lost him again.

"But it is done now, isn't it?" she added softly. "We cannot be friends anymore, can we?"

"No. We cannot."

He didn't move. She was missing something, she felt, like listening to a conversation between scholars, and understanding the words but missing the meaning.

"My invitation stands," he said quietly. "You remain the cousin of my friend. I cannot make up for how I treated you yesterday, but allow me to assist you in this predicament today. What do you wish to do?"

"I don't know." She was not good at dissembling. She tumbled straight back into speaking the truth. "I am still angry with you after yesterday, and confused because we kissed. Yet I am happy to see you, and sad to know we must part, and… Not for a minute did I imagine I might see you today, or ever again, and now I do not know what I feel or what to do with myself."

She glanced across the square. It might be lovely to finally see inside his home. Then again, it might be a terrible mistake.

Oh, it was so very tempting. One more hour. Then she'd say farewell and stop seeing him. Just one more hour and then she'd stop.

Yet she said, "It seemed to me, after yesterday, it would be best for all concerned if we never spoke again."

His expression did not change. "Certainly."

"And you were right—we should completely sever our connection."

"That would be best."

Silence fell. Neither moved. Juno studied her cotton gloves. A seam was fraying. Leo studied his walking stick, then lifted his chin and studied the sky.

It was he who broke the silence.

"Right. Would you like to come in?"

"Yes, please."

CHAPTER 14

L eo's house was a wonderland.

Juno left him in the lobby, introducing Mrs. Kegworth to his housekeeper, and ducked through the first doorway into what ought to be a front parlor.

It was no ordinary front parlor, but a splendid gallery.

Daylight streamed in through the broad windows, to ricochet from one gleaming object to the next. She hardly knew where to turn her hungry, dazzled eyes: a music box painted with constellations, a perfume burner shaped like a dancing ballerina, a red porcelain vase stuffed with gardenias.

She paused at a pair of candlesticks carved from rose marble: one showed Apollo reaching out, the other was Daphne, turning away.

Leo had told her about these, she recalled. He had spoken fondly of the workshop in Derbyshire and related the myth about Apollo's obsessive pursuit of Daphne, who had been compelled by Cupid's love-repelling arrow to deny the love of men. Apart, the candlesticks told a tale of hopeless yearning; when placed close together, Daphne fit perfectly into Apollo's embrace. She had thought of drawing the myth, but had not. She didn't remember why.

She ran her fingers over the cool marble of Apollo's outstretched arms. Leo's collection might be dismissed as the vanity of a bored, wealthy man, but to Juno it reflected his need for connection. His position isolated him from the world, though he might not realize it, for it was simply how he had been raised. But to seek out artisans, to learn their stories and sit with them while they worked? That was not the behavior of a duke who believed himself above others. It was the behavior of a man who wanted to be connected to the world.

Her heart squeezed. The house was so big. Leo ought not to be alone.

She wandered on, pausing before a teardrop-shaped mirror. The wooden frame was carved in an autumnal theme, with playful birds pecking at blackberries and field mice peering out from under leaves.

Her own reflection stole her attention. She looked well enough, she thought. Composed, at least. Her hair was not as messy as she'd feared, nor her cheeks so pink.

This was the woman whom Leo desired, she thought a little smugly. The knowledge of their mutual desire had forged something new between them. They could do nothing about it, but it was there all the same.

A movement in the mirror: Leo had entered. She studied his reflection, his unguarded expression as he raked his gaze over her back.

Yes, he desired her.

He looked up. Their eyes met in the mirror.

And as if the mirror had magical properties, she was transported to some other world: an imaginary world where Leo crossed the room to wrap his arms around her, where he pressed his lips to her neck, then turned her to claim her mouth in a sweet, sweet kiss.

She slapped her hand to the mirror's lies and whirled around.

Too much lay between them. The air pulsed with it. With that kiss yesterday, they had broken a thousand little rules, whose shards now shimmered and bounced around the room like the sunlight itself.

"I recall you talking of this mirror," she said. Her voice sounded unnaturally loud. "A former soldier, am I right? He sings opera as he carves, you said, but he doesn't know the words so he makes up his own."

He smiled faintly. "You remember."

"I enjoy your stories. These items feel like my friends, as if I'm already familiar with your collection. It is so clearly your passion."

He reached out one hand—such beautiful hands, he had— and rippled his fingers over the perfume burner like he was playing the flute.

"I have long dreamed of expanding the scope of the Dammerton Foundation," he said slowly. "It will require a large sum of money to execute. But my expenses are considerable and the divorce was costly." His gaze was steady with meaning. "You do understand?"

"Yes. I understand."

He was speaking of his marriage. He must marry for the usual reasons, of course: duty, family, heirs, and so forth. But also for money, for the Foundation that was his one passion. Presumably the lady in question did not object to being used thus. Juno didn't ask. Miss Macey already haunted the conversation. Besides, Beatrice had revealed enough: Susannah Macey would bring to her marriage twenty-five thousand pounds, which would buy her status, stability, security, and a life with Leo.

Juno wore a sad smile as she turned away to continue her explorations of his home. Leo trailed after her.

The rose-colored muslin of her gown swayed around her. She caressed the objects as she passed, fondled and petted and stroked, as if it demanded all her senses to experience them. She didn't mean to be provocative, but he couldn't stop watching her hands, his chest boiling with jealousy, as if he envied mere objects for receiving her touch.

Neither spoke again. She had understood his meaning. She would not understand everything, but she understood enough.

Dimly, he remembered they had agreed to sever their connection. That was the most sensible thing. But he was not feeling sensible now, with the memory of their kiss and his dream more vivid to him than the room itself, with her dress skimming over her hips and thighs, while every object seemed to come alive in her presence, the peculiar magic that belonged to Juno and Juno alone.

The way she brought him alive.

Still he said nothing. If he spoke, he might say something foolish.

I had a dream about you last night, he might say.

You are more beautiful than any of these decorative objects, he might say.

Foolish indeed. She would roll her eyes because such meaningless words were worthy of only the most inept libertine. Leo was not a libertine, and he had not invited her into his house to seduce her.

Had he?

The silence continued until she reached the dining room, where she clapped delightedly at the sight of the tea services covering the table.

"Good heavens! There are so many. You weren't exaggerating. I revise what I said the other day. You may indeed send me a new tea service or six."

"Choose whichever ones you want."

She roamed about, eager as a child at a fair, before asking, "Which would you choose for me?"

He guided her to a small set, with only four teacups. Each took a season as its theme, personified by a nymph. The autumn nymph wore leaves of red and orange, the spring nymph danced amid pink blossoms, summer was draped in green, and winter twirled in white.

She lifted the cup for summer. "Oh, but they're exquisite."

"Look," he said.

He edged behind her, his coat brushing her back, and slid his fingers under her wrist. He wrapped his hand around hers and the cup, tilted them gently to bring the panel into the light.

He did not need to stand so close. He did not need to wrap his hand around hers. He did not need to breathe in her floral scent, or revel in the warmth of her skin, or enjoy the tickle of her curls as he bent his head too close to hers. She tensed, then relaxed. She did not move away. She became complicit in his pretense that this was all quite reasonable.

"Do you see that flaw on the nymph's gown?" he said softly. "That mistaken brushstroke."

Surely she saw it, with her trained eye, but she asked, "Show me?"

And, of course, the only possible way to show her was to bring his other arm around her and envelop her, before he slid a zigzag caress over the cool porcelain.

"Such imperfections are my favorite part," he said. "Proof of the human touch."

She murmured her assent, as they continued to pretend this

was a perfectly normal way for two people to examine a piece of porcelain.

He had not invited her in for seduction, but if he had, well, he made an inept rake. Other men seduced with flowers, poetry, moonlight; it seemed Leo was trying to seduce her with a teacup.

It *was* a nice teacup, though.

Then came the sound of whistling. Leo eased away from Juno and was on the other side of the table by the time St. Blaise appeared in the doorway, grinning from ear to ear.

"Miss Bell, what a wonderful surprise!" he said. "Have you come to beg me to become your kept man after all?"

Juno rolled her eyes, and Leo said, "She had business with Lord Renshaw, who has some compromising papers of hers."

St. Blaise screwed up his face. "No! What? Renshaw is *blackmailing* you?"

Laughing, Juno carefully returned the teacup to its fellows. "This is how rumors get started. The simple fact is: Mr. Prescott sold Lord Renshaw a painting of mine. But its frame has a secret compartment in which I keep some … personal documents. Mr. Prescott had the painting delivered before I could change the frame or remove the papers."

"How thrilling!" St. Blaise said. "They're love letters, aren't they? Are they very naughty?"

Juno denied it, so swiftly and firmly Leo suspected she was lying. Jealousy bolted through him. He gripped a chair and willed away his fury at the unknown man who had penned love letters, whose words she treasured enough to keep.

She huffed out, her eyes avoiding his. "It does not matter what they are. What matters is that I must retrieve them before they are discovered, and Lord Renshaw will not allow me into his house." She shook her head. "Though I cannot fathom by what arcane magic Lord Renshaw was induced to buy my painting in the first place. The earl despises me."

"No! What? You're adorable."

"I am adorable, true. But it is less about who I am than what I am. You should try being an unmarried woman who makes her own living."

"You should try being a bastard."

She pursed her lips. "Let's call that a draw."

Leo agreed: If Renshaw had grasped that Juno was the painting's artist, he would surely have refused it. Most likely Prescott had bamboozled the old earl, or at least taken advantage of his occasional confusion. Perhaps it was an honest miscommunication, but Leo didn't like Prescott, so it was much more satisfying to think the worst of him.

"And now you are here in Polly's house, where he will rescue you, like a knight in shining armor?"

"I'm not sure that he can. This is rather delicate."

Leo rubbed his hand, as if to rub off the lingering sensation of Juno's skin. Inviting her in had been a mistake. The sooner he ejected them both from his house, the better.

First he'd remove Juno by resolving her problem. Then he'd remove St. Blaise by carrying him up the stairs and throwing him off the roof.

"I have an idea," he said, and made his escape.

CHAPTER 15

J uno blinked at the doorway through which Leo had made his abrupt exit and then chased after him. She still felt a bit fuddled, still felt his solid heat against her back, the wicked thrill at their absurd complicity. Not to mention her surprise: Leo made an unlikely libertine. Perhaps her wantonness was contagious.

Could she provoke him into behaving like a rake? Serve him right if she succeeded.

But she mustn't try. It was a terrible idea. And terribly tempting.

Just one hour, she reminded herself, *and then I'll stop.*

Besides, she did need help, even if it was from Leo, and she was curious as to what he might do.

She caught up to him as he disappeared into another room. His study, it turned out. He strode straight to his desk and consulted a large leather-covered diary, without even acknowledging that she was there.

St. Blaise barreled in after her and hurled himself into an armchair. She was oddly grateful for his presence. Everything with Leo felt jagged and raw, and she was not used to feeling jagged and raw over anyone, especially not Leo.

"I'm invited to some sort of political meeting at Renshaw's residence tonight," Leo said. "I had not intended to attend, because I would find it more diverting to be stuck with spears, but it would grant me entry into his house. I could find the painting and retrieve the papers for you."

Juno shook her head. "Thank you, but I must retrieve them myself. It is imperative that no one else sees them."

With a sigh, he rested both hands on the open diary. "Juno, I would not read your letters."

"They aren't letters."

St. Blaise laughed with lascivious delight. "They're bawdy drawings, aren't they? Wicked, wanton ones." He leaned forward. "Are they drawings of you? Please tell me they're drawings of you."

"No." Juno's cheeks heated again, which would likely convince the two men that the papers were, indeed, nude drawings of herself.

Still, preferable to them knowing the truth.

"Are they secret government papers you mean to pass to the French?" St. Blaise persisted. "Or you are blackmailing someone else and it is their papers?"

Juno had to laugh, as she sat. "I am not nearly that interesting. No spying, treason, or criminal matters at all. Look, it does not matter what is in the frame. What matters is that I must retrieve them myself."

"There must be some way to smuggle you inside." Leo dropped into his chair, barricaded behind his grandiose desk. "Let us try."

They began with modest proposals, such as infiltrating a ball or musicale, but with no Renshaw events planned, they moved on to disguising Juno as a maid, and, before long, they had magicked up a scenario where Juno, dressed in men's clothing—all black, naturally—hoisted herself up a wall, over a balcony, and through a window, retrieved the papers, and then fled across the rooftops. Which was terrific fun, but ended in defeat when Juno admitted that she was not fond of climbing stairs, let alone balconies and walls.

"I am very disappointed in myself," she said with a dispirited sigh. "That my creativity does not extend to criminal activities."

"*You're* disappointed?" Leo said. "I am a duke. I should be much better at crime than this."

"We don't even know where in the house the painting is."

Leo sat up. "Think you could find out, Tristan?" he asked. "Run over there and charm a servant or something?"

St. Blaise tilted his head as if considering. "I suppose I could do it for Miss Bell … in exchange for a kiss."

"I'll give you fifty pounds," Leo said, before Juno could reply.

St. Blaise grinned. "I think I'd prefer the kiss. Don't look at me like that, Polly. It is traditional to ask for a kiss as a reward for gallantry."

"It's hardly gallantry if the kiss is your motivation, and not merely a reward for doing something you'd have done anyway."

Juno carefully did not look at Leo. "It is very flattering to learn my kisses are worth fifty pounds, but they are not for sale, to anyone, at any price."

"Fifty pounds it is, then." St. Blaise yawned and settled more comfortably into his chair. "Painting of Pandora, you say. Are you a student of mythology, Miss Bell? Forgive me, but I have a hard time imagining you studying books."

She chuckled at his apt observation. "Poring over dusty old tomes, most written by dusty old scholars whose main talent is taking a fascinating subject and rendering it dull? Never, I fear. I like other people to read the books and tell me the interesting bits so I can draw them."

"And which kind soul told you the tale of Pandora?"

"Not only Pandora. He told me many such myths."

"'*He*,' Miss Bell?"

St. Blaise could sniff out mischief like a hound sniffing out a fox, and chase it down as doggedly, no doubt. A thorny silence prickled around them.

Leo unfolded from his chair. Very casually, he selected a red-feathered dart from a painted tin box. Even more casually, he threw it at the dartboard on the wall.

Thud.

Liar, Juno wanted to yell at this show of indifference. He was jealous, and she was just wicked enough to be pleased about that.

She turned a bright smile on St. Blaise. "A Greek architect, who was studying in London." She paused. Leo kept his back to her. She added, "He proved a very pleasant way of passing the time."

"Those Greek gods." St. Blaise nodded sagely. "They do know how to have a good time, don't they?"

"They do, indeed."

Another dart hit the oaken board. Thud.

No need to be more explicit; they understood. It was not wise to allude so openly to a lover, but it was suddenly important for Leo to know she needed nothing from him. *You see, Leo?* she wanted to say. *I can get kisses from whomever I please, and I shall not miss you at all.*

Happily, St. Blaise was doing the work for her. "Paint a portrait of me intrigued and hang it on the wall!" he said with relish. "I say, Polly, are you very shocked to learn of this Greek's existence?"

"The world holds millions of Greeks," came his cool reply. "'Tis hardly a shock some might find their way to London."

Thud.

St. Blaise leaned forward eagerly. "What happened to this

Greek Adonis? Did he break your heart, Miss Bell? I must hear your tale."

"And I must disappoint you," Juno said. "He never had my heart."

Thud.

"He left me. That is all. He went back to Greece. He was homesick, poor darling."

Thud.

"Homesick for what?" St. Blaise said. "There's nothing in Greece. We stole all the good bits and brought them over here." He shook his head theatrically. "Preposterous, I say. What does Greece have that London doesn't?"

Juno sighed. "Decent food and actual sunlight."

"But that's—that's—" St. Blaise sighed too. "That's an excellent point, actually."

Thud.

Juno risked a glance at Leo. He was scowling down at the tin box: no more darts. All his throws had landed wide of the center. Ha! Serve him right.

He looked up. Their eyes met. His blue gaze pierced her like one of those darts. Dimly, she was aware of him saying, "The painting?" and St. Blaise repeating, "Ah yes, the painting." A movement from the other chair, the door clicking shut.

And the room narrowing around them, now they were alone.

Juno wished she could play Leo's game of studied indifference, but that fluttering had started up again inside her, an intense fluttering from her throat to her thighs, the sort of fluttering that could be relieved only by a lover's touch.

Desperate to move, she rose, crossed to a glass-fronted cabinet, and stared unseeingly past her own ghostly reflection to the wooden toys within.

"He was your lover, this architect," Leo said.

His atypical bluntness startled her. She pivoted to face him. "And if he was?"

"You mentioned you have criteria. For your liaisons."

"Just as you have criteria for your marriages." She gave him what she hoped was an arch look. "At any rate, you do not meet my criteria."

"I never imagined I did."

"Then my intimate affairs are none of your concern."

Conducting affairs was a risky business; slow, careful negotiations were required. She pursued liaisons for sensual pleasure and release. She pursued them because she did not want to lock parts of herself away. She pursued them because sometimes she felt lonely and craved another person's touch.

She did not pursue them for passion.

But better Leo did not know that. Better to portray herself as a passionate lover, and for Leo to lie awake at night, ruing what he had missed.

Yes, she would very much like for Leo to rue what he had missed. It would serve him right, for casting her off like a troublesome lover when she'd never even enjoyed the pleasures of his bed.

He eased away from the desk, toward her. "If your lovers are none of my concern, why the effort to ensure I knew of them?"

Heat slithered over her at being caught out. "How very self-centered to imagine my story had anything to do with you. St. Blaise was asking questions and I had to answer them. Rules of etiquette."

"You blithely ignore any rule you don't like. If you didn't want to answer his questions, you wouldn't have. Come, Juno. You say you prize candor. Try some candor now."

Still he advanced. Her heart fluttered with each slow, deliberate step. An answering pulse beat between her thighs. For Leo to speak so bluntly, to look at her so intently… How greatly everything was changing, and how fast.

"Very well, my criteria." Leaning back against the cabinet, trying to appear worldly, she marked the items off on her suddenly shaky fingers. "I appreciate a lover with attention to detail, someone who is creative, someone who takes his time. He must promise mutual pleasure and commit to protecting me from consequences. Most importantly, he must be planning to leave London."

"So, your ideal man is one who will not stay. Tell me." He halted before her, just out of reach. Her fingers tangled around themselves. "Of all your lovers, were any special to you?"

Juno choked. "Of *all* my— How many do you imagine there were?"

"I am trying very hard not to imagine it." He scrubbed a hand over his face. "It is irrelevant how many in total. I'm asking how many were special to you."

"I liked them all. I would never have … if I didn't." She shifted uncomfortably. Foolish of her to start this, but there was no stopping now. "My first drawing master in Vienna was very intimidating. He was so scathing about my work, I nearly gave up and came back home. Finally, I pressed him to tell me more clearly what I was doing wrong. He said, 'The skill and talent are there. But to create true art, you must free yourself of that uptight English morality.' So I did. It was easy enough to do, in Vienna. The world of European artists is far removed from the English gentry. I miss living in Europe sometimes, the freedom of those experiences."

His expression told her nothing. She raised her chin defiantly. She knew she was no lady; she had burned her bridges to respectability, and she had done it deliberately. She had no regrets and she would not suffer his judgment. After all, it was his judgment—his rejection of her—that had sent her running down that path in the first place.

"I enjoy it, if you must know," she went on. "The sensuality, the intimacy. I know how to take pleasure, and I know how to give it, and I won't be made ashamed of it. When I was younger, what with my large bosom and low-born mother, men assumed I must be wanton, and I blamed myself for their unwanted attention. But I won't do that anymore. I won't be made to feel ashamed of it," she repeated, almost belligerently.

"I don't want to make you ashamed of it." A new roughness edged his mild words. "I enjoy bedsport too. But you still haven't answered my question."

She examined her fingers, picked at a stubborn fleck of paint under one nail. "I've forgotten the question."

Leo stepped closer. Her head jerked up. Another step. Every inch of him was taut and intent like a beast on the hunt. She did not recognize him like this; she wondered if he recognized himself. Call her terrible for provoking him, call her weak for wanting him, but oh, she *did* enjoy watching Leo grapple with his own control.

He planted his hands on the polished cedar on either side of her, trapping her between his body and the cabinet. His scent and heat infused her. She straightened, but that served only to bring her face closer to his: to his firm jaw and tempting mouth and the pulse pounding at the edge of his cravat.

"Were any of them special?" he repeated in a low, velvet voice, better suited to pillows at midnight. "Did they keep you awake all night, aching with longing? Did they become so essential to you that losing them felt like slicing out a piece of your soul? Did their kisses seep so deeply into your blood that you would have burned down your world for one more kiss?"

She had no words. No thoughts. Only sensations remained: a

fierce hunger, a wild fever, and somewhere deep and forgotten, a gaping emptiness that ached.

And Leo's eyes, imprisoning hers, promising heady adventures like a distant mountain range.

He was going to kiss her and they both knew it.

This time, he would kiss her first, she vowed. She would wait for him.

He kept his arms braced on the cabinet behind her, caging her. He eased so close his legs nudged hers, with an electrifying touch that cavorted up her thighs, and he lowered his head to brush his lips along her jaw: soft, tempting, teasing. His warm breath tickled her. Need blossomed in her breasts and between her thighs and spread over her skin like watercolors.

Kiss me, touch me, want me. The plea pulsed through her veins, in time with her frantic heart. She had provoked him to this; she had won. But it would only end with hurt. She was no longer his friend, yet never his lover. She would never accept the unequal role of mistress, and heaven knew she could never be a duchess. No other options remained. They floated in a limbo, with nowhere to stand, nothing to hold on to, no future to dream of.

If we have no future, then all I have is now, she thought. *Even if it is just an hour or a minute, Leo, be mine.*

More butterfly kisses: His warm lips burned a trail to her temple, then he rested his cheek against hers.

She slid a hand over his chest, taking refuge in the wild thud of his heart under her palm, forcing herself to be patient.

Please, Leo, she silently willed him. *Don't stop now.*

THERE WAS NO STOPPING NOW.

Not with Juno so close, her breath trembling around them,

her palm on his chest, her leg pressed to his. Not with this mix of fury and desire churning inside him.

She had been deliberately taunting him, and he had fallen for it, what with St. Blaise eyeing her as she eyed chocolate truffles, what with the specter of her past lovers hammering at his bones.

Her lovers had never bothered him before. Well, one couldn't be bothered by something if one never thought of it. Not that they need bother him now either. This Greek architect was gone, and Juno had likely not given him another thought since the day the fellow said "*adio.*"

Besides, it was Leo who had kissed her last. That made him her current lover … didn't it? That meant she was his. At least for now.

And if she was already his lover, in a manner of speaking, it was too late for him. She was already in his blood.

He must not kiss her.

He trailed his thumb over her jaw. Her lips parted, soft, pink, alluring.

He must not kiss her.

His fingers wandered down the side of her neck, skimmed over the pulse fluttering in her throat.

He must not kiss her.

He traced the edge of her bodice, slipped beneath it to caress her silken skin. Her breasts were rising and falling rapidly. She made a small noise that shot straight to his groin.

He kissed her.

He brushed his lips over hers, again, again. Caught her lower lip between his teeth, earned a soft moan. Still his hand wandered, over the swell of her breasts, the curve of her waist. She pressed into him and he kissed her more hungrily, sweeping his tongue into her mouth.

Withdrawing on a groan.

She opened her eyes slowly to meet his.

"Well?" he demanded, his voice low and rough. "Is that what you wanted?"

She swallowed, moistened her lips, breathed out, breathed in. "I don't know what you mean."

"You were provoking me, and you know it."

"Then you are vulnerable to provocation." Her expression was triumphant. "You parade about under that facade of indifference, but you desire me."

"Yes."

"Did you desire me before I kissed you yesterday?"

His jaw tightened. "Yes. And you?"

"That kiss yesterday did not come from nowhere."

"You were angry with me."

"I do not kiss everyone I get angry with. My life would become rather complicated if I did."

He stepped back so they no longer touched. She caught his hand.

"Is that it, then?" she whispered. "Is that the mystery that has distorted our friendship? Is that why you keep me at a distance, hold these invisible walls between us? Because you desire me and wish you did not."

It was no surprise she sensed there was something. It was a profound relief she had guessed wrong. Let her think it was lust that made him keep his distance. Let her think anything, so long as she never learned the truth.

He tugged his hand. She let him go. He strode to the dartboard, started to tear out the darts, tried to get his body back under control.

"When did it start, Leo? How long since you first wanted me?"

"Approximately ten years, I'd say."

He was losing control, now he had freed the jealousy and

desire to rampage through him. He needed to deal with this desire. Take control of it. Master it before it mastered him.

Suddenly, the solution appeared in his mind, all at once, the steps as clear as the outline of an embroidery design before the first silken stitch is sewn.

Only one course of action would end his entanglement with Juno. Only one course would put an end to this desire, once and for all.

First, though, he must solve her problem with the drawings. Their previous attempts at planning were a distraction. They did not need to smuggle Juno into Lord Renshaw's house. They needed only to smuggle the painting out.

And Leo knew exactly how it could be done. He would have to pay a price for it, but no cost would be too high.

"Stay there," he said.

She immediately began to speak, but he was already spinning away. The wind itself blew through his limbs as he raced out of the study and out the front door, tore through the garden in the middle of the square, and hammered on the door of Lord Renshaw's house. When a flustered footman answered, Leo demanded to see Thomas Macey at once.

"You want my help with your father?" Leo said when Macey appeared, still gulping down a mouthful of cake. "You want my protection?"

"Yes, Your Grace. Please. I—"

"In exchange, you will do something for me. You will ask no questions and never breathe a word of it to a soul."

"Of course, sir. Anything."

Macey listened to Leo's curt instructions with growing confusion. "But why do you want me to bring you that painting?"

"That sounds like a question, Macey. Is that a question?"

"No, sir. But how will I—"

"Is that——"

"A question. Sorry."

"Prove your ingenuity. Be useful, for once."

Without waiting for confirmation, Leo charged back to his house, the breeze ruffling his hatless hair. In the study, Juno peppered the air with questions. He ignored them, instead rummaging through drawers until he found an empty leather portfolio, tooled with vines and bunches of grapes. He shoved it at her with a curt, "Your drawings are coming. Use this. Stay here. Don't move," then slammed out of the study to pace on the front steps.

An age later, Macey and a footman crossed the garden toward him, carrying between them an open wooden crate, a tablecloth covering its contents from prying eyes.

There followed some juggling of bodies and rooms, to ensure Macey never saw Juno: the painting placed in the front room, the visitors herded off to the drawing room, Juno enclosed with the painting. Once she had retrieved her drawings, he reversed the dance: ushered Juno out, ushered Macey in, put the painting back in its crate, and put Macey and the footman back on the street.

He found the study empty: Juno had wandered off. The leather portfolio beckoned him from a side table, pregnant with her secret sketches.

How tempting it was. He traced the portfolio's vines, poked its plump bulge. She would never know if he took a peek. Just a little peek. She was usually so candid: What secrets could she hold so close?

No. Prying into another's private papers simply was not done.

He huffed out air and abandoned the temptations of the folio for the much greater temptation of her.

CHAPTER 16

H e found her in the garden.

She was wandering along the path that wound among the rose bushes, bending to sniff a rosebud the same color as her gown. The rose garden had been planted by his great-grandfather, the third duke; his great-grandmother's contribution had been the stone rotunda overlooking the roses, where she passed her days, curled up to read on the cushioned seats. Juno kept nothing of her ancestors; Leo encountered his at every step.

She drifted as if she hadn't a care, just as she had at their first early morning encounter in the woods, over a decade ago. Perhaps, like that day, she was singing to herself; he was not close enough to hear.

He stepped onto the path. Gravel crunched. He froze. She stilled too, head cocked like a deer in the woods. Then she continued, neither turning nor fleeing.

He continued to trail after her, his ferocious desire softening in the pleasure of simply watching her as she soaked up the beauty of the garden. That was Juno Bell, with her scavenger's eye for beauty and her conqueror's determination to make it her own.

Suddenly, Thomas Macey's taunting words filtered through his mind: *For whom do you make yourself so beautiful?*

Leo shoved the thought away. Absurd to think he chose his clothing to attract Juno's attention.

The path took her to the small fountain, commissioned and installed by his grandmother, the fourth duchess, based on her own design. In it, the three Fates held hands and danced in a circle, while water rained down over them.

Juno wriggled her fingers under the spray and pressed her wet fingers to her cheeks. She patted her hair, paused, then bent to fiddle with the hem of her gown. She withdrew a pin, closed her eyes, kissed it lightly, and tossed it into the water.

She was making a wish.

He stepped out behind her. She turned her radiant smile on him; it warmed him so thoroughly he ran a lazy hand under the spray too. The sun gifted them with a tiny shimmering rainbow.

"Do you ever make wishes?" she asked. "Or are you the man with everything, who need ask for nothing more?"

"There is something I want very much right now."

"Then make a wish and maybe it will come true."

Leo didn't believe in wishes or fairies or superstitions. Juno did; she saw the world with a dusting of magic.

"I haven't a pin," he said.

"Or a coin. I believe they work too." She pressed a finger to the ruby stickpin nestled in his cravat. "Here's a pin. You could throw this in the fountain to make a wish."

"If I were to throw my beautiful hand-crafted ruby cravat pin into the fountain, my only wish would be to get it back."

"Then maybe I'll use it to make a wish," she said. "A stolen ruby will grant a better quality of wish than a dressmaker's pin. Then maybe I'll get what I want."

Her smile was wickedly flirtatious, her eyes suddenly sultry, and so he said, "Or maybe that is a devious plan to get me out of my clothes."

"If you wished for that, it would be granted before you could blink." She shook her head, serious. "Listen to us, flirting now. Everything is changing, and I don't know what to think."

"Have you been thinking about it, then?"

"Thinking about what?" she scoffed. "You wanting to be my lover? You denying our friendship? Or you charging about like you were chasing a greasy pig at a country fair? Though I do thank you for getting me my drawings." She sighed. "I came into the garden to stop thinking about it. There is nothing to be gained from thinking but a headache. And there are enough parts of me aching now without adding my head to the mix."

Leo sympathized: He had a fair few aches of his own. "What aches the most?"

"My heart, I suppose, at you denying our friendship."

"Perhaps this was never a friendship," he said. "Perhaps it was always a love affair that never had the chance to bloom."

"What do you mean?"

He met her eyes steadily. "Ten years ago, something began between us, but we were too young and naive to know what to do. Ten years have passed, but the desire has not. It's time we finished what we started."

Silence. For once, even her expression told him nothing.

But he had decided. Time now to act.

"Let us lay this unfinished business to rest," he continued. "I have a cottage in Surrey. We could meet there very discreetly. Spend a few days together, then part."

She folded her arms, looking spectacularly unimpressed. Had he misjudged her yet again? For all her flirting, it was possible she was still angry and hurt, and perhaps one did not propose an affair with a woman who was angry and hurt.

"Is this how you always conduct your love affairs?" she said.

"I've never conducted one before. Likely I never will again."
He sighed and shook his head. "I have new respect for rakes and
libertines. The logistics alone are troublesome, and that's even
without securing your consent. How am I doing so far?" She
raised her eyebrows and he answered his own question. "Ah. I am
not doing very well."

"You make it sound very rational."

"It is very rational." He focused every ounce of his concen-
tration on ensuring he remained rational. He had come dangerously close to losing control back in the study: never again. He
would conquer the desire; the desire would not conquer him.
"Desire feels urgent because it never lasts. It erupted yesterday
only because we know we must part and because we never dealt
with it all those years ago. By indulging it, we will get it out of
our blood, put this behind us before we say farewell. Scientific
fact."

"Good heavens. You could write a book on the subject. I'm
sure the scholars at the Royal Society would be fascinated."

No, she was definitely not impressed. He should have just
kissed her here among the flowers, carried her upstairs to his bed,
and had his way with her before she could think twice.

But that might give her ideas, wrong ideas, about being swept
away by passion and other impossible things.

There must be some way to persuade her.

He took her hand. "I want you, Juno." He kissed her knuckles, his eyes not leaving hers. "I cannot put it more plainly than
that, and I believe you want me too. Are you not even a little
tempted, to have an affair?"

JUNO STARED down at their joined hands. She had always admired his hands—so elegant and strong—and she now knew a mere brush of his fingertips could fire up her blood.

Making love to Leo would be a splendid experience, and suddenly it felt too long since she had had a splendid experience.

Of course she was tempted. Yet if she was to have an affair, she wanted an affair with a man, not with an automaton in pretty clothes.

Tugging her hand free, she followed the path to the small rotunda, planted with pink and white petunias around its base. She climbed the three low steps and leaned against a column, looking out over the garden, aware all the while of Leo at her back. She glanced over her shoulder: He was lounging against the column opposite. Oh, what a delicious painting he would make, titled *The Most Vexing Man in the World*.

"I don't know why you even bother to proposition me in person." She sounded as disgruntled as she felt. "Why not simply send a gilt-engraved invitation: '*The Duke of Dammerton requests the pleasure of your nakedness*.'"

Lazily, he pushed off the column; hastily, she turned back away. She stared unseeingly at the garden, all her other senses focused on him as he drew near.

His voice was low in her ear. "I think I see. Do you wish to be seduced?"

"I wish for something more persuasive than some nonsense masquerading as scientific fact."

She kept her gaze fixed on the garden, on the rosebuds bobbing in the breeze, while her skin tingled at the sensation of Leo's closeness.

One hand landed on her hip. His palm burned her through the layers of muslin. He trailed a finger down the nape of her neck. Helplessly, she arched. His breath tickled her hair. He nipped her ear, nibbled the side of her neck. Delicious shivers danced through her, all the way to her suddenly weak knees. She pressed a hand to the column, her palm feverish against the cool stone. Still encircling her with one arm, Leo edged forward beside her. She tilted her head. Their eyes met.

"Am I to understand, then, that you are amenable to an attempt at persuasion?"

His words were formal, but he colored them with such low wicked tones that they slid over her like warm water. Her clothes felt too hot and tight. If only she could tear them off right here, right now, release her hungry body to the cool breeze, the gentle sunlight, his ruthless smolder.

A few words. All it took was a brush of his fingers and a few words.

How foolish of her to quibble: Of course she would say yes. If this was her only chance to experience him, she would not squander it. He was, after all, the first boy who ever inspired her to daydreams, the first to arouse secret midnight urges in her changing body. "Unfinished business," he called it. He was not wrong. Her secret drawings told the truth: A part of her was not yet finished with him. Perhaps an affair would give her some peace, make it easier to forget him once he was wed.

"I confess I am curious," she said coolly. "Though I daresay we shall find the experience a disappointing one."

He flinched, but she must have betrayed herself, for then his eyes narrowed and a tiny smile twitched at the corners of his lips.

"Yes," he agreed blandly. "That is the most likely scenario."

"Dull, even, probably," she said.

"Exceedingly dull. But at least then we'll know."

He shifted back behind her and moved his hand from her hip to press her palm against the stone column. His chest was against her back now, trapping her in the space between the column and his body.

It was an excellent place to be trapped.

His other hand slid down her thigh. In slow bunches, he gathered up her gown, dragging the hem higher inch by torturous inch. Air caressed her ankles, her calves, her knees.

"I shall make every effort to rouse some enthusiasm when I see you unclothed," she said, striving for detached tones. "But I have seen many naked bodies, and I doubt yours will be of much interest by comparison."

"Indeed." His bored tone matched her own. "When I see you naked, I daresay I'll be so unimpressed, I'll continue out of honor and courtesy alone."

He slid a hand under her now exposed knee, and she did not resist as he lifted her leg to place her knee on the cushioned seat. Under her skirts, his hand stroked upward, over the garter of her stocking, up the inside of her bare thigh. On the stone column, their fingers tangled. He nibbled her ear with a low growl.

She breathed deeply, unsteadily, and said, "I would endure your touch out of sheer boredom. Simply because I have nothing better to do."

"I shall make every effort to pleasure you, as a gentleman ought," he murmured. "But you will forgive me if I yawn."

"I shan't notice your yawns. I'll be mentally reorganizing my paints."

Finally, his searching fingers touched her quim; a gasp escaped her lips. He hummed with satisfaction and nipped her neck. She let her head drop back on his shoulder, surrendering to sensation as he slid his fingers through the tender folds, caressing and teasing until— Oh! Pleasure spiked through her anew; she twitched, arched, gasped again. He responded with that low burr of triumph; those wicked, skilled fingers stayed to pleasure that spot.

"Perhaps we should delay," he said. She tensed, and he added, "Just long enough for you to paint a mural on the ceiling, as the sight will provide welcome distraction from the act."

She gathered her fast-scattering wits. "That's a thoughtful gesture," she managed to say. "But studying a mural I painted myself will not relieve the tedium of you thrusting away."

"You misunderstand. The mural is to relieve my tedium while you bounce around on top of me."

She could not see his smile but she could *feel* it. Pleasure in their game mingled with the pleasure from his dancing fingers, and the sheer thrill of being wicked with Leo, after all these years, Leo so familiar and yet so new.

She forced her mind back to their conversation. "If I must exert myself thus, do be so kind as to read aloud to me during the act, for I'll surely need a diversion."

"I shall pack a book for precisely that purpose. *Fordyce's Sermons*, perhaps."

She bit back her laugh. "I might require something a touch more erotic, if I am to succeed in faking any enthusiasm at all."

"Something like that?" he murmured low in her ear, as his magical fingers sent a new wave of sensations whirling through her delighted, desperate quim.

Her response was only a quivering moan: She had no more breath for words, nor wit for games. She surrendered to his touch, until the pleasure grew so potent it demanded release. Leo held her up with strong arms as bliss hurtled through her and her gasps flew into the garden like startled birds.

Once it passed, she freed herself and fumbled for his breeches, desperate to touch him, to watch him surrender to pleasure too—but somehow he escaped. She reached and reached, but he was sliding away. She could not chase him, with her knees so weak. Instead, she tumbled onto the seat amid tiny persistent shocks of pleasure, her skirts in wild disarray, not to mention her thoughts.

And there stood Leo, on the other side of the rotunda, not two yards from where she sat, yet somehow, suddenly, a thousand miles away. A mere glance provided evidence of his desire. He ignored it, flexing his thighs while he straightened his lapels, his cuffs, the hem of his stupid bloody coat.

How dare he play her game and pleasure her senseless, only to hide once more behind his carefully tailored facade.

That was why she must agree to this affair, she thought fiercely. True: She desired him. True: She could not resist. But she saw his intention now, she saw his true plan: He meant to give her unforgettable pleasure and a final farewell, but without giving her the smallest piece of himself.

Very well. Let him have her body, her surrender, and every-thing else he demanded too, but in return she would exact her price: nothing less than a piece of him to keep with her once he was gone.

"I take it I have your agreement then," he said, as coolly as if his fingers did not still carry her scent.

"You know you do. You always did."

Something flickered in his gaze, a perplexing hint of uncer-tainty. *I will tear you open,* she vowed silently, *even if I must tear myself open too.*

If her thoughts showed in her face, he would never know, for he was already heading down the steps, saying, "I shall finalize the arrangements and send a messenger to inform you how matters will proceed."

CHAPTER 17

The comfortable carriage deposited Juno at Leo's ivy-covered cottage late on a cold, rainy afternoon. Leo was not there when she arrived, but a cheerful maid showed her to a well-appointed chamber, and Juno happily availed herself of the offer of a hot bath.

She emerged from the water, her skin pink and fragrant, to discover a gorgeous robe had been laid out for her. It was painted with cherry blossoms, and its cool silk flowed over her skin; she whirled about on the plush rugs just to feel its caress.

The cottage was simple, the garden under her window small, but everything in the room was the height of luxury, from the robe to the flowers to the bowl of fruit. Leo must have roused a small army of staff.

Whether making her wait was part of his plan, she found herself enjoying the anticipation immensely. She savored a juicy peach and some hot chocolate, then she lay back and dozed off to a gallery of deliciously lewd thoughts.

A sound from the next room roused her from her stupor. It was early evening now, the lingering summer daylight muted by soft rain. Juno eased open the connecting door and peered into an enormous chamber, furnished with a sitting area and an over-sized bed, already warm despite the chilly night.

Her eye was drawn directly to Leo, crouched before the fire, stoking the flames. He still wore his shirt and breeches, under a dressing gown embroidered with suns and moons and stars. He glanced up and smiled, that familiar smile that stirred both warm pleasure and a wicked, spiraling thrill.

Yet this room, too, was opulent, from the silken sheets to the red velvet chaise. Here a platter of fruit, cheese, and cakes, there a tray holding crystal goblets and red wine. Candles bathed the room in a soft, alluring glow, and a golden perfume burner filled the air with a heady scent.

It was lavishly luxurious. Deliciously decadent.

Infuriatingly impersonal.

"I confess I'm a touch confused," she said. "Did you bring me here to tup me or feed me?"

"You'll need to keep your strength up."

He raked his eyes over her, heat flaring in his hungry gaze as if he could see right through the fastened robe.

"The robe is to your liking?" he asked.

"It's splendid. Yours too."

And she would strip it off him the first chance she got.

This opulence betrayed him: He had not come as Leo, but as the duke. She would strip him of his remoteness, along with that embroidered silk.

He unfolded upward, the silken threads of his robe shim-mering in the firelight as he stood. She tiptoed toward him, as if he were a prey animal about to startle, and boldly fingered the embroidery on his sleeve.

"I always want to touch your clothes, but you make yourself untouchable," she confessed softly. "I mean to touch you, Leo. All of you."

She pushed the silk up his arm, revealing the fine tendons and veins of his inner wrist. His skin here was so soft, in contrast to the rougher hairs beyond. She pressed her fingertip against his pulse, and he swiftly evaded her to capture her wrist and explore her skin in return.

"All this luxury!" she said. "Do you mean to seduce me with lavish compliments and gifts?"

"You don't like it?"

"Oh, I *like* it. But you need not shower me with pretty things and pretty words. I'm here because I want you."

His thick lashes screened his expression, as he lowered his head and trailed promising kisses along her forearm. Bliss danced inside her like a fire sprite, igniting sparks from her breasts to her quim.

Answering sparks lit in his eyes when he looked up at her.

"You don't need me to seduce you with luxury," he repeated.

She smiled. "Nice but not essential."

"Or lay you down on the velvet couch, feed you grapes and sips of wine."

"No need."

"While I recite odes to your beauty?"

"No, no, and no."

"In that case." He released her and gestured at the table. "Lift your robe, bend over, and we'll get right to it."

A bright shard of laughter flew out of her. The fire crackled in the hearth; desire crackled in the air around them.

When he spoke again, it was in his pillows-at-midnight voice.

"If you won't indulge your own senses, perhaps you'll indulge my dreams of seeing you on that red velvet chaise in nothing but silk stockings and your hair loose around your breasts."

Craving rippled through her. She bit her lip. "I'm but a humble artist. Do you think I can afford silk stockings?"

With one lazy knuckle, he traced the edge of her robe,

starting at her shoulder and sliding down, down, to the valley between her needy breasts. "If I know you at all, Juno Bell, then I know you are wearing silk stockings. Am I right?"

Of course he was right, and he knew it. Smiling faintly, he plucked the combs from her hair and tossed them aside. Her curls hesitated, unusually coy, then all at once surrendered and unfurled down her back.

With both hands, he shook out her hair, flicking her long curls sensuously over her shoulders. She feasted her eyes on his chest, on the burnished skin peeking through the open triangle of his shirt.

"Then tell me, if you know so much, what color are the garters that hold my silk stockings?" she asked.

"Ah, that I don't know, though I know you delight in pretty, colorful things. Perhaps your garters are blue, to match the morning sky, for that is one of your favorite sights."

He abandoned her hair and skimmed his hands down her front, carelessly brushing her breasts, their nipples hard under the silk. He found the first button fastening her robe and slipped it through its hole.

"Perhaps your garters are pink and embroidered with white flowers, because you do love flowers," he murmured.

His eyes imprisoned hers, as his nimble fingers released each button. The silk parted helplessly, as did her lips.

"Or perhaps today your garters are red and embroidered with flames, in honor of the way a mere glimpse of you heats my blood."

"Only one way to find out."

The robe fell open. He stilled as he took her in, naked but for the robe and those famous silk stockings, tied above her knees. His gaze roamed over her hungrily.

"Well?" Her voice was husky. "What color are my garters?"

He kept staring. "I have absolutely no idea."

"Perhaps this will help," she murmured, and slipped the robe over her shoulders. It slithered down her body and puddled at her feet. Fire-warmed air kissed her bare skin.

A shuddering breath racked his chest. His mouth worked, swallowing, moistening his dry lips, seeking sips of air. Finally, he looked up. His eyes smoldered.

"Lie on the chaise," he ordered roughly. "Your bare skin on velvet. I think we'll both like that."

Breathy laughter danced out of her. "I think we'll both like a lot of things."

She tripped backward to the chaise, nestled her bottom into its soft velvet embrace, and reclined back, one knee bent. She let her thighs fall open under his hungry gaze. Her own brazenness thrilled her.

"Is this what you had imagined?" she asked.

"My imagination fell far short of the reality."

He loomed over her, then he sat too, his silk-clad hip hot against hers. She wriggled in anticipation of his touch, but he reached past her, with a tickle of his robe and a hint of his spicy scent.

"And what is this I see, draped over the top of the chaise?" he said. "Why, it's a swansdown tippet."

Slowly, lazily, he reeled the tippet toward him, dragging the long line of white downy feathers over her shoulder, to curl and coil around her breasts. Under his sensual teasing, her back arched; a breathy moan escaped. She pressed one hand into the velvet of the chaise, while the other clutched his iron-hard thigh.

"I thought you'd like that," he murmured with rough triumph.

"What else are you planning to do with it?"

With a sigh, he dropped the tippet alongside her. "I guess you'll never find out now."

She giggled. "Are you sulking?"

"Why would I sulk? I'm not the one depriving myself of a thousand sensual pleasures."

Juno began to regret her earlier words. He had given this thought, she realized warmly, anticipated what might please her. She idly tangled her fingers in the tippet. How might he respond if she were to trail it over his body? How magnificent, to torture him in this exquisite fashion, to make him shudder and moan under her touch.

Again he reached past her, this time to pour a large glass of red wine from a carafe.

"To think I even decanted a bottle of fine wine, and you don't want to taste it," he said. "But I intend to indulge. A toast to your glory."

He raised the crystal goblet in a toast and then tilted his wrist. Wine splashed onto her breasts. She gasped. Grinning wickedly, he set down the glass. He dipped a finger into a puddle on one breast.

"A fine vintage," he said, smearing the wine over her nipple. "Notes of blackberry, oak, and sin."

He licked the wine off, his tongue rough and hot as he swirled it around her sensitive nipples and nibbled the soft curves of her breasts. He took his time, not missing a drop. When he was done, he shot her a knowing, heavy-lidded look.

"So you do like the wine," he drawled huskily.

She laughed, breathy and high. "It's very potent. Goes straight to my head."

"Oh dear, I wasn't aiming for your head. I shall have to try again."

He drizzled a trail of droplets over her breasts, her belly, her thighs.

Juno watched, nibbling on a finger, her breathing shallow. Her hips shifted against the velvet chaise.

Once more, he chased the drops of wine with his lips and

tongue, scraping her feverish skin with his teeth, dipping his tongue into her navel. All the while, his fingers frolicked on the softest part of her inner thigh.

This was true luxury, she thought hazily, not silk and velvet and swansdown, but the luxury of time and space and attention. The luxury of being pleasured and served.

His eyes glinted. "You like that," he said.

"I like you touching me."

"I like touching you. Your body is a marvel."

As he spoke, he shifted his hand on her thigh, becoming more adventurous. His thumb boldly glided upward, ruthlessly venturing over her most sensitive part.

"Here?" he murmured. "Or here? Like this?"

A breathy cry escaped her, and a triumphant, satisfied smile spread over his face, like a man who had struck gold and was very pleased with himself indeed.

Through the haze of pleasure, doubt fluttered in her like a trapped moth: how deliberate this was, how cleverly strategic, as if he was applying a learned technique. She'd almost prefer enthusiastic incompetence to this ruthless strategy.

But the thought fled as the skills of his thumb sent fresh pleasure rippling down her legs.

Very well. Ruthless competence was not entirely unwelcome.

"You are truly enchanting," he murmured, his lips against hers. "So real and intoxicating and potent. There isn't a wine in the world that can get into my blood like one taste of you."

"But you haven't had a taste of me yet."

Desire flared in his eyes as he caught her meaning.

Yes! He liked her brazenness, her wantonness, her familiar disrespect. He enjoyed her readiness to issue commands as much as he enjoyed her willingness to surrender to his.

I just learned something very intimate about you, Leopold Halton, she thought triumphantly. *You try to hide from me, but I am seeing you all the same.*

He slid onto his knees beside her, parted her thighs, and lowered his mouth to take that taste. With his tender lips and strong tongue, he skillfully caressed and teased, taking his time, responding to her every move or sound, which she gave freely.

But even as she basked in the molten sensations swirling inside her, something niggled: his ruthless machination, his purposefulness in wringing pleasure from her.

Fury churned through the whirlpool of wanting. She wanted more than this sensation.

She wanted *him*.

He was giving her pleasure, but nothing of himself. He was reducing her to a puddle of desperate desire, but staying in control. Maybe if she had a thousand nights with him, ten thousand, she would relish such strategy and skill. But not when time was against her. She could seize pleasure any day of the week. This was her only chance to seize *him*.

She sat up and glared at him.

He stopped, questions in his glazed eyes. "You don't like that?"

"I like it very much," she said. "But I told you what I want is you. I haven't even seen you yet."

She lay back, one arm behind her head, legs still parted, brazen as you please, and eyed him lasciviously. She nudged him with one foot. "It's no fun being the only naked one in the room."

"As you wish."

He stood, bare feet on the plush rug, and undressed for her, unhurriedly, nonchalantly, with a casual insolence that mirrored her own.

But her trained eye noted the tension in his muscles, the faint trembling of his hands, the moment when he got awkwardly caught in his own shirt, his unusual clumsiness as he rolled down his trousers and drawers.

Part of her wanted to protect him, cocoon him. But part of her—that part that was still angry with him for keeping himself from her—vowed to make him tremble more.

Finally, he stood before her, naked.

At attention.

No longer an untouchable painting. Not an artwork of any kind, but a glorious man, ready for her touch.

Juno rose up onto her knees on the velvet sofa, happily taking command. She pressed one hand to one knee. His eyes tracked the movement. She feathered her fingers up her thigh, dipped into her own hot, wet core. His hands flexed, fisted.

"Show me," she ordered.

He wrapped a hand around his cock. A sigh escaped her.

"Does that please you, madam?" His insolence delighted her.

"It pleases me that you please yourself."

His hand moved obediently, in long, hard, mesmerizing strokes. "Is that all you want?" he said. "To look at me?"

"Oh no," she purred. "I want much, much more."

She crooked her finger. He sauntered closer, only to stop just out of reach. Wasn't that just like him? To show her what she could have and then deny her.

She licked her lips.

"Juno," he murmured on a note of protest. "This isn't…"

She was wise to his ways. He did not want to be vulnerable. He wanted her incoherent and begging with pleasure, while he stayed in control.

Not a chance. If they were doing this, they were doing this together.

She extended one arm, dipped into the goblet of wine, then slipped her wine-soaked fingers between her lips and sucked them.

"I've changed my mind," she said. "I do want to try the wine after all."

His battle with himself was almost visible, but then he surrendered to her will: As obediently as a prisoner of war before a queen, he approached. He released himself and slid his hand into her hair.

She dribbled the wine over his cock and took her own sweet time in licking it off. Each leisurely stroke of her tongue earned a growl from him. Her scalp tightened as his hand gripped her curls.

His control was slipping away. She was shattering him slowly.

She trailed her fingers over his ribs, his belly; over his waist and hips, where the skin was outrageously soft; over his tight buttocks; over the rough hairs of his muscled thighs.

"I like this," she murmured. "I like touching you very much."

"Tormenting me, you mean."

Breaking him into pieces, so there'd be a piece for her to take with her when they parted.

She knelt back. "Do you want me to stop tormenting you?"

"No."

"What do you think I should do next?"

Once more, he took command. "I think you should have some more wine."

Leo watched in a haze of desire as Juno dipped her fingers into the goblet and painted streaks of wine down his stomach. He wound his fingers more deeply into her hair, as she leaned in and licked it off. Then she looked up, nibbling her lip.

"You missed," he said sternly.

Her smile was both brazen and triumphant. He was issuing the commands, but they both knew she was the one in control.

If he begged, it would be her will.

It wasn't meant to be like this. He had vowed to give her pleasure, to savor the experience, but no more. The point was to lose his desire for her; he was not supposed to lose his mind.

But oh, how fascinating her mouth was! How enchanting her bold sensuality!

She gripped him in one hand, doused him so liberally that wine trickled down his thighs and splashed onto his feet. Without hesitation, she took him into her mouth, sucking and swirling, until she stole his breath, his soul, his veneer of civilization, until he was barely holding on to the shreds of his control.

Too much! He pulled away. She let him go, questions in her eyes.

"I haven't finished with you yet," he said and, before she could protest, he had swooped and hauled her into his arms.

She cried out in delight, laughing and kicking her feet and arching back so her hair swung down over his arm. He found himself laughing too, as he carried her across the room and tossed her onto the covers, where she stretched luxuriously, provocatively. Savage desire zigzagged through him like a lightning bolt.

The miracle of it, to be looming over her, Juno Bell, naked and sensuous, eager for his touch, ready for him to devour.

Not yet, he told himself. *Stay in control.*

He would not lose himself in her.

He would not lose himself.

He would not.

He ran his hands and mouth over her, nuzzling her neck, plucking her nipples, molding her breasts, exploring her quim. He noted her every move, breath, gasp: The more he focused on her response, the more controlled he could be.

She moaned, she writhed, she sighed. She held back nothing; Leo vowed to seize it all. He would make her see stars, make her hoarse with screaming his name. He would watch pleasure shatter her with an intensity she had never known and that she would never, ever forget.

Yes, he thought triumphantly, he was doing it right.

"I know what you're doing, Leopold Halton," she said.

He froze. Beyond her blatant desire lurked something darker, fiercer. Before he could name it, she raked her hands over his scalp, the scrape of her nails sending pleasure shivering through him.

"But you like that," he stammered. His brain wasn't working very well; his rational faculties were absorbed in restraining himself from plundering her like a pirate. "I know you do."

"Oh, I do." A flintiness, almost like a warning, hardened her voice. She squeezed his bicep as if she wished to throttle him.

"Then let me give you more," he said.

"That's what I want from you. More."

"More what?"

She sat up. Confused, he reared upward, and she shoved his shoulder, hard. He rolled onto his back. She pounced on him, her curls flying, and pushed his shoulders into the mattress, her eyes as wild as her hair.

"More you," she said, in a voice like a growl.

He caught her hips. "Are you angry with me?"

She leaned over him, so her breasts brushed his chest, her mons smothered his cock. His last shreds of sanity began to flit away like a dandelion puff in the wind. That new ferocity seemed to shadow her eyes and tugged at his very soul.

No, he thought, *not like this*. This tryst was meant to be light and lusty, full of laughter and play. He had planned to tease her and tup her, and then escape, untouched, unscathed, untrammeled, untied.

But her expression was hungry and demanding, and it swept through them both like a hot desert wind. Gone was the merry maker, the woman who laughed off trouble with bawdy jokes. The woman looming over him was ruthless and fierce.

This was the woman who drew that siren, that possessive, passionate mermaid who dragged the sailor down into the dangerous depths. He recalled the sailor: besotted, enchanted, happy to go to his death, so long as he went with her.

Oh hell, Leo thought. *I'm doomed.*

"You think I don't know what you're doing," she said.

"Am I not doing it right?"

"You're doing it right. Too right. You want me to see stars."

"Yes," he confessed.

"You want me helpless with wanting you."

"Yes."

"You want to be inside me."

"Oh hell, I want to be inside you," he groaned. "But we must be careful. There are many other things——"

"But we want to. I want you inside me. I want all of you, Leopold Halton, every last inch."

She lifted his hands off her hips and pressed them up over his head. His knuckles brushed the hard wood of the headboard. With one hand, she pinned both his wrists to the pillow. He let her, though they both knew she could not hold him if he did not wish to be held.

His heart pounded; his every muscle burned with sensation. Her gaze dismantled him as she reached between them and positioned his cock at her entrance, her hot, wet promise teasing the sensitive tip.

Leo hissed in breath through his teeth. "Juno, what do you want?"

"You. How many times must I tell you that what I want is you?"

"I want to give you pleasure," he rasped out.

"And I want you to give me a piece of you, to take with me when you're gone."

Take it, he wanted to say. *Take whatever you want. Take it, take me, take everything.*

But his voice wouldn't work, and then her hair was a curtain unfurling around them as her mouth hovered over his. Oh, yes, to kiss her again. To spend their first day together just kissing. Their lovemaking was moving too fast. Too much. He wanted to—

"Tell me again that our friendship meant nothing," she said, her tone taut and intense.

Leo blinked at her, confused. "What?"

"You said our friendship was of no consequence, merely duty, it meant nothing." Her anger was palpable now. "You claimed it was never truly a friendship. Say it again now."

"Say…" His voice failed him. He swallowed. Her thighs were tense on his, as if he were a wild stallion she needed to tame.

"I thought I was a friend to you, but you denied it," she went on, in that low, intense voice. "So, say it again. Tell me our friendship was of no consequence. Tell me it wasn't real."

"I can't."

He lifted his hands, but she pressed them back down into the pillow. He had never felt so vulnerable, so exposed, not only his body but his very heart.

"Tell me you never cared and I'll take you inside me. I'll let you do anything you want to me. Just look me in the eye and tell me again our friendship meant nothing to you." She shoved at his hands. "Say it, curse you."

"Our friendship meant everything to me." The confession poured out of him. "I lied in London. I called on you these past years because I wanted to see you. I needed to see you."

She froze, as if stunned by his admission. Then her ferocity dissipated. Sorrow seemed to wash over her, as if she had wanted him to keep lying, so she could hate him just a little. Leo understood that. He understood how hatred and anger were essential sometimes, as the only protection against losing oneself.

"Oh, Leo," she breathed, and sank down onto him, with a sigh.

LEO FILLED HER COMPLETELY.

Not only her body, but her heart, which suddenly seemed full of empty places for him to fill. The secret places where she ached alone, he filled them all. All those dark crooked corners where no one else ventured, he filled those too. Juno almost wept at the sublime wonder of their union. Her anger had risen unbidden, almost consuming her while she seized control and won his confession, but it was a hollow victory, because it did not change a thing. Their friendship was still over, he would still leave her to marry someone else, they still had no future together, and the world they lived in—the worlds between them—meant she had no choice but to let him go.

She had thought all she had wanted was to hear him admit the truth, but that small piece was not enough. Still she wanted more.

More and more and more.

He reared up, arrowing more deeply inside her, and claimed her mouth in a desperate kiss. Something had changed: His kiss seared her with a savage passion, new to them both. Yes! No more control! No more of his careful calm or cursed curation.

She wanted to release his wild heart.

She wanted to taunt him into forgetting himself, into taking what he wanted, and giving her nothing less than a piece of his soul.

"You make me wild," she breathed. "Be wild for me too."

He gripped her hips but, once more, she pinned his hands overhead. Once more, he let her.

She slowly slid up his shaft, then slowly, so slowly, slid back down. She tightened her muscles around him, reveling in the feel of him, in his harsh groans, in the ecstasy and agony painting themselves across his face. His hips rose, to thrust into her; she rose too, to deny him. This felt almost like a war, a war of attrition. She didn't care.

Whatever happened next, she knew she would lose. But when she flew off that cliff, she would take him with her over the edge.

"Is this too tame for you?" She nipped his ear. "What a gentleman you are, Leo."

She raked her nails down his inner arm, his bicep, down his ribs, his shuddering chest.

"Be careful what you ask for, Juno," he warned in strained tones.

She laughed, low and breathy. "Cheap, easy words. You hide behind them like you hide behind embroidery and silk. Show me who you truly are."

She lifted right off him, hovered over him, daring him with her eyes.

Cast off your control and show me the parts you show no one else, she willed him silently. *Give me that, for I want nothing less.*

She made to leave him. With a roar, he surged up beneath her. Strong hands gripped her, flipped her onto her back like a rag doll. It felt like flying and she cried out with breathless delight as he thrust deep inside her, grunting and growling, eyes savage, teeth bared, a solid quivering mass of muscle and desire.

"More," she urged him. "Give me more."

Again, she shoved his shoulder; again, he rolled over, bearing her with him. But a heartbeat later, he rose to flip her onto her front. Those relentless hands hauled up her hips and he drove hard into her from behind.

Frenzied passion coursed through her, until her muscles and skin and blood sang like a choir, as she lost herself to him, to this messy wildness of two people giving each other their all.

Then he stopped, his chest heating her back, his breath rough and ragged against her neck. He slid a hand enticingly up her inner thigh and unerringly found that one spot created to make her scream.

"Wild enough for you?" he growled in her ear.

"Almost," she gasped. "Give me more."

His fingers worked their magic, and his teeth grazed her shoulder. Bliss broke over her like a thunderstorm, and his strong arm cradled her as pleasure rippled through every inch of her being.

She came back into herself, with Leo gently turning her onto her back and hovering over her.

Hazily, she fumbled for him, gripped him hard, reveled in his groan, in his fingers wrapped over hers. Their mouths met and their tongues tangled, until he reared back, face turned to the heavens. He released a strained shout and shuddered as he spent his seed onto her belly.

Juno sank back onto the pillows, feeling wrung out and ragged and blissfully alive. Leo collapsed too, half on top of her. Their chests raggedly moved in time.

Slowly, they recovered. The warm air glided over their damp, feverish skin. She dimly identified another sound as the rain pouring down outside.

"Well," Leo mumbled beside her. "That was about as tedious as expected."

"Oh, is it over?" she replied. "I hadn't noticed."

Laughter welled up inside her. He began to laugh too. Her spent muscles protested at the effort, as the mattress shook beneath their shared mirth.

CHAPTER 18

Leo stared up at the pale-blue canopy of the bed. Rain drummed softly on the roof, and ghostly evening light haunted the edges of the curtain, lending the room an air of mystery, of a place out of time. He must have dozed after cleaning them both up, while Juno had eyed him with the smug air of an overfed cat.

She was still dozing, her breaths soft and even, her hair a tangle spread over his chest. It felt wonderful, this sweet intimacy, and he did not know what to do with it. There was a possessiveness in the way she draped her limbs over him. He could never possess her, though. She would dance away again, as she had before, and leave him holding air.

And their lovemaking, if that was what it was. He still felt raw with it, as if the power of that passion had bruised his nerves. How blithely she had torched his careful plans and smashed his expectations. The woman in his bed was not the merry, light-hearted friend, the flippant pleasure-seeker. She played a different game; she had transformed their pleasure into something complex and powerful.

Like a goddess, he thought. When he'd been young and foolish, and read so much mythology and classical poetry that his brain turned soft, he'd thought of Juno as a pagan goddess, a goddess of nature, of flowers and spring, that life force bursting from the earth to create pretty things. He had berated himself for his lazy thoughts: Just because she had the name of a goddess, didn't mean she was one.

Perhaps he had never quite shaken the idea, and now his mistake loomed, along with the truth. Nature was ruthless; goddesses were too. It was all flowers and moonbeams till she gripped your cock in her fist.

Her power had stripped him of all his lies, leaving him raw and open, so that he felt everything, and everything felt too much.

He had never felt so close to anyone in his life. He had never felt so close to losing himself.

She stirred. Yawning, she spanned a hand over his chest and slid a foot up his leg.

"You were right to bring so much food," she said with a sleepy smile. "I will indeed need my strength to survive another romp like that." She stretched languorously and flipped back her hair, so at ease with herself and the release of their secret, wild selves. "If only I could keep you in my studio after all, for my pleasure when I will. But I suppose you must go and be a duke, and I'll have no use for you then."

Leo said nothing. He stared at the canopy. There was a small tear in the fabric. How did a tear get up there?

She raised her head, the pressure of her hand on his chest increasing as she gave him some of her weight. He had to look at her.

She searched his eyes. "Is something troubling you?"

"Not at all."

"You're tense."

"I'm fine."

She ran her hand over his muscles with easy familiarity, like a hostler with a horse. "You shouldn't be tense after that." She narrowed her eyes. "You weren't tense. You too were beautifully, blissfully relaxed. Then I fell asleep and you became tense. Do you not like this part?"

"What part?"

She sank back down. He rescued his arm as she lay on her side, head propped up, studying him. "Did you not intend to sleep with me? You prefer to have your own room for sleeping? Is that how you… Never mind, I suppose, if that is what you prefer."

The sleeping part, as if it was simply one part of the experience. A continuous stream of holding her, feeling her arms around him, making love, sleeping, waking, eating, doing it again. Again and again and again.

Until she found something else to interest her and wandered away.

"No. I…" He wasn't sure what to say.

"You want to leave? It must have been difficult for you, with me all over you like a blanket. Or am I the one who is supposed to leave?"

"No. I was merely … thinking."

"Oh."

His brain was tense too, moving everywhere, settling nowhere.

"Leo?"

"Hmm?"

"Would you like to tell me what you're thinking?"

"No."

"No. Of course not."

"That is, I don't know. Nothing in particular."

Her hand drifted over him again, over his chest and shoulder and arm. His mind traced her touch, while his eyes stared at that little tear in the canopy.

"I can feel you leaving me already," she said. "Ever since you walked into my studio four years ago, I have known that one of those visits would be your last. It is sad to know that last visit has been and gone."

He made to sit up, but she pressed on his chest.

"Wait. Let me take this chance to speak. When we leave here, we'll not speak again, except perhaps polite niceties when necessity demands it. You will … go about your life, and I shall miss you. That is all I wish to say. That I will miss you very much. I don't know what I shall do without you." She sighed and flopped down onto the pillows. "I suppose I shall have to eat more cake."

"How comforting to know I'll be so easily replaced."

"Oh, not easily. It will have to be very fancy cake." Then she laughed, a mirthless sound. "Listen to me, hiding behind a joke. As if things will not hurt me if I take them lightly. As a strategy, it is an utter failure. How does your strategy serve you?"

Her words were bouncing through his brain like the ball on a roulette wheel, and somehow his mouth said, "My strategy?"

"You hide behind your clothes."

"We all hide behind our clothes," he said. "That is the entire point of clothes."

She sighed. "There it is. Your clever words, so you never give away anything of yourself. So very contained. Careful. Curated."

She wasn't touching him now. He missed the warmth of her hand. There were inches between them, close enough that he could feel her presence.

She truly saw him, didn't she? Saw right through his defenses, his deceptions. She accepted him anyway. Juno always welcomed him, just as he was, and he needed that.

Then he should tell her, he thought. Tell her he would miss her too.

But before he could speak, she spoke first.

"I was very wrong to liken you to cake," she said.

"Is that an apology?"

"It's an epiphany. With cake, I can have a whole piece. With you, I only get crumbs." Melancholy shaded her usual light tone.

He did not know how to have conversations like this. But he said, "You're angry with me."

"You pretend to the world that you care about nothing but your teacups and clothes, but you don't have to pretend with me."

But he did have to pretend. She didn't know how he had waited for her and planned their future together. She didn't know how he had forged an elaborate story so no one would stop him from traveling a thousand miles to ask her to be his. She had no idea that his youthful heart had shattered into pieces that day in the gardens in Vienna when she laughed away their love as a silly infatuation. She could not conceive of the way she then trampled those pieces into dust when she kissed another man while Leo sat in the room. As far as she was concerned, whatever had lain between them had long since passed.

It wasn't her fault; it was his fault for misunderstanding. And it was his pain.

He didn't want it to end like this, but he knew what would happen if he let himself go down that path again.

"If…" She stopped, swallowed, breathed. "If I were to say I love you, would that horrify you again?"

His mind blanked. His muscles braced.

Juno sat up abruptly, sheets spilling about her like sea foam about Venus. "Easy, there. Calm down." She flipped her hair to one side. "I know this part: This is where you make that speech to remind me we have no future together because you are a duke. Save your breath. That was not a marriage proposal. I do not aspire to be a duchess. I know we have no future together. I merely wished to express how I feel. And what I feel is that I love you. I can love you without wanting to marry you.”

Her words spun around him, gossamer and tensile as a spider's web. He rolled away from her and off the bed, landing so heavily the floorboards groaned through the plush rug.

“You may say what you please,” he said, as he crossed the room to hunt down his clothes. “Those are your sentiments. Perhaps they are even true.”

“*Perhaps*? You do not believe me?”

“I believe that you believe it. But what is this love of yours anyway? You feel it, you indulge it, and then it fades. You fall in love three times a day, you said, and no doubt fall out of love four times. Today, you say you love me. In a month, you will say, ‘Oh yes, the Duke of Dammerton. I knew him once.’”

“You think I will forget this? Forget you?”

“No doubt I shall inspire some lovely paintings before then.”

He found his drawers, his breeches, tried to sort them out, one from the other. They were not cooperating.

“You love easily and generously, but it is not your nature to love long or with any constancy, is it?” he continued.

He shoved his feet into his clothes. Nothing seemed to work. He felt like a fool, hopping around, unnaturally clumsy. He scrubbed a hand over his face and caught her scent.

“Is this what you think of me, then?” she persisted. “That I am inconstant? I have no true, lasting emotions?”

“You said you loved me before, and that lasted how long? You feel emotions, deeply even, but they are nothing but fuel for your art.”

“You resent that my first love didn't last? All those years ago?”

She was sitting upright, uncaring of her glorious nakedness, so comfortable in her own skin. He hunted down his shirt and went back to trying to remember how to dress.

“Let me tell you what lasted,” she said, in a hard, quiet

voice that followed him around the room. "My memory of your face as you stared at me in the meadow. How *appalled* you looked when I said I loved you. Then you spouted that nonsense about duty and honor and assured me we had no future together. And then—" She uttered a sharp, scoffing laugh. "Then you took up gambling like every other mediocre young gentleman. Even in Vienna I heard tales of how you practically lived in London's gaming hells. You ran wild in Vienna, drinking and reckless. You married a *princess*, for heaven's sake! And I was— What? Was I supposed to pine for you? Weep and moan and wring my hands or whatever other nonsense is expected of a lady who is unlucky in love? Let myself waste away to nothing, let life pass me by and refuse to allow myself any happiness because I attach that happiness to only one man? Perhaps I should have thrown myself at your feet and wept. Perhaps I should have died of a broken heart. Would that have satisfied your definition of love?"

He said nothing. Dressing. Dressing was all he had to do. The arm goes through the sleeve, the button goes through the hole, the heart goes straight to hell.

"For heaven's sake, Leo, when I told you I loved you back then, your response was to point out that I was not good enough for you."

Leo froze. His heart seemed to stop. He straightened, the linen of his shirt falling over his stomach and thighs, and took her in. The curls tumbling around her face made her look younger. Her eyes were both hard and full of appeal.

"I never said you weren't good enough for me," he ground out.

She waved an arm, loose and uncontrolled. "Of course you never *said* it. You're too well-mannered for that. But oh, 'my family, my duty, my honor'—it amounts to the same thing, when you speak to someone low-born like me. Tossing me aside as unworthy of a duke's heir, making it clear you've no place for me in your life."

His blood iced.

His throat tightened.

No. Dear heaven, no. All these years she believed he spurned her because she wasn't *good enough*? Juno Bell, the most wonderful person he had ever met?

Realization slammed into him like a fist. He had been so young, trying to do the right thing, and instead he had broken even more than he knew.

Not once had it occurred to him that she might have believed he thought of her as inferior. He'd been too busy battling with himself, torn between his family and his duty on the one hand, and his feelings for Juno on the other. Cursing himself for his weakness in meeting her each morning when he had known he must not.

Too late the pieces fell together. Her flinty refusal to even think of her parents, because they had rejected her; of *course* she had dealt the same to him. She had been young and hurt; she had coped the only way she knew how. And he had been young and selfish, and so wrapped up in his own struggle he had never dreamed she might have experienced their conversation so very differently to him.

Now, ten years later…

I do not aspire to be a duchess.

I can love you without wanting to marry you.

Finally he understood how his reaction in the meadow had hurt her, but it was too late.

Ten years too late.

He sat on the edge of the bed. "I never thought you less than me. Never. I was trying to do the right thing by everyone, but then I…" He sighed. "You must believe me."

He could not bear to tell her the full story, this sensitive secret he had nursed so long.

But neither could he bear her thinking that she had earned the poor opinion of anyone on this Earth. He especially could not bear her thinking that of him.

She pulled the sheet up to her shoulders. "Why should I believe you?"

"It's the truth."

She scoffed. "You try to be kind, but this is—"

"The truth," he repeated. "I came to Vienna to ask you to marry me."

"No."

The denial came instantly, thoughtlessly, to Juno's lips. The world shifted, as if the bed were on a ship and she was far out at sea.

She stared at his back, the muscles flexing under his shirt as he sat on the bed, but her mind was in another place and time. She could picture him still, Leo at twenty-one, walking with her among the autumn trees in Vienna, while she hastened to assure him she no longer loved him and thought of him as only a friend.

How had he looked when she said that? She did not remember; she did not know.

"No," she repeated. "You... You were touring. The Grand Tour. You were visiting your mother's relatives, all your royal cousins in Prussia."

He raked a hand through his hair. "That was only an excuse to travel. I left England the day I turned twenty-one. Old enough to marry without anyone's permission."

"But you..." She gripped the sheet, as if it was all that kept her from flying away. "In the meadow, you said we had no future. We could not be together in any way."

Rueful laughter huffed out of him. "I was trying to do the right thing. I argued with myself for months after that. Then I argued with my father and my mother. They both insisted I had been right to turn you down, as I should never encourage affections from an unsuitable lady. But I decided they were wrong, we were all wrong, the whole world was wrong. By then, you'd already left England. I waited until I reached my majority to ensure the marriage was legal, as my parents would most certainly not agree."

"You…" She squeezed her eyes shut, remembering. "I never knew." Her eyes flew open. "You never wrote."

"I didn't have your address. And if I'd written via Hadrian, he'd have wanted to know why."

She clenched the sheet, clenched and released, as she stumbled through her memory. The past shifted and changed around her. "The gambling. My family told me how you lived in gaming hells."

"Gaming is the only way for a dependent young lord to earn money, so I built up a nest egg, enough to support a wife and family for years, should my father cut me off. I spent it all on decorative objects in the end. That gambling funded the start of my collection." He paused. "I had a ring made for you. My own design. A very patient silversmith worked on it with me."

Sorrow washed over her as she pictured him again in Vienna. Oh, how very young they had been! She hugged her knees, and there, tangled in sheets that still smelled of him, her heart ached for that lovely, sensitive youth. For the dreams he had nurtured, the months he had waited, the hundreds of miles he had traveled, only to find her absorbed in her new life, barely sparing him a thought. She had not lied when she said her love for him was gone by the time they met in Vienna; by then, it was the truth.

But what even was the truth? For ten years, her truth had been that Leo rejected her because she was not good enough for him. For ten years, resentment for that rejection had hummed in her breast, like the cello in an orchestra.

For ten years, that was the truth by which she had defined the course of her adult life.

For ten years, she had been wrong.

He was bowed over, his face buried in his hands, his shirt pulled tight over the muscles in his back. She wanted to curl her arms around him, thread her fingers through his hair. Loll against him while they fed each other snacks and chatted about nothing. With this conversation, she had robbed them of their only chance for such sweet domestic intimacy. She ought never to have said a word. If only she could return to that innocent time of believing that he, and he alone, was wrong.

But this new truth was part of her now, crystallizing in her brain.

"You mean," she said slowly, "that if I had not decided to study art in Europe, if I had stayed in England, waiting for you, you'd have come after me and we would have married and our whole lives would be different."

The room felt haunted by those other versions of themselves, this other Duke and Duchess of Dammerton. If they had made different decisions all those years ago, they would be different people now.

He sat up. He didn't look at her. "But it didn't happen like that, and there is no point thinking about it."

And Vienna? He had said he preferred not to remember Vienna. Because of his wife, she had assumed. She searched for memories of him in Vienna. She had a thousand wonderful memories of those years, and he was not in them.

A new anger blossomed. "You called me inconstant," she said. "Yet back in Vienna, I didn't see you running after me, fighting for me. Indeed, a few months later you married someone else. You say you loved me and dare scorn my love for fading. Why, if you loved me so much, why did you not even *try*?"

"Why try when you—" He surged to his feet, took two aimless steps then pivoted. "You were thriving, Juno," he said. "You always had verve, but studying art, free from England's restrictions, you had become so alive. So *luminous*. Marriage is not only about choosing a spouse, but choosing a life. And what life could I offer you? Only more rules, more duties, people always watching, judging, demanding. I offered wealth and status, but you care nothing for those. Had I married you and taken you home to England, I would have had to watch your spirit fade and wither away."

She pressed her lips together and hugged her knees more tightly.

Leo threw back his head, briefly squeezed his eyes shut. "If I had chased you, fought for you, and asked you to marry me back then, would you have accepted?"

A deep breath shuddered through her, as she swiped at the tears burning her eyes. "No. I would have refused you." Her voice was barely more than a whisper. "Those were such wonderful days."

He nodded. "So I married someone else. Erika knew about you from the start."

"Your wife. Erika. Did you..." She gathered her courage. "Did you love her?"

"Erika was what I needed, as I was for her. We were terribly ill-suited, though we did not realize it at first. I was young and drunk and..." He shook his head, as if disgusted and impatient with his younger self. "I told myself it did not matter whom I married, if I could not marry you."

"But it does matter, doesn't it?" she said. "You are a duke, and it matters to the whole country whom you choose as your wife. And to your family, and your Foundation, and your future heirs."

He didn't answer.

The silence rumbled on around them, louder than the fire in the hearth and the drumming of the rain. The room seemed as real as a stage, with Juno naked on the bed, Leo dressed on the floor, and a scattering of props: food, drink, a swansdown tippet, a velvet couch.

There was nowhere to go from here. They had torched their bridges, and everything was in flames. There was no other way it could have ended, not with them being who they were, with their choices and lives. Not in this world.

She would not regret this, she vowed. She had succeeded in claiming a small piece of him to take with her when they parted. This pain was simply the price she must pay.

"You did love me then, once?" she asked.

"Maybe. Maybe not." He seemed exhausted. "Did you truly love me, when you said those words? Is it still love if that love fades over time?"

"You called it desire. Unfinished business."

"Yes. Desire is all it was."

"And is all the desire now spent?"

A foolish and futile question: She knew he would not answer. And sure enough, he didn't. He went to the door.

"Forgive me," he said. "I fear this has been a mistake."

Her heart cracked a little more. "You said you valued our friendship."

He paused in the doorway. "Yes. I did. Very much." He stepped back toward her. She sat up. He stepped away. "But as you are always the first to say, nothing ever stays. Not even this."

CHAPTER 19

Leo fled to his estate in Richmond, where he lingered several days. A private retreat, he had claimed before leaving London. Now, he made his lie true, and was grateful to avoid contact with the outside world.

There was only a skeleton staff, but he didn't need much. He was happy enough to subsist on bread and cheese, to bathe in the lake, to wear whatever came to hand. No one would ever know about the night in Surrey. They would hear only of his days in Richmond, rowing and riding until his muscles screamed and his palms blistered and bled.

He tried to steer his thoughts away from Juno, but his thoughts proved as obedient as her cats: They went where they pleased, pounced on small things, and toyed with him mercilessly.

And when he laughed—like a madman, laughing alone at night—it was at his own folly. Had he truly believed that sleeping with Juno would dissolve his feelings for her? Behold the madness caused by thwarted lust: It burrowed into a man's brain like a worm in an apple and made him believe all manner of foolish notions as if they were the wisest ideas in the world.

It was always going to end like this. He had examined their relationship like a cut-glass teardrop, turning it this way and that, exploring every facet. No matter how the light shone through it, he could not see how it could have ended any other way.

I can love you without wanting to marry you.

I do not aspire to be a duchess.

She could not have put it more plainly than that.

They had hurt each other. He had made mistakes. But the differences between them were stark. It simply wasn't meant to be and that was all there was to it. Nothing had changed, in the end. No more options were available. He had decided to marry Susannah Macey, and that was what he would do.

So it was that, five days later, Leo rode along the mews behind his London house.

Ashen daylight pressed down on him like a headache. His horse shied away from the gate. He did not want to set foot inside that house.

Perhaps he wouldn't. Perhaps he would hunt down Hadrian Bell, take him to some new club in London, get roaring drunk. Excellent idea. Except his face was unshaven, his clothes were dirty, Hadrian was out of town, and drinking had not solved any of his problems yet. But after days of seclusion, Leo needed company. He was exceedingly sick of himself.

An image arose: a parlor with shabby, mismatched furniture, and cats that shed on his clothes, and a warm, crooked smile that always, unfailingly, welcomed him in.

He shook off the image and forced his skittish horse through the gate.

Outside the stables, he swung out of the saddle, landed on the flagstones with tired legs, and scowled up at his house. How dare it look the same as always. But it would never change. The house and title endured; the men who claimed them came and went, irrelevant.

Sainted stitches. He *was* in a gloomy mood.

He turned as two grooms came running out of the stables. Their faces broke into such broad smiles, one might think he was their savior.

"Your Grace, you've returned, praise be," one said, as the other took the reins.

"Thank you, Jones, Allan. It's, ah, lovely to see you too."

How odd. Leo liked to think he treated his staff decently, but he never imagined they actually missed him during his absences.

A moment later, the stable master came striding out to greet him too.

"Your Grace," he said, his rough voice breathy with relief. "Your secretary said you were on a private retreat in Richmond and were not to be disturbed, and the butler wasn't sure if he should write to you."

"About what?"

Shrill laughter flew from an open window on an upper story of the house. The window revealed a man and woman laughing and kissing and disappearing from view.

The stable master gave a world-weary sigh. "Mr. St. Blaise has guests."

THE AIR INSIDE was thick with perfume and smoke. Delicate pianoforte music floated down the halls, dueling with shrieks of raucous laughter. Light peered around the closed curtains like a voyeur. Fine gentlemen and fine courtesans, in various states of undress, pranced drunkenly through the rooms, except where they were sprawled on furniture in interesting arrangements of limbs.

Reigning over this bacchanal was, of course, St. Blaise, as beautiful and destructive as Lucifer himself. He lounged in a green brocade armchair wearing nothing but his breeches and one of Leo's waistcoats, with a horde of admirers at his feet.

Upon seeing Leo, St. Blaise leaped up and raised his crystal goblet in an exuberant toast.

"Brother dear! Welcome home! The prodigal duke has returned! What a thrill to see you at long last!"

Every exclamation slammed into Leo like a fist. Even the drunkest guests were suddenly sober enough to remove themselves from his orbit.

"And what a thrill to come home to this welcoming party," he said.

"Not a welcoming party. It's a search party!" St. Blaise beamed. "You disappeared, so we gathered to search for you."

Leo cast his eye over the once-elegant salon, now looking disheveled and mildly ashamed. Searching for him? The only thing anyone here was searching for was a good time and a rotten ending.

He was something of an expert in good times and rotten endings.

"You don't seem to be searching very hard," he observed.

"But we found you. Because look! Here you are! What a frenzy London was in, wondering where you ran off to."

Leo whipped his head around. "Why the devil should anyone care? I retired to Richmond for some peace and quiet." He repeated his alibi like a criminal in the dock. "Hardly cause for concern."

"Ah, but in the circumstances, it looks like you scarpered."

The wicked glee in his half-brother's expression gave him pause. "What circumstances?"

"Absconded. Fled. Decamped. Escaped. Run off."

"*What circumstances?*"

"Of course, *I* never believed you would behave so dishonorably as they said," St. Blaise went on blithely. "'My dear brother

Polly would never have disappeared willingly,' said I. 'Maybe he's been kidnapped or robbed by highwaymen, and while all of London is maligning his good name, he's bleeding in a ditch while wild dogs eat his face.'" St. Blaise grinned. "But here you are, face uneaten. Surprisingly unshaven, but also uneaten, and I am very glad about that."

"So am I." Leo rubbed the stubble on his itchy—but uneaten —jaw. "Now, what circumstances?"

"The circumstances of you getting engaged to Miss Susannah Macey and running off without informing her family or publishing the notice in the papers, as only a scoundrel and cad would do."

"I'm not engaged to Miss Macey."

"And now he denies it! The scandal!" St. Blaise fell back, as if in a swoon. "You used to be so honorable, yet there's that poor lady become a laughingstock for fancying herself engaged to you while you go running off."

What the devil had happened? Had Renshaw become confused, mistaken Leo's request to court her as an actual betrothal? Surely Miss Macey herself would have not said a word?

Or...

"Perhaps this rumor was started by someone with a vested interest in my getting engaged to Miss Macey," Leo said. "For example, someone who would win a sizable sum of money in some asinine bet."

St. Blaise's eyes opened wide. "No! Polly, my dear brother, you cannot be referring to *me?*"

"Yes, Tristan, my dear brother, I am referring to you."

St. Blaise studied him, suddenly not as drunk as he had appeared. "Then it's true what they say," he said softly. "Nothing will rile you up these days. Remember the scraps we used to get into whenever Papa Duke forced us together? You would go wild. What happened to you, Polly?"

Leo ignored the question. "So, you attempted to win not only the bet on my engagement, but also a few hundred pounds for making me angry, is that it?" he said. "Tell me, amid all the fun and games, did you give a single thought to the consequences for Miss Macey?"

St. Blaise spread his palms. "Wasn't me."

"Give me one good reason why I should believe that," Leo said and turned for the door.

"Because it was Thomas Macey," St. Blaise called after him.

"Thomas Macey is a smug, immature numbskull with a history of deplorable tailoring and worse decisions, but he would not harm his own sister thus."

"In White's. He shoved his friend and yelled that his sister would be your duchess and his friend had better watch his mouth as he was under your protection."

Damn. Too late Leo recalled his hasty promise to help the lad with the problem of his secret, inappropriate marriage, a promise Macey had apparently taken to heart.

He turned back. "Macey said that?"

"Everyone heard and so he doubled down, said you and his sister were engaged. Then Renshaw said it wasn't so, but everyone knows the man's memory is shaky, so they went looking for you to confirm, and you'd scarpered, and then Miss Macey developed a prolonged headache, and when no one could find you for days, well, it all got very exciting after that."

Sainted stitches. If only these people had a *hobby*.

"Ask Macey, he'll tell you," St. Blaise went on.

"I intend to. If he knows what's good for him, he'll have scarpered too."

"Clearly he doesn't know what's good for him. He's in the next room."

STEPPING into the next room was like stepping into another house, this one pleasant and wholesome. A pretty young lady was playing a sonata on the pianoforte for Thomas Macey, who lolled tipsily in a chair. He bolted upright when Leo sat beside him. The lady stopped playing but Leo waved at her to continue; if she knew who he was, she gave no sign.

Leo said nothing. Macey said nothing. But Leo said nothing better and harder, and Macey launched into a stream of chatter as fervently as if Leo were holding his feet over a fire. His friend had seen him with his wife, he gabbled, and asked awkward questions, and he'd tried to *distract* his friend, and it slipped out that his sister would be a duchess, and he hadn't *meant* to lie, but everything got out of control, and now he'd made a *mess* and he needed Leo's *help* so very *much.*

With a wave of Leo's hand, the painful confession whimpered to a halt. "Where's your lady now?"

"Right there."

The lady at the pianoforte looked up and met Macey's eyes. An intimate smile passed between them.

"You brought her *here*?"

"It's not fair to her." Macey slumped back down. "She knew the risk, marrying the grandson of an earl, and she never asks for anything. We thought it might be diverting, see inside a duke's house. She plays beautifully, doesn't she?"

Leo thought her music was rather ordinary, but Macey was clearly besotted. "Why did you marry her, if you're so worried about it?"

The younger man's face screwed up, as if trying to explain a complex mathematical theorem. "She's so thoughtful, so… When I'm with her, I feel right. Usually, I feel like I'm pretending. One goes through the motions—school, society, trying to impress the other fellows—but it's not real, is it? With her, I feel real. Sometimes I think it wouldn't be so bad if my father disowned me. I'm only the younger son; he won't care. But she deserves better than some outcast for a husband."

"Real," Leo repeated to himself. The boy was not such a fool after all; nothing felt real to Leo now.

He shook off the feeling and resolutely shifted his thoughts onto Macey's dilemma. Society depended on stability, so it insisted upon rules. Those who wanted society to stay the same had to enforce those rules. Those who wanted society to change had to break those rules. And pay the price.

And here were young Macey and his wife, who had found each other against the odds, who had decided to throw their lots in together, despite all the excellent reasons why they should not.

Suddenly, he could not bear it, to let a rigid society and an angry father tear these young fools apart.

"When you married her, were you already twenty-one?" he asked.

"I was twenty."

"A minor. Your father could simply petition the courts to annul the marriage on the grounds that you wed without your guardian's permission."

"He can do that? That's exactly what he'd do. She'd be completely ruined. No, I shan't allow it."

Leo hesitated then added, "It's a way out for you. Dissolve the marriage, pay her off, and then carry on as if it never happened."

Macey bounded to his feet. The music stopped. "A disgusting notion! Till death do us part, I said, and that is what I meant. How dare you think I'd ever treat her like that!"

Leo smiled. "Well said. There's hope for you yet. Sit down."

Deflated, Macey plonked himself back down.

"First, you must marry her again, legally," Leo said.

"Elope? Then everyone would know."

"Special license, then."

"Ha! As if the archbishop would give me the time of day."

Leo nodded. "I'll write to him, see if I can squeeze a special license out of him. Perhaps I could find you a posting abroad somewhere. No one need know of her family if you do not tell them."

"You'd do that? Thank you, a thousand times thank you." He twisted his hands together. "And I do apologize, for starting that other game, about baiting you to anger. I tried to put a stop to it, but these things take on a life of their own. The prize money is nearing one thousand pounds, and I don't know what to do."

Leo found he no longer cared. "You're not the first person to make sport at my expense."

"It's that you're always so *calm*." Macey had apparently developed a taste for confession. "Jane said—that's Jane, my wife— that the traits that vex us in others are either traits we dislike in ourselves, or traits we wish we had. I suppose I wish I could be like you, so unflappable, and I suppose I wished to see what might make you lose control. But nothing does."

Leo wiped a hand over his face and laughed.

"Forgive me, Dammerton, what is so droll?"

"Nothing. Nothing at all."

Within a couple of hours, the guests were ejected, the servants were soothed, Leo's body was bathed, and his smooth face tingled from the ruthless scraping of a very sharp blade. Clean pantaloons, clean stockings, and a clean shirt billowing over his head, and Leo felt almost himself again. Almost.

"And which waistcoat today, Your Grace?" his valet asked.

The huge wardrobe gaped open, full of brightly colored

silken treasures, like a magical cave in a fairy tale.

And there, on the wardrobe door, a scar. Erika had thrown a hairbrush.

You have no passion, she had yelled, during one of their fights, near the end, when he was trying to impress upon her why her behavior must change, the damage she was doing to his family name. *So boring, all this silk and china and crystal. You used to be* fun.

No passion?

Juno might disagree. She had ruthlessly torn him open, until so much wild passion flooded out of him, he almost drowned in it.

That was the wild passion that had him lurking on street corners in Vienna, longing for a glimpse of her. A wild passion he channeled into the bright colors and textures of his collection and his clothes.

Yes, he and Erika had had *fun*, at first, endless wild soirees and adventurous bedsport. But as his interest in artisans grew, his interest in drinking waned. He changed, but Erika did not. She detested his sobriety; he detested her hedonism. He begged her to change; she refused. And as Leo trudged behind his father's coffin in the softly swirling snow, he had made the decision he had long known was necessary, for the sake of his title, his heirs, and the family name.

One did the right thing. One did what had to be done.

He had gone to Erika's room, at midday, when she was still in bed.

"Every morning for years they bring me tea and every morning I do not drink it," Erika had said, smiling. "I think this is the peculiar English sense of humor."

Leo climbed onto the bed beside her and took her hand. "This cannot continue. I warned you."

"Are you finally sending me away? I enjoy life in London."

"You enjoy it too much for English tastes."

He had explained what would happen next: Leo would sue Erika's current lover for criminal conversation, which was the law's way of saying "sleeping with another man's wife." Given the substantial eyewitness testimony, the jury would most likely pronounce her lover "guilty" and order him to pay damages.

Erika listened, curious, unconcerned. "He won't be able to pay."

"I won't expect him to pay. But the guilty verdict is a necessary step to secure an Act of Parliament permitting a divorce."

"And then you'll send me away."

"You won't be welcome in English society once divorced."

"I'm not sure I've ever been welcome here, but they find reasons not to shun me, because I am never dull. In the story of our marriage, I am the villain, the wicked adulteress." She laughed freely. "Of course, I *am* a wicked adulteress, but at least I am honest. You misled me about the sort of man you are. You led me to think we are the same, but where I am wild and wicked, you were merely heartbroken and drunk. I cannot even blame you for being terrible, which makes you the worst sort of villain of all."

He brushed his lips over her knuckles. "I have done badly by you. Believe me, I have regret and guilt too."

"I do hope you feel guilty enough to give me a nice house. Maybe in Paris—they will *adore* me."

How she baffled him, viewing her own ruination as nothing more than another adventure. Nevertheless, he had tried to warn her about the scandal.

"We will be the talk of England," he said. "Every detail of our lives will be made public. It will be very unpleasant."

She poked him in the ribs. "For you, maybe. I shall revel in every moment."

Indeed. She even stirred up more excitement by releasing a set of her own carefully edited letters and commissioning a series of cartoons about herself. Now she made a comfortable home in Paris, with a wide circle of similarly disgraced friends.

And here he was, the past firmly behind him, ready to start again.

"That one," he said to his valet, pointing to a waistcoat that was striped blue and gray. It was a little dull for his taste, but the stripes struck him as orderly, and Susannah Macey liked order. It would make as good an outfit as any in which to start his new life.

MISS MACEY BLEW into the drawing room at Lord Renshaw's house like a hat on a gust of wind, with only Lady Renshaw's hand on her elbow stopping her from flying away. Her complexion was like chalk, and her jaw was set, and she eyed Leo with a mix of trepidation and hope.

"I would like to request a private conversation with your granddaughter," Leo said to the countess.

Lady Renshaw lifted her chin mutinously. "Your Grace. All of London is speculating about what you might have done to her."

"Others' speculations are of no interest to me," he said shortly. "I have come to ask Miss Macey for her hand in marriage, which will repair any damage to her reputation, and I should like to do so in private."

Susannah tugged her arm from Lady Renshaw's grip. "It is all right. Please, Grandmother."

The countess darted sharp looks from one to the other. "Five minutes, mind. I'm sure that will be ample, Your Grace."

"Thank you, my lady," Leo said, and politely maneuvered her to the other side of a firmly closed door.

Miss Macey had regained her poise, hands clasped at the waist of her neat russet dress. Despite her composure, her thumbs were worrying each other. He would come to know those hands well, over the years. He would learn her mannerisms, her turns of phrase, her moods.

All was as it ought to be: a formal and slightly awkward marriage proposal in a drawing room, while relatives guarded the door. Their start was not ideal, but otherwise, this was the correct order of things. Leopold Halton and Susannah Macey: not a match written in the stars, but in accord with what was written in *Debrett's*.

I can love you without wanting to marry you.

I do not aspire to be a duchess.

When he spoke, the words came smoothly, without hesitation, as if recited from his memory like a nursery rhyme. "I assure you, Miss Macey, Susannah. This situation has not forced my call on you today, but only hastened it. I would be honored if you would agree to become my wife."

She moved her head, three small nods in one. "I do agree. Thank you. Yes."

They were engaged.

How easily matters unfolded, when one did as one was supposed to do. Weddings were easy too, as he recalled. Say what they wanted you to say, and the rest followed nicely.

Silence slid into the space between them. It was not an awkward silence. It was merely … there. A beige sort of silence. The sort of silence they could expect to join them at meals for the next forty years.

Everything was fine.

Leo rested his hands on the crest of a chair, his thumb finding the rosette carved in the smooth, cool wood.

"I should like us to be in accord on certain matters," he said. "I do not wish to mislead you as to my character or my feelings. I like you and esteem you, and I am honored to marry you, but from my side, this is not a love match."

Her thumbs stopped fidgeting. "Nor from mine either. What

a relief that is clear!" She smiled for the first time. "It's so silly, isn't it, this chatter about love? I am never so astonished as when I witness a capable friend reduced to stammering over some man's eyes. Love seems sweet enough in books and on the stage, as in, oh, I don't know, *Othello*, or one of those plays. But love is not like that in real life."

Ah, yes. *Othello*. That famously sweet play about a man who is driven by jealousy to murder his beloved wife. Either Susannah Macey did not pay attention at the theater, or she held peculiar notions about love.

But all he said was, "I agree. Books and plays rarely reflect love as I have known it."

"But you don't know love, really, do you?"

Her comment startled him. Visibly, he surmised, for she tilted her head, looking puzzled.

"Forgive me for speaking of an indelicate matter, but I recall the letters of your—your former wife, which were published during the—" She rippled her fingers through the air, thus dispensing with the months of trial and divorce. "In one letter, she wrote of you that 'He cannot love anyone.' When I read that, I thought: There is a man of excellent good sense."

He frowned. "You could have been no more than sixteen at the time."

"And I was a sixteen-year-old of excellent good sense."

"Clearly."

She was nineteen now, ten years younger than him. Suddenly, that decade felt like a century. When Leo was nineteen, he had experienced his first kiss and the blissful agony of love. When Juno was nineteen, she was studying in Vienna and taking a lover.

The light glinted on the pins holding up Susannah's dark hair. She was pretty, he thought. He felt no desire for her, not yet, not today, but today was not their wedding, so that was all right.

She was fidgeting with her thumbs again.

"While we are clarifying matters, I would like to express my interest in the work of the Dammerton Foundation." She smiled shyly. "It is wonderful that you will be able to expand its operations after our marriage. I should very much like to be involved."

Well played, Susannah, Leo thought. A neat and subtle reminder that his plans depended upon her money. She was much sharper and smarter than her pretty, genteel demeanor let show. She would mature into an excellent duchess.

"What sparked your interest?" he asked.

She considered her words, as if shuffling through a pack of cards to choose which ones to play. "Some years ago, we visited the house of the Duke and Duchess of Northumberland, and I was shown the first duchess's collection of decorative objects. Have you seen it?"

"It is quite marvelous."

"When I learned how she had been a renowned patroness, I thought: That is something I can do." She bit her lip. "I adore art, but I confess my skill with watercolors leaves much to be desired, and my embroidery..." The word slipped out on a defeated sigh. "The threads get so tangled up, and I don't understand why. I always seem to pull the thread too tight or not tight enough. I cope with simple designs, but anything complex turns into a horrid mess."

A charming confession, he found. "And you do like to impose order on the world."

"I do, yes." She smiled. It was a pretty smile. "Thank heaven for lists: They never get tangled up. My household accounts are a thing of beauty, and I can prepare social events down to the last detail. I promise our household will be very orderly."

Leo managed a reassuring smile. "And what more could any man ask?"

CHAPTER 20

When Juno stumbled out of the carriage and into her house the day after her tryst with Leo, she felt more tired than she could ever remember feeling before.

Mrs. Kegworth greeted her with surprise. "We'd not expected you back from the country so soon. Oh, my dear, is aught amiss? You look distressed."

Who knew what stories her face was telling? Juno schooled it to pleasant neutrality.

"A friend told me some news," she said.

"Nothing bad, I hope."

"Something from the past. It made me think."

Juno did not enjoy this sort of thinking. She did not like the way her thoughts spun around like autumn leaves in a whirlwind. She did not like the way Leo's revelation had sent every choice from the past ten years dancing through her mind like frenzied drunkards.

But how could she regret her choices? She was happy as an artist. She cherished her experiences. She was proud of what she had achieved. She liked who she had become.

Yet beside him in that bed, their bodies melded as one, she had felt more alive and whole than she had in years.

Longing swept over her like a river after a storm. She blinked it off as she became aware of Mrs. Kegworth repeating her name, her kindly face etched with concern.

Juno forced a smile. Enough! No point in yearning for Leo. He cared for her, she knew he did, but she had broken his youthful heart, and then strayed so far from the path of respectability that he had no room for her in his life.

And what of it? She could hardly fit a duke into her life either. Dukes took up an awful lot of space.

She squeezed the housekeeper's hand. "Mrs. Kegworth. Alice. Have I ever said thank you?"

"Several times a day, Miss Bell."

"I mean, really thank you. To you and Mr. Kegworth for agreeing to our arrangement."

Mrs. Kegworth laughed and patted her hand. "No need to thank us, my dear. With the money we save on not paying you rent or board, Mr. Kegworth has saved a nice little nest egg. Besides, I enjoy keeping house and meeting your lively guests. I'm certain we've the better end of the bargain, as all we do in exchange for our rooms is to tell a little lie."

"If not for that lie, I would not be able to have this studio. Some things money cannot buy."

Juno glared at the kitchen, as though it were the stove's fault that an unmarried woman could not run her own household, not if she earned her own living and wished to keep her good name. The scheme had been a gift from her friend Arabella, now Lady Hardbury, who created schemes the way other people ate breakfast. It was Juno who rented the house, but Mr. Kegworth, a lithographer, led the world to believe it was his household and that he was her mother's cousin. This nice fiction gave Juno the cloak of respectability that came with living in the household of her male kin. Such stupid rules! At first it had amused her, like a game. How weary she was, now, of treading the tightrope of respectability.

"But I like my life," she said to Mrs. Kegworth as if they'd been arguing over this point. The kitchen felt overheated. Her eyes were hot too; she swiped at a surprising tear. "I break their rules and I tell lies and I do what I must because there is always a price to pay. But it's all right because I like my life. I'm happy," she cried, and turned and ran up the stairs.

WHAT SHE NEEDED to do was draw.

But her studio looked shabby and threadbare. It felt like a stranger's space, even as Angelica and Artemisia came bounding across the room to greet her. She crouched down to pet them and smiled as their heads bumped her chin, but her eyes roamed hopelessly, seeing all the places Leo would never be again.

Never mind: She did not need him. She had her art, and art had been enough for years.

She pulled out her sketchbook and sharpened the pencil and pressed that pencil to the page, and pressed and waited and pressed and waited and pressed until the pencil broke. Her Muse was silent. Her imagination felt numb.

Again she took up the blade, again she sharpened the point, and this time caught her skin with a yelp. She stared at the little jewel of blood in wonder. She had not cut herself since the first time Hester had let her sharpen her own pencil.

If Leo were here, he'd shake his head and gently wash off the blood, saying, "I warned you about becoming addled. The adverse side effects of drawing nudes!"

The image was so solid it stole her breath, and she shivered as she washed and bound the little cut herself.

WHAT SHE NEEDED to do was lose herself in diversions.

She had scores of friends. Why, she would not even notice Leo's absence. Bohemian circles in London were large and full of drama. There was always some entertainment to be found, from salons and musicales to picnics and games.

But even among such entertainments, Leo haunted her. Everywhere she went, her friends would say, "Oh, but you know the Duke of Dammerton, do you not?" Juno would ignore her pounding heart and say something like, "We are acquainted," at which they'd lean in eagerly and ask if the rumors were true: Had the duke really become engaged to a lady without informing her family and then run away? Each time she would say he'd never behave so dishonorably, to which they would say "Where is he, then?" and she would say she didn't know, and they would say, "Of course not," and the conversation would move on. Until someone else recalled her acquaintance, and the exchange would repeat itself all over again.

How funny people were. Every now and then, during these past years, someone would speculate that she was Leo's mistress, simply because she was a woman and he was a man and what other evidence of an affair could anyone need? But in the end, no one truly believed a spinster and minor artist to be of any real interest to such a grand public figure as a duke. No one knew of their history, not even her family. No one knew they had loved each other and broken each other's hearts. No one would guess they had each unwittingly shaped the course of the other's life.

And no one ever would know. Did it happen if there was no one to witness it? If there was no record of something, was it even real?

Oh, how she despised such questions, for they were impossible to answer, yet they itched at her brain until other conversations became meaningless, and even discussions of art felt trite. When an artist she admired was explaining how to capture the ocean at sunset, Juno wanted to throw her wine in his face and say, "Forget the stupid sunset!" She wanted to know how to capture the way Leo made her feel. How might she paint her regret for her errors, or her confusion over her desires, or her stark new loneliness in the company of her friends?

How irritating they had become, how unbearable their chatter, how insufferable their witticisms about The Disappearing Duke of Dammerton.

Where was he, anyway? Why had he not returned to London? Worry gnawed at her, but she could ask no one. She did not have that right.

At salons and soirees, she caught herself imagining him sauntering through the door, draping himself over a chair, singing along with everyone else. At the theater, she imagined him at her side, holding her hand, whispering wry commentaries, stealing a kiss.

Every facet of her life seemed scarred with a Leo-shaped hole, as if an empty space moved alongside her. As if there were another world where they had married in Vienna all those years ago.

As if the ghost of that other Leo, her husband, was always by her side.

WHAT SHE NEEDED to do was spend time with her family.

Hadrian was out of town, and Phoebe was visiting Oxford, but her aunt and uncle and Livia were still in London for the final weeks of the Season.

As luck would have it, Hester planned to redecorate the family home in Longhope Abbey and was eager for Juno's advice.

But as Juno paged through a thick wallpaper catalogue, she hardly saw the colorful designs. Did Hester know if Leo had returned to London? Did Juno dare ask?

"You've not heard a word I said," Hester said, abandoning her newspaper to stand at Juno's side. "Are the wallpapers so engrossing?" She peered over her shoulder. "Parrots and pineapples? You would not inflict such horrors upon me."

Juno said, "I beg your pardon?" and realized she was staring at a sample of wallpaper that featured green parrots and yellow pineapples arranged in circles. The pineapples seemed cheerful enough, but the parrots looked very solemn.

"Forgive me. I was thinking." She paused. "I don't like it."

"That wallpaper?"

"Thinking. I don't like thinking." She scowled at the gloomy parrots. "The wallpaper is hideous too."

She turned the page and absently traced a pale blue fleur-de-lis design. "I'm sorry."

Hester shifted to see her face. "For what, my dear?"

"I wasted years as a child, drawing pictures for my parents. I was so sure if my drawing was good enough, they would come back for me. I wasted time wanting them back, when I could have been enjoying my life with all of you."

"That is not how I remember it at all." Hester looked baffled. "You were very much part of our family. Yes, you spent hours every day drawing, but your cousins passed hours every day with their Greek and Latin and other books. We adored having you in our family. You livened us up no end. I thought you were happy."

"I was. I am. But I missed them."

"You could be happy with us and miss your parents too. It's possible to love more than one thing in your life."

Something in those words tugged at her weary brain. Oh, enough of these thoughts fogging up her mind! She whirled away and tumbled onto the settee. "When I was fourteen, I found a letter my father wrote to my uncle. He was asking for money. He did not even mention me."

"Oh, my darling." Hester sat beside her and took her hand.

"He wrote that he would transform art forever. I know artists like that, the ones who do nothing but talk." She studied their joined hands. "Did my uncle Gordon give them money?"

Hester adjusted her spectacles. "Every time. They said if we did not give them money, they would take you away."

"I don't understand."

"We did not want them to take you away from us and they knew it, so they made us pay to keep you." She squeezed her fingers. "The state you were in when you arrived: ill-kempt, poorly behaved, barely able to read. We feared they would neglect you again, or simply leave you with someone else, and we loved having you. You do not blame us, I hope?"

"I am glad you kept me." Juno adored them, she always had, yet she had never felt she truly belonged. Not until Leo. "But … I am so very different to the rest of you, with your books and your *thinking*. I'm not nearly so clever as all of you."

"One need not be bookish to be clever, and you are very clever in your own way. We are all awed by your skills."

The day Juno found that letter from her father she had run into the woods, where she sat in her favorite glade and hugged her knees and cried. Nothing could be relied upon to stay, she had thought. She had vowed, with all the fervor of her fourteen-year-old heart, never to waste her energy on anyone who made her feel unwanted. In time, that included Leo.

Hester put a knuckle under her chin. "Juno, is something amiss? This is not like you at all."

"It is too terrible. I cannot stop *thinking*." She rubbed her aching temples. "What if I had made different choices in the past? What if I had not left England to study art? What if—" She sighed. "Who would I be? If I had made different choices, I would have a whole different life, and I would be different too, and what if that life had been better? But what if it had been worse?" Her head thunked back against the settee. "I do not wish to alarm you, but I have become very philosophical and I fear it is endangering my health."

"I'm sure you'll pull through. You are very robust. Besides, you have always been philosophical." Hester nudged her shoulder. "But it is a waste of good time to wish to change the past. We can never go back to the beginning and start again. All we can ever do is look at where we are and start there. We make new choices, knowing that we are someone different now, and one day we'll be someone different again."

"You are very wise."

"Has something happened?"

"Nothing. A peculiar mood, I suspect." She bolted to her feet and returned to the book of wallpaper samples. "You were saying something and I wasn't listening."

Hester frowned, adjusting her spectacles, then her face brightened. "Oh, yes. I asked if you'd seen the notice in the paper: Dammerton is back in London and is engaged. I've met Miss Macey once or twice. She's sharp, I think. Have you met her, Juno?"

A yellow floral design rippled before Juno's eyes. "No," she said.

"I must write him a note. We might host a dinner and invite them both. You'll come, won't you?"

"I'll be out of town that night," Juno said hastily and escaped before her aunt could point out she'd not yet chosen a date.

What she needed to do was get out into the world.

Livia, who loved running around the countryside as much as

she loved sitting motionless with books, indulged her with an array of outings, but London had too many people, and too many carriages, and sour, acrid air. Wherever Juno walked, the words pounded in her mind like a drumbeat.

Leo was engaged. Officially, properly, formally, publicly engaged.

Her uncharacteristic irritability earned more than one remark from her cousin.

"But I thought you liked London," Livia said, as Juno cursed the horrors of Hyde Park at the promenade hour.

"I love London," she replied, and scowled at the crowd around them, all gorging on gossip as they milled about in their finest summer clothes. "But sometimes I miss the freedom of life on the Continent. There are so many wretched rules here, and people watching and judging all the time."

"If you do return to the Continent, you must take me with you. I am so ghastly tired of English society."

"Which is surprising, considering how assiduously you avoid it." Juno looped her arm around her cousin's and guided them away from the Serpentine, in search of somewhere she could breathe. "Why do you hate society so? If anyone is unkind to you, you must tell me, and I shall poke them in the eye with my paintbrush."

Livia sighed. "I can never think of anything normal to say, so I talk about the conquest of Byzantium or Aristotelian principles and this awkward little silence falls until they discover somewhere better to be. I told a group at a ball that I had translated a poem for *The Lady's Magazine* and they just stared at me and one said sadly, 'But why?'"

Juno elbowed her. "You are not the only bluestocking in London, you know. Find the others."

"Mama introduced me to some, daughters of old friends of hers. Now there was someone who was unkind and well deserves a poke in the eye. She said she'd translated that same poem two years ago and my version was a waste of space."

"She's jealous because your translation is superior."

"How would you know? You've not read the poem or the translations."

"I just know," Juno said and bumped her shoulder against her cousin's and made her smile.

Finally, they escaped the crowds. Livia's coltish stride ate up the grass easily, much faster than Juno liked. She called a halt and leaned back against a tree with a sigh.

"You inspired me, you know," Livia said. "To submit my translation to *The Lady's Magazine*. You are so brave and determined, and I thought, there is Juno with her own studio, and plenty of ladies make money from their pen. Why can I not do that too? I should very much like to write a travel memoir, but first I shall need to travel."

"Brava." Juno reached out and lazily picked a leaf. "But take care not to follow me too closely, or you'll trip over the mountain of mistakes I've left in my wake. I don't regret choosing my own path, rather than a safe, genteel marriage, but it is not always an easy choice."

"Why did you choose it? You never mentioned a career to anyone, until suddenly you were insisting you must study art in Europe. I always wondered if it had something to do with Leo. Dammerton, I should call him now."

Juno made a show of scrutinizing the leaf she had picked, while saying, in an admirably casual tone, "Hmm? Don't know what you mean."

"Liar," Livia laughed, snatching the leaf from her hand. "You went to the schoolroom one day and we hardly saw you for a fortnight while you painted up a storm. You hardly ate or drank, and Mama was ever so worried, and then you said you wished to study art abroad and become an artist. And Phoebe said, but then no one would marry you, and you said you had no wish to be married and if Father meant to give you a dowry, you'd rather it went to your studies than to a husband."

Juno gaped at her. "That was ten years ago. You were barely thirteen. How do you remember all that?"

Livia shrugged. "I remember things. And I remember that your painting frenzy started the same day that Leo, I mean, the duke, abruptly announced he had to leave."

Juno had no response to that.

"No one else noticed anything, and I'll never tell a soul," Livia said. "I just wondered. And?"

"And I'm afraid you'll have to keep on wondering."

She clapped her hands. "I knew it! But you and the duke are friends now, which is nice. Anyway, you are my inspiration, to make my own money. I'm perfectly content to be alone, just like you."

~

WHAT SHE NEEDED to do was scrape Leo from her mind like paint off an old canvas.

All these wretched questions could fly out the window too. Livia's memories had only roused more questions. Had Juno become an artist because she had truly wanted to? Or had it been nothing more than an adolescent impulse driven by a broken heart, for the same reason Leo had married?

Back in her studio, Juno opened the leather portfolio holding her secret drawings of him. She did not know why she had kept them. She never looked at them. She simply did a drawing, when the urge came upon her, and shoved it in with the rest.

Time to burn the lot. After one final look.

She leafed through the pages, moving back through time, the

artist in her noticing the changes in her skill and style, the woman in her reliving where she was as she drew each one.

And there was her record of the day it began: a messy sketch of Leo in the meadow of wildflowers, under the old oak tree, rejecting her and breaking her heart.

On this page, her seventeen-year-old self had written: "*I have two passions: Leo and art. I cannot have them both, so I shall devote myself to art. If I cannot have Leo, I shall have no one.*"

Oh, dear heaven, how very *dramatic* she had been.

She had completely forgotten these vows, yet she had made them come true, like wishes.

Or curses.

There was a sort of magic to that.

With otherworldly calmness, she reached for her sketchbook and she began to draw. No surprise that the image that emerged was of him. Again and again. She put them in the dossier.

She had loved him, the foolish infatuation of a girl. Now she loved him again, or still. Before, she had been a girl, looking for a place to belong. Now she was a woman, with a wealth of experience, who had carved her own place in the world.

Nothing ever stays, she always said. If only that were true. She wished her heartache over her parents hadn't stayed. She wished her feelings of inferiority toward her cousins hadn't stayed. She wished her feelings for Leo hadn't stayed. But all these feelings stayed. They haunted her.

Enough, she scolded herself, and shoved the drawings back into the portfolio, and shoved the portfolio into the armoire with all her other secret things.

She was veering dangerously close to moping and pining. Juno did not mope, and she most certainly did not pine. It was like crying for the moon to come down, which was pointless and even undesirable, because the moon was much better off up there in the sky, and what would she even do with the moon if she had it? She ought to simply cherish the wondrous experience of joining with him, body and soul, if only for a few minutes. True, he had hurt her, but she had always known it would hurt in the end.

But what she had not known—what she saw now, in the tip of a pencil digging into a mockingly blank page, in the emptiness of her studio, in the loneliness of her bed—was that she would keep throwing glances at the doorway, looking for him: leaning in the doorway, his eyes crinkling as he favored her with one of his playful smiles. Another image formed in her mind, with painful vividness: their eyes meeting, Leo shouldering off the doorjamb, pacing toward her with that lazy, focused intent, taking her in his arms, kissing her—

A sound came from below. She froze, listening.

Was that—a male voice, talking to Mrs. Kegworth? Were those—booted footsteps, coming slowly, easily, up the stairs?

He was here. *He was here!*

WHAT SHE NEEDED to do was see Leo one more time.

But the man who entered was Mr. St. Blaise.

Impatiently, she looked past him, to the empty doorway. She listened for more boots, another voice, another man.

There was no one else. Only St. Blaise and his angelic smile.

"Miss Bell, as beautiful as ever! Are you not delighted to see me?"

"I am delighted," she said, and it was true because he was undemanding and uninteresting and made for a jolly distraction. "Entertain me."

He obeyed, regaling her with amusing anecdotes and provocative opinions and not one mention of Leo at all.

Until he stretched and said, "My timing lacked finesse last

time I was here, as Polly was also present, but perhaps you have given some thought to my proposition?"

Juno searched her memory for a proposition, but came up as blank as one of her own canvases.

His eyes widened with incredulity. "You and me? Naked? Kept man? Except I don't actually expect you to keep me. I have Polly for that."

Laughter poured out of her then, bright and merry. An affair with St. Blaise? What a marvelous joke.

He did not seem to think so. "The jest was not so diverting as that. It is not fair to tease me so. If you laugh so loudly at something that is only a little amusing, I must assume you are flirting with me."

"If a woman passes you on the street, you assume she is flirting with you."

"Yes, but that's only because they usually are."

She shook her head. "The only time I want to see you unclothed is if I am drawing you. Which, in the circumstances, will not happen again. So."

He shrugged one shoulder, suddenly looking very French. "That's too bad. We could have a good time together, indulge a passing passion, a fleeting fancy, a temporary tup. We are similar creatures, you and I."

Something jolted down her spine. She sat bolt upright. She was *not* like him.

Was she?

He was still talking, in a low voice no doubt honed for the purpose of talking women into bed.

"We are both creatures of sensuality. We take enjoyment in life's transient pleasures. Why should you not fall lightly into my bed?"

Juno leaped up to pace about the sitting room. Leo also had

claimed that her emotions did not endure. Was this truly her nature? Was this who she had become?

But of course she enjoyed life's transient pleasures. Because they *are* transient, she wanted to yell, at St. Blaise, at Leo, at the world. Nothing was permanent. Seasons changed. Bodies aged. Friends moved away.

Parents left their daughter on a doorstep and disappeared.

Dukes married other, more suitable women.

One could hold on to nothing. If everything was transient, all one could do was enjoy it in the moment and never try to hold on.

That was why she had devoted herself to art, because art alone would never leave her.

She looked through the doorway to her studio, with its array of empty easels, and laughed again.

Well. Now art had left her too.

St. Blaise was watching her, eyebrows raised. She was falling to pieces.

"I'm not like you," she said desperately, fists clenched. "I'm not."

"Oh, but I think you are."

"You have no morals, no purpose."

He dismissed those with a lofty wave. "I have no need for those."

"I have clients and a studio and a patroness. I have responsibilities. I have bills. I have a housekeeper. I have *cats*."

"I don't quite see the connection between cats and—"

"You may leave now."

He rose, palms spread wide in conciliation, and sauntered toward the door.

So, your ideal man is one who will not stay, Leo had said. *It is not your nature to love long.*

She was not like this rake. She was *not*.

In the doorway, he shot her a sly, calculating look. "You cannot pine over Polly forever. He was always going to marry someone else. You are not the sort of woman a man like Polly marries."

She itched to throw something at him. Her own violence startled her.

"I'm not pining," she snapped. "Pining is for people who refuse to accept reality, and I never dreamed for a heartbeat that I might marry Leo. I would certainly never want to be a duchess."

A smile lurked in his features. She had revealed too much. She scrounged up a show of cheerful indifference.

"I thought your mind broader than that, Mr. St. Blaise, but clearly you are as narrow-minded as the rest of them, to imagine my former friendship with Leo was anything more than just that. Are you yet another of those fools who assume that if a man and woman are alone in a room, they must be up to no good?"

"If I am, it is only because when I am alone with a woman, we get up to no good." He released a woeful sigh. "Usually, anyway."

His attitude was so self-mocking that Juno's anger melted away.

"I don't think that is something to be proud of," she said.

He grinned. "What can I say? One must pass the time somehow, and I'm a terrible conversationalist." Then he sketched a lazy bow, said, "A pleasure as always, Miss Bell," and was gone.

WHAT SHE NEEDED to do was curl up in bed with her cats and stay there until the end of time.

CHAPTER 21

"Oh, but it is hopeless!" Beatrice wailed. "I don't know why I even bother!"

Juno glanced at Beatrice's profile and then back at the painting that had apparently inspired this outburst of despair.

To be fair, it was not exactly a cheerful painting—women weeping over the bloody corpses of their men—but that was in keeping with the spirit of this new exhibition of Spanish art.

She had been eager to join Beatrice at the viewing but, unfortunately, Beatrice had insisted on attending the exhibition on its opening day, along with the rest of London. With everyone determined to be among the first to see the paintings, there was such a crush it was difficult to see any paintings at all. Although, she supposed, many of them cared less about seeing the art than about being seen to be seeing the art.

Then Juno realized Beatrice's gaze was fixed on a stout, bland-faced lady, conversing in a group nearby.

"She did not grant me so much as a second glance," Beatrice said in a broken whisper.

"Is she someone important?"

The question livened Beatrice right up, as her jaw dropped and her eyes went wide. "Juno Bell, how can you not know?" she whispered. "Why, that is the Viscountess Newhurst. To think we'd see someone so grand here today! I was introduced to her at Prescott's art contest last week. She was most gracious and I invited her to my ball." Her shoulders slumped. "And now she does not care who I am! Even after she expressed interest in your new work."

New work? If only. Juno had hoped this exhibition might spark an image inside her, but the paintings only made her feel more on edge and dull, as if the art was building up inside her like so much sludge on her brain.

"It is nearly the end of the Season and still society hardly knows I exist," Beatrice said.

"Your garden party was well attended," Juno pointed out. "And you said you have had an excellent response for your ball next week."

"Yes, but none of my guests are peers!" she wailed. "I thought the duke's attendance at my party might make them notice me, but still they ignore my invitations."

"Aristocrats are just ordinary people too," Juno said.

"*Ordinary!* What are you saying? They are not ordinary people. They are the best people! If only they would acknowledge me. I might be nothing more than the daughter of a squire, but that would prove to everyone that I have a right to be here too. I know more about art than most of the clowns at the Royal Academy, though when I do venture an opinion or offer a fact, they immediately assume I am repeating Prescott's views."

She hooked her fingers around Juno's elbow and dragged her on to the next painting, grumbling all the while. "Mr. Prescott does deals with these fine lords, but only in their clubs. I suppose they never tell their wives—because why would a man bother to tell his wife anything?—so the peeresses do not even know I exist."

Juno abandoned all hope of studying the art. Just as well, for here was a painting of a slender, elegantly dressed gentleman, brandishing flowers for his blushing, dark-eyed love.

She looked away.

"What if Mr. Prescott were to show some paintings, at a dinner party perhaps?" she suggested. "Everyone would be sure to attend. It is something of a peculiarity with your husband, the way he has such a marvelous collection but refuses to share."

Beatrice sighed. "We had such a wonderful time when we first married, when he took me to Europe and showed me the art galleries and private collections. I loved learning. People think I'm silly, because I talk too much, but he saw my talent and he liked my enthusiasm. But now he says I should concentrate on passing my knowledge on to our children. The pair of them are not yet five! I thought he enjoyed tutoring me, but now I fear he might tutor some other young lady, if you grasp my meaning. If only I could triumph in society, at least I'd have that. But to fail as a wife, to fail as a patroness of the arts, to fail as…"

She stared glumly at the next painting: One powerfully built Titan was beheading another, while a crowd of demons cheered. Perhaps Beatrice, too, enjoyed beheadings, for barely a heartbeat later, she was grinning at Juno again.

"You know what will cheer me up? A new project. I shall get you married."

"Because misery loves company?" Juno asked dryly, and added, as she always did, "I have art. I have no interest in marriage."

A voice inside whispered: *Why not? Why not?*

Beatrice waved that away. "One can be both married and an artist. What about Mr. Adair, the frame maker? His business is thriving, and when he rolls up his shirt sleeves, well, let me say I quite enjoy the sight. Don't tell Mr. Prescott, will you?"

The very idea Juno might tell Mr. Prescott that his wife was admiring the frame maker's forearms!

They were lovely forearms, though.

"An excellent idea," Juno agreed solemnly. "Frames are expensive and marrying him would give me a lifetime's supply for free."

She moved on aimlessly, navigating through the chattering crowd. The hall was hot and stuffy, and her head was starting to ache. She would come back when it was quieter and she could study the art in peace.

Beatrice was still at her side. "You will be twenty-eight at your next birthday. Time's running out."

Twenty-eight. Hardly decrepit, but an old maid nonetheless. And what of it? *She* didn't care.

If I cannot have Leo, I shall have no one, she had written. Well, she could not have Leo, and here she was with no one.

She had received exactly what she'd wished for.

"I suppose I am yet to meet a man for whom I would turn my life upside down," she said.

Beatrice waggled a scolding finger. "One of these days, some man will sweep you off your feet like a gale."

Juno wasn't sure she wanted to be swept away by a love like a howling wind. She preferred love like a sunrise, gently creeping up through the darkness of one's solitude, brightening one's life with an array of colors, rising, spreading, growing in light and warmth until it filled her whole world, and watched over her all her life.

～

MERCIFULLY, Beatrice did not persist. "Oh look!" she cried. "We've reached the main painting by Señor de Goya!" She whipped out her quizzing glass to examine the famous art.

Which meant she didn't notice that Juno had gone very still and was staring across the gallery.

Right at Leopold Halton, the Duke of Dammerton.

Despite the crush, a space had opened up around him and the fashionably dressed dark-haired lady by his side. How very ducal he was: polished, flawless, shiny. He was spinning his quizzing glass on its chain, a blur of energy that belied his lazy demeanor.

He ought not to be here. How dare he be here! There had been a special opening of the exhibition for exalted invitees, so they did not have to share their space with the rabble.

Perhaps her surge of energy was too strong, for the crowd parted as if she had fired out a lightning bolt, and he twisted to look over his shoulder as if she had called his name.

He looked right at her.

Their eyes met.

The world receded. The noise dimmed. Everything and everyone blurred into the background. All she saw was him.

For long, frantic heartbeats, their gazes collided and tumbled over each other like stones in a landslide. But his gaze revealed nothing, nothing, and then he twisted back and bent his head to hear the words of his affianced bride.

Something fierce seared through Juno's veins. *No, he's mine!* she wanted to yell. She wanted to tear out that lady's hair and scratch out her eyes and hurl her out a window for good measure. *You don't know him. You'll never know him, never own him, not until you've seen his wild heart. He's mine!*

Her feet began propelling her forward; she realized her madness and yanked herself back, only to trip and stumble on nothing. She knocked into someone: a middle-aged gentleman.

Their catalogues fluttered to the floor; she scooped them up while he straightened his hat. Her cheeks burned as they exchanged apologies and assured each other no harm was done. Then the gentleman moved on, and Beatrice was there, eyes wide.

"What are you up to, Juno?" she said. "It is not like you to be clumsy."

Juno smoothed down her pelisse and patted her bonnet. She imagined Leo's amusement at her collision, Leo saying, *See? Your mind is already addled.*

"The adverse side effects of drawing nudes," Juno muttered to her poor mistreated catalogue.

Then she remembered herself. Oh no! Please let Beatrice not have heard her careless words!

No. Fortunately, Beatrice's attention was directed elsewhere. Her eyes shone.

"Juno, darling, look! Look!" Juno didn't need to look. "'Tis the Duke of Dammerton and Miss Macey. Shall we talk to them? Would it be an imposition? We have been introduced. No, I ought not to talk to him. But you could talk to him. No, you ought not to talk to him."

Juno swiveled and catapulted herself toward another painting. "They are here to enjoy the art. It is best if we leave them alone."

Beatrice agreed, but she kept twisting her head for another look, like a spaniel straining against her leash. Juno forced her eyes onto the sliver of painting visible through the bodies. She would not so much as glance at Leo again.

Or at the lady he meant to marry, that clever, virtuous earl's granddaughter with twenty-five thousand pounds. Miss Macey looked very well. Stylish, nicely put together, pretty, young. And what of it? Juno thought grumpily. She could look well too, if she could spare a few hours each day on dressing, and had pots of money and a team of skilled maids. People always judged ladies by how accomplished they were, and never stopped to think how much more accomplished they would be if they didn't have to spend so much time fussing about their hair and their clothes. Of course, when Miss Macey was a duchess, every eye in the room would be on her, so she had to look good. *Rather her than me*, Juno thought, and resolutely turned to march on.

But suddenly Leo was there, right in front of them.

No, not Leo. The duke.

She searched his face hungrily, seeking something, anything. A hint of a smile, a glint in his eye, a shared memory, a whisper of intimacy.

Nothing. His face was an exquisite mask, indifferent and aloof.

Beatrice sank into a low curtsy and yanked at Juno's skirts, so she lowered her eyes and curtsied too.

"Your Grace, my husband and I would like to offer our sincerest felicitations upon your engagement," Beatrice said.

"Thank you, Mrs. Prescott. Are you enjoying the exhibition?"

"Very much indeed."

Then he turned his cool blue gaze on Juno. "Miss Bell. Your family is well, I trust? Your art progresses well?"

"Thank you, Your Grace. It is proving adequate."

There: pleasantries successfully exchanged. Now they would nod and part. Again.

Indeed, he was going. One foot slid back, just an inch, and his chin came up and his lips parted. He would bid them farewell and, once more, he would be gone.

"Will you stay in town for the summer?" she asked.

He blinked as if that were a shocking question. Then he gathered himself and said, "Brighton."

It was her turn to blink. Leo never went to Brighton. He held opinions on the *ton's* summer revelries there.

"I will accompany Miss Macey and her family," he added.

She should end this torture. She must stop talking. Release him. Let him go.

"When is the wedding?"

"September."

"Will your mother and sister have returned from Prussia by then?"

"My mother has indicated her intention to spend another year with her family."

Such trite nonsense! If only she could speak her true questions: *Under that aloof mask, are you roiling and tumbling, like I am? Do you still feel my touch as I feel yours? Do you think of me with pleasure, then rise to come and see me, only to catch yourself with a sharp pain as you realize it can never be? Or did our tryst achieve its aim? Have you made peace with the past? Do you feel nothing from this encounter but the awkwardness of meeting a former lover in a public place?*

She despised herself for her weakness, for she had no claim to him, not anymore. She had chosen to tread her own path, and that path had taken her further from him than ever before. She had burned her bridges, rendered herself permanently unsuitable for a respectable gentleman.

Now he was engaged to someone else, and that someone was in this room, and Juno had lost any right to ask for anything anymore.

Summer stretched before them. By the time the air cooled and the leaves turned orange, when children picked hazelnuts and men shot birds under crisp skies, skies the color of Leo's eyes, the eyes she would never paint, the mouth she would never again kiss, the heart she would never own—

By that time, Leo would be wed.

She must stop this. She must let him go.

Finally, she found the strength and grace to say, "I hope you'll be very happy."

But he was already looking elsewhere, saying absently, "I don't see any reason why not." Then he inclined his head. "If you'll excuse me, I must return to my party."

Beatrice was still there, though Juno had forgotten her, and Beatrice said, "And if I might be so bold, if Miss Macey were to want her portrait done——"

"Beatrice!" Juno stared at her in horror.

"Hush, Juno. It is my duty as your patroness to put you forward. Mrs. Green painted a portrait of the Duchess of Clarence, and you are more than her equal. His Grace doesn't mind, do you, Your Grace?"

"Not at all, Mrs. Prescott. I bid you both good day."

Having neatly sidestepped her offer, he moved away through the crowd.

Juno stared at the long, lean lines of his back. She had last seen that back covered by only a shirt, as he sat on the side of the bed, making the confession that upended her world.

But then the crowd had the kindness to close around them, and all Juno could see was his departing hat.

CHAPTER 22

W hen the hackney cab stopped outside Juno's house late that evening, she scrambled out of it as fast as she could. The wretched day had dissolved into an even more wretched evening, haunted by Leo's coldness. Her heart was as crowded with emotions as that art gallery had been with Londoners. Anger, hurt, bewilderment, longing, regret: They were all milling about inside her and treading on each other's toes.

As the cab trundled away, a figure emerged from the shadows across the street. Her heart thumped. Fear hurried her feet toward the door.

Only to stop: The figure was Leo, looking less than impeccable. Indeed, he looked downright disheveled, as he weaved his way across the street toward her.

The glow of the full moon, peeking out from behind its blanket of rainclouds, lent him an ethereal look, casting eerie shadows over his face and shimmering over the white of his waistcoat and cravat. If this were a painting, she'd title it *The Haunting.*

"Leo? What are you doing here?"

"I was in the neighborhood." He spoke carefully, as if he needed to create each word anew.

"What, pray, brings a duke to this neighborhood in the middle of the night?"

"There was a dinner. Then a ball. Then a game of cards."

"I suspect there might have been some drinking too."

He considered this, then said, "I concede there may have been some drinking too."

The clouds shifted. Moonlight filled the street. Leo's gaze shifted too, focused on her. Suddenly, all the parts of her he had touched with his fingers, and the parts he had touched with his tongue, and the parts he had touched with his words—all those parts seared into life as his gaze swept over her.

But he was engaged to someone else, and there was nothing she could do. Because he had made a choice and he had not chosen her, and this was the way the world worked, and it was all for the best.

Yet still his confession echoed in her mind: Once upon a time, when they were different people, the one he had chosen was her.

The moment passed, as a cool breeze rippled around them and blew the clouds back over the moon. The air grew heavier with the threat of rain.

She did not know what he wanted.

She did not even know what *she* wanted.

"I saw you today," he said, words ever so slightly slurred. "Spanish art, and sad-eyed madonnas, and there you were."

"Yes."

"I *saw* you."

She waited. She had never seen Leo drunk before.

"That must not happen again," he added.

"Encountering each other in a public place?"

"Should not happen."

"Are you to dictate where in London I may go, for fear of

treading in your path? Duke or not, you do not tell me where I can go. *You* can avoid *me*."

"I'm doing a fine job of that so far."

A single fat raindrop fell on his cheek. Another landed on the street. Neither moved.

Then words were raining out of her too.

"You turned my world upside down," she said. "With what you told me about … Vienna."

"I swore I'd never tell you."

"Why not?"

"Man has his pride."

"I always sensed walls between us and now I know why. Why did you tell me?"

He breathed out audibly. "You thought I thought you were not good enough for me. For ten years, you believed that. I did not want you to think I think—" He paused, frowning, and started again. "I do not want you to think that *anyone* thinks you are not good enough. You are good enough for anyone. They —*we*—they must try to be good enough for you."

Was he speaking as a friend? As a lover? He cared for her. Maybe he even loved her, though "love" was such a complex, circumstantial word, it really was quite useless.

Love had no relevance now, anyway. Not for them.

"You will be happy, won't you?" She stepped closer, her chest tight with urgency. "With … your next marriage? She understands you, doesn't she? It matters, Leo. It matters for you to be…"

"Happy. That is what you think?"

She sniffed. "I think you are drunk."

"Yes."

"And I think you are saying things you would not say if you were sober."

"Perhaps. But perhaps they are things I should say. I don't drink much normally. I wanted to stop seeing you."

"You've not seen me in a fortnight."

"I see you all the time. Do you know... My life is order. Society is order. You see the stars and the planets up there?" He waved wildly at the thick clouds smothering the sky. "All in order. Until you. One kiss and my life is havoc. And that mermaid. That bloody mermaid."

He stared at her accusingly, as one stared at the perpetrator of a crime. Then he swiped his hand over his face and spun and pressed his palm against the wall. His fingers curled as if he wished to claw out a handful of stone.

"Leo? Why are you here?"

His only response was to slap the wall. He winced.

"Did that hurt?"

"Yes."

As if she were drunk too, she took his hand in hers. Her fingers sought out the newly abused skin and slid over his palm. She was surprised to trace the rough ghost of calluses. His palms had been smooth when they caressed her skin.

She wished to press this hand to her mouth, her cheek, her breast. She wished to tangle her fingers with his and lead him upstairs.

"If there are consequences," he said, "you must tell me."

"Did you come here to say that?"

"We were not careful. I meant to be careful. But I lost control."

"We were careful enough. You have no awkward obligations looming." Her monthly had come as usual. "You said it was a mistake," she added. "When you were leaving, after we argued. You said it was a mistake."

"I regret..." he started.

243

She did not know if he withdrew his hand or if she dropped it. "You regret... What?"

He fumbled in a pocket, found a glove.

"You regret ... our night together?"

He merely shook his head.

"So you still believe it was a mistake." Her mouth was dry, her words hoarse.

"A mistake!" He laughed, a soft, rueful sound. "Yes, I would say that. I can't..." He looked around, as if coming out of a fugue state and realizing where he was. "I'm doing it again," he said, as if to himself, and she had no idea what he meant. "I swore I wouldn't, but I am."

More fat insistent raindrops fell, slow and heavy like a funeral drum.

He would get wet. She should ask him inside. She could not ask him inside. He would have a carriage. Indecision froze her.

Then he shook his head and stumbled back away from her.

"I'm foxed," he said. "Don't listen to me. I should never have come here. Forgive me."

Then he was gone, down the road, to where a carriage waited, she now saw. He climbed inside, and she stared at its lights as it trundled away, while the heavy raindrops slapped her skin.

THE NEXT MORNING, Juno awoke on the daybed in her studio with a crick in her neck. She winced at the aggressive daylight, then at the pages of useless drawings carpeting the floorboards, and then at a bright-eyed Beatrice bounding in.

From the sitting room came the sound of Mrs. Kegworth rattling around with a tea tray. Yawning, Juno tugged on her dressing gown and blinked blearily at her guest.

"You must forgive me for calling on you like this, but really!" Beatrice poked her. "Still abed at this hour. What are these drawings? Surely these are not yours?"

The offending drawings were simple sketches of cats, flowers, hands. At least she drew.

I regret… A mistake…

How did one draw regret?

"I was practicing technique," Juno mumbled.

Beatrice wasn't interested. "I have decided on the solution to our problem," she said.

Rubbing her eyes, Juno stumbled into the sitting room and sat down. Steam rose from the teapot. It took her a moment to understand what she was seeing: The teapot was from the service Leo had promised to send over, the one painted with a goddess for each season.

"Our problem?" Juno repeated. "We have a problem?"

"Have you forgotten so soon? The question of how I shall gain entry into the highest echelons of society. Which is important for you and your career."

"Oh. That problem."

"I do hope you haven't been drinking. Prescott cannot abide it when a woman drinks."

Juno let her head fall back on the settee. "Prescott's views on my activities are irrelevant. Your husband can dictate your behavior, but he has no say over mine."

"But what you do reflects on me. He was very clear about that when I took you on." Beatrice peered at her and laughed. "You're quite grumpy when you don't get enough sleep, aren't you?"

"Apparently."

"The Duke and Duchess of Dammerton," Beatrice announced.

Juno bowed forward and pressed her palms into her eye sockets until little lights appeared.

"You must persuade the duke to let you paint them together as a wedding gift. Suggest we meet them in Brighton. Once society learns they are to sit for you, everyone will want your art and my acquaintance."

"No," Juno said into her hands. "Let them be."

"It is a useful connection. He came to speak to us yesterday. Do you not realize what an honor that was? No more coyness, Juno. We can use your connection with the duke—"

"No!" Juno's head jerked up. "Leo—the duke, he and his wife —betrothed—person. They are not *things* to be used for our benefit."

"Of course, of *course*, but you could ask him—"

"I could not. I will not."

Beatrice narrowed her eyes, hands on hips. "I need this, Juno."

"If you must use someone, use your husband. London's foremost art critic, remember? Talk to him."

"I tried." Her mouth trembled. "It's so easy for you, isn't it? Living independently, not following anyone's rules. I cannot ask my husband—"

"You cannot speak to the father of your children, but you expect me to impose upon a duke of the realm and a lady to whom I have never been introduced? I shall not, Beatrice. No."

"If you want me as your patroness, you will do this."

"Then the cost of your patronage is too high."

A harsh silence tumbled around them, broken only by Beatrice's shuddering breaths.

"You ungrateful wretch!" she hissed. "You are just another artist in London, Juno Bell. But I can elevate you. You know I can. I can make you into something more."

"You cannot make me into anything." Juno jumped to her feet so violently the tea things rattled. "I make myself."

"You need me."

"I need no one." Suddenly it was important for everyone to know that. "You can go, everyone can go, but I have myself and my art and I need nothing else."

"That is it? You refuse to help me and you refuse my patronage?"

"I don't need you," she repeated shakily.

"So be it then."

Without another word, Beatrice gathered her skirts and her dignity and swept out.

Groaning, Juno lay back on the settee, staring unseeingly at her paintings on the wall. She tried to rouse some anger or concern, but everything felt flat. All she could see was Leo the night before. All she could hear were his drunken words. Saying he regretted— What did he regret? He had not been clear. But he thought their tryst a mistake: He had been clear about that.

And something about the mermaid drawing.

Suddenly alert, she dashed into her studio and dug the drawing out of the armoire. It was as good as she remembered, from the passions of the figures to the turmoil of the storm.

Excitement surged through her, and she leaped into action like an opera dancer at her cue. She set a blank canvas on an easel, opened her box of paints, ran her fingers over the bladders of hues, closed her eyes, and imagined the scene in full color.

And then she was back in that bed with Leo, reliving those moments when he had opened himself to her, when they created a storm together, when that fierce, possessive hunger claimed them both. She had possessed him. Only for a few minutes perhaps, but in those minutes, he had belonged completely and utterly to her.

"Mrs. Kegworth!" she called, hearing the housekeeper in the

parlor. "Bar the doors. I will receive no guests. I am going to paint."

Paint she did. Over the next few days, that painting came to life, while Mrs. Kegworth steadfastly kept friends and visitors away.

Until her aunt Hester appeared in the studio door, twitchy and distressed, a twisted newspaper in her hands.

"Oh, Juno, my dear," Hester said sadly. "What have you done?"

CHAPTER 23

T he cut-glass goblet was exquisite. It was gently curved and beautifully weighted right down its teardrop stem. Sunlight caught in its diamond-shaped cuts and danced over the green velvet on which it was displayed.

Leo found it hard to care. *It's just a glass,* he thought. *Just a stupid bloody glass.*

But a hushed silence awaited his verdict. His visit to this small glassworks in Kent was of great consequence to its owners, who were desperate for a grant: He could change their lives with a stroke of his pen. And it was of consequence to Susannah, who had brought the glassmakers to his attention. She sought to impress him, he thought.

And he was impressed. It wasn't the glass's fault he didn't care, or the glassmakers' fault, or Susannah's.

It was nobody's fault but his own. He was the one who had approached Juno at that exhibition. He was the one who drank too much for the first time in years. He was the one who wound up on her street to make a fool of himself and say he knew not what.

But that temporary insanity had passed along with the hangover, which itself was just departing when they arrived at Susannah's aunt's house in Kent for a week-long stay. Susannah and her aunt had a range of activities planned: walks, boating, carriage rides. It sounded blissfully dull, and it removed him from London, and anywhere that was not London was an excellent place to be.

So Leo feigned interest, toured the workshop, asked simple questions to put them at their ease. Then he accepted their gift of a set of goblets and left with his smiling betrothed.

It was a fine day. When Leo suggested they leave the carriage and walk the few miles back to her aunt's house, Susannah agreed.

A dim memory stirred: Juno mentioning Susannah that night. Saying … what? That she hoped Susannah understood him. Well, of course Susannah understood him. Would any other lady in England think to take him to a glassworks in Kent?

"What do you say?" she asked. "Might they be a candidate for a grant from the Dammerton Foundation?"

"If you wish."

"I shall put them on my list. There is an interesting Norman church in the village," she added. "We could look at the carvings."

Leo did not give a damn about the Normans or their carvings. "Excellent," he said.

Susannah seemed to feel no need to say anything more. As usual, she displayed no interest in sharing her thoughts, or in any aspect of Leo at all.

Just as well, considering.

He had not kissed her. She made no sign of expecting a kiss, nor had she said anything that even the most hopeless romantic might mistake for flirtation. They were becoming friends and she seemed content with that. Leo was too, of course. Perfectly content.

He liked Susannah. Trouble was, he wasn't sure he liked himself when he was with her. He felt artificial, somehow. Guilt made him try too hard, though he had no reason to feel guilty because he had tried to be honest with her, at least as honest as she would allow. But somehow his essence seemed to be draining away, rendering him no more substantial than a title in a suit of clothes.

Beautiful clothes, to be sure, but mere clothing nonetheless.

In the churchyard, Susannah guided him past an ancient yew tree and pointed at an old stone archway. She launched into an animated history of the church, something about the Normans and saints and grotesques. Lots of facts. Susannah liked facts. She liked lists. She liked order.

"Susannah," he said, interrupting her recitation.

She turned, ever pleasant, a familiar stranger. "Yes?"

"I thought perhaps I might kiss you now."

"Very well." She folded her hands and lifted her chin.

"This is an important part of marriage," he said.

"Yes. I do hope we are blessed with children."

Kiss her now, he told himself, but his hands remained clasped behind his back. A kiss to his betrothed did not demand an explanation, yet still he said, "I'm sure your mother or grandmother has explained it to you."

"I'm aware of the facts, yes."

"I shall do everything in my power to make it pleasant. You have no cause for concern."

She cleared her throat. "How very considerate."

"Although I suppose saying there is no cause for concern makes it sound as if there might actually be some cause for concern. Which of course there isn't."

She looked perplexed. "I never expected to discuss it," she said after a pause.

"Neither did I. Which might be why I am making such a hash of it."

It was only a kiss. She was pretty. He liked her. They would marry soon. He could do this.

Her gaze flicked from side to side. She fidgeted with her thumbs.

"Of course, there's plenty of time," he said. "No need to rush into anything."

"Of course."

She sounded relieved. She stepped back and, in tacit agreement, they left the churchyard for the road.

Yes, Leo reminded himself, no need to rush her into a kiss. He had plenty of time.

Indeed, he had the rest of his life.

BACK AT THE HOUSE, they learned the party had been enlivened by the arrival of Susannah's cousin with a trio of his friends. The pack of young gentlemen were now making merry in the drawing room with the ladies.

Not quite together, however: The groups had segregated, as groups of English were wont to do, with the ladies at one end and the gentlemen at the other.

Leo headed past the ladies toward the lively quartet of young men, grateful for the letters a footman had handed him, which gave him a reason not to talk. He leaned against the mantelpiece to read them. One letter was from the archbishop's secretary: The special license for Thomas Macey was ready for Leo to collect.

The other letter was franked from Leo's household and addressed in his half-brother's hand.

What an astounding notion: St. Blaise actually knew where the writing desk was. Perhaps he had stumbled upon it while stealing an ink pot.

The letter was a mere note, short, cryptic, and surprisingly legible:

Polly—Have you seen this? She won't receive me. T.

"This" turned out to be a clipping from *The Times*. How impressive: St. Blaise had exerted the effort to cut something out of a newspaper. More impressive: St. Blaise had actually read a newspaper.

Dear Sir— the item began, as all letters to the editor of *The Times* began. Leo glanced at the bottom. This letter writer was William Prescott.

Dear Sir—

It has come to my attention that a woman in London, styling herself as an artist, has engaged in the immoral behavior of drawing figures, male and female, in a state of undress.

Leo gripped the clipping in both hands. He fell back against the mantel. Its edge dug into his back. He took a deep breath. He scanned Prescott's letter.

No respectable woman would ever… Miss J— B—… My lady wife cruelly misled… Only certain genres of art are suitable… Moral indecency…

He had ruined her.

With this letter to the editor of *The Times*, William bloody Prescott must have ruined Juno. Her career in London would be over, for who would accept a woman who drew figures in a state of undress?

Leo scrunched the cutting into a ball. Straightened it out. Folded it in half. In half again. Put it back into St. Blaise's letter. Folded the page over it.

This letter needed burning, but no fire was lit in the hearth. He slid the page into his pocket. Withdrew his trembling hands.

It was none of his concern.

Juno made her own choices. She knew the risks. It was not his concern.

"Any interesting correspondence, Dammerton?"

Susannah had entered the drawing room, having refreshed herself. For a moment, Leo was confused as to where he was.

"Ah." He glanced down at the other letter and forced his memory to work. "An appointment with the archbishop," he said. He had not told her he was acquiring a special license for her brother. "He has requested my advice."

Her eyes widened.

"On matters decorative, not ecclesiastical, I assure you." He tried to inject some levity into his tone, but only sounded like a buffoon, and like a buffoon he added, "Cloths and clocks and so forth."

"How lovely."

She was already moving, to sit with the ladies.

Leo leaned back against the mantelpiece.

It wasn't his concern. Whatever Prescott had done, whatever Juno had suffered, it was not his concern. Honor came first. He owed his loyalty to Susannah, not to Juno.

Loud laughter burst from the party of young men, quickly suppressed.

"Don't see the problem," one said, then added, in a lower voice, "Art is full of nude pictures."

"Those nude pictures you look at ain't art," one of his friends joked.

"'Tis not right for a woman to draw nudes."

"Right, women should *be* the nudes!"

Once again they laughed, then once again hushed each other, aware of the ladies down the other end of the room.

London would be alive with such bawdy chatter and jokes at Juno's expense, and she would—

It was *not* his concern.

"It's nonsense, this notion that women are more delicate than men," one young fellow said. "Last woman who saw me in the buff, she didn't so much as blush."

"They say that every year at the Royal Academy, some student faints the first time a model drops her robe."

"Think I fainted my first time too!"

Then Leo was moving, his legs propelling him down the drawing room, so fast the air seemed to rush around him. The ladies stopped talking and stared at him in surprise.

"Dammerton?" Susannah said.

"I must return to London," he heard himself say. "Urgent matter."

"The archbishop's decor?" She sounded incredulous.

"Yes. Do excuse me. I must go."

They were staring at him as if he were a madman. Perhaps he was a madman. No matter: He was a duke. If he said he must leave, then no one would comment on it. At least, not to his face.

He bowed. Spun on his heel.

He walked until he was out of the room.

Then he ran.

Juno's task was simple: Take each prop out of her cabinet and pack it into the crate.

But all she could do was stare at the array of whimsical gifts she'd received from Leo over the years. His first gift: a violin so she could complete a commission. His final gift: the conch shell.

She still had to pack her secret paintings too, secret because the figures wore no clothes. What a scandal! For a woman to paint like a man! How dare she paint a mermaid claiming a ship-wrecked sailor, or Hypatia being dragged over stones by a murderous mob. What on earth was she to *do* with these paint-ings? Mustn't let anyone see them. Mustn't let anyone know she painted nudes.

Laughter erupted out of her, so wild she feared losing control. She looked for the cats to soothe her, but Livia and Phoebe had already taken them away, and now her studio was truly nothing more than an empty room.

Her family had stood by her while her world collapsed, though they really ought not to. Her uncle Gordon said he did not care for others' opinions; his career was fine. Phoebe said she did not care, for she'd already ruined herself by leaving her husband. Livia said she did not care, for she did not even want a husband. Daniel said he did not care, for it only made him more interesting among the lads. Even Hadrian came rushing back to London, once he heard the news, and said he did not care, because the government needed him too much. They'd all gath-ered around her, and she did not deserve them when she had been such a fool.

But their support changed nothing. She was finished in London and there was nothing anyone could do.

It was the letters that convinced Juno she had truly lost everything.

Of course, she had known as soon as Hester showed it to her that Prescott's letter to the editor of *The Times* spelled the end, but it hadn't seemed quite real.

Then the other letters came.

Letters from future clients, canceling their appointments. Letters from past clients, expressing their disgust. Some even returned the portraits she had painted of them; apparently, one could catch a nasty case of moral indecency simply by viewing a painting by Juno Bell.

There were kind letters too, from her friends in the countryside, Arabella and Cassandra. They could not be with her, both now in the business of producing babies, but they offered to send carriages, promising her a home, somewhere to rest until it all blew over.

It would not blow over. An aristocrat could weather a scandal. An artist could too, provided that artist was sufficiently charming, talented, and male. But an unmarried woman? Her career in London was finished.

And that was nobody's fault but her own.

Oh, she could rant about Prescott, or the injustices of society, but she had known the rules and the risks. She had done as she pleased anyway. Why? Because she had *wanted* to.

Because she was headstrong and foolish and arrogant enough to think the rules did not apply to her. As if she were someone special.

She was no one special.

Restless, she roamed away from the cabinet, stared out the window at the dismal London day. Well, at least in Italy she would see the sun.

She was still staring out the window when she heard footsteps, slow, steady, somewhere in the next room. She ignored them. Until the glass reflected a movement behind her.

A slender male figure stood in the doorway of her studio.

As Leo had stood in that doorway so many times.

She closed her eyes and hugged herself. It could not be Leo, which meant she was finally going mad, but she didn't care. She let her senses track the movements. The gentle thud of bootheels on wooden floorboards. The stirring of the air. The warmth of a presence behind her, close enough that she could feel his essence, catch his scent.

His arms slid around her. Enfolded her in their warmth.

She let herself rest against the solidity of his chest. His hands found hers. He entwined their fingers. He rested his head lightly against hers. His hair tickled her temple.

Hot tears escaped her shut eyelids and trickled down her cheeks.

"Hush," he murmured. "Hush."

"You're here." Her voice came out as a broken whisper. She swallowed, tried again. "You're here."

Everything felt right, in color, in harmony, in balance. Leo was with her; the rest of the world could go hang. Nothing else mattered.

Nothing except the fact that he was promised to someone else and she was London's newest scandal.

Suddenly, she could not bear it. She could not bear his presence, his kindness, his support, his friendship, because he would take them all away when he left her again.

He had rejected her love. Called her inconstant, ended their friendship, got engaged to someone else, brushed her off coolly, and then he had come to her when drunk and dismissed their one hour of true intimacy as a mistake.

She wrenched herself from his arms, swiped at her eyes, and turned to face him.

Oh, but he looked wonderful, a balm to her soul, with his expression soft and caring, his eyes deep with concern.

"You ought not to be here," she said dully.

"I just heard," he said. "If I can offer assistance."

"There is nothing to be done."

"What do you need?"

She needed him to hold her. Just hold her and hold her and hold her.

Shaking her head, she backed away. Her knees hit the window seat, which halted her retreat. "Perhaps you mean to be kind, but this is too…"

Cruel, she wanted to say.

It was too cruel of him to offer her kindness. Not when his kindness could only be temporary and she needed it so much.

He glanced around the threadbare studio. "Where are your family and friends? Who is helping you?"

"The artists will not come near me. The adverse side effects of painting nudes are contagious and they have put me in quarantine so no one catches my shocking moral indecency."

"You have powerful friends, wealthy friends. Lady Hardbury? Mrs. DeWitt? Have they abandoned you?"

"Arabella and Cassandra cannot leave their babies, but they offer to send carriages. They will put me in their attics to paint pictures and hide from their respectable guests." She twisted her fingers in the curtain. "My aunt and uncle have taken the cats to live as lazy mousers in their London house. They will have a nice life and soon they will forget me, because that is what cats do." Then, because anger always proved an excellent defense against sorrow and fear, she added, "That is what I do too, I hear. Forget people."

"I—" He stopped short.

"You—what? You would wave some ducal wand and fix everything? Will you hide me in your attic too, and keep me secret from your lovely lady wife? 'Tis all right, Leo. You don't have to look after me. I have no one to blame but myself."

"Prescott is a pompous, narrow-minded prig."

She laughed shakily. "Yes. He is. But he is the voice of a society, and it is stronger than me and it is stronger than you. There is nothing you can do. I want nothing from you anyway."

He didn't answer. He turned to pace through the studio. His footsteps echoed through the hollowed-out room. She drank in the sight of him, so impeccably dressed, all familiar lines and fluid grace.

"I have booked passage to Italy," she added jauntily. "I leave late tomorrow night, and that is how it goes. Mrs. Prescott has behaved well and I have behaved badly, so she will host a ball and I shall flee on a boat. Maybe after Italy, I'll go to France. There are so many places in Europe I can go. They do not care about some silly English scandal. It is not so bad, you know. I'll be free of London's rules, at least. I'll paint whatever I please and have whatever experiences I want."

He stopped before her row of secret paintings and studied them in silence.

"Here they are," he said softly. "The paintings you did not want me to see."

Fondness infused his expression as he looked at her. No, not *at* her: He looked right *into* her, seeing her deepest parts. He saw her dark shadowy corners, her secret landscapes, her foolishness, her regrets, her loneliness, her passions.

Curse him. How dare he! How dare he understand her and accept her, when he had not chosen her. He cared about her, she knew that, but that was not enough, not enough for him to show up here and—

"Go," she said, the word tearing through her.

"Juno—"

"There is nothing you can do. You cannot help."

He waited.

"Leo, please leave. I cannot bear to see you anymore."

CHAPTER 24

J uno's usually rosy complexion was pale. Her eyes were dull and shadowed. Even her boisterous hair looked defeated.

Leo would burn down the world if it brought warmth into her cheeks, command the sun to shine if it might dispel those shadows. He would hold her until her tears went away.

It was not the tears she wanted gone, but him.

It occurred to him that this was the first time she had ever sent him away. He had always taken her welcome for granted. Today, he was no longer welcome.

And today, when she needed him most, when the world had stolen her verve and livelihood and dreams, he could do nothing.

Those other paintings—he had never seen them before, but he recognized them all the same. They formed the gallery of her hidden heart. She had shown him her secret places, and he had shown her his. She had seen him flawed and foolish and out of control, and she had claimed to love him anyway.

He had not dared to believe in her love, for fear she might break his heart again, yet his heart was shattering anyway, because she had lost everything, and there was nothing—nothing—*nothing* he could do.

She stood straight and did not relent.

He stepped back. He bowed. He turned. He left.

On the street, the horses were stamping their feet after the hazy, too-fast drive from Kent. He told the coachman to take the carriage home, tend to the horses; he would walk.

Rage propelled him through the streets, his usual unhurried pace transformed into a relentless march. He hardly knew where he went or what to do. The only place he wanted to be was by Juno's side; the only thing he wanted to do was fix everything for her.

He could not. She was right: It was bigger and stronger than he was.

He could marry her. That would save her reputation. No one would dare snub a duchess. But she did not want to be a duchess. She did not want him.

I have booked my passage to Italy. I leave tomorrow night.

How brittle she had looked, how desolate and lost. She was crumbling, and he could not hold her together.

All his money and power, and he could do nothing. He was a duke, a bloody *duke*, but one spiteful letter from one nasty small-minded hypocrite could destroy her world and he could do *nothing*. She was hurting—*Juno was hurting*—and he could not stop her pain. He could not even hold her because he was promised to another woman, and besides, she did not want him; she had made that plain.

On and on he marched, faster and faster, slicing his walking stick through the air. He found himself passing through Leicester Square, along St. Martin's Lane. He found himself passing a coffee house popular with artists. He found himself staring at a square, compact man, in crisp black and white clothes, holding court before a group of hangers-on.

William bloody Prescott himself.

"Prescott!" Leo yelled, and hurtled toward him like a cannon-ball, half blinded by the blood rushing behind his eyes.

A dozen faces turned. He saw only one. The circle of artists scattered like goats.

"You pompous, prick-faced parasite," Leo spat. "I'll pull you apart with my bare hands and feed you to the rats."

Prescott stepped back, hands wide. "Dammerton! Your Grace!"

He kept advancing. "You lily-livered lump of—"

"Please. Your Grace. Calm down."

"I am calm," Leo roared. "I am completely bloody calm!"

Again like goats, the scattered artists re-formed into a circle to watch, along with a few other passersby.

Leo backed the critic up against the stone wall, pressed the head of his walking stick under his chin, and loomed over him.

"Does it feel good, Prescott?" he hissed in his ear. "To play God with others' lives? To make yourself the righteous judge of how people are to behave?"

Prescott's mouth twisted into something like a sneer. "I shine a light on art. I guide people. I provide a service."

"The only service you provide is saving other people the trouble of having to think for themselves."

"If an artist behaves badly—"

"Artists are supposed to behave badly!"

Prescott sidestepped toward the door of the coffeehouse; Leo swiftly blocked his path.

"I had to protect my wife," Prescott said. "Her reputation could have been harmed."

"If you'd kept your mouth shut and she'd quietly severed the connection, no one's reputation would have been harmed. But you *wanted* to expose her."

"It is unacceptable for a woman to—"

"Poor little Prescott, how scared you must be. If the world changes, you'll lose your position and power, so you must make sure the world doesn't change." Leo stepped back. "You call yourself a critic, but you are nothing but a narrow-minded, lily-livered, yellow-bellied coward."

Prescott set his shoulders. "I'll thank you not to malign my honor as a critic and a gentleman."

Leo smiled. That was, he bared his teeth. "How can I malign your honor when you have none?"

An intake of breath whooshed through their audience: That insult was a shootable offense. A gentleman's honor was too valuable a concern to withstand such a slight.

Prescott looked uncertain. "For the sake of my wife, I—"

"Oh, sod your bloody wife!"

Everyone fell quiet. Half of London fell quiet. First Prescott went very white, then he went very red. He began to tussle with his glove.

"Your Grace, you will not speak of my wife thus."

"What will you do about it, Prescott?" Leo taunted him. "Write a letter to the editor of *The Times*?"

Prescott pulled off his glove and flapped it in the air between them. One flaccid finger slapped Leo's chin. They both stared at it, surprised.

But, having launched his challenge, Prescott committed. "Name your second, Dammerton."

Leo's rage subsided. "A duel. Nice. Thank you. I would very much like the opportunity to shoot you." He laughed roughly. "You deserve it, for ruining an innocent with your—"

"She's no innocent. I wrote nothing but the truth from my wife. I am only glad she herself never saw such sordid filth."

Leo cocked his head. "If Mrs. Prescott never saw the artwork, then how did she know of it?"

"She wouldn't say, only that she heard of the drawings from someone else."

A fresh ribbon of rage waved inside him. "So, you ruined her based on rumor alone."

He had assumed Mrs. Prescott had seen the drawings herself, or Juno had confided in her. But if Mrs. Prescott had learned of the drawings from someone else…

He spun around. A small crowd had gathered to watch. A larger crowd had gathered to find out what the small crowd was watching.

Leo raised his voice to address them all. "Anyone know where I might find my fair brother, Tristan St. Blaise? Think before you speak, for I mean to kill him. Who'd like to watch?"

A DUKE STALKING through the streets on a mission to murder his own half-brother was exactly the sort of entertainment London was in the mood for.

Leo had attracted something of an entourage by the time he stormed into the gaming hell in Covent Garden where St. Blaise was rumored to be.

Rumor was right.

St. Blaise lolled at a gaming table, cards in hand, looking slightly drunk and eminently punchable. Leo shoved through the other men and grabbed his brother by his lapels. Playing cards fluttered madly. He hauled him away from the table and up against a wall.

The confused hubbub of excited chatter faded into silence.

"Polly dearest!" St. Blaise said. "I'm very happy to see you too. What have I done to deserve such brotherly affection?"

"Why did you do it?" he hissed.

"Do what? There are so many possibilities to choose from."

Leo didn't dare speak her name. "Why reveal her secrets and ruin her?"

"I say, you are in a state, aren't you?" A half-smile twisted St. Blaise's lips. A sly, calculating look entered his eyes. "The gentlemen of London have been waiting a long time for this. Shall we see what happens next?"

An alert sounded somewhere in Leo's brain. He ignored it.

St. Blaise craned his neck to bring his face close. "How about I marry her?" he offered softly, on a brandy-scented breath. "You'll have to give me lots of money, but we'll leave England. And if she's pregnant with your whelp, I'll raise the child."

Leo shoved him back against the wall. "She trusted you. What did she ever do to you?"

"Refused to tup me," St. Blaise sighed. "Maybe now she will. I don't even mind that my little half-brother had her first. You did, didn't you? Maybe you should thank me. Maybe now she'll be desperate enough to become your mistress. That's what you want, isn't it? Marry your earl's girl, like the good boy you are, then keep that luscious lady on the side, just like Papa Duke did with our mothers. I saw the way you looked at her. With hungry eyes."

He kept going, but Leo didn't hear. He released him long enough to draw back his fist and fire off a punch.

St. Blaise stepped aside. Leo's fist slammed into air. He stumbled, then spun, to see his brother's cheeky grin.

It occurred to Leo that this was his first fistfight in approximately fifteen years, whereas St. Blaise probably fought other men nightly for fun.

He feinted, swung again. This time, he somehow caught his target's cheek.

"Not the face," St. Blaise protested, and lunged for Leo's head.

"Not the hair," Leo said, and jerked his head away.

They stared at each other, ten years old again, reliving the day Papa Duke first brought them together, so hopelessly, optimistically sure that his two eldest sons would take to each other. They had taken to each other, all right: They had taken to each other with their fists. Leo cursed him: Tristan St. Blaise, usurper, heartbreaker, mischief maker. This had been a long time coming.

With a cackle of laughter, St. Blaise spun away and bounded up onto the nearest card table, chips and cards scattering under his feet. Leo leaped up after him. Again he swung. Again he missed.

Still laughing, St. Blaise jumped from table to table, Leo bounding close behind.

On one of the larger tables, Leo finally snared his elbow. He yanked him around. This time, St. Blaise stayed to fight, while the table creaked under their feet and the crowd cheered from the floor. He was making a fool of himself, Leo realized through the haze of anger. His fists never made contact, and St. Blaise was doing nothing more than dodging Leo's punches and messing up his clothes and hair.

He stopped, breathing heavily. St. Blaise was a trained, experienced soldier, for pity's sake.

Although he did have a gratifyingly red welt on one cheek.

St. Blaise shook his head, looking Leo over. "How do you do that? I messed you up, but still your hair looks superb."

"And I punched you, but still your face looks—"

"Superb?"

"In need of a punch."

He advanced, determined to wipe that smirk off once and for all.

"Polly, Polly, Polly." St. Blaise held up his hands in a sign of peace. They both knew, now, that he could easily wrestle Leo to the ground and pummel him to a pulp. "Face it. You don't know how to throw a decent punch."

"But I do know how to fire a gun."

"Do you?" He sounded genuinely curious. "Really?"

"Yes. Really. Name your second. I'll shoot you tomorrow at dawn."

St. Blaise sighed. "Could we do it in the afternoon, though? Let me have some sleep."

"You'll sleep when you're dead."

Leo took his time straightening his clothes, then lightly jumped down onto the floor.

Grins faltered before his glare. Silence rippled outward and a path opened up before him. He'd taken barely two steps toward the exit when another cheer burst through the room.

St. Blaise, still on the table, was making his bow.

"It is done and won!" he cried. "The Duke of Dammerton yelled at me, struck me, *and* called me out. The pot is mine! One thousand pounds!"

St. Blaise met Leo's eyes. Grinning broadly, he bowed again.

"You ruined someone to enrage me for a *wager*?" Leo said. "Cold comfort when you die."

"I didn't do it, in truth. I only said I did because I saw an excellent opportunity to anger you."

"I'll still shoot you. No one speaks of her like that and lives."

"You won't shoot me, Polly. Papa Duke told you to look after me."

"I'll look after your corpse. Give you a nice funeral and send your winnings to your mother." He touched a finger to his brow. "See you at dawn, brother mine."

He spun back around. The crowd subdued before his scowl. Among the faces was a slack-jawed Thomas Macey. His mouth snapped shut when Leo informed him that he would be his second in the duel.

"But my—" Macey stepped closer and whispered, "I mean to be married again soon, recall. You promised a special license."

"And a license you will have." Leo clapped him on the shoulder. "So long as neither of us gets shot."

CHAPTER 25

The hammering on the front door vibrated through Juno's house, at the in-between hour when the first faint hints of daylight edged the corners of the sky.

She was already mostly awake, thanks to the eerie howling of a cat fight and the general discomfort of having slept in her clothes. But she had, at least, finally managed to pack up the last of her things.

Rumpled, bleary, and mumbling curses, she stumbled down the stairs to open the door. There was Beatrice Prescott's coachman, fist raised mid-thump, and Beatrice herself, face creased with worry.

Juno was suddenly very, very awake.

A swish of her arm sent the door slamming toward them, but the coachman caught it and Beatrice cried, "Oh, Juno. You must help me."

A bark of disbelieving laughter flew out of her. "*I? Help you?*"

"I know you detest me, and you'll never forgive me, for what I did was unforgivable, but they mean to shoot each other and I don't know how to make them stop."

"Who is going to shoot each other?"

"Have you not heard? Dammerton went mad! Completely mad! He assaulted Prescott, who called him out, and then Dammerton assaulted his own half-brother and called *him* out, and now they're all in the park counting their paces as we speak!"

Juno's heart stopped, then thumped, then did a few somersaults for good measure. Her eyes were on Beatrice, but all she saw was Leo: his face like stone when she sent him away, his bow so formal before he went. She had ordered him to leave, insisted he could do nothing, and he had— Started fights? *Leo?* How could this be? His weapons were chilly silence, a slicing set-down, a disappointed sigh. He didn't go around hitting people. He certainly didn't shoot them.

Or, heaven forbid, be shot.

Because of her?

"But why?" she asked.

"There is no time to discuss this! Our civilizing influence is required at haste! It is my ball tonight, and with Prescott in the middle of a scandal—"

"Do you think I care tuppence for your wretched ball? What if someone gets hurt?"

"Precisely." Beatrice leaned closer, as if confiding a terrible secret. "How often in one's life does one have the opportunity to stop a duel? Hmm?"

A herd of emotions stampeded right through Juno's feeble efforts to think. She grabbed up her outerwear and they piled into the carriage. The coachman near yodeled in excitement as he set the horses moving.

In the cramped space, Juno struggled to pull her pelisse over yesterday's gown and her bonnet over her morning hair. She had no choice but to tolerate Beatrice's help, along with her stream of insufferable chatter.

"Oh, Juno, I am so, so sorry for what we did to you. I wish I could undo it. There is no excuse. None! I was just so angry after those things you said, and so tired from how hard it's been, and I ranted at Prescott, and I said— Oh, I don't even know what I said, but I never dreamed the man would repeat it, let alone publish a letter for the entire world to see!"

Dressed, Juno fell back onto the seat. Beatrice fell back too.

"If only I could fix it for you, but I have ruined everything! I am a terrible patroness, a terrible friend, a terrible *person*. Oh, please forgive me! No, *never* forgive me."

Juno had little patience for this self-flagellation. "How did you even know about the figure drawing?" she asked. "Those drawings were well hidden. Was it Mr. St. Blaise who told you?"

"Heavens, no! I've never exchanged a word with that dreadful man in all my life."

"Then who told you?"

Beatrice's jaw dropped. "Why, you did, Juno. At the Spanish art exhibition, you said something about the effects of painting nudes."

Her fingers flew to cover her own open mouth. "I thought you didn't hear."

"I pretended not to. It was hardly a surprise. And, in truth, I don't care, though I could never admit *that* in public. But honestly, one cannot take two steps in an art gallery without seeing some man's painting of naked women, and I swear, if I see one more depiction of some mythical *ravishing*, I shall scream! Then those same men have the gall to pontificate about morals. Oh, I wish I hadn't told him, Juno. I've wrecked your career and destroyed our friendship, and now Prescott will be killed."

"And your ball will be ruined!"

"I know!" Beatrice wailed, then stopped short. "You are making fun of me. Precisely as I deserve."

Juno slumped back against the squabs. "It seems so unlikely

for the duke to brawl or duel." She forced a deep breath through her tight lungs. "What is the nature of their quarrel?"

"All Prescott told me is that the duke insulted me and his honor." She rolled her eyes. "Men say they keep such matters secret to preserve our delicate sensibilities, but I suspect they won't tell for fear we'll laugh at their shenanigans."

"But Leo—Dammerton—he doesn't hunt or shoot. I doubt he even knows how to duel."

"Oh, this lot are born knowing how to duel, aren't they? They have little practice duels in the nursery before their nanny brings their tea."

Leo was in this mess because of her, Juno was sure. What a fool he was, to risk his life at worst, his future at best. It was just as well that at four in the morning, less than twenty-four hours from now, her ship would sail for Naples. Their first kiss had thrown his life into a decade of chaos, he had told her. Once more she was creating havoc without meaning to. It was better she left.

But, by all the stars in the sky, she would ensure he was still alive and well when she left England's shore. Or she'd shoot the foolish man herself.

"You really don't want to do this, Polly."

"Oh, I really do."

Leo leaned back against a plane tree and stretched his legs out before him. The bark roughed his back; the ground chilled his seat. His clothes would be dirty, but he was too tired to move. His first duel and he was already bored with it. And how the devil was he supposed to shoot straight when he'd not had a wink of sleep?

St. Blaise, still in his evening clothes, was sprawled out on the grass alongside him.

Around them, mist billowed over the park and wreathed the trees, blending into the indecisive blue-gray of the pre-dawn sky. A few birds were beginning to stir, but nothing else moved. Three duelists meant three men were serving as second, yet not one of those three men had remembered to bring a surgeon, so the duel could not begin. Prescott's second had gone in search of one.

Meanwhile, St. Blaise's second had fallen asleep on the grass beside Thomas Macey, who cast occasional worried glances at his watch. Prescott sat alone on a log, with the air of a man who was reconsidering all his recent decisions, and possibly some of his older ones too.

Leo shifted on the hard, cold ground and studied the gun on his lap. An intricate mother-of-pearl inlay adorned its grip. It was nice to admire the mother-of-pearl, so he did not think about what came next. Once a gentleman was committed to a duel, it was out of his hands and he must go through with it, whether he wished to or not.

A duel was like a betrothal that way.

"Let's call it off," St. Blaise persisted. "You do realize a duel involves shooting? Of the two of us, one of us knows a lot about shooting and one of us knows a lot about embroidery."

"Papa Duke insisted I learn to shoot as a boy."

"And have you fired a gun in, say, the past fifteen years?"

Leo considered the gun. "Surely the mechanism has not changed much. Bullet, trigger, and so forth."

"I will have shot you and be tucked up in bed before you've even found the trigger."

"No, you won't. Because you'll do the decent thing for once in your life and stand still while I shoot you."

St. Blaise rose up onto his elbows. "I'll apologize to you, you apologize to Prescott. Everyone's honor will be satisfied, no blood shed, and we can chuckle about it over bacon and eggs. Come, doesn't bacon and eggs sound better than getting shot?"

Leo said nothing.

"I swear I told no one about modeling for Miss Bell," St. Blaise said. "I like Miss Bell. This is twice now, you've accused me of doing something I didn't do. Why must you always think the worst of me?"

"It's easier that way, I suppose." Leo sighed. "That was badly done and I apologize. But that doesn't excuse the way you spoke of her."

"Not my finest moment, I admit. I never touched her either, if that's your real reason for wanting to shoot me. She did refuse to tup me, but fair enough, I'd refuse to tup me too, if I had any say in the matter. You know I said those things only to make you livid and win that game. Gambling debts make a demanding mistress."

The sky was lightening. More birds stirred. It looked like Thomas Macey had nodded off too. Soon it would be too late for the duel, if this bloody surgeon didn't hurry up. Why bother with laws to prevent duels when ineptitude and liquor were so much more effective?

"What happened, Tristan?" Leo asked. "The gambling, the women, selling your commission... I thought you liked the army. You were an excellent cavalry officer, they said."

St. Blaise plucked a blade of grass and shredded it slowly. "There was a war on," he said after a while. "Not that war was enjoyable, but we had each other, and we had the horses, and we had a reason to get up each day. Then they sent me back to London, and they pinned a medal on my chest, and gave me plumes for my helmet and more plumes for my horse and..." He sighed. "I'm the first to admit I look very fetching in plumes, but there doesn't seem to be any *point*. That excitement of war—at the time, you hate it, but then you don't know how to carry on without it."

"So you make your own excitement."

"Because if you don't, there's too much time to think. It's nice to stop thinking. Just as you use your clothes and knickknacks to avoid thinking." He paused. "No mystery what you're avoiding thinking about. Or whom, rather."

Leo did not bother to reply. The gun was pleasantly cool in his hands. Did guns become hot when they were fired? He couldn't recall.

"It was Juno Bell for whom you made that little silver ring years ago, wasn't it?" St. Blaise asked. "I knew something was afoot when I first heard you say her name. Then I met her at some salon, thought I'd find out more. Stroke of luck you showed up the day I modeled. There seemed to be something between you, but it looked messy. And here we are."

"If you want excitement, I could find you a position as a spy. Seems you'd be good at it."

"I'd certainly be very dashing," he said. "What will you do about Miss Bell?"

Leo caressed the barrel of the gun. "I am engaged to someone else. It is the height of dishonor for a gentleman to end his engagement."

"And you could never marry Miss Bell anyway."

I can if I want to, Leo thought sulkily, stubbornly. Yet everyone said it. Even Juno said it.

"She doesn't want to marry me, so it hardly matters anyway."

"So—what? You'll keep her as your mistress?"

Leo contemplated the damp toes of his boots and ignored the question. "Did you mind that Papa Duke never married your mother?" he asked instead.

St. Blaise sat up, his back against the other side of the tree. "We were his true family, not you and your siblings," he said. "He lived with us, loved us, but he had this whole life we could never be part of." He paused. "Was it he who taught you to shoot?"

"He left instructions that it be done. He assessed my performance on his next quarterly visit."

"See, he taught me to shoot, to ride, to fish. Everything that mattered, he taught me. I thought the world of him and wanted to be just like him. But he was a duke above all else, and that was something I could never be. Every time I'd ask about his other life, his public life, it was always, 'No need to worry about that, that's for Leopold.' No wonder I wanted to punch you."

Leo snorted. "He visited me four times a year and spent every single visit boasting about you. How you ran faster, rode better, shot straighter. No wonder I wanted to punch you."

Being a duke entitled Leo to a lot, but it had never entitled him to be loved. He realized that, at some point, he had learned not to ask for what would not be given.

The futility. The absurdity. All his life Leo had been jealous of St. Blaise, their father's favorite, and all his life, St. Blaise had been jealous of him, their father's heir. Each of them had only half a father; their mothers each had only half a husband. All because an English duke could not marry a French Catholic, and why not? Because that simply wasn't *done*.

"He split himself into pieces," Leo said. "He shouldn't have done that."

"He shouldn't have had to do that." St. Blaise peered around the tree to grin at him. "I would have made a better duke than you."

"Gambling, fighting, and whoring?"

"I wouldn't do those things if I were the duke." Leo sliced him a look. "Very well, I'd still do them, but in a much more ducal manner," St. Blaise amended. "But as a duke, I'd have a purpose, wouldn't I? Let's swap. I'll become the duke, and you can be a ragged artist starving in a garret with Miss Bell."

Across the park came the sounds of wheels and hooves and the jingling of a harness. They both stood to watch a carriage emerge from the mist.

"The surgeon," said St. Blaise. "You can still put a stop to this."

But when the carriage doors opened, it was not the surgeon who jumped out, but Mrs. Prescott, followed by Juno.

Her eyes went straight to him. She stopped short, gripping the carriage door as if to hold herself up, while the mist dissolved behind her back. As their gazes tangled over the dew-covered grass, a bittersweet peace settled like a blanket around Leo's soul.

I want you to give me a piece of you, to take with me when you're gone, she had said.

What fools they both were. He had given her a piece of himself ten years earlier, and she still carried it with her. That, surely, was why he only felt whole when she was near.

The absence of that piece had left a hole inside him. He had tried to fill that hole with alcohol, with marriage to Erika, with pretty objects and prettier clothes, with artisans and his Foundation, and with a sensible marriage to a suitable lady, with family and duty and honor.

But when Juno was there, he had no empty spaces needing to be filled.

She was not disorder. He'd had it wrong. The whole bloody world had it wrong. For Leo, loving Juno was the natural order of things. The disorder, the chaos, the disruption: They were the result of denying his love for her, of trying to follow society's blinkered rules.

Then Juno looked away, and reality flooded back. Only a few seconds had passed since their arrival, he realized, and in those few seconds, Mrs. Prescott had been running and shouting, charging at her surprised husband like a bull.

~

JUNO DRAGGED her eyes off Leo—how her heart ached at the sight of him, unshaven, tired, in yesterday's rumpled clothes, with a gun in his hand—as Beatrice cried, "I'll not stand for this, Prescott!" and shoved her husband so hard he stumbled backward and nearly tripped over a log.

At her shouts, the two young men dozing on the grass jumped up like startled cats.

"You've ruined Juno's life, but you'll not ruin mine nor our children's either, nor our ball tonight," Beatrice cried. "End this, Prescott. Apologize to the duke. Now."

Prescott folded his arms like a sullen child. "He must apologize to me."

Beatrice looked around, perplexed. "I cannot tell him what to do. He's a duke. Juno, could you ask the duke to apologize?"

"I would be very glad if no one shot at anyone, but I cannot tell a duke what to do either," Juno said. "That's the trouble with dukes. They are terribly difficult to command." The duke in question was advancing across the grass, his half-brother yawning along behind him. "I must note that St. Blaise did not reveal my secrets," she added. "I spoke out loud where Beatrice could hear. It was my own doing."

"They ruined you," Leo said.

"I'll still be ruined if you kill each other. We cannot change the past. Even if we want to."

He went very still. His gaze seemed soft and full of meaning. The rest of the world disappeared.

"*Do* you want to the change the past?" he asked her.

"We cannot." She smiled sadly. "I've considered it from every angle, and my only conclusion is that I should not attempt philosophy."

His eyes widened. "Philosophy?"

"Please don't worry. It was a very painful five minutes, but I believe I shall pull through."

A smile eased over his face then, slow and warm like the rising sun, that familiar intimate smile that made his eyes crinkle and her heart dance.

Someone cleared his throat, a reminder that they were not, in fact, alone.

Once more, Leo's aloof mask fell into place. "Prescott: I insulted you, in defense of my friend. I apologize for that insult, at the request of my friend."

"There." Beatrice nudged her husband. "The duke has apologized. Dukes do not do that often."

Prescott snorted. "He insulted us both."

"And you both ruined Juno," Leo said. "You ruined her for your own gratification." With each word, his tone sharpened like an axe. Fresh anger rolled off him in waves. "How about I dedicate myself to ruining your career, the way you ruined Miss Bell? Day after day, I shall— Ah, sod it." He aimed the gun, prepared to fire. "I'll just shoot you anyway."

His jaw hardened. His finger caressed the trigger. Time stopped. Juno stumbled forward, crying his name. In that same moment, Beatrice hurled herself in front of her husband, and St. Blaise hurled himself at Leo, grabbed his arm with both hands, and discharged the gun into a tree. A squawking flock of indignant birds fluttered into the sky.

St. Blaise released Leo, who shot him a dirty look and straightened his clothes, only to once more raise the gun.

Prescott did not notice. He was staring at his wife and sipping little gasps of air. "You threw yourself in front of me," he said.

"He threatened to shoot you."

Prescott was pale. "He might have shot you."

"He might still shoot you," Beatrice said.

St. Blaise grinned. "Gun only had one bullet," he said cheerfully. "It's gone."

"Accept the apology, William. Do it for me."

"Beatrice, I— Right." Prescott held out his hand to Leo. "I accept your apology, Your Grace."

Leo ignored his hand. "You can't put this right. She must leave her home because of you. A whole life she's built here, and you take it away with your selfish, narrow-minded, pompous…" He punctuated each word with a jab of the gun in Prescott's chest.

"Reparations!" Beatrice said. "He'll make reparations."

"I'll make reparations," Prescott repeated. "A sum of money. To support her new life abroad."

Leo waved the gun like an enthusiastic highwayman. "And write another letter to *The Times*. Tell them you were mistaken. Give her that Botticelli, too. Juno," he added, without looking at her. "Does he have any other paintings you want?"

She chuckled, light-headed with relief. "If we really want him to suffer, force him to exhibit all his paintings, for everyone to see. Even the rabble."

Prescott gulped visibly, but gamely said, "Whatever my wife asks." He repeated, as if to himself, "She was willing to take a bullet for me."

Beatrice remained unaffected by her brush with death. "Oh, I have the most marvelous idea! Let's show your collection at our ball tonight." She dipped her hand into her husband's pocket and consulted his watch. "Look, 'tis barely five o'clock in the morning. We have a good sixteen hours until the first guests arrive. That's sufficient time for you to hang all the paintings, isn't it?"

His eyes bulged.

"But of course it is," she carried on blithely. "All else is ready. I can see it now: The Prescott Art Ball. Society will be amazed!"

Juno sighed. Somehow, Beatrice was going to triumph from her own treachery.

"Perhaps, Your Grace," Beatrice ventured, "it would aid Miss Bell's reputation if she painted a portrait of you with your new duchess."

"No!" Juno tried to compose herself. "Not a brilliant strategy."

Leo did not look at her. "Leave my betrothed out of this," he said coldly.

His betrothed. He was still promised to another.

Yet he was here because of Juno. Leo, always so calm and in control: He was disheveled and violent because of her. Oh, the poor darling. How she longed to slide her arms around him and feel his arms holding her.

With one of his sighs, Leo transferred the gun to his left hand and extended his right hand to Prescott. There followed one of those peculiarly gentlemanly transactions, where hands were shaken under sour glares and a murmured ducal threat. Then Beatrice was clapping her hands and cajoling her husband to hurry along for there was so much work to do!

Hand in hand, the newly happy couple trotted away. Beatrice had clearly forgotten Juno, but Juno would not get into a carriage with Beatrice and her husband right now for every Botticelli in the world.

St. Blaise smiled at her winningly. "Wasn't that exciting, Miss Bell? I say, the morning air becomes you. You look——"

Leo shouldered him aside. "Get away from her," he snarled. "Don't talk to her. Do not even look at her."

"You would be more intimidating if the gun were loaded, Polly. But I merely wish to apologize to Miss Bell. If I might?"

Leo extended his arm in front of St. Blaise's chest like a bar. "You can apologize from there."

"'Tis Leo to whom you owe apologies," Juno said.

"You might disagree had you heard what I said about you."

"I do not pay much mind to whatever nonsense comes out of your mouth."

"That nonsense won me a thousand pounds. Show it some respect. I had to provoke him into a duel to win, but the rules say nothing about actually fighting the duel. Which is just as well, since Polly cannot tell one end of a gun from the other, and it would be very unsporting of me to shoot him. So, apologies and all that. Now, I'm hungry." He waved at the two other men, who had watched the proceedings in silence. "Oi, lads! Let's visit one of your clubs for some ale and eggs, and celebrate our escape from the jaws of death."

Grinning jauntily, St. Blaise gathered the other gentlemen. Arms linked at the elbows, the trio paraded off to their hard-earned breakfast.

Suddenly, the park was empty but for Leo, Juno, and the birds. The sun spread sleepy rays across the grass, gilding Leo's hair and dispelling the last wreaths of mist.

It was on similar mornings that she first came to love him, all those years ago. Soft, gentle mornings, when they were alone in the world, when they were wholly themselves, when the air was crisp and unsullied and full of hope.

And just as the sun dissolved the mist, so it dissolved the carefully constructed lie of her life: the lie that she remained a spinster for the sake of her art. It was a nice lie, and everyone did such a good job of believing it that Juno had believed it herself. She had embraced her light-heartedness, her air of frivolity. She had cultivated that air as carefully as Leo had cultivated his indifference. It enabled her to step lightly through life and never fall too hard.

Yet she had fallen, and her whole edifice of lies came crashing down around her.

How on earth had she ever thought he was only a small part

of her life? Loving Leo was as much a part of her as art itself, as the heart beating in her chest, as her hopes and joys and sorrows and dreams.

She nodded at the gun. "*Do* you know how to use that?"

He glanced at it. "Sort of. Mostly. In theory."

"What happened, Leo? Fistfights and duels? Why did you do this?"

His beautiful, untouchable face creased in astonishment, as if he could not believe how simple she was.

"They hurt you. They should never have hurt you." His eyes searched hers. "I would not change the past, because I would not want to change who you have become. But I would change the future, if it were in my hands."

"You said…" Her breath was shaky. "You regret our tryst. You called it a mistake."

"It was a mistake to ever believe I felt nothing for you but desire."

"But you said you regret…" She frowned, trying to remember. He had not specified what he regretted; she only assumed he meant being with her.

Just as she had once wrongly assumed he thought her not good enough for him.

"What do you regret?" she asked.

"I regret…" He glanced down at the gun, his thumb sliding over the gleaming mother-of-pearl, and when he looked back up at her, it was with eyes as tender as the petals of a forget-me-not. "I regret it lasted only a few hours. I regret all the years I never saw you, all the nights I never slept beside you, all the days I did not spend with you. I regret not telling you that you are life itself, a wonder, the goddess of my heart. I regret all the times I hurt you and all the times I left you. I regret all the chances I missed and all the mistakes I made and all the fear that diminished me.

And more than anything, I regret that I do not know how to be the man you need me to be.

"But I do not regret any minute I spent with you, and I will never, *never* regret having you in my life."

She had no words, no breath. She blinked away tears; they clung, cold, to her lashes.

He raised his eyes to the pale heavens, squeezed them tight for a heartbeat, then said, "I must——" He stopped and breathed out heavily. Finally, he added, his voice hoarse, "And I regret that I am not at liberty to say more, for I have embroiled an innocent lady in my affairs, a lady who does not deserve my treatment of her and to whom I owe an obligation. Forgive me."

With his warm palm, he cupped her cheek. With his gentle thumb, he caught a runaway tear. He lifted that thumb to his lips, tasted that tear, and without another word, he turned away and was gone.

CHAPTER 26

Leo pounded on the front door of Lord Renshaw's house until finally it swung open, revealing the wide eyes of a harried-looking maid. He realized how he must appear: wild-eyed, unshaven, disheveled. Possibly even his hair did not look good.

"But they are all abed," the maid protested, when he demanded an immediate interview with Lord Renshaw and Miss Macey. She sucked on her teeth, likely calculating whether it was a greater evil to turn away a duke or rouse her employers. "They won't be awake for hours."

And the staff had work to do, and Leo's demands would upset everyone, and he was making enough trouble as it was. He would be back later, he said.

In his house, he demanded the newspaper. It had not been ironed, he was informed, but he did not care, he insisted, and ignored the black ink gleefully transferring itself onto his fingers as he flipped the pages in search of the shipping news. Here it was: A ship bound for Naples would depart at the next high tide, about four in the morning. Twenty-odd hours from now.

"Get me a ticket," he ordered. "Pack me a bag. I will be on that ship."

❧

NEXT ORDER OF BUSINESS: Thomas Macey's special license. Leo tracked down the archbishop's secretary to a crowded coffee house.

With the excessive politeness unique to an Englishman who feels unfairly imposed upon, the secretary informed the duke he would not be opening his office for another hour, as he meant to enjoy his morning ritual of breakfast and newspaper first. An excellent program, Leo agreed, and sat and stared at the man, while the other residents of the coffee house took turns staring at Leo. It turned out that a ducal stare improved the secretary's reading speed vastly, and the man, still grumbling, soon rose to open his office early.

With the special license tucked into his pocket, Leo went in search of Thomas Macey. He found him at his club, where he and St. Blaise were engaged in their post-duel breakfast.

"Come along, then," he said, and Macey, startled, sent a forkful of sausage into his chin instead of his mouth. "I have acquired the special license. The wedding will be today."

Silence fell over the neighboring tables. Interest rose from every gentleman in the club like steam off a galloping horse. He ignored them; he was giving London all sorts of entertainment these days, and he wasn't even close to finished.

St. Blaise grinned over his ale, but Macey looked around, panicked. "Please, Dammerton, do lower your voice," he whispered. "I don't want a scandal."

"He doesn't want a scandal!" Leo laughed. "Why, Macey, you do have some wit after all."

The silence had erupted into murmurs.

"Besides," Macey added, "there's no time to make arrangements to hold it today. It really ought to take place in a church."

Leo seized the fork from Macey's hand and threw it onto the plate. "Today, I say! He who hesitates is lost! Between the three of us here, we have a special license, a groom, and two witnesses. We need only collect the bride and I assure you, somewhere in London is a vicar willing to open up his church and say the right words. There will be a wedding today, Thomas Macey, mark my words."

LEO ARRIVED home after Macey's wedding at the same time as a footman bearing a letter from Lord Renshaw.

He fumbled it open, shakily unfolded the page. The letter was a furious torrent of phrases such as "disgraceful behavior" and "shame on my family and your own" and "undeserving." Leo agreed with every word, the sum total of which was: The engagement was off.

But no sooner had he read the last word than Susannah Macey herself marched into his study, a cowed-looking butler in her wake.

"Is that the letter from my grandfather?" she asked.

"It is."

Without breaking stride, she ripped the page from his hand, tore it in half, then in half again, and again. She tried to tear it a fourth time, but the pieces were too thick.

"Would you like me to light a fire so you can burn it?" he offered.

With an exasperated look, she slapped the pieces down onto a table. They fluttered about in indignation.

"My grandfather is being premature."

"He is also right," Leo said. "I have behaved dishonorably, I have disgraced my name and my title, and I shall do it all again before the day is out."

She gave an impatient huff. "And again, when one of my relatives challenges you to yet another duel."

He considered this. "Renshaw won't. Your father would, but by the time he returns to England, I'll be gone, and I believe your eldest brother is hunting in Scotland."

"Then Thomas—"

"Doubt it. An hour ago, he married the daughter of a warehouse clerk with my help."

"What on earth…?" She sank into a chair. "What a mess."

"I know. Beautiful, isn't it?"

Her eyes narrowed. "This is about that woman artist, isn't it? Spare me that look, Dammerton. Everyone knows. Right now, every lady in London is donning her best bonnet so they can crowd into my grandmother's drawing room full of gleeful commiseration. And yes, if I remain engaged to you, they'll laugh at me. Then next week, there will be someone else to laugh at, and then they'll leave London for the summer. By next year, I'll be a duchess and everyone will have forgotten."

"Susannah. Forgive me but I cannot—"

She stood so abruptly the chair rocked behind her. "I'll not release you. I shan't. You've been swept away by one of those peculiar passions people get into. All the excitement of duels and so forth, and perhaps you are panicking about the wedding; I hear that happens. This is nothing more than the effect of hot blood and cold feet. You simply need to calm down. In a few days, this whole frenzy will be over."

"It will never be over. Even if I never see her again, it will never be over. I tried to sever my connection with her, but—" He raised his hands, let them fall. "It quite simply cannot be done."

"But…" She looked baffled. "Your former wife's letter. She said you cannot love anyone. And surely not this artist."

"It's not that I cannot love anyone. It's that I cannot love anyone but her."

"But you cannot marry her."

Leo scowled. "Why does everyone keep saying that?"

She paced the length of his study. At his desk, she paused, drumming her fingers on the wood. It made a soft sound like distant horses. "She cannot be a duchess. Do as your father did and keep this artist as your mistress." She turned back around with a swish of her skirts. "After this conversation, I shall go back to pretending she doesn't exist. If you refrain from making further public displays over her, everyone will look away, I'll be spared further humiliations, and your honor will be spared further pain. It worked well enough for your father and mother."

"It caused rifts between my father and his children, and led my mother to withdraw from society."

She snorted. "Your mother had an excellent arrangement: all the privileges of being a duchess, but without having to pander to a husband."

"I see you did not exaggerate your aversion to sentimentality," he observed dryly.

The silence shuffled between them. How fascinating to see her true character at last. How sobering to see how ill-suited they were.

It was Susannah who broke the impasse. "So, you truly mean to marry her. This ... artist."

"I mean to ask. She has already stated quite clearly she does not wish to marry me."

"She does not love you?"

"She loves me. The question is whether she loves me enough." He rubbed the newspaper ink still smearing his fingers. "She leaves England in the early hours of the morning."

"Then she is lost to you anyway."

"She is only mostly lost to me. If I marry another woman, she will be lost to me forever."

"And if she refuses you, you will be forever alone."

"Yes," Leo agreed softly. "I suppose I will."

Susannah resumed her pacing, her gaze darting over the various decorative objects as she circumnavigated the room. "And the title? You have a duty, Dammerton."

"I also have younger brothers. In the end, I am irrelevant as an individual to the title. I suspect I am also irrelevant as an individual to you. You have surely received plenty of other offers. The Earl of Normanby, for example."

She made an exasperated sound. "Lord Normanby insisted on showering me with nonsense compliments and protestations of love."

"My sole attraction cannot be that I do not love you. Is it so important to be a duchess?"

"Your Foundation, Dammerton," she said impatiently. "That is what I want. To be involved with that. It's something I can actually do."

His Foundation! Sainted stitches, Leo had completely forgotten the Dammerton Foundation. His greatest obsession for years and it had entirely slipped his mind.

Susannah was still explaining. "When you showed me your offices and the manager showed me the books and the box room…" With a sharp shake of her head, she added, "There are so many ways it could be organized better. There truly are."

"Did you make a list?"

"Oh, I made several lists." She held up a porcelain figurine of a minstrel playing a harp. "Do you see this? This is me. A pretty little ornament. I won't do it," she said, suddenly forceful, as if mid-argument. "I try to do the pretty things, I really do try, but it all comes out a mess. I am better at useful things, lists and plans, but they want me to be an ornament. I'll not do it. I won't."

The figurine slipped out of her hand. It landed on the carpet and broke neatly in two. Her hand flew up over her mouth. "Oh, forgive me. I did not mean to do that. My family is always scolding me for being so clumsy."

She clasped her hands. Her confident impatience had vanished, and she looked distressed and very young. Her thumbs were attacking each other again.

He was leaving England with Juno, though Juno didn't know it yet. He was abandoning his beloved Foundation without a second thought, with no one to oversee it. He had already struck several blows against the social order today. Perhaps he could encourage a touch more disorder here too.

He crouched down to tidy up the pieces of the broken figurine. "If given the choice," he said as he stood, "would you choose to marry or to run the Dammerton Foundation?"

She frowned. "I don't understand. I could only be involved in the Foundation by marrying you."

"You could be involved if I said you were involved."

"I know nothing. I'm a lady."

He shrugged. "Half the ladies of the *ton* occupy themselves by overseeing charitable organizations and whatnot. If you were given the chance to learn? Would you make that choice?" he repeated.

The clock ticked on and on as she stared at the broken figurine and fidgeted with her thumbs. Then her thumbs settled. Her shoulders straightened. Her face cleared.

"Is such a thing possible?" she asked.

Leo waited.

She answered herself. "It could be, I suppose. But if you marry that artist—"

"You will refer to her with more respect."

At the chilly rebuke, she gulped. "My apologies. But if she becomes your wife…"

"She will support you, I am sure. She is not as judgmental as some."

She had the grace to flush at that. "If I am to take on this task, I will need all the support I can get. My family will not approve. It can be difficult to learn new ways to think."

"I shall write to the director to make arrangements," he said. "Your education can begin."

A ghost of a smile crossed her face. "And perhaps I shall be fortunate enough to find another eligible lord who does not love me."

"If you are very fortunate, you might find one who does not even like you."

She made a soft sound of laughter. "It's too bad, Dammerton, really it is. We would have rubbed along well enough."

Alone again, Leo wandered through the rooms, through his collection, saying his farewells. Juno had not spent much time here, but her spirit filled every room. He trailed out to the garden, to the stone rotunda where they had agreed to have an affair. What a fool he'd been, thinking a few nights of passion would burn his desire for her right out of his blood.

All it had done was seal her place in his heart.

He would not have it any other way.

And here: the fountain, the three Fates dancing, where she had thrown a pin into the water in hope of magic. The spray dusted his cheeks.

Leo could use a little magic now. He fumbled for the ruby stickpin in his cravat, closed his eyes, and touched it to his lips. Then he tossed it into the water and made a wish.

CHAPTER 27

Juno ran. When she could run no more, she walked. When she could walk no more, she ran.

Upon bursting into her house, she learned from a bewildered Mrs. Kegworth that the men had already taken her trunks to the docks for loading onto the ship. Once more she set off, racing to her aunt's house, where she begged to borrow the carriage that she might chase after her trunks. Hester and Livia, exchanging confused, concerned looks, abandoned their breakfast and insisted on coming too.

The docks bustled with noisy activity, crowded with stevedores and sailors, passengers and prostitutes. Juno and Hester battled through them, finding the quay with her ship, and there —her trunks, a stevedore just now bending his knees to hoist one onto his shoulder.

"No! Wait! Stop!" Juno cried.

She slapped her hands onto the trunk. When he snarled at her to get away, she plonked her bottom on the trunk instead.

"If you think I'm carrying you onto that ship, lady, think

again," he said. "You have to walk like the rest of us. Now, I've got a job to do."

"Do it elsewhere, please," she said. "I need a moment to think."

With a huff of tobacco breath and a muttered curse, he turned away to hoist a more amenable trunk onto his brawny shoulders, and then he joined the ant lines of workers, loading the ship for its departure at high tide. On the deck of the ship, sailors moved about, doing whatever it was that sailors did.

They were very picturesque, these docks, with the masts and people and gulls, all rough energy and the promise of adventure. An image rose in her mind: a painting of a young woman, eyes shining with either excitement or tears, walking up the gangway to board a ship. Title: *The Great Mistake*.

"Juno, what are you doing?" Hester stood before her, arms folded, the bonnet shadowing her thin face.

Juno sighed. "I haven't the faintest idea."

"Do you mean to stay in London then?"

"I cannot stay in London."

"Then you mean to leave for Italy."

"I cannot leave for Italy."

Hester perched on the trunk beside her. "If you can neither stay nor leave, you are in a very difficult position. What is going on?"

Juno gripped the edges of the trunk and considered the ships. A decade ago, she had come to these same docks and departed England for the first time. Because Leo had rejected her, because she believed he was saying she wasn't good enough for him. And she had been wrong.

She had thought he regretted their tryst. She had been wrong.

She had thought she could never marry a duke. Perhaps she had been wrong about that too.

For someone who made such a song and dance about making her own decisions, Juno Bell did seem to get a lot of them wrong.

"Can I tell you a secret?" she asked, but did not wait for Hester's reply. "Years ago, when Hadrian first brought Leo home from Oxford, I fell in love with him."

Hester widened her eyes. "You did? You hid it well. I don't recall you two ever speaking much."

"We used to take long walks together, in the mornings while you were all sleeping."

"Good heavens, your uncle would have been furious." Hester shook her head. "I had no idea Leo was such a scoundrel."

"Oh no, please don't think poorly of him." Juno gripped her arm, pleading. "*I* was the scoundrel. He was always honorable and proper, but I threw myself at him, right at his head. He very politely pointed out we could never be together. I thought he meant I was not good enough for him."

Her aunt frowned. "I don't believe he would have said that. Perhaps he meant he had to consider his duty to his family first."

"Yes, that's what he said."

"When?"

"The other day. When he told me he wanted to marry me."

A statue-like stillness fell over Hester, as she said, very carefully, "The Duke of Dammerton wishes to marry you?"

"Years ago, he wished to marry me," Juno clarified. "And now… Now I am leaving England in disgrace, and he is engaged to someone else."

"And you have sworn all these years you were content to remain unmarried. That you chose art above all else."

Juno sighed. What was it Hester had said about her parents? It was possible to love more than one thing in one's life.

"There was some gossip about him last night," Hester said thoughtfully. "A public brawl with his half-brother. And even duels, I think I heard?"

Juno said nothing.

"Juno, did these fights and duels have anything to do with you?"

"I believe so." She met her aunt's eyes. "Yes."

She was more than a distraction for Leo; she was a disruption. She was disrupting his plans, his dreams. It was best she leave him to the proper order of things.

Yet he loved her. She loved him. They were right together. Why must they be separated by silly rules about who could marry whom? Was that not the proper order of things, for two people who loved each other to be together, to share their lives?

And how was she to convince Leo of this? After all, she had told him she loved him. Back in that cottage, lying in that bed, she had said "I love you" and then he——

No. And then *she*——!

Oh, dear heaven, what had she done?

In that cottage, she had spoken of love. In the very next breath, she claimed to have no interest in marrying him. At the time, she had even believed it was true.

Because it was better that way. Because if she failed to make that clear, he might have felt obliged to remind her she did not fit into his world. Because she could not have borne it, if he rejected her again.

Clever trick, that: He could not reject her if she rejected him first.

And now he must believe she did not want to marry him, for the simple reason that she had said she did not want to marry him.

But if she offered herself to him now, and he told her she misunderstood? Suppose he told her, "I said I would change the future if it was in my hands, but it is not. You know I can never marry you."

She would not be able to bear it.

TWICE MORE THE man came to take her trunks. Twice more she sent him away. She sat tensely with Hester, while Livia explored the docks with greedy, shining eyes.

"Juno! Oh, Juno, darling, there you are!"

Beatrice? Surprised, Juno turned. Beatrice Prescott, skirts raised high to show her half boots, was picking her way through the mud and mess.

"I thought I would never find you!" Beatrice said brightly, with a nod at Hester. "They said you had left for the docks, but your ship is not leaving yet, is it? Oh, do say it isn't!"

Juno stared at her uncomprehendingly. "What are you doing here? Haven't you a ball to organize?"

"Oh, that's all in hand." She waved dismissively. "Mr. Prescott has summoned an *army* of helpers, to carry and hang the paintings, and he found a printer willing to print off his personal inventory, which shall be distributed to all invitees, even those who declined. I swear, once everyone learns of the paintings on display, the queen herself will beg to be let in. Here, an invitation for you." Beatrice handed Juno a thick, embossed card. "Of course, I already gave you an invitation, but … here is another one?" She patted Juno's trunks. "I was so hoping you might not leave after all, what with the Duke of Dammerton fighting duels over you…" She trailed off meaningfully, seeking information.

Juno would give her nothing. "Then I am more of a disgraceful scandal than ever, and you ought not to be talking to me," she said coolly. "What *would* Mr. Prescott say?"

Beatrice winked. "Mr. Prescott has become very amenable. Do say you'll come. And you too, Lady Bell, and all your family if they are in town."

Juno flicked the sharp corners of the card. "Do not waste your invitation on me. I am a scandal. No respectable lady would suffer to be in the same room as me. If your art ball succeeds in attracting a single peeress, she'll run away the minute she knows of my presence, and you'll be ruined too. You'll never achieve your grand ambition of being embraced by the aristocracy then."

Beatrice's fingers were white where she squeezed her parasol. "The decorations in the ballroom look amazing," she said sadly. "Prescott is hanging the paintings. It will be like nothing London has ever seen. Yet all I can think of is you. It is you who has paid the price for my success and I cannot bear it."

"But it is done now. Without me there, perhaps you'll finally win the admiration of the best people."

Beatrice lifted her head gamely. "You *are* the best people. I should rather have you there than all the peeresses in the world. If the queen herself should demand you be ejected from the room, I would be proud to stand by your side and say no."

Juno traced the embossed edges of the card with one gloved finger, while Beatrice squeezed her bottom into the space between her and the edge of the trunk.

"I will never be able to express my sorrow for what I did to you," Beatrice went on. "It was like a maggot in my brain, this need for society to admire me. I would rather put everything back the way it was, and keep you and lose them." She kicked the trunk with her heels like a child. "What foolish mistakes we make, when we lose sight of what truly matters and let ourselves believe in the wrong thing."

Juno snorted softly. That was a foolish mistake she knew too well.

Beatrice tried again. "I do wish you did not have to leave England, but the ship does not leave for hours, so perhaps you could drop by, just this one last night…"

Juno turned an incredulous look on her. "Do you really think I would wish to spend my last few hours in London at a ball, hosted by you, with judgmental ladies giving me the cut?"

"You should hold your head up high. You belong among the highest in society."

The highest in society? That was Leo's world. She could not enter his world.

Could she?

Did she dare?

She did not want to be the sort of woman who broke up someone's engagement and started a huge scandal and hurt a young lady who did not deserve the scorn.

But neither did she want to be the sort of woman who spent her life alone and in exile because she never had the courage to ask for what she wanted from the one and only man she'd ever loved.

And he loved her too, she knew that. She could only hope that he loved her enough.

She bounded to her feet, just as an officious-looking man brandishing a roll of paper approached.

"Miss, we must load your trunks now. We cannot delay, not for you or anyone. The ship must leave at the next high tide."

Juno smiled. "There will be another ship. And another tide. And another day."

"Ye-es?" he said uncertainly.

"But there might never be another chance. And Leo and I— We've missed too many chances as it is."

LEO STIRRED ON THE BED, emerging from the cobwebs of sleep, reaching for Juno, to hold her close for the rest of the night.

His hand touched emptiness. He opened his eyes: The room was bright with daylight. He still wore his clothes.

From deeper in the house came angry voices, a mistreated

door, and footsteps approaching his chamber in what sounded like a purposeful stomp.

Then his bedroom door slammed open and Hadrian Bell stood glowering in the doorway.

Leo blinked at him sleepily. Suddenly, memory flooded back in. The docks! Juno's ship!

"Bloody hell," he muttered. "What time is it? What's the bloody time?"

He leaped off the bed but Hadrian caught his shoulders and shoved him back so hard he bounced on the mattress.

"It's time you gave me an explanation," Hadrian said. "What the devil have you done to Juno?"

Leo sat up, hands raised in a show of peace. "Hadrian, old friend, I did not survive two duels this morning only to be shot by you."

"I know." He sank onto the bed beside him. "Juno won't let me shoot you."

"She doesn't want me dead?"

"No. Quite opposed to it, actually."

Leo grinned. "That's a promising start. Good to see you back in London. Why are you here?"

"I brought you a gift. From Juno. It's a painting, I guess, as she was running around buying a new frame. She is behaving very oddly, odd even for her, and I have no idea what is going on."

THE PACKAGE WAS A WOODEN CRATE. Leo called for a crowbar and tore off the planks with splintering haste.

In the crate was indeed a painting, in a large, ornate frame. With Hadrian's help, Leo lifted it out and rested it against a table.

He dusted off the packing straw and folded back the protective cloth.

It was her depiction of the mermaid laying claim to the shipwrecked sailor, now painted in oils and brought to stormy, passionate life. The faces on the figures did not look like Leo or Juno—they did not look like anyone he knew—but he recognized their expressions.

The expressions of two people who yearned for each other, but had no place in each other's world.

With one unsteady finger, Leo traced the line of the mermaid's back. "What the devil is she trying to say?" he muttered.

Hadrian jerked his chin. "There's a note stuck to the back of the frame."

But Juno did not write notes. The piece of card turned out to be an invitation to the Prescotts' ball that night. What an odd thing for her to give him. What a *very* odd place for her to stick an invitation.

So, if Juno was trying to tell him something…

Leo carefully examined the place where the invitation was stuck. Frames were so big these days, something to do with the new composite material, she had once explained. It wouldn't be difficult to hide a cache of secret documents in them. Some frames were so big it wouldn't be difficult to hide a family of four. Leo fiddled about until— There! He found the seam. And then the mechanism.

And then the frame split open like a very large book.

Hidden within was a portfolio made of tooled leather, the very same one Leo had given to Juno to hide her secret drawings.

He tumbled back onto the floor to open it.

The first page showed a drawing of himself, sprawled out naked on a bed, covered by nothing but the corner of a bedsheet, strategically placed.

Well. He looked very peaceful, though he was not at his most, ah, impressive while asleep. Another showed him standing with his naked back to a rumpled bed, his face in profile.

At a groan of "Oh, my eyes," Leo looked up to see Hadrian turning away, scrubbing a hand over his face.

He yanked out all the pages and spread them over the rug. His gaze bounced from one to the next. Every single page held a drawing of him. He could see himself growing younger under her hand, as he moved through the pages, back through more than ten years, back to the very first drawing of him as a naive boy, completed when she was sixteen.

None of them offered any more information than a date and her name. Except one, in her careless handwriting: *If I cannot have Leo, I shall have no one.*

She had never forgotten him. He had remained with her all these years.

He looked at the invitation again. Nothing on this Earth would induce him to set foot in Prescott's house.

Nothing except a request from Juno.

Leo packed up the drawings, hid them once more in the painting, and sent word to his valet that tonight he would attend a ball.

CHAPTER 28

L eo was surprised by the squeeze at the Prescott house, and especially by the presence of fellow aristocrats and their families among the guests.

Then he saw that everyone was flapping a page, on which were printed names that such high-ranking guests might deem almost as important as their own: Rubens, Titian, Turner. In less than a day, the "Prescott Art Ball" had become the talk of the town, and no self-respecting member of society could bear to miss such an event. Everyone was an art connoisseur tonight, even those who could not tell a Caravaggio from a cartoon.

The announcement of Leo's name met with the familiar two-step: a collective hush, then a collective murmur. He ignored Prescott, who returned the favor, and gave Mrs. Prescott a cool nod.

"Congratulations on your ball, Mrs. Prescott," he said.

"Thank you, Your Grace, and if I might—"

"It takes a very special sort of person to triumph from another's troubles."

Her color heightened and she started to splutter a response, but Leo turned away to move through the crowd. The orchestra was playing: A country dance was about to get underway. Some couples headed for the floor; other guests continued to examine paintings, each other, or him.

He ignored them all, seeking only Juno, not seeing her. Why had she sent him here? What was she playing at?

OH, what did she think she was playing at? Juno tried not to fidget in her lavish ballgown, as she climbed down from her uncle's carriage outside the Prescott house.

She was playing at being a duchess, she reminded herself sternly, so she straightened her shoulders, lifted her chin, and followed her aunt and uncle and cousins through the doors with a most regal air. Were those speculative looks directed at her? Was she the subject of those murmurs? Or was she extremely conceited to imagine anyone here cared tuppence about her?

The trick was to keep her gaze fixed ahead, at what artists called the vanishing point. If she must look at anyone, she would look at them down her nose. But she was a novice at this duchess game: As she turned around after relinquishing her cloak, she accidentally met someone's eyes. His face was vaguely familiar, one of those noblemen who enjoyed artists' salons. "Good evening, Your Grace," he said with a nod. Juno froze, then gathered her courage and twisted to look over her shoulder. The only "grace" she spotted was the Duchess of Sherbourne; when she turned back, the gentleman was gone.

By some miracle, no one was giving her the cut. Perhaps she did belong here. Or perhaps they dared not issue insults at the art ball. Or perhaps she simply wasn't that important to anyone in the end.

And what of it? Only Leo mattered tonight. But how on earth was she to find him in this crush?

HOW THE DEVIL was he to find her in this crush?

Leo scowled his way through the rooms, peering past feathers and flowers and turbans, for a glimpse of her.

But all he found was a grinning Tristan St. Blaise, accompanied, surprisingly, by an anxious-looking Thomas Macey. Sainted stitches, it was the fellow's second wedding night and he was spending it at a *ball*? When Leo had his second wedding night, he would spend it in the company of his wife, and his wife alone.

If he got a second wedding night.

"Polly! How fine you look! You are looking for Miss Bell, I presume?"

"I certainly didn't show up here to waltz with you," Leo said.

"But I waltz so beautifully." St. Blaise stepped closer, mischief writ plain across his face. "I thought you'd like to know that I placed a very large wager this afternoon. I bet you married Miss Bell today by special license."

"You did what?"

St. Blaise beamed. "And then Macey here also placed a very large wager, that you married Miss Bell today by special license."

Leo looked from one to the other. "You blithering clowns! When people learn it's not true, she'll be a laughingstock and then I'll have to shoot you all over again."

Macey's eyes widened and his head whipped about to face St. Blaise. "You told me he got two special licenses," he accused. "You told me it was true. You—"

St. Blaise clapped him on the shoulder. "It *might* have been true," he said. "The other men heard you in the club, Polly, talking about special licenses and weddings, and you know gossips always leap to the most exciting conclusion. I merely encouraged them in that conclusion. Stroke of genius on my part, really. Now, no one is sure whether Miss Bell is a duchess or not, so they won't dare cut her if she shows up. After all, there are not so many duchesses in the world that anyone can afford to offend one."

Leo shook his head. "Neither of you has two farthings to rub together, not with your debts. Where did you get the funds to place a large wager?"

"Well, Polly, you did say you wanted to solve your problem with the excess china. Got me a pretty penny, selling that."

Leo couldn't help it: He laughed. "You are so annoying. But if you helped her, thank you." He slapped his brother on the back, and Tristan slapped him back, and somehow it devolved into a half-hug. Then Macey was saying, "Are we hugging now?" and threw his arms around them both.

"I'm leaving London tonight," Leo said quietly to his brother, once he had extricated himself and was straightening his coat. "Look after everything for me, would you?"

"Be happy to." St. Blaise's eyes glinted. "And what about Miss Macey? Shall I look after her too?"

Before Leo could hurl him off the balcony, a hush wafted over the crowd.

"Sir Gordon and Lady Bell," the butler announced.

Leo went very still. A million faces turned his way.

"Mr. Hadrian Bell," the butler said. "Mrs. Grayshott. Miss Livia Bell."

Leo turned around. A million whispers rustled across the room.

"Miss Juno Bell," the butler said.

Leo looked up. A million stars exploded in his heart.

Somehow, Juno had procured a stylish evening gown in a dark red, trimmed with gold braid on its bodice and around its hem. Red rosebuds bloomed from her carefully coiled hair, and garnets adorned her throat. She looked radiant and full of verve. She looked elegant and full of grace. She looked like a goddess. She looked like a—

"Duchess," someone whispered behind him, hastily shushed, but that too was lost in the chorus of murmurs, before the guests remembered themselves and tried to behave as if everything was normal.

Juno was searching the crowd. She stilled when she saw him. Their eyes met. He waited, desperately, for her crooked grin to spread over her beloved face. It never came. Her expression went remote. She lifted her chin haughtily. She looked at him right down her nose.

But even from this distance, he saw the smile and love in her eyes.

Even across the room, Juno saw the smile and love in Leo's eyes. It warmed her so thoroughly, she had to remember to maintain her appearance of aristocratic aloofness and not shove aside this pestilent crowd and hurl herself into his arms. He eased toward her; she drifted away. A heady new confidence rushed through her.

Just as well, for she'd not gone far when a lady claimed her attention.

"You are an artist, are you not? I remember you from Mrs. Prescott's garden party," the lady said, and fired a glance at another pair of ladies who were watching, their lips tight with suppressed giggles. Juno suspected she had become the subject of a dare.

The lady waved her list of paintings like a fan. "My friends and I are so intolerably ignorant," she said, as her friends crept closer. "We know many of the artists listed here, but we've never heard of this Leyster chap. That's an English name surely? But you must know him."

Juno managed a smile. "Judith Leyster was neither a chap nor English. She was Dutch and was born nearly two centuries ago. Many notable women artists were working during the Dutch Golden Age."

This stunning fact invited gasps from the ladies.

An older gentleman joined their conversation. "*Many* of them?" he repeated. "How interesting. Why did Holland produce so many talented women artists, do you think, given there are so few elsewhere?"

Or maybe she was the butt of a joke, Juno amended. But she must remain polite and gracious. A duchess was always gracious and polite, even when asked questions like that.

"Because of the tulips, of course," she said.

"The tulips?"

Her new friends looked at her expectantly, as if desperate for her next pearl of wisdom. Yet before she could feed them another scrap of nonsense, their attention shifted to someone behind her.

She felt Leo's presence at her side even before she heard him say, "Yes, the tulips. When Dutch children play among the tulips, the beauty awakens artistic sentiments in boys and girls alike." He paused. "Scientific fact."

As they exclaimed on this marvel of nature, he slid his fingers around her elbow and gently drew her away.

"The tulips?" he said, one eyebrow raised.

She laughed, then hastily covered her mouth. Fine ladies did not laugh. "It was the first thing to come out of my mouth. I had no idea how to answer his question without being rude." She faced him. "I am trying very hard to be polite and gracious, and to behave like a—"

She stopped, lacking the courage to say "duchess," when she did not know what Leo wanted, or if anything had changed.

"Proper lady," she finished weakly. She took a deep, steadying breath.

His hand slid down her arm to curl around hers. Even through two layers of gloves, she could feel his warmth, his strength. His very essence of Leo.

And it was a heady delight to see him in evening clothes, too. His coat was black and his cravat white, but his waistcoat was magenta silk, upon which were embroidered plump carnations, roses, and tulips within golden foliage scrolls.

"You look beautiful," he murmured.

"So do you. And it is most peculiar, but no one has snubbed me. Even though my career as an artist in London is irrevocably ruined."

"I am very sorry you lost your career. But perhaps being a duchess might prove a tolerable alternative?"

Her heart stopped. "You are at liberty to speak, then?"

"Yes. Miss Macey has been so kind as to release me. Forgive me for departing so abruptly earlier. It felt only right to speak to her first." He huffed out ruefully. "It is rather difficult, juggling all these women."

Her chin jerked back. "*All* these women?"

"Well, only two. But that is twice as many entanglements as I have ever dealt with before. I am not a libertine, I am sorry to say."

"I am not at all sorry to hear it."

He entwined their fingers. "You have very neatly avoided my question. But neither have you fainted, nor run away, which I'll take as an encouraging sign. Juno, we——" He stopped short. "We are not alone. Let us go outside."

"To be alone in the dark?" She squeezed his hand. "You are behaving like a libertine already."

310

Leo was feeling like a libertine, to be honest. Juno looked ravishing in that gown. The light of a flaming torch on the balcony glinted off her garnet necklace and bathed her in its glow.

Yet her expression was sad. "I shan't marry you just so you can save me from ruin," she said. "I don't need you to salvage my reputation."

"I don't care about your reputation." He slid his hands around her waist. "Take me with you to Italy. I'll wash your paintbrushes and shower you with kisses and sweep the studio floor and sweep away your cares. I'll carry your easels through the countryside, and I'll read books just to find stories for you to paint, and I'll make love to you so thoroughly that your dreams will be as full of me as mine are of you."

Her hands landed on his chest. "But everything you love is here in London. Your life is here. I cannot ask you to give that up."

"You are my life. More than ten years, Juno, and still it's not over. It will never be over. These feelings between us, they endure. I must believe it is the same with you. Those drawings you sent me." He squeezed her waist. "It seems I have a rather fine pair of buttocks."

"Oh, you really do."

Soft laughter curled out of him. "Anywhere you go, I will come too. If you do not want me, I shall wait in the street, rain or shine, until you come to your senses and realize our lives must be as one. No matter where you go or what you do, I will not part from you again. You will just have to get used to it."

She ran her fingers down his cheek. He caught them and held them to his lips.

"Forgive me," he whispered. "I so feared loving you again

that I was determined to keep a distance between us and all I have done is hurt us both."

"Is loving me so terrible, then?"

"Loving you is a wonder. But I am fated to love you immoderately—with all that I have and all that I am. I fear I would suffer greatly, should you have no need of my love."

Her smile was like a blessing from the angels. "Then it is as well for both of us that I have very great need of it indeed. You are happiness and hope and home. You took up residence in my heart years ago, and could not be shifted. I drew you to get you out of my thoughts, but you kept coming back. Even after I left you, still you never left me."

"Because all those years ago, I gave you a piece of myself, the very best part of me. You have carried that part of me with you, and I am only whole when you are near. I ask only..." He took a deep breath. "I ask only that you take the rest of me too. I cannot stop loving you, but neither can I stop being a duke. Only say that you will marry me."

"Yes, I will marry you," she said softly. "I wish I had claimed you sooner. I could not let myself believe you would still want me, not when I had become so disreputable, and I could not bear for you to reject me again, so I rejected myself first. But the truth remains, Leo, I shall make a terrible duchess."

"You'll make an unconventional duchess," he corrected gently. "Besides, the Italians won't care about that. They think the English are all mad anyway."

"And here, in England?"

He shook his head. "No need. I could not bear it, if marriage to me stole away your verve. I could not bear to watch you fade away under the demands of society, and their restrictions and rules."

"Not if I am with you." She traced one of the golden scrolls curling over his chest. "If you had not come back into my life, I might have gone on believing I had no need of you. But that was a lie. You have stolen my dearest lie from me, and it was all that was holding up my world. I cannot go on as I was without it, which means I cannot go on without you." She flounced out her skirts. The scallops of golden braid around the hem glinted in the light. "Hence this gown and this ball. I wanted to prove that my love for you is such that I shall happily go anywhere and behave properly, so long as it is with you. Besides, I love London too, so why let them chase us out of it? Parliament sits for only half the year. Why not spend that half-year in London, as the Duke and Duchess of Dammerton?"

A smile eased over his face. "And the other half of the year in Europe, as Leo and Juno, a pair of eccentric English artists. You do realize that half the people here think we are already married?"

"I heard a rumor that you acquired a special license."

"I did, but not for us. What sort of wedding would you like? I could acquire another special license, or we could have an enormous wedding in London and rub everyone's nose in it. Or the ship's captain could marry us, if you wish to go straight to Italy. Or we could take the more traditional route and elope to Gretna Green."

"Scotland! The light in Scotland at this time of year must be marvelous. But surely an elopement would be more of a scandal?"

"I hope so." He brushed a kiss over her lips. "You must understand, my love, that we have an important duty to the good people of England: We are duty bound to provide them with a source of entertainment, which means giving them a jolly good scandal every now and then."

She wrapped her arms around his neck. "Do you mean to say that my first official duty as a duchess will be to run away with you to Scotland?"

"Definitely. With such scandalous behavior, you'll be everyone's favorite duchess before the night is out."

His head lowered, their lips met, but muffled laughter and the faint strains of music forced them to break apart.

She cocked her head. "Is that a waltz? You know we've never danced before."

"Then we shall remedy that immediately. We'll waltz before all of society and they won't know where to look." He took her hand to lead her inside. "Let's give them something to talk about."

EPILOGUE

Regency Duke Still A Scandal After All These Years

The Times

17 May 1976

L ONDON—Drawings of a naked man hidden in a nineteenth-century picture frame are believed to be of Leopold Halton, the sixth Duke of Dammerton, who inherited his title during England's Regency era.

The set of drawings was found during restoration of a painting depicting a mermaid with a shipwrecked sailor. The painting, found hidden in an attic, was painted by the duke's second wife, Juno, Duchess of Dammerton.

The drawings were found by art historian Dr. Elizabeth Cranston, who says she had been seeking Juno's mermaid painting for many years.

"The duke mentions the mermaid in his journals, but it had never been found," Dr. Cranston said. "Their descendants probably hid it during the more restrictive Victorian era, given its unashamed portrayal of female desire by a female artist."

Before her marriage, the duchess, Juno Bell, was an artist working in London. She sparked a scandal in the art world when it was revealed that she painted nudes, which was forbidden for women at the time, Dr. Cranston said.

Notable for his colorful clothing and generous patronage of the decorative arts, Leopold Halton also worked up an impressive list of scandals. He made an impulsive marriage at age twenty-one, later divorcing his wife for adultery, making him one of the very few divorced men in England at the time. He also brawled in public and famously fought two duels in a single day, one of which was with his own half-brother. Following the duels, he was jilted by his respectable fiancée, before he eloped to Scotland with Juno Bell.

"He really was a one-man scandal," Dr. Cranston said. "And judging by these racy drawings by his wife, he remained naughty well into his later years."

Once married, the couple divided their time between Europe and London. The duchess continued to paint and exhibit after their marriage, while using her new position to mentor young women. She is best known for her painting titled *Hades and Persephone Duel with Flowers*, a gift to her husband on their tenth anniversary. It is said that the two imps in the painting represent their two children. The painting forms part of the collection at the Tate Gallery in London.

RESEARCH NOTE

The professional women artists mentioned in this novel are the following historical figures:

Élisabeth Louise Vigée LeBrun (born Paris; 1755–1842). She began painting portraits professionally in her early teens, and later painted more than thirty portraits of Marie-Antoinette and her family. In her memoirs, published when she was in her eighties, she gives her impressions of life in London.

Maria Anna Angelika Kauffman, known in England as Angelica Kauffman (born Switzerland; 1741–1807). She was one of the founding members of the Royal Academy of Arts in London in 1768.

Mary Linwood (born Birmingham; 1755–1845). She was famous for her embroideries, including embroidered copies of old master paintings. Admirers of her work included Catherine the Great and other royals across Europe.

Margaret Sarah Geddes Carpenter (born Salisbury; 1793–1872). She was a noted portrait painter, and first had a portrait exhibited at the Royal Academy in 1814.

Mary Byrne Green (born England; 1766–1845). She

exhibited at the Royal Academy and painted a miniature of the Duchess of Clarence.

Judith Jans Leyster (born Dutch Republic; 1609–1660). I took some liberties in mentioning Leyster. She was well known during her lifetime, but after her death, her body of work was attributed to her husband. It was not recognized as hers until late in the 19th century.

And Juno named her cats for **Angelica Kauffman** and **Artemisia Gentileschi** (born Rome; 1593–1656).

ACKNOWLEDGMENTS

My thanks to May Peterson, Melinda Utendorf, and Deb and Debbie of DP Plus, for their valuable feedback and editorial skills, which immensely benefited this book.

THE LONGHOPE ABBEY SERIES

Main Series

A Dangerous Kind of Lady

A Wicked Kind of Husband

A Scandalous Kind of Duke

Prequel

A Beastly Kind of Earl

Holiday Novella

A Christmas Affair to Remember

The Brothers DeWitt Bundle

A Wicked Kind of Husband, including A Christmas Affair to Remember

Each book in this series can be read as a standalone, and the books can be read in any order. As the characters move through the same world, they do appear in each other's stories, but without any overarching plot.

For news on release dates, future books, and more, sign up at miavincy. com/news or visit miavincy.com.

ABOUT THE AUTHOR

Mia Vincy wandered the world for years, sometimes backpacking, sometimes working variously as a journalist, communications specialist, and copyeditor. She always carried a tattered book or three in her backpack, until the advent of the e-reader meant she could carry thousands of books at once.

Mia eventually settled in a country town in Victoria, Australia, to write historical romances, in between bike rides through the countryside and muttering at the walls.

For more, visit miavincy.com.

facebook.com/MiaVincyBooks
twitter.com/miavincy
instagram.com/miavincywrites

Printed in Great Britain
by Amazon

33123849R00187